LEO TOLSTOY (1828-1910),
born of a noble Russian family, is universally acknowledged to be one of the world's great writers. Always an
idealist, he began writing to further certain reform
ideas he cherished and by the end of his life was the
most conspicuous literary figure in the world and one of
its greatest single moral forces.

TOLSTOY portrays not only the physical milieu but also
the intellectual and spiritual revolution of his time in
his works, which emphasize love, faith, simplicity and
the Christian brotherhood of man. The six short stories
which comprise this volume span almost a half century
of the author's writing and furnish representative ex-
amples of Tolstoy at his early and late best.

F. D. REEVE, who has written the Introduction to this
collection, teaches Russian literature at Wesleyan University. He has translated numerous short stories, plays
and novels from the Russian and has made extended
visits to the Soviet Union.

Other books by Tolstoy
available in Laurel Editions:

WAR AND PEACE

ANNA KARENINA

Short Masterpieces by
TOLSTOY

TRANSLATED BY MARGARET WETTLIN

Introduction by F. D. Reeve

A LAUREL EDITION

Published by DELL PUBLISHING CO., INC.
750 Third Avenue, New York 17, N.Y.

Introduction © Copyright, 1963 by F. D. Reeve

Laurel ® TM 674623, Dell Publishing Co., Inc.

First printing—October, 1963
Second printing—May, 1970

Printed in U.S.A.

CONTENTS

Short Masterpieces by

TOLSTOY

INTRODUCTION

In 1903, asked by his friend P. I. Biryukov to supply some autobiographical information for the first edition of a book on himself, Tolstoy cited the tone of moral crisis which he felt had pervaded his life and listed four periods into which, he said, his life divided:

. . . Remembering my life, i.e., thinking back on it from the point of view of the good and evil I did, I saw that my life falls into four periods:

That wonderful, especially in comparison to what followed, innocent, joyful, poetic period of childhood up to fourteen.

Then the second—a terrible twenty years or period of vulgar licentiousness, of ambition-serving, vainglory and, chiefly, lust.

Then the third, an eighteen-year period from my marriage to my spiritual birth, a period which from the world's point of view may be called moral, i.e., during these eighteen years I lived a proper, honest family life, not yielding to any of the vices castigated by public opinion, a period during which all my interests were limited to egoistic concern for my family, for augmenting my wealth, for achieving literary success, and to pleasures of all sorts.

And, finally, a fourth, twenty-year period in which I am now and in which I hope to die, from the viewpoint of which I see the whole significance of my past life and which I would not wish to alter in the slight-

est, except in those evil habits acquired by me in previous periods.

> . . . I think that, despite great inadequacies, such
an autobiography would be more useful for people
than all that literary chatter which fills the twelve vol-
umes of my works and to which people nowadays attach undue importance.

Though the reverse is true—the actual importance of
Tolstoy's literary work has required that attention be paid
to all aspects of his biography—Tolstoy's life itself is a rare
and edifying example of aristocracy. In "Two Hussars" the
genuine count is the one who has the courage of his passions, the skills of a long memory, and a consciousness of
vitality that encompasses in one night a ball at the Marshal's
of nobility and wild gypsy dances. The first Count Tourbin
extends the privileges of class to affirmation of life: he
controls others by sympathy and devotion, asserting his will
on them to their satisfaction. He unmasks the fraudulent,
risks his own life to emphasize its realness, and pretends to
no standards he cannot exemplify by his self-control. A
count, he is an aristocrat by birth. His largeness of spirit,
his daring, his sophistication, his integrity and love—he
goes back to kiss the sleeping Anna Fyodorovna good-bye
—his irreverence for the dead and the effete—he appears
at the gypsy debauch in Anna Fyodorovna's dead husband's
overcoat; he deliberately insults the cavalryman for an attempt at specious friendship—his manner and the sympathies it expresses, define both himself and the sort of aristocracy to which inherited privilege is entirely natural.

The count's son is a travesty of the father. We are kept
in suspense to the end of the story by our doubt that the
integrity with which the father seized life can be actually
subverted by the son's manner. After all, Anna Fyodorovna
is now given over to cards and to her daughter with the
same simple, even if narrowed, intensity with which she
one night gave herself up to a hussar. Liza is a paragon of
modesty and rural elegance, but, as Anna Fyodorovna
muses, stroking her head, "It isn't what my hair was at her

age . . . Oh, Lizochka, I could wish for you. . . ." The twenty-three-year-old girl, like the twenty-three-year-old boy, not only recalls Anna Fyodorovna's memories and arouses in her the desire to relive the past, but also points up the discrepancy between the past and the present.

At the beginning of the story, this theme is presented by a catalogue of socioeconomic changes which visibly measure changes of manner (deportment). It is recapitulated at the beginning of the second part of the story (chapter nine). The change is considered historically—from 1825 to 1848, from the spirit of the Decembrists to the tone leading up to the Crimean War—and marked by births, deaths, and the usual chronology of our social world. The story as a whole may be read, then, as a study in the meanings of manner. The aristocracy of manner which Tolstoy defines through the first Tourbin fits, partly, Tolstoy as count and especially Tolstoy as a writer, a man whose skill and integrity included all levels of social activity and all habits of thought that shape human life.

The periods into which Tolstoy divided his own life may be considered equivalents to the catalogue of changes given in "Two Hussars." Consciousness of life in all its details—which Tolstoy called his own highest quality—and sympathy for life in terms of an understanding of a harmonizing, eternal, and nonmaterial principle, or God, are analogous to the interlacing of details of manner and the pattern of life which this story is about. In the story, as in life, the relations are neither infinite nor nonmaterial, which Tolstoy's *theory* about their spiritual source suggests they must be. In his notebook for July 1908, however, among passages celebrating virtue and exhorting all men to live in God, he notes laconically: "Can't feel sorry for flies—there's a limit." It is the "fly"-quality in the cavalryman for which the first Tourbin slaps him down. It is this improper claim to possession which Tolstoy feels required by his own nature to hound down and expose, and which forms a central thread in all of the stories presented here.

"Two Hussars" was written in St. Petersburg in the spring of 1856. Tolstoy had moved to the capital in the late fall of 1855 and was traveling in the best literary and social circles. His earlier stories had given him immediate recognition and extensive praise. "Two Hussars," published in the May 1856 issue of *The Contemporary*, was saluted by the literary world but adversely criticized by the social. Dedicated to Tolstoy's sister Mariya Nikolayevna and signed "Count Lev Tolstoy," the story had as epigraph two lines from an 1819 poem by Denis Davydov, a campaigner against Napoleon and himself a dashing figure and poet. Davydov's "Song of an Old Hussar" cites differences between two generations of hussars and refers to Henri Jomini, the then widely known Napoleonic strategist. Davydov says the younger generation is

> Smarter now, supposedly,
> Yet what do we hear from all?
> Jomini, more Jomini,
> And of vodka—not at all.

The elder Tourbin is a fictionalized portrait of Fyodor Ivanovich Tolstoy (1782-1846), a first cousin once removed, nicknamed "The American" for an extended voyage he had undertaken—a wild, brave man, a duelist, rake, lover of gypsy singing, and inveterate gambler. In the story, the son is less debauched and less interesting than the father. Although we know, of course, with whom Tolstoy's sympathies lie, it is from an entry in his diary on May 16, 1856 that we know definitely how he felt about the story. He cites Truzson as having "said perfectly that the second hussar is portrayed lovelessly."

The stories presented here document the scope, the perseverance, and the acuity of Tolstoy's examination of the actual and the possible relations between a man and the society which gives him his living. They sharpen our understanding of the power of Tolstoy's literary universe—of that vision which he was continually refurnishing with absurd (when isolated) fancies and strange political notions, that vision which yet in his writings bears down brilliantly on almost all parts of our own lives.

The stories here are not particularly "Russian"; they reach through beauty of language and literary style to exemplify terms and values celebrated in any Western country. If you will, their power is peculiarly Tolstoyan—a haunting search for "truth" moves each story.

These stories all present their search within the context of habitual lives in the world of the upper and upper-middle classes—even Yardstick, though "an ugly duckling," is an upper-class horse—and in the forms of social activity by which members of those classes express their personal power and desires for self-fulfillment. Tolstoy, of course, was a member of the upper class. His ethical studies were analyses of the obligations of the individual in regard both to necessary and possible social functions, but we understand the substance of his scholarship only through his transformation of it into fiction.

Tolstoy's own notes and letters all certify that the source, so to speak, for "A Happy Married Life" was his affection for and near-engagement to Valeriya Arsenyeva, a girl eight years younger than he. The relationship was finally terminated—whether before or during his work on "A Happy Married Life" (1857?-1858-59) is not accurately known—but the available biographical facts contradict the substance of the experience given in the story. Valeriya Arsenyeva was, apparently, not clever or imaginative or resourceful; after having broken with her, Tolstoy was left with a certain indifference, even dislike of her. In the story, of course, the marriage is repaired as the romance ends. The moving force behind the "plot" is Masha's energy and passion, her desire to possess herself. Young and naïve, she has to proceed through the social school Sergei Mikhailich has already passed, in order to be at all aware of the limits she may claim to that self which she would be master of and to that position in the world to which she asserts she has a just right.

If there be weakness in the story, it is, I think, that the authority by which she proffers her claims is obscure—we grasp this by comparing the resolution of "A Happy Married Life" with the end of *Anna Karenina*. In both, an older

husband and a lovely young bride move onto an unexpected plane of understanding through affection for their infant
children—symbols of their status and of the future—and
through awareness of mutual support of one set of values.
The title "A Happy Married Life" is fitted ironically to the
narrative, as its only use indicates. Sergei Mikhailich is having an argument with Masha (chapter seven): "You . . .
sacrifice (he stressed the word) . . . and so do I. What
could be prettier? A contest as to who is more magnanimous. What other happy married life is there?"

Masha's complaint is obliquely put as criticism of her husband's weak will. She says that he betrayed her by tolerating
her inquisitiveness and by allowing her to satisfy what she
called her wish to "live." The wish is satisfied, though it
leads to nothing conventionally more serious than a decla-
ration of love by a stranger. However, Masha interprets
her desires as themselves the instruments and measures of
betrayal and reproaches her husband for not having kept
her in his possession when he had the authority to do so. He,
in turn, denies the validity of his authority—all along,
Masha has appealed to conventional definitions; indeed, that
is how and why she married—if the passion it protects is
gone. At the end, their love is reaffirmed but their passion
is exhausted.

The irony of the story is that nothing has happened—
the conventions which restrict Masha's search for life turn
out to be finally and wholly adequate for her. Like her, her
husband, who greatly feared his happiness would change,
finds new happiness in the tranquillity of sure affection.
Husband and wife have come to possess each other more
than they at first desired—a carnal attraction and desire
for self-assertion has changed into the maintenance of a
condition in which each partner is gratefully possessed in
peace by the other.

By March 1859, Tolstoy had finished the first draft of "A
Happy Married Life" and read it at "evenings" in the drawing rooms of relatives and friends in St. Petersburg. At first
delighted by his new composition, Tolstoy turned sharply
against it—even considered publishing it under a pseudo-

nym not to sully his reputation—and, in a letter to Botkin
on May 3, 1859, wrote, having received the proofs of the
second part, that "I saw what shameful crap, what a blotch,
not just as writing, but as morality, this foul composition
is . . . I'm now buried both as a writer and as a man.
This is for certain. Especially since the 1st part is even
worse. . . ." To his relative A. A. Tolstaya he wrote that,
on rereading, the story "appeared such shameful filth that
I can't pull myself together from shame and, I think, I'll
never write again."

Of course, he did go on writing, and much of his indignation was directed not only against himself but also against
the world—as in the story "Lucerne." In May 1856, not
long after he had finished "Two Hussars," Tolstoy noted
in his diary that he wanted to write the story of a horse.
Horse stories were rather popular in the 1850's and 1860's,
as Eikhenbaum has pointed out. Tolstoy's idea, which was
so vivid and sympathetic that at one point Turgenev was
prompted to say, "Lev Nikolayevich, really, at some time
you were a horse yourself," was given further impetus and
shape by the story of Kholstomer, which he probably heard
from one of the Stakhoviches, his friends.

"Yardstick" ("Kholstomer"), dedicated to the memory of
the writer M. A. Stakhovich, goes back to an account relat-
ed by the writer's brother, A. A. Stakhovich, a great horse
breeder in Oryol province and founder of the Petersburg
Racing Club. Stakhovich had heard of a great horse named
Kholstomer who, in the early 1800's, had covered 200 sa-
zhens (about 2⅕ furlongs) in 30 seconds. After much in-
vestigation, he had learned that a stallion called Muzhik I,
born in 1803 out of Baba by Lyubezny I and gelded in 1812,
had been nicknamed Kholstomer by its owner Count Orlov
for its great stride—as if it were measuring off *kholsty*,
or big squares of burlap. M. A. Stakhovich prepared an
outline for a story but was killed by his serfs in 1858 before
he had written further.

Tolstoy returned to his notion for a horse story after a
ride from Moscow to Yasnaya Polyana with A. A. Stakhovich in 1859 or 1860, during which Stakhovich recounted

to Tolstoy his brother's projected "The Adventures of a
Piebald Gelding." In spring 1863, in the midst of settling
down to new family life, Tolstoy worked on the story but,
he felt, unsuccessfully. By 1864, the story was finished. After a fruitless attempt at publishing it (in a magazine that
never got started), it lay in Tolstoy's desk until 1885, when
his wife brought it out in the third volume of her edition of
Tolstoy's works (1886). The story was checked by A. A.
Stakhovich, and Tolstoy was helped in historical details by
Stakhovich's son: "My son stood behind his chair and in
ecstasy watched the wonderful lines flow out onto the paper; and the great writer would keep saying to him with
a smile: *'There's* something for you, and now something
more.' "

The story is both sentimental and fantastic, of course:
the history of a creature who must outlive his glory in what
a politician has recently called "the long twilight struggle"
and who communicates with other horses in a skillful Russian literary style. The story is poignant and moving, behind its apparent simplicity, because of Tolstoy's skill in
manipulating the point of view: we "see" Yardstick as author of his autobiography, as an outsider among the other
horses, as the mere property of several owners (shifts in
price reflect shifts in owners' viewpoints), as a romantic
figure, as a beast or bundle of expendable energy, as an
annoying job or duty for the stableboy, as the "subject" of
a story, as a symbol of the change that marks all life, cul-
minating in the knacker's complaint about the quality of
the hide and the parallel but "useless" death of Serpukhovskoi, who, like the horse, has lost his central function in
life and has no resources to find another. The story is highly moral, illustrating the inevitability of life's continuing on
any terms except those of loss of consciousness. The horse
accedes to his death with a natural grace which the man
has long ago abandoned by turning love into self-pity and
adventure into drink.

In 1895, Tolstoy published a story that indirectly comments on "Yardstick" and explicitly extends the moral to
human life. In "The Master and the Workman," Brekhunov

saves peasant Nikita's life by warming him, though he himself freezes to death. In this way he exculpates a useless life and promotes that continual birth in nature which Tolstoy associates with genuine love. "The Death of Ivan Ilyich," one of the very greatest stories ever written, first published in that 1886 edition of Tolstoy's works, focuses less on a summary moral (though, to be sure, one may read the ending as announcement of Ivan Ilyich's identification with the love that moves the world) and more on the psychological responses a man makes to, and in, his function in the world. As life is, literally, an approach to death, so a man's social performance is an ever more nearly apt definition of his value. At the end of the story, of course, the terms are altered: the values behind social performance are defined as contradictory to eternal human values.

Ivan Ilyich Golovin has possessed many *things;* he slowly shucks them all off, with the support of gentle Gerasim's ministrations, until, in a sort of epiphany, he finds himself literally self-possessed. Encircled by an indifferent world— the image early in the story of the "mourners" around the coffin, each occupied with a separate duty—he reaches a mystic vision—"There was light instead of death"—in which he experiences charity toward his family and finds he has transcended pain. The power and loneliness of his discovery are emphasized by its inaccessibility: "For those present his death agony continued for another two hours." The story is framed by third-person response, which, of course, is our point of view. Ivan Ilyich is made so skillfully to respond to it that we, in turn, are converted to Ivan Ilyich's point of view. The deepest understanding of death is affirmation of the highest vitality of life. This aesthetic formulation is comparable to the strongest philosophic analysis; only, its instruction is presented as experience and, therefore, much closer to us.

The closeness of the experience is enforced above all by the literalness of detail. As the eighteenth century conveyed its understanding of a man by his "humor," so Tolstoy presents a man in any given moment as equal to a detail. Each of the characters in the opening scene, for example, is fitted to a pattern composed of all their separate details. We are taken into the dead man's room by the eyes and reflections of Pyotr Ivanovich, who is worried about the proper manner: "He knew it never did any harm to cross oneself on such occasions." The phrase "like all dead men" is repeated several times, each time modified by a detail: how the stiff limbs have sunk into the bedding of the coffin, how the waxy yellow forehead and nose stick up, how the face seems more important than in life.

The motifs of death are threaded through with the motifs of dead, i.e., unconscious, life, symbolized by the game of whist.

The details of Ivan Ilyich's disease are presented so literally that, as N. F. Golubov asseverated, "the actual facts in the portrayal [of the disease] are so clear that not only a doctor but also any third-year medical student could make an almost exactly accurate diagnosis. . . . Having read Tolstoy's story, one may say with nearly certain conviction that Ivan Ilyich died from cancer of the abdomen, somewhere in the region of the caecum or the right kidney. The cause of the disease (the contusion), its picture, development—and even the necessity of [the patient's] lying with his leg raised high—everything confirms it." The description of the disease parallels the description of Ivan Ilyich's life. That is, selected details are presented in an ever-increasing intensity leading to a central, or final, apotheosis by which the process of selection is explained and justified. We see the "progress" of Ivan Ilyich's life, the progress of his disease, and the progress of his philosophic speculation which follows from the two. Throughout the story, we are aware of a purpose toward which the whole terse narrative is moving. The last detail—the *fact* of the ultimate vision—is something we can never confirm, but here it is something we must assent to as both the source and the consequence of that progress of life—Ivan Ilyich's and our own—to which we are addicted, body and soul.

The story is "characteristic" of much of Tolstoy's later work: the language moves with economy and severity to a denouement that is simultaneously a moral lesson. Yet the terms of that morality are not reducible to precepts or commandments. Of course, Tolstoy also preached, and I think we tend somewhat to confuse his homilies with his fiction. The reordering of chronology itself—the story moves from the dead man, as a fact, back through his life to his death as meaning—reminds us how Tolstoy has reordered life that we may *see* it forever. "Errors" in time should help keep us in the story: both children, for example, are about five years older at the end of the story than they should be if their dates of birth in the story are remembered. The story is, literally, foreshortened. Tolstoy's absorption with death—an absorption found in all his important works, and from his early works to his last—is the direct expression of his consciousness of life. From inside one's self death is the dreaded possibility of existence. It is the ultimate experience which the individual confronts alone. It is the difference between all or nothing. By the end of the story Ivan Ilyich has triumphed over the futility of his life, has ceased to pretend, has grown to care for others, and for the first time, loves. Tolstoy has so sharply presented the values by which alienated inauthentic existence is overcome, that "The Death of Ivan Ilyich" has become part of existentialist scripture.

In "real life" Ivan Ilyich was not Golovin but Menchikov, brother of the well-known scientist Ilya Ilyich and lawyer in Tula, prosecutor of the District Court. Tolstoy's wife's sister remembers that "during Menchikov's stay at Yasnaya Polyana, Lev Nikolayevich became extremely fond of him, with artistic flair having realized that he was an outstanding man." She adds that "afterwards his wife told me his last thoughts and conversations on the futility of the life he had led, which I passed on to Lev Nikolayevich." Tolstoy said that Menchikov was "intelligent, very intelligent." He died of cancer, forty-five years old, on July 2, 1881. Tolstoy immediately thought of a story "The Death of a Judge," a "description of the simple death of a plain man." Turgenev's very painful death in 1883 and Urusov's in 1885—both men were close to Tolstoy—undoubtedly pushed him on to finish the story left in embryonic form

since 1881. In the early winter—November-December—of
1884, he read portions of it to his family. By October 1885,
he noted that work on the story was coming to an end. Set
up in galleys in early 1886 for the edition of his works
which his wife was publishing, the story was corrected de-
finitively on March 25, 1886. Ivan Ilyich Golovin, born in St.
Petersburg in 1837, dies on February 4, 1882—not long
after, in fact, Sarah Bernhardt and her troupe had visited
Moscow and St. Petersburg, as referred to in the story.

Historical accuracy is incidental, of course, to Tolstoy's
design. *War and Peace* may seem a web of military and
social analyses; *Anna Karenina* may appear a textbook sum-
marizing the main philosophic and sociopolitical issues of
the 1870's—but, accurate as these "footnotes" may be, they
are the excuses, the symptoms of literary provocation.
"The Kreutzer Sonata," first published with Tolstoy's au-
thorization in Volume XIII of his *Works* in 1891, drama-
tizes the difficulty of achieving technique when the provocation is equally referrable to "hot" social issues. The story,
unfinished but released by Tolstoy's relatives, was circu-
lated widely in St. Petersburg and Moscow in 1889-90 in
lithographed form, and was read numerous times at literary gatherings. N. N. Strakhov, who heard the tale on October 28, 1889, wrote Tolstoy to the effect that, though he
felt the observations on music, medicine, children, continence, and so on were true and powerful, he thought the
tale had certain flaws: the author is closely tied to the narrator because of the first-person form, yet the narrator en-
gages in long discussions before getting to his story; it is
unclear whether or not Pozdnyshev has an honest understanding of himself and whether or not he is repentant; the
denouement too quickly follows the violinist's appearance,
making the narrator seem suddenly mad and hasty, who
previously had been cool and judicious; and the long in-
troductory discussions—important in themselves—lose ef-
fectiveness because of the reader's loss of suspense as he
goes through them, waiting for the story.

Tolstoy subsequently made some not extensive changes,
but his immediate reply to Strakhov said: "In aesthetic

terms, I know that this piece of work is beneath all criticism: it is the result of two devices, and the two are incompatible, and consequently there's this deformity you heard. But nevertheless I'm leaving it as is and don't regret it, not from laziness, but I can't change it—don't regret it because I'm sure that what's written there is not just something better than useless but something very useful for people, and to a certain extent new. If it were going to be a real piece of fiction, which I don't promise not to do, it would have to be done over from scratch and right away."

For a long time, the story was not passed by the censor "and not only . . . for the improper expressions in it." Only after strenuous intercession by Tolstoy's friends and wife with the Court and the Tsar himself was permission granted "but not for separate publication." The "undigested" sociopolitical materials which made it a sort of scandalous treatise were, of course, the reason.

They were not in the first version. In the late 1860's, after *War and Peace*, Tolstoy wrote a little untitled fragment (published in 1936 as "The Wife-Killer") about a man who murdered his wife out of jealousy and immediately went to the police to confess and be punished. In 1887, he returned to this idea after the actor Andreyev-Burlak had told him "that once, riding in a train, a certain gentleman had told him of his misery from his wife's infidelity, and Levochka used this idea." As Tolstoy worked on the tale in the following three years, he kept adding materials on the sex question, influenced in this especially by his readings on the American Shaker movement. Abstract discussion of the consequences of sexual passion and of the roles of men and women in conjugal life became more important than the emblematic revenge story. Much of what Pozdnyshev says is essentially the same as what Tolstoy wrote in letters to Chertkov at the time. The "Afterword," appended in reply to the many letters and comments Tolstoy received after the story had become clandestinely known, propounds a theory of continence, based on religious dogma, which would lead to annihilation of humanity. The very extremism of Tolstoy's position, of course, gives his attack authority, though not credibility. He "goes all the way"; the personal disaster which Pozdnyshev experiences is explained in general social terms. The argument demands response, just as society requires reform.

In his 1886 article "Nikolai Palkin," Tolstoy recalls an officer he knew, presumably when a student in Kazan: "I knew one . . . who in the evening danced a mazurka with his beautiful daughter at a ball and went home early in order to be up early to take charge of a Tartar soldier's execution by running the gauntlet, beat this soldier to death, and returned home to dine with his family." Tolstoy never saw such an execution, but in 1898-99 he had heard a detailed description of one from his friend the writer I. N. Zakharin-Yakunin. In April 1903, Sholom-Aleichem (S. N. Rabinovich) asked Tolstoy to submit something for a literary anthology the proceeds from which were to help the Jews who had suffered in the Kishinev pogrom. Tolstoy replied that what he wanted to say—that the government was at fault—could not be printed in Russia. In June, he noted in his diary a plan for a story, originally called "Daughter and Father," which he wanted to submit for the anthology for Jewish relief. He wrote the story in a few days in August, but then set to revising it. He never completed the revisions, and the story was first published in Chertkov's 1911 edition of Tolstoy's posthumously published fiction.

"After the Ball," Ivan Vasilyevich's story, proceeds from theory—the relation between environment and coincidence —to example—"Often he became so absorbed in the story that he forgot his reason for telling it, especially since he always spoke with great fervour and sincerity"—to moral —"And so my love . . . petered out . . . that is what sometimes happens, and it is incidents like this that change and give direction to a man's whole life."

Ivan Vasilyevich cannot endure the perversions of consciousness he has perceived in the contrasts of the father's and the daughter's behavior. His compassion for life prevents him. His career, his "brilliant" future in the army and in society, is gone. His own nature has compelled him to abandon the uniform and the girl that he thought were his proud possessions in order that he may unquestionably possess himself. After he had become aware of what really was—"after the ball," after the second, the military "quadrille"—he "didn't fit in," even as Tolstoy himself in 1910 ran away from his wife and Yasnaya Polyana and the world he did not fit in, to reach another world, perhaps to join the Dukhobors in Bulgaria. The articulation of consciousness—of *things* and feelings and patterns and meaning—remained behind in these stories, remained forever.

F. D. REEVE

TWO HUSSARS

In the early years of the nineteenth century, at a time when there was no railways or highways, no gas lights, no low spring-cushioned sofas or unlacquered furniture, when there were no disillusioned youths with monocles in their eyes, no liberal-minded lady-philosophers, no *dames aux camélias* who have sprung up in such numbers in our day—in those innocent times when anyone traveling from Moscow to St. Petersburg loaded his cart or his carriage with a whole kitchenful of cooked victuals, drove eight days and nights over soft dusty or muddy roads and put his faith in fried cutlets, hot *bubliki,* and Valdai carriage bells —at a time when wax candles smoked in long autumn evenings, casting their light on family circles of twenty or thirty members, and when the candelabra in ballrooms were filled with wax and spermaceti candles and furniture was distributed symmetrically and the youth of our fathers was indicated not only by the absence of wrinkles and gray hair, but also by the duels they fought over ladies and the agility with which they leaped from one corner of a room to another to pick up the handkerchiefs dropped accidentally or otherwise; when our mothers wore high-waisted gowns with enormous sleeves and decided all household problems by the drawing of lots; when adorable *dames aux camélias* shrank from the light of day—in those innocent days of Masonic lodges, Martinists, and the Tugendbund, in the days of Miloradovich, Davidov, and Pushkin—in those days there was an assembly of rich landowners in the town of K, center of the gubernia, and final elections of representatives of the nobility had just been held.

I

"No matter, I shall put up in the public room if needs be," said a young officer in a greatcoat and hussar cap who had just climbed out of a sleigh and was now entering the finest inn the town of K could boast of.

"It's such a big assembly, Your Excellency, something extraordinary," said the page boy who had already learned from the officer's servant that he was Count Tourbin and therefore addressed him as "Your Excellency." "The mistress of the Afremovskaya estate has promised to leave with her daughters this evening, so if you wish I can put you up in room eleven," he said, stepping softly down the corridor in front of the count and continually glancing back.

In the public room, at a small table below a time-darkened full-length portrait of Czar Alexander, sat a few men drinking champagne. They were, apparently, members of the local gentry, and near them was a group of traveling merchants in dark blue cloaks.

When the count had entered the room and called Blücher, an enormous gray dog, he flung off his coat before the hoar frost had melted on the collar, ordered vodka, sat down at the table in his blue satin tunic, and began talking to the gentlemen who, instantly attracted by his handsome figure and open countenance, offered him a glass of champagne. The count first tossed off a glass of vodka, then ordered another bottle to treat his new acquaintances. The sleigh-driver came in at this point to ask for money for a drink.

"Sasha!" cried the count. "Give it to him!"

The driver went out with Sasha and returned presently, holding the money in his outstretched palm.

"Look at this, Y'r Excellency, after the way I put myself out on your account and you promising me half a ruble and he gives me a quarter!"

"Sasha! Give him a ruble!"

Sasha stared sulkily at the driver's boots.

"It's enough for him," he said in a deep bass voice. "And besides, I haven't got any more money."

The count took two five-ruble notes out of his purse (the last it contained) and gave one of them to the sleigh-driver, who kissed his hand and went out.

"A pretty pass I've come to!" said the count. "My last five rubles."

"That's a true hussar for you!" said one of the gentlemen with a smile. Judging by his mustache, his voice, and a certain energetic looseness in his legs, he was a retired cavalry officer. "Do you intend staying here long, Count?"

"I wouldn't stay at all if it weren't that I must get some money. There aren't even any rooms to be had in this accursed inn, devil take it!"

"Allow me to share my room with you, Count," said the cavalry officer. "I'm in room seven. If you have no objections to putting up with me, you must try to spend three days here. Tonight the Marshal of Nobility is giving a ball. He will be delighted to have you."

"True enough, Count, do stay," put in another of the company, a handsome young man. "What is your hurry? After all, they only take place once in three years, the elections. You might at least have a look at our young ladies, Count."

"Sasha! Get out my linen: I'm going to the bathhouse," said the count, getting up. "After that we'll see—perhaps I really will look in at the Marshal's."

He called one of the waiters and said something to him that made the man chuckle and reply, "Everything's possible, Y'r Excellency." Then he went out.

"So I'll have them put my portmanteau in your room," the count called back from out in the corridor.

"I'll consider it a great favor," replied the cavalry officer, running over to the door. "Room seven, don't forget."

As soon as the count's footsteps had died away the cavalry officer came back to the table and, drawing his chair closer to the clerk and smiling straight into his eyes, said:

"He's the very man!"

"You don't say!"

"He is, I tell you—the hussar famous for dueling. Tourbin's his name, everyone knows him. I'll wager he recognized me—he must have. He and I were on a spree at Lebedyan that lasted three weeks that time I was sent there for remounts. A little incident took place—he and I were responsible for it; that's why he pretended not to recognize me. A fine fellow, eh?"

"A fine fellow indeed. And what nice manners! Nobody would guess he was that sort," said the handsome young man. "And we made friends so quickly. I don't suppose he's more than five-and-twenty, is he?"

"He doesn't look it, but he is. But one has to really know him to appreciate him. Who ran off with Madame Migunova? He did. And who killed Sablin? And who dropped Matnev out of the window by his legs? And who won three hundred thousand from Duke Nesterov? You cannot imagine what a reckless chap he is! A gambler, a duelist, a seducer. But he's got the soul of a hussar, a true hussar. People are fond of maligning us, but they don't appreciate what a true hussar is! Ah, those were the days!"

And the cavalry officer launched into an account of his debaucheries with the count at Lebedyan that not only never took place but never could have taken place. They could not, first of all, because he had never before set eyes on the count and had retired from the army two years before the count entered it; and in the second place because the cavalry officer never served in the cavalry; he had been for four years the humblest cadet in the Belevsky Regiment and had resigned as soon as he got his commission as ensign. But ten years before, on coming into his inheritance, he really had made a trip to Lebedyan where, in the company of some remount officers, he had squandered seven hundred rubles and ordered himself an Uhlan uniform with orange cuffs with the intention of joining the lancers. So great was his longing to enter the cavalry that the three weeks spent in the company of remount officers in Lebedyan remained the happiest days of his life, and he mentally transformed this longing into reality, then into recollection, so that he himself came to believe firmly in his cavalry career, a thing which in no way prevented his being, in respect to honesty and amiability, a truly worthy gentleman.

"Ah, yes, none but those who have served in the cavalry can appreciate our sort." He straddled his chair and thrust out his lower jaw as he went on in a deep bass voice: "Time was when I'd be riding at the head of my squadron with a horse between my legs that was more of a devil than a horse; there I'd be sitting, a devil myself, and up rides the squadron commander to review us. 'Ensign,' says he, 'we can't manage this without you. Be so kind as to lead the squadron on parade.' 'Very well, sir,' say I, and no sooner said than done. Round I whirl, shout a command to my mustachioed bravos, and away we go! Ah, those were the days!"

The count came back from the bathhouse with a flushed face and wet hair and went straight to room seven where the cavalry officer was sitting in his dressing gown with a pipe between his teeth, reflecting with a delight tinged by apprehension on the good luck that had fallen to his lot— that of sharing his room with the famous Tourbin. "But what," thought he, "if he should suddenly take it into his head to strip me naked, lead me outside the town, and bury me in the snow, or smear me all over with tar, or simply . . . but no, he wouldn't treat a comrade-in-arms like that," he comforted himself.

"Sasha! Feed Blücher!" shouted the count.

Sasha, who had had a glass of vodka and was fairly tipsy, put in an appearance.

"Couldn't wait! Drunk already, you ruffian! Feed Blücher!"

"He won't die without it; see how sleek he is," said Sasha, patting the dog.

"No back talk if you please! Feed him!"

"All you care about is your dog; if your man takes a glass you shout at him."

"Aye, I'll strike you!" shouted the count in a voice that made the windowpanes rattle and frightened the cavalry officer a little.

"You might ask whether your Sasha's had anything to eat today. Go ahead and strike me if you think more of a dog than a man," said Sasha. But at this point he got such a blow on the nose that he fell down, striking his head against the wall; the next instant he had leaped to his feet with his hand over his nose; he rushed out of the door and threw himself down on a trunk in the corridor.

"He's knocked my teeth out," he muttered, wiping his bloody nose with one hand while with the other he scratched the back of Blücher, who was licking himself. "He's knocked my teeth out, Blücher, but he's my count all the same and I'll go through fire and water for him, and that's the truth, because, you see, he's my count, Blücher. Are you hungry, Blücher?"

When he had lain there for a few minutes, he got up, fed the dog, and, almost sober, went to serve his count and offer him tea.

"I'll take it as an affront," the cavalry officer was saying meekly to the count, who lay on the officer's bed with his feet up on the bedpost. "I, too, am an old soldier and comrade, so to speak. Rather than have you take money from someone else I would gladly give you two hundred rubles myself. At present I don't have that much—only one hundred—but I will get the rest this very day. I would simply take it as an affront, Count."

"Thanks, old fellow," said the count, slapping him on the back and divining at once the relations that were sure to arise between them. "Thanks. Well, if that's how matters stand, we'll go to the ball. But what shall we do for the present? Tell me what goes on in this town: are there any pretty girls here? Any rakes? Any cardplayers?"

The cavalry officer said there would be a bevy of pretty girls at the ball, that the greatest rake in town was the newly elected police captain Kolkov, but that he did not have the recklessness of a hussar, but was a good sort; that Ilyushka's Gypsy chorus had been singing here ever since elections began, that Styesha was the soloist, and that *everyone* was planning to go and hear the Gypsies after the ball.

"And there's quite a lot of cardplaying," he said. "Lukhnov, a wealthy visitor, plays all the time and Ilyin, in room eight, a cornet in an Uhlan regiment, has been losing heavily. They've begun already. They play every evening, and you wouldn't believe what a nice chap that Ilyin is, Count; nothing mean about him—why, he'd give you the shirt off his back."

"Then let's go and see him. We'll have a look at who's here," said the count.

"Let's go, let's go. They'll be awfully glad to meet you."

II

Ilyin, the cornet in the Uhlans, had only just waked up. On the eve he had sat himself down at the card table at eight o'clock and had lost for fifteen hours at a stretch, until eleven o'clock in the morning. It was a great sum he had lost, but he himself could not have told exactly how great, for he had with him three thousand of his own money and fifteen thousand from the regiment treasury which he had long since mixed up with his own and was afraid to count lest he be confirmed in his fears that his losses had already encroached on the treasury money. It was almost noon before he had fallen into the heavy dreamless sleep that comes only to the young, and then only after heavy losses at cards. On waking up at six o'clock in the evening, at the very hour when Count Tourbin arrived at the inn, and seeing the cards and the chalk scattered over the floor and the stained tables in the center of the room, he remembered with horror the night's gaming, and especially his last card, a knave, that had brought him a loss of five hundred rubles; but, unwilling to accept the reality of his situation, he took his money out from under his pillow and set to counting it. He recognized certain banknotes that had passed from hand to hand in "corners" and "transports," and this brought to mind the whole course of his playing. His own three thousand were gone, as well as some two and a half thousand of the regiment money.

The Uhlan had been playing for four nights running.

He was traveling from Moscow, where he had been entrusted with the regiment's money. In the town of K he had been detained by the overseer of the posting station on the pretext that there was no change of horses, but as a matter of fact by a secret agreement with the innkeeper that all travelers should be detained overnight in this town. The Uhlan, a gay young lad who had just been presented with three thousand rubles by his parents on the occasion of his being appointed to a regiment, was only too glad to spend a few days in the town of K during election festivities, for he hoped to have his fill of enjoyment here. A country gentleman of his acquaintance, a family man, lived in these parts, and just as he was making ready to drive out to see him and pay court to his daughters, the cavalry officer turned up and made his acquaintance. And that very evening, with no ill intentions, he had introduced him to his friend Lukhnov and some other cardplayers in the public room. From then on the Uhlan had been sitting at the card table. He had forgotten all about his friend the country gentleman; he had even forgotten to ask for horses; he had, in fact, not so much as come out of his room for four days running.

When he had dressed himself and had his breakfast, he sauntered over to the window. A little walk, he thought, would help drive the insistent thoughts of the cards out of his mind. He put on his greatcoat and went outside. The sun had already sunk behind the red-roofed white houses; twilight had settled over the land. The air was warm. Flakes of wet snow were falling softly on the dirty streets. The thought that he had slept away this day, now drawing to a close, filled him with deep sadness.

"Never will this lost day come back," he thought. "I've squandered my youth," he said to himself, not because he really thought he had squandered his youth—indeed he harbored no thoughts at all on this subject—but because the phrase suddenly came into his mind.

"What am I to do now?" he reflected. "Borrow money from somebody and go away?" A young woman passed him on the pavement. "What a foolish-looking lady," he thought for some odd reason. "There's no one I could borrow from.

I've squandered my youth." He went on to a row of shops.
A merchant in a coat lined with fox was standing in the
door of one of them touting for customers. "If I hadn't got
rid of that eight-spot I would have made up my losses." An
old beggar woman whimpered as she followed at his heels.
"There's no one I can borrow from." A man in a bearskin
coat drove past; a watchman stood on duty. "What could I
do that would cause a sensation? Fire at these people? Too
dull. I've squandered my youth. What a fine set of trappings hanging on display! Oh, to go dashing off in a sleigh-
and-three! I'll go back to the inn. Lukhnov will come soon
and we shall begin playing."

He went back and counted his money again. No, he had
made no mistake the first time: two thousand five hundred
rubles were missing from the regiment money. "I'll stake
twenty-five on the first card, then a 'corner' on the second,
then seven times the stake, then fifteen, thirty, sixty times,
up to three thousand rubles. Then I'll buy those trappings
and go away. But he won't let me win, the ruffian! I've
squandered my youth."

These were the thoughts that were passing through the
Uhlan's mind when Lukhnov came into his room.

"Have you been up long, Mikhailo Vasilyich?" asked Lukhnov, slowly removing his gold spectacles from his bony
nose and polishing them deliberately on a red silk handkerchief.

"No, I just got up. Slept beautifully."

"A hussar has just arrived. He's staying with Zavalshevsky. Have you heard?"

"No, I haven't. Where are the others?"

"They've dropped in to see Pryakhin. They'll come directly."

And, true enough, they were soon joined by the others:
an officer from the local garrison who always accompanied
Lukhnov; a Greek merchant with an enormous hooked
nose, brown skin, and deep-set black eyes; a fat, cushiony
landowner who ran a brewery by day and gambled by
night, always for half-ruble points.

Everyone was anxious to begin playing, but no hint of

this was given by the principal players, especially Lukhnov, who spoke with great composure on the lawlessness in Moscow.

"Just to think!" he said. "Moscow, one of our greatest towns, a citadel, and at night ruffians roam the streets with hooks in their hands, dressed up as goblins, terrifying the foolish rabble, robbing travelers, and nothing is done about it. What are the police thinking of? That's what I should like to know."

The Uhlan listened attentively to his account of the lawlessness, but at last he got up and quietly gave orders to bring the cards. The fat landowner was the first to give voice to their desire:

"Well, gentlemen, why should we waste the golden hours? Let's get down to business!"

"I can understand your wanting to, after all the money you took home with you last night," said the Greek.

"But it really is time," said the garrison officer.

Ilyin glanced at Lukhnov. Lukhnov looked him straight in the eye and calmly went on talking about the ruffians disguised as goblins with long claws.

"Shall we deal the cards?" asked the Uhlan.

"Isn't it too early?"

"Belov!" called out the Uhlan, reddening for some reason. "Bring me some dinner. I haven't had a bite to eat yet, gentlemen. Bring champagne, and give us the cards."

Just at that moment the count and Zavalshevsky came into the room. It turned out that Tourbin and Ilyin were in the same division. They quickly became friends, toasted each other in champagne, and in five minutes were talking like bosom friends. Ilyin made the best possible impression on the count, who smiled as he watched him and teased him for being so young.

"There's an Uhlan for you!" said he. "Such whiskers! Such ferocious whiskers!"

The down on Ilyin's upper lip was perfectly white.

"Are you getting ready to play cards?" said the count. "Well, I hope you win, Ilyin. You're a first-rate player, aren't you?" he added with a smile.

"We are getting ready," replied Lukhnov as he opened a pack of cards. "Won't you join us, Count?"

"No, not this evening. I'd strip you clean if I did. Any bank cracks wide open when I play. But I have nothing to play with now. I lost everything at the posting station near Volochok. A deuced infantryman with rings on his fingers cleaned me out. He must have been a cardsharper."

"Why, did you have to wait long at the station?" asked Ilyin.

"Twenty-two hours. I'll never forget that accursed station, but the postmaster will never forget me, either."

"How is that?"

"I drive up, out leaps the postmaster, with his sly, ugly little mug. 'No horses,' says he. I must tell you I've made the following rule for myself: whenever I'm told there are no horses, I go straight to the overseer's chamber without taking off my coat—not to the public room, mind you, but to his private chamber, and order all the doors and windows opened, as if the place were full of charcoal fumes. So that's what I did in this case. Cold! Remember what frosts we had last month? Four below. The postmaster tried to argue with me, but I just gave him one in the nose. An old lady and some wenches and females began screeching, picked up their pots, and were about to run off to the village. I blocked their way and shouted, 'Give me some horses and I'll go; if you don't, you can freeze to death; I won't let anyone out!' "

"That's the way to treat 'em!" said the cushiony landowner, going off into peals of laughter. "Like freezing out beetles."

"But I didn't keep my eye on them—went off somewhere —and the postmaster and his women gave me the slip. The only hostage left me was the old lady lying up on the stove-bunk, who kept sneezing and saying her prayers. After that we opened negotiations: the postmaster came back and urged me from a distance to let the old lady go, but I just sicked Blücher on him—Blücher has a nose for postmasters. But he didn't give me horses till the next morning, the blackguard! That's how I got to know that deuced infantry officer. I went into the next room and began playing with him. Have you seen Blücher? Blücher! Come here!"

Blücher came. The gamblers paid him condescending attention, but it was clear they were anxious to be doing something else.

"But why aren't you playing, gentlemen? Don't let me keep you from your game. I am something of a windbag, you know," said Tourbin. " 'Love me, love me not'—a good game."

III

Lukhnov drew over two candles, took out an enormous brown purse stuffed full of money, opened it with the slowness of one performing a mystic rite, drew out two hundred-ruble notes, and slipped them under the cards.

"A bank of two hundred rubles, just as yesterday," he said, putting his spectacles straight and unsealing a new pack of cards.

"Very well," said Ilyin without looking at him and continuing the conversation he was holding with Tourbin.

The game began. Lukhnov dealt with machinelike precision, stopping from time to time to mark a point unhurriedly, or glancing severely over his spectacles to say in a feeble voice, "Your lead." The cushiony landowner made more noise than anyone else, making calculations to himself aloud and smudging the cards with pudgy fingers as he bent down the corners. The garrison officer jotted down his points in a neat hand and turned down the edges of his cards ever so slightly under the table. The Greek sat next to Lukhnov, who was keeping the bank, and his deep-set black eyes followed the game with the strained attention of one waiting for something to happen. Zavalshevsky, standing at the table, suddenly became all movement: he took a red or blue banknote out of his pocket, put a card on it, clapped his hand down on it, cried out for luck, "Come along, seven!" bit his mustache, shifted from one foot to the other, grew red in the face, twitched all over, and kept on twitching till he got a card. Ilyin ate veal and cucumbers from a plate that was placed beside him on the horsehair sofa, hurriedly wiped his fingers on his jacket, and threw down one card after the other. Tourbin, who from the very beginning had been sitting on the sofa, instantly saw what was happening. Lukhnov did not so much as glance at the Uhlan and said not a word to him; he would only glance through his spectacles at his hands from time to time. Most of the Uhlan's cards were losing ones.

"That's a card I should like to take," said Lukhnov, referring to the card of the cushiony landowner, who was playing for half-ruble stakes.

"You take Ilyin's cards—why bother about mine?" said the landowner.

And true enough, no one's cards seemed as ill-fated as Ilyin's. Each time he lost he nervously tore at the offending card under the table and chose another with shaking hands. Tourbin got up off the sofa and asked the Greek to allow him to sit next to the player keeping the bank. The Greek changed his seat and the count, taking his chair, fixed his eyes on Lukhnov's hands.

"Ilyin!" he said suddenly in a voice which, though in his ordinary tone, drowned out all other sounds. "What makes you think that card's lucky? You don't know how to play."

"However I play, it all comes to the same thing."

"You're certain to lose if that's how you feel. Here, let me take your hand."

"Oh no, thank you: I never let anyone play for me. Play for yourself if you want to."

"I told you I didn't want to: I was just offering for your sake. I'm sorry to see you losing so."

"That seems to be my fate."

The count said nothing else; he merely put his elbows on the table and once more stared at Lukhnov's hands.

"Very bad," he suddenly drawled in a loud voice.

Lukhnov glanced at him.

"Very, very bad," he repeated still louder, looking Lukhnov straight in the eye.

They went on playing.

"A dirty business," said Tourbin as Lukhnov took another one of Ilyin's cards.

"Just what are you displeased with, Count?" asked Lukhnov in a tone of polite indifference.

"The way you take Ilyin's cards. That's what's bad."

Lukhnov made a slight movement of his shoulders and
brows that seemed to say one must accept one's fate, and
went on playing.

"Blücher! Come here!" cried the count, getting up. "At
him, Blücher!" he said quickly.

Blücher nearly knocked the garrison officer down as he
leaped out from under the sofa, rushed over to his master,
and stood beside him growling, wagging his tail, and eyeing
the company in a way that said, "Which is the recreant,
eh?"

Lukhnov put down his cards and pushed back his chair.

"It is impossible to play under the circumstances," he
said. "I can't abide dogs. How is one expected to play with
a whole kennelful of dogs in the room?"

"Especially dogs like that—leeches they're called, I believe," chimed in the garrison officer.

"Well, Mikhailo Vasilyich, are we to go on with our
game or not?" said Lukhnov to his host.

"Please don't interfere, Count," said Ilyin to Tourbin.

"Come here a moment," said Tourbin, taking Ilyin by
the arm and drawing him out of the room.

Everything the count said could be heard distinctly, for
he spoke without lowering his voice. And his voice was such
that it could always be heard three rooms away.

"Have you gone quite daft? Can't you see that that gentleman in the spectacles is an accomplished cardsharper?"

"Oh, come. What are you saying?"

"Drop it, I tell you. What matters it to me? At any other
time I myself would be only too glad to take your money
away from you, but tonight for some reason I'm sorry to
see you taken such advantage of. Are you sure it's all your
own money you are playing with?"

"Yes! . . . er . . . Why? What have you in mind?"

"I've traveled that same road myself, friend, and so I know all the tricks of these sharpers; and that fellow in the spectacles is a sharper, I tell you. Drop it, do; it's a bit of comradely advice I'm giving you."

"I'll only play one more round."

"I know what 'one more' means. Well, we'll see."

They came back. In one round Ilyin threw down so many cards and so many of them were beaten that he sustained heavy losses.

Tourbin spread out his hands on the table.

"Enough!" he cried. "Come away!"

"I can't now; be good enough to let me alone," said Ilyin in vexation, shuffling the bent cards without looking at Tourbin.

"Then the devil take you! Go on losing if you enjoy it so much, but I must be going. Zavalshevsky! Come along with me to the Marshal's!"

They went out. No one said a word, and Lukhnov did not deal until the sound of their steps and the click of Blücher's claws had died away down the corridor.

"What a fellow!" said the landowner, laughing.

"Well, he won't interfere with us now," added the garrison officer hurriedly, still speaking in a whisper.

And they went on playing.

IV

The musicians, the Marshal's house serfs, standing in the pantry that had been cleared for the occasion, had already turned back the cuffs of their coats and, at a given signal, had begun to play the old-fashioned polonaise "Alexander-Elizabeth," and in the soft bright light of the wax candles the couples had begun to step gracefully out on to the parquet floor of the large hall (first the governor, a general of Catherine's court, wearing a star on his breast and holding the arm of the Marshal's thin wife; then the Marshal holding the arm of the governor's wife; then all the others, members of the gubernia's ruling families in various groupings and combinations) when Zavalshevsky in a blue frock coat

with puffs on the shoulders and an enormous collar, in long
hose and dancing shoes, diffusing the scent of jasmine which
had been so generously sprinkled on his mustache, his la-
pels, and his handkerchief, entered the room accompanied
by a handsome hussar in tight blue riding breeches and a
gold-embroidered red tunic ornamented with the Vladimir
Cross and the Medal of 1812. The count, though not above
average height, was extremely well built. His clear blue
very bright eyes and the large ringlets of his thick chestnut
hair added something particularly winning to his beauty.
His appearance in the ballroom was not unexpected: the
handsome young man who had seen him in the hotel had
informed the Marshal of his intention to be present. The
news had been variously received, but on the whole without
great enthusiasm. "He may make fun of us," said the men
and the elderly ladies. "What if he should elope with me?"
was the thought that occurred to most of the girls and
young women.

As soon as the polonaise was over and the dancing partners had bowed to each other and parted, the women to
join the women, the men the men, Zavalshevsky, proud and
happy, led the count to the hostess. The Marshal's wife, inwardly fearful lest the count reduce her to ridicule in front
of everybody, turned her head and said with proud con-
descension, "Charmed. I hope you will dance," following
the words by a glance of distrust that seemed to say, "You
would be a ruffian indeed if you insulted a lady after this!"
But the count soon overcame all prejudice by his courtesy,
attentiveness, gaiety, and elegant appearance, so that in
five minutes the expression of the hostess's face said to all,
"I know how to manage such gentlemen; he instantly understood to whom he was talking. Wait and see, he will be
paying me attention the whole evening." But at this point
the governor, who had known the count's father, came up
to him and drew him aside so that he might engage him in
conversation, a thing that further served to calm the fears
of the local gentry and raised the count in their estimation.
A little later Zavalshevsky introduced him to his sister, a
plump young widow who had not taken her large black

eyes off of him from the moment he had entered the room.
The count invited her to dance the waltz that the orchestra
was then playing, and his skill in dancing finally overcame
the last remnants of prejudice against him.

"He certainly dances marvelously," said the fat wife of a
country gentleman as she followed the legs in the blue riding breeches whirling about the room, and counted to herself, "One, two, three; one, two, three—marvelous!"

"What a tripper! What a tripper!" said another woman,
a visitor in the town, who was considered rather vulgar in
local society. "How is it he doesn't strike anyone with his
spurs! Marvelous! So light on his feet!"

In his performance the count eclipsed the three best
dancers in the gubernia: the tall, tow-headed adjutant to
the governor who was famous for the swiftness with which
he danced and the closeness with which he held his partner;
a cavalry officer, who had a particularly graceful way of
swaying as he waltzed and of tapping his heels very lightly
and rapidly; and still another gentleman, a civilian, who
everyone said was a superb dancer and the life of any ball,
even if he was not gifted with a great mind. And indeed
this gentleman did not rest a moment from the beginning
to the end of a ball, asking all the ladies in order as they sat,
stopping only on rare occasions to wipe his tired but beam-
ing face with a moist handkerchief. The count outdid them
all and danced with the three ladies of most consequence at
the ball: a large one—rich and handsome and stupid; a
middle-sized one—thin, not very pretty, but elegantly
dressed; and a little one—very plain but very clever. He
danced with others, too; with all, in fact, who were pretty,
and there were many pretty women at the ball. But the
one who pleased him most was Zavalshevsky's sister, the
widow. With her he danced a quadrille, an *écossaise,* and
a mazurka. He began by paying her many compliments
during the quadrille, comparing her to Venus, Diana, a
rose, and some other flower. The little widow responded to
all these civilities by bending her fair white neck and lowering her eyes as she gazed at her white muslin frock and
shifted her fan from one hand to the other. When she said,

"Dear me, Count, you are only jesting," and other things of the same sort, her voice, which was rather husky, expressed such innocent candor and comic simplicity that as he gazed at her he could not help thinking that she really was more like a flower than a woman; and not a rose, but some full-blown pink-and-white wildflower without any scent, growing in a pristine snowbank, all by itself, in a far country.

Her artlessness and lack of the usual affectations, combined with her fresh beauty, made such an odd impression on the count that on several occasions during their conversation, as he gazed mutely into her eyes or at the lovely line of her arms and neck, he was seized by so strong a desire to take her in his arms and kiss her that he had difficulty in controlling himself. The little widow was pleased to note the impression she made, but there was something in the count's behavior that began to disturb and frighten her, even though, besides being fawningly attentive, he was respectful to a fault, judging by prevailing standards. He rushed off to bring her refreshments, picked up her handkerchief, snatched her chair out of the hands of a scrofulous-looking young rival, and performed innumerable other small services.

Seeing that all his efforts to play the gallant made little impression on her, he attempted to be amusing by recounting funny stories and assuring her that at her bidding he would stand on his head, crow like a cock, throw himself out of the window or through a hole in the ice on the river. He was entirely successful in this. The little widow became very gay, breaking into peals of laughter that showed her beautiful white teeth. She was highly pleased with her cavalier. And with every passing minute the count became more infatuated, so that by the end of the quadrille he was truly in love.

When the idle eighteen-year-old son of the richest landowner in the region, who had long worshiped the widow (that same scrofulous-looking youth out of whose hands Tourbin had snatched the chair) came up to her at the end of the quadrille, she received him coldly and displayed not a tenth part of the perturbation excited in her by the count.

"A fine person, you!" she said to him, her eyes fixed on Tourbin's back as she unconsciously calculated how many yards of gold braid had gone into the making of his coat. "A fine one, you! You promised to come and take me for a sleigh ride and to bring me some chocolates."

"But I did come, Anna Fyodorovna. You were not at home and I left a box of the very finest chocolates for you," said the youth, who, despite his tallness, spoke in a small, shrill voice.

"You always find excuses. I don't want your chocolates. Please don't think—"

"I can see how you have changed toward me, Anna Fyodorovna, and I know why. And it is very wrong of you," he added. He seemed to have something else to say, but his agitation set his lips to trembling so violently that he could not speak.

Anna Fyodorovna did not listen to him and went on watching Tourbin.

The Marshal, the host of the evening, a stout, toothless, majestic old gentleman, went over to the count and, taking him by the arm, invited him into his study to smoke and have a drink if he felt so inclined. As soon as Tourbin went out, Anna Fyodorovna, for whom the ballroom was now as good as empty, took the hand of a thin spinster with whom she was friendly and drew her into the dressing room.

"Well, do you like him?" asked the spinster.

"But it's awful the way he makes up to me!" said Anna Fyodorovna, going over to a mirror and gazing into it.

Her face was shining, her eyes were laughing, she was even blushing, and suddenly, in imitation of the ballet dancers she had seen perform at the elections, she pirouetted on one toe, then gave that charming deep-throated little laugh of hers and leaped into the air, kicking up her heels.

"And what do you think? He asked me for a keepsake," she said to her friend. "But he'll not get a s-i-n-g-l-e th-i-ng!" She sang the last two words, holding up one finger sheathed in a kid glove.

In the study to which the Marshal guided Tourbin were various brands of vodka, liqueurs, and champagne, and plates of hors d'oeuvres. Members of the local gentry were sitting or walking about in a fog of tobacco smoke, discussing the elections.

"If the nobility of our uyezd honored him by election," the newly elected police captain, already quite tipsy, was saying, "he had no right to shirk his duties, he had no right to—"

The talk was interrupted by the advent of the count. Everyone was introduced to him and the police captain shook his hand with particular cordiality and begged him over and over again to join the party he was treating to supper after the ball at a new tavern where they could hear a Gypsy chorus. The count accepted the invitation and drank several glasses of champagne with him.

"But why aren't you dancing, gentlemen?" he asked as he was about to leave the study.

"We're not much when it comes to dancing," laughed the police captain. "We make a better showing with the bottle, Count. By the way, they've all grown up under my very nose, these young ladies, Count. And sometimes I do step out in an *écossaise*, Count—I'm still up to it, Count."

"Then let's step out now," said Tourbin. "Let's enjoy ourselves here before we go to hear the Gypsies."

"Why not, gentlemen? Let us do it to please our host."

And three red-faced noblemen, who had been sitting in the study and drinking since the very beginning of the ball, drew on their gloves, one a pair of black kid gloves, the others silk knitted ones, and were just about to go out into the ballroom when they were stopped by the scrofulous-looking young man who, white-lipped and scarcely able to restrain his tears, went up to Tourbin.

"You think that just because you are a count you can push people about as if you were in the marketplace," he said, breathing with difficulty. "It's rude and . . . and . . ."

Again the trembling of his lips put a stop to the rush of his words.

"What?" cried Tourbin, suddenly scowling. "What? You puppy!" he cried, seizing the youth's hands and squeezing them so hard that the blood rushed to his face more from fright than insult. "Is it a duel you want to fight with me? If so I am at your service."

As soon as Tourbin let go of his hands, two gentlemen took the youth by the arms and led him away to the door in the rear.

"Are you mad? You must have taken too much to drink. We'll tell your father. What in the world is the matter with you?" they asked him.

"I am not drunk, but he pushes people about without so much as apologizing. He's a swine, that's what he is," wailed the youth, now crying openly.

But his complaints were ignored and he was taken home.

"Pay no heed to him, Count," said the police captain and Zavalshevsky, eager to mollify Tourbin. "He's a mere child; why, he still takes spankings. He's only sixteen years old. Whatever could have got into him? He must be mad. And his father is such a highly respected gentleman—our candidate."

"Well, the deuce with him if he doesn't want satisfaction."

And the count went into the ballroom, danced an *écossaise* as gaily as ever with the pretty little widow, laughed wholeheartedly on seeing the performance of the gentlemen who had come out of the study with him, and gave a roar that rang throughout the ballroom when the police captain slipped and fell down amidst the dancing couples.

V

While the count was in the study, Anna Fyodorovna, feeling that she ought to feign indifference to him, went up to her brother and asked nonchalantly, "Tell me, brother, who is that hussar who danced with me?" The cavalry officer did his best to explain to her what a very great hussar Tourbin was, adding that he had remained in town and come to the ball only because his money had been stolen from him on the road, and that he himself had lent the count one hundred rubles, but that that was too little and could not his sister lend him another two hundred? At the same time he asked her not to mention this to anyone, especially the count. Anna Fyodorovna promised to send her brother the money that very evening and to keep the matter a secret, but during the *écossaise* she was seized by an irresistible desire to offer the count any sum he needed. It took her some time to pluck up the courage to do it; she blushed and hesitated, but at last, with a great effort, broached the subject.

"My brother told me you met with misfortune on the road, Count, and that now you have no money. If you are in need of any, perhaps you would accept it from me? It would make me exceedingly happy."

No sooner were the words out of her mouth than Anna Fyodorovna grew frightened and turned red. All the joy went out of the count's face.

"Your brother's a dunce," he said curtly. "As you are aware, when a man insults another man he is challenged to a duel. But do you know what happens when a woman insults a man?"

Poor Anna Fyodorovna felt her neck and ears burning with shame. She dropped her eyes and said not a word.

"The woman is kissed in front of everybody," whispered the count, bending down to her ear. "Allow me to kiss your hand," he added softly after a long pause, taking pity on the lady for the confusion she was suffering.

"Oh, but not now," said Anna Fyodorovna with a deep sigh.

"When? I am leaving early tomorrow. And you owe it to me."

"But under the circumstances I cannot pay it," said Anna Fyodorovna with a smile.

"Give me the opportunity of seeing you tonight so that I can kiss your hand. But I shall find it myself."

"How will you?"

"That is my concern. I would do anything to see you. You don't object?"

"No."

The *écossaise* came to an end. They danced another mazurka, during which the count performed wonders, catching handkerchiefs, dropping on one knee and clicking his spurs together in the peculiar Warsaw manner, so that the old men left their card tables to watch the dancing, and the cavalry officer with the reputation of being the best dancer acknowledged himself defeated. Supper was served, a final "Grandfather" was danced, and the guests began to depart. All this time the count had not taken his eyes off the little widow. It had been no exaggeration when he had said he was ready to throw himself through a hole in the ice for her sake. Whether for love, a whim, or mere obstinacy, all his faculties were concentrated on one desire that evening —to see and make love to her. When he saw Anna Fyodorovna taking leave of the hostess, he ran to the footman's room and from there, coatless, to the roadside where the carriages were waiting.

"The carriage of Anna Fyodorovna Zaitsova!" he called. A high carriage for four with lanterns on it moved toward the entrance.

"Stop!" he called to the coachman as he ran up, knee-deep in snow.

"What do you want?" called back the coachman.

"I want to get in," replied the count, opening the door as he ran alongside, trying to climb up. "Stop, damn you! You blockhead!"

"Stop, Vaska!" cried the coachman to the postilion, and he drew in his horses. "Why should you get into somebody else's carriage? This carriage belongs to Anna Fyodorovna, not you, Your Honour."

"Hold your tongue, idiot! Here, take this ruble and get down and close the door," said the count. But since the coachman did not stir, he himself pulled up the steps, opened the window, and managed somehow to slam the door to. The carriage, like all old carriages, especially those with gold braid ornamenting the upholstery, gave off an odor of mustiness and burnt bristles. The count's legs, which had been up to the knees in wet snow and were clad only in thin boots and riding breeches, were badly chilled, and indeed his whole body was shivering. The coachman was grumbling up on his box and seemed about to climb down. But the count heard and felt nothing. His face was burning, his heart pounding. He seized the yellow strap in tense fingers and thrust his head out of the side window, his whole being concentrated on this moment of anticipation. It did not last long. Someone at the entrance called out, "Madame Zaitsova's carriage!" The coachman flicked the reins, the carriage rocked on its high springs, and the lighted windows of the house marched past the carriage windows one after another.

"Mind you say nothing to the footman about my being here, you rogue," said the count, poking his head through the front window that communicated with the coachman. "If you do I'll give you a flogging; if you don't—ten rubles."

Scarcely had he slammed down the window when the carriage stopped with a lurch. He shrank back into the corner, held his breath, and even shut his eyes, so fearful was he that something might thwart his passionate hopes. The door opened, one by one the steps slapped down, there was a rustle of a woman's gown, into the musty carriage floated the scent of jasmine, little feet pattered lightly up the steps, and Anna Fyodorovna, brushing the count's legs with the hem of her cloak, sank silently, breathlessly, onto the seat beside him.

Whether she had seen him or not no one could have said, not even Anna Fyodorovna, but when he took her arm and murmured, "Now I shall certainly kiss your hand," she showed very little alarm and said nothing, and instantly the arm she surrendered to him was covered with kisses at a spot high up above her glove. The carriage set off.

"Say something. You're not angry, are you?" he asked her.

She only shrank further back into her corner, but suddenly, with no apparent reason, she burst into tears and her head dropped of its own accord upon his breast.

VI

The newly elected police captain and his party, the cavalry officer and other gentlemen, had been drinking and listening to the Gypsies in the new tavern for some time when the count, in a blue broadcloth cloak lined with bearskin which had belonged to Anna Fyodorovna's husband, joined them.

"Ah, Your Excellency, we had almost given up hope of your coming!" said a black-haired, cross-eyed Gypsy, who greeted the count with a flash of white teeth as he rushed into the entranceway to help him off with his coat. "We haven't seen you since Lebedyan. Styesha's pining away for you."

Styesha, too, came running out to meet him; she was a graceful young Gypsy with a warm flush on her swarthy cheeks and with deep-set black eyes whose brilliance was softened by the shadow of long lashes.

"Ah, the little count! The little darling! What a joy!" she murmured, smiling happily.

Even Ilyushka ran to meet him, pretending to be glad to see him. Old women, middle-aged women, young wenches, jumped up and surrounded him. Some claimed kinship with him for his having stood godfather to their children, others for his having exchanged crosses with them.

Tourbin kissed all the young Gypsy girls on the mouth; the old Gypsy women and the men kissed him on the shoulder and hand. The noblemen, too, were delighted to see him, the more so since festivities, having reached their height, were now on the decline. Each was beginning to feel surfeited. The wine had lost its power to stimulate the nerves and was only a strain on the stomach. Having indulged in all the hilarity of which they were capable, the guests now sat staring at one another. All the songs had been sung and got mixed up inside their heads, leaving an impression of noise and dissipation. However original or daring the tricks now performed, no one found them amusing. The police officer was lying in an ugly pose on the floor at the feet of an old woman.

"Champagne!" he cried, kicking his feet. "The count's come! Champagne! He's come! Bring on the champagne! I'll fill a bathtub with champagne and bathe in it! Gentlemen of the nobility! How I do love to be in such select society! Styesha! Sing 'The Open Road'!"

The cavalry officer was quite as muzzy as he was, but he gave different expression to it. He was huddled in the corner of a sofa very close to a tall and handsome Gypsy girl named Lyubasha, blinking his eyes and tossing his head to get rid of the blur of his drunkenness, and urging her over and over again, in one and the same phrase, to run away with him. Lyubasha, smiling, listened as if what he was saying was at the same time extremely amusing and slightly pathetic, and now and again she cast a glance at her husband, the cross-eyed Sashka, who was standing behind a chair opposite her. In reply to the cavalry officer's protestations of love, she bent down and whispered a request that he buy her some ribbons and some scent, provided nobody learned of it.

"Hurrah!" shouted the cavalry officer when the count came in.

The handsome young man, now wearing an anxious look, was walking back and forth with unnaturally firm steps and humming a tune from *The Revolt in the Seraglio*.

An aged paterfamilias who had been lured to the Gypsies by the insistent entreaties of the gentlemen of the nobility, who assured him that their fun would be spoiled and it would be better for none of them to go if he refused to join them, lay on the sofa where he had stretched himself out as soon as he arrived, and no one was paying the slightest attention to him. A government official had taken off his frock coat and perched himself, feet and all, on top of a table, where he sat ruffling his hair to show what an awful rake he was. As soon as the count came in he unfastened the collar of his shirt and hitched himself further back on the table. On the whole, the party became more lively with the arrival of the count. The Gypsies who had been sauntering about the room sat down again in a ring. The count put Styesha, the soloist, on his knee and ordered more champagne.

Ilyushka seated himself with his guitar in front of the soloist and made a sign to begin the "plyaska," which is the singing of Gypsy songs such as "Whenever I Walk Down the Street," "Eh, You Hussars!" and "Hear and Understand" in a given order. Styesha sang beautifully. Her rich and flexible contralto voice that came from deep down in her chest, her winning smile, her laughing passionate glance, the little foot that involuntarily tapped in time to the song, the wild little cries she gave at the beginning of every chorus—all of these things set some resonant but rarely touched string to vibrating. She threw her whole soul into whatever she was singing. Ilyushka accompanied her on the guitar, expressing his oneness with the song in little movements of his back and legs, in his smile, in his whole being, and as he nodded his head rhythmically, he fixed his eyes upon her and listened as anxiously and attentively as if he had never heard the song before. When the last note died away he suddenly straightened up, and as if feeling himself above everyone else in the world, proudly and deliberately gave his guitar a little toss with his knee that sent it spinning in the air while he tapped with his heels on the floor, tossed back his hair, and swept the Gypsy chorus with a scowling glance. And then he began to dance with every fibre of his body. And twenty strong and vigorous voices rang out, each of them vying with the others to offer the most unique and original rendition. The old ladies gave little jumps without getting up, waved their kerchiefs, grinned, and shouted each other down in time and tune to the song. The men poured out their deep bass voices as they stood behind their chairs, their heads tilted, the cords of their necks swelling.

Whenever Styesha took a high note Ilyushka would bring his guitar closer as if to help her, and the handsome young man would cry out in ecstasy that now they would hear her high C.

When a dance tune was sung and Dunyasha stepped

forth, shoulders and breasts quivering, circling in front of the count and then sailing out into the middle of the floor, Tourbin jumped up, flung off his jacket, and joined her, performing such feats with his legs that the Gypsies glanced at one another and exchanged smiles of approval.

The police captain sat with his legs crossed like a Turk, beat his chest with his fist, and shouted, "Bravo!" then, seizing the count by the leg, confided to him that he had come here with two thousand rubles and had only five hundred left, and that he would do anything he liked provided the count gave his sanction. The old paterfamilias woke up and wanted to go home, but he was not permitted to. The handsome young man coaxed one of the Gypsy girls to waltz with him. The cavalry officer, eager to make a show of his friendship with the count, emerged from his corner and put his arms round him.

"Ah, my dear fellow," he said, "why in the world did you leave us?" The count said nothing, his mind evidently on something else. "Where did you go? You're a sly one, Count! I know where you went!"

For some reason Tourbin was displeased by this familiarity. He stared into the face of the cavalry officer without smiling and without speaking, and suddenly let out a string of such coarse and stinging abuse that the cavalry officer was taken aback and could not make up his mind whether to take it as a joke or not. At last he smiled and went back to his Gypsy, assuring her that he would certainly marry her after Easter.

The whole company sang another song, and yet another, danced some more, sang songs in one another's honor, and fancied they were having a glorious time. There was no end to the flow of champagne. The count drank a lot. His eyes grew moist but he did not stagger; he danced better than ever, spoke in a firm voice, joined in when the Gypsy chorus sang, and harmonized with Styesha when she sang "The Gentle Flutter of Love's Wings."

In the middle of a song the proprietor of the tavern came and asked the guests to leave, as it was nearly three o'clock in the morning. The count seized him by the nape of the neck and ordered him to do a squat-dance. He refused. The count snatched up a bottle of champagne, turned the proprietor upside down, and had the others hold him while, amidst general merriment, he poured the whole bottle over him.

It was already growing light. All but the count were pale and exhausted.

"But it's time for me to be leaving for Moscow," he said suddenly, getting up. "Come back to the hotel with me, gentlemen, and see me off. We'll have some tea."

Everyone consented except the sleeping paterfamilias, who was left behind. They all packed themselves into three sleighs standing at the door and set out for the hotel.

VII

"Harness the horses!" cried out the count as he entered the public room of the hotel with all his guests and the Gypsies. "Sasha!—not the Gypsy Sasha, but my Sasha—tell the postmaster I'll tan his hide for him if he gives me bad horses. And bring us some tea! Zavalshevsky, you see to the tea while I drop into Ilyin's room and find out how he's getting on," added Tourbin, and he went out into the corridor and made for the Uhlan's room.

Ilyin had just finished playing. Having lost all his money down to the last kopek, he was now lying on the torn horsehair sofa, pulling out the hairs one by one, putting them in his mouth, biting at them, and spitting them out. Two wax candles, one of which had burned right down to the paper, were standing on a table littered with cards, their light struggling feebly with the light of dawn peeping in at the window. There were no thoughts at all in the Uhlan's mind; all his mental faculties were wrapped up in the dense fog of his gambling fever; he did not even feel remorse. True, at one point he had tried to think what he was to do next, how he was to leave this place without a kopek, how he was to pay back the fifteen thousand belonging to the regiment, what the regiment commander would say, what his

mother would say, what his comrades would say—and he
had instantly been seized by such fear and disgust with himself that in order to forget everything he had jumped up
and paced the floor, taking pains to tread only on the
cracks between the floorboards. Once more he went over
in his mind in the most minute detail all the games he had
played. He recalled how he had almost won—he had picked
up a nine and the king of spades, staking two thousand
rubles on it: on the right—the queen; on the left—the ace;
on the right—the king of diamonds, and—all was lost. If
the six had been on the right and the king of diamonds on
the left he would have won everything back and would
have staked it all and won another fifteen thousand clear.
Ah, then he would have bought a saddle horse from his
regiment commander and a pair of horses besides and a
phaeton! And what else? Why . . . why . . . oh, it would
have been wonderful, wonderful!

Once more he lay down on the sofa and began chewing
hairs.

"Why are they singing in room seven?" he thought.
"Tourbin must be entertaining. Perhaps I ought to join
them and get good and drunk."

Just then the count came in.

"Well, have you been cleaned out?" he asked.

"I'll pretend to be asleep," thought Ilyin. "Otherwise I'll
have to talk, and I'm too tired."

But Tourbin came over to him and stroked his hair.

"So you've been cleaned out, my good fellow, eh? Lost
everything? Speak up."

Ilyin made no reply.

The count gave his sleeve a tug.

"Yes, I lost. What is it to you?" muttered Ilyin in a sleepy
voice that expressed annoyed indifference; he did not so
much as turn over.

"Everything?"

"Yes. What of it? Everything. What is it to you?"

"Listen, tell me the truth, as a comrade," said the count.
The wine had awakened tender sentiments in him, and he
went on stroking the youth's hair. "I've really come to love

you. Tell me the truth: if it is regiment money you've lost, I'll come to your aid; tell me before it is too late: is it regiment money?"

Ilyin leaped up off the sofa.

"If you really want me to tell you, then don't speak to me as if . . . as if . . . please don't speak to me at all. The only thing left for me to do is put a bullet through my head!" he cried in genuine despair, dropping his head in his hands and bursting into tears, although only a moment before he had been dreaming of a saddle horse.

"Come, you're behaving like a girl! We've all been through it. No particular harm is done; I think we can patch things up. Wait here for me."

The count went out.

"In what room is Lukhnov, the landowner, staying?" he asked the page boy.

The boy offered to show him.

Despite the valet's protests that his master had just got in and was about to disrobe, the count went in. Lukhnov was sitting at the table in a dressing gown, counting a pile of banknotes that lay in front of him. There was also a bottle of Rhine wine, of which he was extremely fond, standing on the table. His winnings permitted him to indulge in this luxury. Lukhnov looked at the count through his spectacles in a hard, cold way, as if he did not know who it was.

"You seem not to recognize me," said the count striding boldly up to the table.

"What can I do for you?" he asked.

"I want to play cards with you," said Tourbin, taking a seat on the sofa.

"Now?"

"Yes."

"Another time I shall be delighted, Count, but at present I am tired and about to retire. Will you have some wine? Excellent wine."

"I want to play now."

"I have no intention of playing any more tonight. Perhaps some of the other gentlemen will play with you; I will not, Count. I trust you will forgive me."

"So you will not?"

Lukhnov gave a little shrug of his shoulders expressing his regret at being unable to comply with the count's wishes.

"Not for anything?"

Another little shrug.

"I am asking you very earnestly: will you play or not?" Silence.

"Will you play?" repeated the Count. "Mind, now!"

Still Lukhnov was silent, then he threw a quick glance over the top of his spectacles at the count's face, which was quickly clouding.

"Will you play?" shouted the count, giving the table such a blow with his hand that the bottle of Rhine wine fell over and spilled. "You know that you won by cheating. Will you play? I am asking you for the third time."

"I told you I would not. Your behavior is very strange, Count. Respectable people do not burst in and hold a knife to a man's throat," observed Lukhnov without lifting his eyes.

There was a brief pause during which the count's face grew whiter and whiter. Suddenly Lukhnov was stunned by a terrific blow on the head. He fell on the sofa, grasping at his money, and let out a wild and piercing cry that one would hardly have expected to come from a man who was always so calm and dignified. Tourbin swept up the money, pushed away the valet who came running on hearing his master's cry, and made for the door.

"If you want satisfaction, I am at your service; I shall be in my room for another half hour," said the count on reaching it.

"Thief! Blackguard!" came from inside the room. "I'll have you taken to court!"

Ilyin, who had given no credence to the count's promise to patch things up, was still lying on the sofa, choked by tears of despair. The count's tender sympathy had penetrated the odd mixture of impressions filling his mind, awakening him to a recognition of his plight, and this was still with him. His youth so rich in hope, his honor, the respect of his fellows, his dreams of love and friendship—all were lost forever. The fount of tears was beginning to run dry, a sense of despair, all too calm, was taking firmer and firmer hold of him, and thoughts of suicide, no longer inspiring a feeling of horror and repugnance, occurred to him with growing insistence. At this point the firm steps of the count were heard.

Tourbin's face still wore a trace of his wrath, his hands were trembling slightly, but his eyes shone with kindly good-humor and satisfaction.

"Here, I won it back!" he said, tossing a heap of notes onto the table. "Count it and see if it's all there. And hurry into the public room, I'm leaving," he added, pretending not to notice the joy and gratitude expressed on the Uhlan's face. He went out of the room whistling a Gypsy tune.

VIII

Sasha, his girdle wound tightly about his waist, announced that the horses were ready, but demanded that they first go and reclaim the count's greatcoat, which, with its fur collar, was worth all of three hundred rubles, and give back the wretched blue cloak to the scoundrel who had exchanged it for the greatcoat at the Marshal's. But Tourbin said there was no need to get back the greatcoat, and went to his room to dress.

The cavalry officer hiccuped incessantly as he sat in silence beside his Gypsy girl. The police captain ordered vodka and invited all the gentlemen to go home to breakfast with him, promising that his wife would come down and dance with the Gypsies. The handsome young man was earnestly trying to convince Ilyushka that there was more soul in the pianoforte and that the guitar could not take an A flat. The government official was sitting in a corner drinking tea, and, now that daylight had come, seemed ashamed of his debauch. The Gypsies were arguing among themselves in their own tongue, insisting that they sing another song in honor of the gentlemen, but Styesha objected, saying that the *barorai* (meaning "count" or "prince," to be more exact, "great nobleman") would be angry. In a word, the last spark of life was dying out.

"Well, one last song in parting and everyone goes home," said the count as he came into the room in his traveling clothes, looking fresher, handsomer, and gayer than ever before.

The Gypsies had just arranged themselves in a ring for the last song when Ilyin came in with a bundle of notes in his hand and called the count aside.

"I only had fifteen thousand rubles of regiment money and you have given me sixteen thousand three hundred," he said. "These others belong to you."

"Capital! Let me have them!"

Ilyin turned a shy glance on the count as he gave him the money and opened his mouth as if to say something, but instead he simply blushed till the tears came and, seizing the count's hand, squeezed it hard.

"Be off with you! Ilyushka! Listen—here's some money; see me off with songs as far as the gates of the town," and he tossed the thousand three hundred rubles Ilyin had given him onto the Gypsy's guitar. But he forgot to give the cavalry officer back the one hundred rubles he had borrowed the night before.

It was now ten o'clock in the morning. The sun was already high over the roofs, the streets were full of people, the shopkeepers had long since opened their doors, noblemen and government officials were riding past, ladies were sauntering from one shop to another in the arcade, when the flock of Gypsies, the police captain, the cavalry officer, the handsome young man, Ilyin, and the count in the blue cloak lined with bearskin came out on the steps of the hotel. The day was sunny, the snow was melting. Three sleighs, each drawn by three horses with their tails tied up short, drew up at the hotel entrance and the whole gay party got in. The count, Ilyin, Styesha, Ilyushka, and the count's servant Sasha, took their places in the first sleigh. Blücher, beside himself with excitement, wagged his tail and barked at the shaft horse. The rest of the gentlemen and the Gypsies got into the other sleighs. As soon as they had left the hotel

the sleighs came abreast of one another and the Gypsies
began singing in chorus.

And in this manner, with songs and the jingling of little
bells, they rode the length of the town, out to the very
gates, driving all the vehicles they met up on to the pavement.

What was the wonder of the shopkeepers and pedes-
trians, especially those who knew them, on seeing these respectable gentlemen riding in broad daylight through the
streets of the town, accompanied by singing, by Gypsy girls,
and drunken Gypsy men!

When they had passed through the town gates the
sleighs came to a halt and everyone took leave of the count.

Ilyin, who had had quite a lot to drink before starting
out and had driven the horses himself, suddenly grew sad
and tried to persuade the count to stay for another day.
When he was convinced that this was impossible, he unexpectedly threw himself upon his new friend with tears in
his eyes and swore that as soon as he got back to his regiment he would put in an application to be transferred to
the hussar regiment in which Tourbin served. The count
was in particularly high spirits. He pushed the cavalry officer, who had been very familiar with him all morning, into
a snowbank, he set Blücher on to the police captain, he
snatched Styesha up in his arms and threatened to carry
her off to Moscow, and at last he leaped into the sleigh and
sat Blücher down beside him, though the dog would have
preferred standing up in the middle. Sasha, having once
more urged the cavalry officer to find the count's greatcoat and send it on to them, leaped up into the driver's seat.
The count shouted, "We're off!" snatched off his cap, waved
it over his head, whistled at the horses in the manner of a
sleigh-driver, and the three sleighs moved off in different
directions.

Far away into the distance stretched the monotonous
snowy plain with the dirty yellow ribbon of the road wind-
ing across it. The bright sun, dancing and sparkling on the
icy crust of thawing snow, brought a pleasant sensation of

warmth to face and back. Steam rose from the sweating flanks of the horses. The sleigh bells jingled. A peasant who was running beside his overloaded sledge pulled hastily on the ropes serving as reins to make way for the count, wetting his bast shoes in the slush of the roadside. A fat, red-faced peasant woman with a baby thrust inside the breast of her sheepskin coat was sitting on another sledge slapping the back of her white nag with the ends of the reins. Suddenly the count remembered Anna Fyodorovna.

"Turn round!" he shouted.

The driver did not understand.

"Turn round! Back to town! Quick!"

The sleigh passed back through the gates and drove swiftly up to the wooden entrance of Madame Zaitsova's house. The count ran up the steps and strode through the entrance hall and drawing room. Finding the little widow still in bed, he put his arms round her, lifted her up, kissed her on her sleepy eyes, and ran out. In her drowsy state Anna Fyodorovna could only lick her lips and murmur, "What has happened?"

The count leaped into the sleigh, shouted to the driver, and with no further delay and without giving another thought to Lukhnov or the little widow or Styesha, thinking only of what was awaiting him in Moscow, he left the town of K forever.

IX

Twenty years have passed. Much water has flowed under the bridge, many people have died, many others have been born, still others have grown up or grown old, even more ideas than people have been born and have died. Much of the good and much of the bad of the old days have vanished away; many good new things have come to maturity, even more bad new things have put in an appearance.

Count Fyodor Tourbin has been dead these many years, killed in a duel with a foreigner whom he struck with his riding crop in the street. His son, the exact image of his father, is now a charming youth of three-and-twenty, an officer in the *Cavalier Gardes*. But in disposition young Count Tourbin does not resemble his father in the least. He has not a shadow of the reckless, passionate, and, to put it bluntly, dissolute propensities characteristic of the last generation. In addition to intelligence, good breeding, and the gifted nature he inherited, his most outstanding qualities are a love of respectability and comfort, a practical way of judging people and circumstances, and a cautious and sensible approach to life. The young count has advanced swiftly in the service; at twenty-three he is already a lieutenant.

When military operations began, he decided his chances of promotion would be greater if he entered active service, so he had himself transferred to a regiment of hussars in which he served as captain, and was soon entrusted with a squadron.

In May 1848, the S. Regiment of Hussars passed through the K Gubernia, and the squadron under the command of young Count Tourbin was to spend the night in Morozovka, the village belonging to Anna Fyodorovna. Anna Fyodorovna was still alive, but so advanced in years that even she had ceased to look upon herself as young, which is going very far for a woman. She had grown extremely stout, and that is said to make a woman look younger. But deep wrinkles had made inroads into her soft white corpulence. She no longer rode into town, indeed she could hardly climb into her carriage, but she was as good-natured as ever, and as silly, as we may admit now that there is no longer any beauty to blind us to the fact. Her daughter Liza, a Russian village beauty of three-and-twenty, lived with her, as did her brother, the cavalry officer of our acquaintance, who, due to his easygoing nature, had squandered all his inheritance and depended on his sister in his old age. His hair was completely white; his upper lip was caved in, but the mustache growing on it was carefully dyed black. Wrinkles covered not only his cheeks and forehead, but even his nose and neck; his back was bent, and yet there was still something of the old cavalry officer in his weak and crooked legs.

On the evening in question Anna Fyodorovna with all her family and domestics was seated in the little drawing room of the old house, whose verandah door and windows opened upon an old-fashioned star-shaped garden shaded by lime trees. Anna Fyodorovna, gray-haired, in a lavender quilted jacket, was sitting on the sofa behind a round mahogany table on which she was playing solitaire. Her old brother, in clean white pantaloons and a blue coat, had seated himself at the window and was crocheting something of white cotton thread, an occupation which his niece had taught him and which he had grown extremely fond of, since he was incapable of doing work of any importance and his eyes were too weak to allow him to indulge in his favorite pastime—the reading of the newspaper. Pimochka, a little girl Anna Fyodorovna had adopted, was sitting next to him and doing her lessons under Liza's supervision, the latter at the same time knitting her uncle a pair of stockings of goat's wool. As always at that time of day, the last rays of the setting sun were falling obliquely through the lime trees, lighting up the furthermost window and the *étagère* that stood next to it. It was so quiet in the room and the garden that they could distinctly hear the quick flutter of a swallow's wings outside the window, Anna Fyodorovna's gentle sighing inside the room, and the grunting of the old man as he crossed his legs.

"Where should this card go? Please show me, Liza; I keep forgetting," said Anna Fyodorovna, pausing in her game.

Without interrupting her knitting, Liza went over to her mother and glanced at the cards.

"Oh, you've mixed everything up, dear Mama," she said rearranging the cards. "This is how it should be. Still, it will come out—your guess was right," she added, slipping off one of the cards when her mother was not looking.

"You're always fooling me, always saying it will come out."

"But it really will. See? It has."

"Very well, very well, you little vixen. Isn't it time for us to be having tea?"

"I've already told them to heat the samovar. I'll go and see. Shall I have it brought in here? Hurry and finish your lessons, Pimochka, and we'll go out for a walk."

And Liza disappeared through the door.

"Liza! Lizochka!" called her uncle, his eyes fixed on his crocheting. "I seem to have dropped a stitch again. Pick it up for me, that's a dear girl."

"In a minute, in a minute! I'll just give them this head of sugar to break up."

And sure enough, in three minutes she ran back into the room, went up to her uncle, and took him by the ear.

"That's what you get for dropping your stitches," she said with a laugh. "You haven't even done what was given you for today's lesson."

"Come, come; do put it right—there seems to be a knot somewhere."

Liza took the crochet hook, pulled the pin out of her kerchief, which was then blown open a little by the breeze coming through the window, caught the stitch with the pin, looped it up two or three times, and handed it back to her uncle.

"Here, a kiss for my labors," she said, offering him a rosy cheek as she pinned her kerchief back in place. "You shall have rum with your tea today. Today is Friday, you know."

And again she went back to the tea room.

"Come and see, Uncle! The hussars are coming!" she cried in a clear, high voice.

Anna Fyodorovna and her brother went into the tea room, whose windows faced the village, to see the hussars passing. Very little could be seen through the windows; they could only make out a crowd moving in a cloud of dust.

"What a pity, sister," observed Liza's uncle to Anna Fyodorovna, "that our house is so small and the new wing is not finished yet. Otherwise we would ask for some officers. Officers of the hussars are always such fine gay youths; I should like to have a look at them."

"And I would rejoice with all my heart to have them; but you yourself know, brother, that we have nowhere to put them. There's only my bedroom, Liza's little room, the drawing room, and your room. Where could we put them? Judge for yourself. Mikhailo Matveyev has made the elder's hut ready for them. He says it is properly clean."

"We would choose you a husband, a brave hussar, from among them, Lizochka," said her uncle.

"I don't want a hussar, I want an Uhlan; wasn't it in the Uhlans that you served, uncle? I'll have nothing to do with those hussars; they are said to be such reckless fellows."

A faint blush dyed Liza's cheeks, but again she laughed her ringing laugh. "Here comes Ustyushka running; we must ask her what she has seen," she said.

Anna Fyodorovna sent for Ustyushka.

"As if there was not enough work to keep you busy! But no, you must go running to have a look at the soldiers!" said Anna Fyodorovna. "Well, where are the officers to be put up?"

"At Yeremkin's cottage, madam. There are two of them, and so handsome! One is a count, they say!"

"What is his name?"

"Kazarov or Tourbin or something of the sort—I don't quite remember, begging your pardon."

"You *are* a simpleton—can't tell us anything. You might at least have found out his name."

"I'll run back and ask if you like."

"Oh, you're very good at that, don't I know! No, let Danilo go; tell him to go, brother, and ask whether the officers are in need of anything; we must show them every civility; and have him say that he was sent by his mistress."

The old people sat down in the tea room again and Liza went into the maids' room to put the sugar away. There she found Ustyushka talking about the hussars.

"My dear mistress, if you ever saw how handsome that count is!" she said. "A very cherub, with dark brows and hair! If you found a husband like that for yourself, wouldn't you make a handsome couple, just!"

The other servants smiled approvingly. The old nurse-maid, sitting at the window darning a stocking, gave a deep sigh and murmured a prayer on an indrawn breath.

"So that's the impression the hussars made on you!" said Liza. "You like nothing better than to talk about such things. Bring us a fruit drink, Ustyushka—something sourish to treat the hussars to."

And, laughing, Liza went out with her sugar bowl.

"I would like to have a look at that hussar," she thought. "Is he fair or dark? And I do not doubt but that he would be glad to make our acquaintance. But perhaps he will pass by without ever knowing that I was here and gave him a thought. And how many like him have passed me by! No one ever sees me but uncle and Ustyushka. What matters it how I do my hair, or what sort of sleeves I wear? There is no one to admire me," she thought with a sigh, gazing at her plump white arm. "I suppose he is tall, with big eyes and probably a little black mustache. Just to think, three-and-twenty already and nobody has ever fallen in love with me, except that pockmarked Ivan Ipatich. And four years ago I was even prettier than I am now. My girlhood is almost over, and nobody has had any joy of it. Oh, how unfortunate I am! A poor country girl!"

The country girl was roused from her ruminations by the voice of her mother calling her to pour out the tea. She gave a little toss of her head and went into the tea room.

The best things are those that happen by chance; the more one tries, the worse things turn out. In the country, little attention is paid to child education, and so in most cases the education turns out to be excellent. So it was in Liza's case. Anna Fyodorovna had too limited a mind and too lazy-going a disposition to give Liza any education at all: she had not taught her music, nor the indispensable French, but quite by chance she had presented her late husband with a very pretty and healthy child—a daughter, whom she placed in the hands of a wetnurse and a nursemaid. She fed her, clothed her in cotton frocks and goatskin shoes, sent her out to play and to gather berries and mushrooms, hired a young student to teach her reading, writing and arithmetic, and in sixteen years' time, quite by chance, she found that Liza was a good friend and a cheery, kindhearted, industrious little housekeeper. Anna

Fyodorovna herself was so kindhearted that she was always adopting some serf child or foundling. Liza, from the age of ten, took care of her mother's wards: she taught them their letters, dressed them, took them to church, and reproved them when they became too mischievous. Then came her feeble, good-natured old uncle, who had to be tended like a baby. Then there were the house servants as well as the serfs from the village who brought all their aches and pains to the young mistress; she treated them with elder-flower water, peppermint, and spirits of camphor. And then there was the care of the house that, quite by chance, had fallen entirely upon her shoulders. And then there was the thwarted yearning for love that found an outlet in her love of nature and in religion. And so, quite by chance, Liza turned out to be a busy, cheery, amiable, independent, pure, and deeply religious woman. True, she suffered little pangs of envy on seeing her neighbors at church wearing modish hats brought from the town of K; she was driven almost to tears by the whims of her querulous old mother; she had dreams of love that took incongruous, even crude forms—but all of these were driven away by the useful work which had become indispensable to her, and at three-and-twenty there was not a blot, not a regret to mar the bright and serene soul of this developing woman, so rich in physical and moral beauty. Liza was of middle height, more round than angular; her eyes were brown and not very large, slightly shadowed under the lower lids; her hair was long and fair; she walked with a wide, easy swing. The expression of her face when she was busy and had nothing on her mind to worry her said to all who saw it: life is good, life is a joy, for those whose consciences are clear and who have someone to love. Even in moments of vexation, indignation, alarm, or grief, when, as if in defiance of her wishes, tears filled her eyes, her lips became set, her left eyebrow scowled— even then the light of a kind and candid heart, unspoiled by sophistication, could be glimpsed in the dimples of her cheeks, the corners of her lips, and in her shining eyes.

x

It was still hot, though the sun had set, when the squadron entered Morozovka. Up ahead, in the dusty village road ran a spotted cow that had strayed away from the herd; it kept casting frightened looks behind it, and from time to time it stopped and mooed, unable to guess that all it had to do was to step out of the path of the horses. Old peasants, village wives, children, and house servants, crowded on either side of the road to gape at the hussars, who advanced in a thick cloud of dust, mounted on short-bridled, snorting black horses. To the right of the squadron rode the two officers, sitting loosely in the saddle. One of them was Count Tourbin, the commander; the other was Polozov, a young man who had but recently received his commission.

Out of the finest hut in the village stepped a hussar in a white tunic, who, taking off his forage cap, went up to the officers.

"What accommodations have been made for us?" the count asked him.

"For Your Excellency?" replied the quartermaster, his whole body stiffening. "We've cleaned this hut for you—the elder's. We asked for a room at the manor house but were turned down. The mistress is a mean one."

"Very well," said the count, dismounting and stretching his legs as he went toward the elder's hut. "Has my carriage arrived?"

"It has, Your Excellency," replied the quartermaster, pointing with his cap at the carriage standing at the gates, then running ahead to the entrance of the hut where a peasant family had gathered to stare at the officers. He almost knocked over one old woman as he flung open the door of the freshly scrubbed hut and stood aside to let the count pass.

The hut was large and roomy, but not entirely clean. A German valet, dressed like a gentleman, had put up an iron bedstead and was now taking bed linen out of a traveling bag.

"Ugh, what beastly quarters!" said the count in vexation. "Dyadenko! Is it really impossible to stow us away somewhere in the manor house?"

"If Your Excellency so orders, I shall dispatch someone there," replied Dyadenko. "But it is a poor sort of manor house—little better than this hut."

"It is too late now. Leave me."

And the count lay down with his hands clasped under his head.

"Johann!" he called to his valet. "You've made a lump in the middle again! How is it you can't make a bed properly?"

Johann was about to remove the lump.

"No, it's too late now. Where is my dressing gown?" the count went on peevishly.

The valet gave him his dressing gown.

Before putting it on, the count examined the hem.

"I thought so; you haven't taken out that spot. I don't know how anyone could serve worse than you do," he added, snatching the gown out of the man's hands and putting it on. "Is it intentionally or what? Is tea ready?"

"I haven't had time," said Johann.

"Dolt!"

The count took up a French novel he had brought for the occasion and read it in silence for some time; Johann went out into the entranceway to heat the samovar. It was clear that the count was in a bad mood—due, no doubt, to his weariness, his dirty face, his tight clothing, and his empty stomach.

"Johann!" he cried again. "Account for that ten rubles I gave you. What did you buy in town?"

The count glanced over the account handed to him and made a few dissatisfied remarks as to the dearness of the articles purchased.

"I shall take rum with my tea."

"I didn't buy any rum," said Johann.

"Marvelous! How many times have I told you to keep rum on hand?"

"I hadn't enough money."

"Why didn't Polozov buy it? You might have taken it from his man."

"Cornet Polozov? I don't know. He only bought tea and sugar."

"Wretch! Get out! No one tries my patience as you do. You know very well that I always take rum with my tea when on the march."

"Here are two letters for you from Staff Headquarters," said the valet.

The count, lying on his bed, tore open the letters and began to read them. Just then the cornet, who had been seeing the men to their quarters, entered with a cheerful face.

"Well, Tourbin? Not a bad place at all, it seems. But I must admit I'm deucedly tired. It was a hot day."

"Not bad! A filthy, stinking hut and no rum for my tea, thanks to you. That fool of yours forgot to buy it, and so did mine. You might have told yours to."

He went back to his letters. When he had finished read-ing the first one he crumpled it up and threw it on the floor.

Meanwhile, out in the entranceway, the cornet was whis-pering to his servant, "Why didn't you buy some rum? You had the money, didn't you?"

"Why should we do all the buying? I stand all the ex-penses as it is; that German of his does nothing but smoke a pipe."

The second letter was evidently not disagreeable, for the count smiled as he read it.

"Who is it from?" asked Polozov, who had come back into the room and was making a bed for himself on some boards next to the stove.

"From Minna," replied the count gaily, holding the letter out to him. "Would you like to read it? What a charming woman! Much better than our girls. Just see how much wit and feeling there is in this letter! There's only one bad thing—she asks for money."

"Yes, that is bad," observed the cornet.

"To be sure, I promised her some; but then we set out on this march, and . . . well . . . but if I am in command of the squadron another three months I'll send it to her. I certainly don't grudge it; charming, isn't she?" he asked with a smile, watching the expression of Polozov's face as he read the letter.

"Awfully illiterate, but rather sweet, and she seems to be really in love with you," said the cornet.

"Indeed she is! It's only women of her sort who truly love, if they love at all."

"And who is that other letter from?" asked the cornet, handing back the letter he had finished reading.

"That? Oh, there's a certain gentleman, a filthy sort, to whom I lost money at cards; this is the third time he has reminded me of it. I can't pay him back at present. A stupid letter," said the count, evidently annoyed by the remembrance.

The two officers said nothing for some time after this. Influenced by the count's mood, the cornet drank his tea in silence, afraid to begin a conversation, for Tourbin, at whose handsome face he glanced from time to time, was staring steadfastly out of the window, deep in thought.

"Oh, well, everything may turn out all right," said the count suddenly, turning to Polozov and giving his head a little toss. "If there are promotions all along the line in our regiment this year, and if we move into action besides, I may get ahead of my friends who are captains in the Guards."

The conversation was following these lines over a second glass of tea when old Danilo came in, bringing Anna Fyodorovna's message.

"And her honor bade me ask if your honor was not the son of Count Fyodor Ivanovich Tourbin?" added Danilo of his own accord, having heard the officer's name and remembering the visit of the late count in the town of K. "Our lady Anna Fyodorovna knew him very well indeed."

"He was my father; tell your mistress that we are very grateful to her for her thoughtfulness and are in need of nothing, but say that we should be very much obliged if a cleaner room might be found for us somewhere, at the manor house or elsewhere."

"Why did you say that?" asked Polozov when Danilo had gone. "What difference does it make? We'll only be here for one night so why should we put them to all that inconvenience?"

"You and your scruples! Haven't we had enough of sleeping in henhouses? It's clear that you are not a practical man. Why should we not take advantage of the opportunity of sleeping in comfort if only for one night? They, on their part, will be very much flattered. There's only one thing I don't like: her having known my father," went on the count, exposing his brilliant white teeth in a slow smile. "I always blush at the memory of that papa of mine—always some scandal or some debt. That's why I can't bear to run into former acquaintances of his. But then, the times were like that," he added seriously.

"I forgot to tell you," said Polozov, "I once met the commander of an Uhlan brigade named Ilyin. He was anxious to meet you and was devoted to your father."

"He seems to have been a worthless fellow, that Ilyin And the thing is that all those gentlemen who claim to have known my father so as to make up to me, tell me tales about him I am ashamed to listen to, though they give them out as charming anecdotes. I cannot deny—I always try to take a cool, objective view of things—that he was too hot-tempered and sometimes did things he shouldn't have. But it was all because of the times. In our day he might have turned out to be very successful, for to do him justice, he was extremely talented."

A quarter of an hour later Danilo returned and brought them an invitation from his mistress to spend the night at her house.

XI

On learning that the young hussar officer was the son of Count Fyodor Tourbin, Anna Fyodorovna was all aflutter.

"Goodness gracious! Bless you, Danilo! Hurry back there and say that the mistress invites them here," she said, jumping up and scurrying off to the maids' room. "Lizochka! Us-

tyushka! We must make your room ready, Liza. You will
move into your uncle's room, and you, brother . . . you,
brother, will have to spend the night in the drawing room.
It won't hurt you for one night."

"Indeed it won't, sister; I will lie on the floor."

"He must be handsome indeed if he resembles his father.
Oh, to have a look at him, the darling! Just you wait and
see, Liza! What a good-looking man his father was! Where
are you taking that table? Leave it here," cried Anna Fyodorovna as she bustled about. "Bring two beds—fetch one
from the bailiff's—and take the crystal candlestick that
brother presented me with on my birthday and put a tal-
low candle in it."

At last everything was ready. Despite her mother's in-
terference, Liza arranged her room for the two officers
according to her own taste. She brought fresh bed linen
scented with mignonette and made the beds herself; she
had a decanter of water and the candle placed on a table
next to the bed, she burned some perfumed paper in the
maids' room and made up her own bed in her uncle's room.
When Anna Fyodorovna had become more composed she
sat down in her usual place and took up her cards, but
before she dealt them out she put a puffy elbow on the
table and fell to dreaming. "How time flies! How it does!"
she whispered to herself. "It seems like yesterday. . . . I
can see him now. . . . Oh, what a reckless fellow he was!"
And tears came to her eyes. "Now it is Lizanka's turn—
but she is not what I was at her age—a pretty child, but
. . . not what I was. . . ."

"Lizochka, you had better put on your *mousseline de
laine* this evening."

"Do you intend to entertain them, Mama? Oh, I don't
think you ought," said Liza, unable to suppress her agitation at the thought of meeting the officers. "I really don't
think you ought, Mama."

In actual fact, she more feared than desired to meet
them, for she sensed that some great and perturbing happiness lay in store for her.

"Perhaps they themselves will want to make our acquaintance, Lizochka," said Anna Fyodorovna, stroking her daughter's hair and thinking to herself: "It isn't what my hair was at her age. . . . Oh, Lizochka, I could wish for you . . ." and she did indeed wish something for her, but she could not hope for her marriage with the young count, and she could hardly want Liza to enter upon relations with the young count such as she herself had had with the elder. And yet she wished for something, and that very ardently. Perhaps she hoped to revive, through her daughter, the emotions she had felt with the late count.

The old cavalry officer, too, was somewhat excited by the count's arrival. He went into his own room and locked the door. A quarter of an hour later he came out in a military tunic and blue riding trousers. Wearing the look of pleased self-consciousness with which a young girl dons her first ballgown, he went into the room prepared for the guests.

"We shall see what the new generation of hussars is like, sister. The late count was a true hussar if there ever was one. We shall see, we shall see!"

The officers went to the room assigned them through the back entrance.

"What did I tell you?" said the count, lying down just as he was, in his dusty boots, on the freshly made bed. "Isn't this better than that hut full of beetles?"

"Of course it is better, but we have put ourselves under obligation to our hosts. . . ."

"Tut-tut! One must always take a practical view of things. You can be sure they are dreadfully pleased. Boy!" he shouted. "Ask them to hang something over that window to keep out the draught at night!"

At this point the old man came in to make the acquaintance of the officers. Naturally he could not resist saying, though he blushed a little in doing so, that he had been a comrade of the late count, that he had enjoyed his kind regards, and was even indebted to him for certain kindly services rendered on his account. Whether under "kindly services" he had in mind the count's neglecting to return the hundred rubles he had borrowed, or his pushing him into a snowbank, or his showering him with abuse, it is hard to say—the old man offered no explanations. The young count was extremely courteous to the old cavalry officer and thanked him for putting them up.

"You must excuse its not being very luxurious, Count," (he almost said "Your Excellency," so unused had he become to addressing people of rank) "my sister's house is very small. We'll have something hung over that window, and everything will be fine," he added, and under the pretense of going for a curtain, but really so that he could give an account of the officers, he shuffled away.

The pretty little Ustyushka came in with her mistress's shawl to hang over the window. Her mistress had also told her to ask the gentlemen if they would not care to have tea.

Decent quarters evidently had a brightening effect upon the count's spirits: he smiled and joked with Ustyushka so gaily that she called him a naughty man; he questioned her as to whether her young mistress was pretty, and when she asked whether he cared to have tea, he said he supposed they might as well bring it in, but that it was more important, since his man had not yet got supper ready, to have some vodka if they could spare it, and something to eat, and also some sherry, if there was any on hand.

Liza's uncle went into raptures over the young count's manners and praised the young generation of officers to the sky, saying that they were incomparably superior to their fathers.

Anna Fyodorovna disagreed—no one could have been superior to Count Fyodor Ivanovich. In the end she even became tetchy, remarking coldly, "For you, brother, the last person who is kind to you is the best. Everyone knows, of course, that people have grown more clever, but Count Fyodor Ivanovich was so polite and danced an *écossaise* so beautifully that everybody, you might say, lost their heads; and yet he paid no attention to anyone but me. And so you see there were good people in the old times, too."

Just then word was brought of the request for vodka, food, and sherry.

"Now just see, brother! You never do the right thing! You ought to have ordered supper," said Anna Fyodorovna. "Liza! Do take things in hand, my dear!"

Liza ran into the storeroom for mushrooms and fresh butter and ordered the cook to broil some steak.

"Have you any sherry left, brother?"

"No, sister. I never had any."

"How is that? You take something with your tea, don't you?"

"Rum, Anna Fyodorovna."

"What difference does it make? Give them that . . . er . . . rum; it doesn't matter. But hadn't we better invite them in here, brother? You know what is right. They won't take offense, will they?"

The cavalry officer said he was certain the count was much too generous to decline their invitation and he would bring them without fail. Anna Fyodorovna went to put on her grosgrain dress and a new cap, but Liza was so busy that she had no time to take off the wide-sleeved pink linen dress she was wearing. And she was dreadfully nervous: she felt that something stupendous was about to happen. She took the count, the handsome hussar, to be a glorious creature, new and incomprehensible. His ways and manners and speech—everything about him must be such as she had never known before. All that he thought and said must be clever and true; all that he did must be upright; every detail of his appearance must be beautiful. She had no doubt of it. Had he demanded not only food and sherry, but a perfumed bath as well, she would not have been surprised and would not have blamed him, but would have been firmly convinced that it was only right and proper.

The count accepted Anna Fyodorovna's invitation the minute it was communicated to him by the cavalry officer. He combed his hair, put on his coat, and took his cigar case.

"Come along," he said to Polozov.

"I don't think we ought to," replied the cornet. *"Ils feront des frais pour nous recevoir."*

"Nonsense. It will give them pleasure. I've already made inquiries—it seems the lady has a pretty daughter. Come along," said the count in French.

"*Je vous en prie, messieurs!*" said the cavalry officer just to let them know he understood French and had caught what they said.

XII

Liza, with blushing face and downcast eyes, pretended to be all absorbed in the pouring out of the tea, for she was afraid to look at the officers when they came into the room. Anna Fyodorovna, on the contrary, jumped to her feet and made a little curtsey, and without taking her eyes off of the count's face, spoke incessantly, telling him how like his father he was, introducing her daughter, offering him tea, jam, and country fruit paste. The cornet was so modest in appearance that no one paid the least attention to him, for which he was duly grateful since it gave him an opportunity to study, as far as that was decent, every detail of Liza's beauty, which he was evidently quite struck by. The uncle sat waiting for his sister to finish speaking to the count, hardly able to restrain himself, so anxious was he to give his reminiscences of life in the cavalry. The count lighted a cigar that was so strong that Liza could hardly keep from coughing. He was very loquacious and courteous, at first inserting a word now and then in the stream of Anna Fyodorovna's talk, later holding forth all by himself. One thing struck his listeners as being rather strange: his use of words which, if considered inoffensive in the society to which he was accustomed, were shocking here. Anna Fyodorovna was a bit frightened by them, and Liza blushed to the tips of her ears. But the count did not notice this and remained his serene and courteous self. Liza filled the glasses in silence and instead of putting them in the hands of her guests, she set them down within easy reach. Still greatly excited, she listened avidly to the count's every word. The triteness of his stories and his faltering manner of speech helped to restore her composure. She did not hear the wise utterances she had expected him to make, nor did she discover that elegance in all things which she had vaguely hoped he would display. During the third glass of tea, when she shyly lifted her eyes to his and he held them with his glance, going on talking quite unperturbed, smiling the faintest of smiles as he gazed at her, she felt a certain hostility rising up within her and soon realized that not only was there nothing extraordinary about him, but he was in no way distinguishable from all the people she knew, and therefore there was no reason to fear him; true, his nails were long and carefully tended, but he was not even particularly handsome. And suddenly, having discovered with a pang of regret that her dreams were unfounded, Liza grew calm; the only thing which disturbed her now was the glance of the silent cornet which she felt fixed upon her. "Perhaps not he, but *he* is the one!" she thought.

XIII

After tea the old lady invited the guests into the other room, where she sat down in her accustomed place.

"Perhaps you would like to rest, Count?" she asked. "How shall I amuse you, my dear guests," she added on receiving a reply in the negative. "Do you play cards, Count? You might see to that, brother—arrange a hand of something."

"But you yourself play 'preference,'" replied her brother. "Shall we have a game? Would you like to, Count? And you?"

The officers declared they were ready to do anything their hosts found agreeable.

Liza brought the old pack of cards with which she was used to telling fortunes, to divine whether Anna Fyodorovna's toothache would soon pass, when her uncle would arrive home from a journey to town, whether the neighbor would pay them a call, and such things. These cards, although they had been in use for two months, were cleaner than the ones with which Anna Fyodorovna told fortunes.

"But perhaps you do not care to play for small stakes?" asked the uncle. "Anna Fyodorovna and I play for half a kopek a point. Even so, she ruins us all."

"Oh, for anything you wish, I shall be only too glad," said the count.

"Then let it be for one kopek—paper money. Anything for such exceptional guests—let them drive an old lady like me to the poorhouse," said Anna Fyodorovna, settling comfortably in her armchair and patting down her lace shawl. To herself she said, "Perhaps I shall win a ruble from them." She had, it seemed, developed a slight gambling fever in her old age.

"If you like I shall teach you to play 'with honors,' " said the count. "And 'with misery.' Very amusing."

Everyone was delighted with the new St. Petersburg manner of playing. The uncle declared he had once known it, that it was the same as playing "Boston," but he had forgotten it a little. Anna Fyodorovna understood nothing, and understood nothing for so long that she found it advisable to smile and nod and declare that now she understood and everything was clear. There was a great deal of laughter in the middle of the game when, with the ace and the king in her hand, Anna Fyodorovna called "misery" and was left with the six. She was quite nonplused, smiled weakly, and hastened to assert that she had not quite got used to the new way of playing. But it was scored against her nevertheless, and scored heavily, especially since the count, due to his habit of playing for big stakes, was cautious, kept exact accounts, and failed to grasp the meaning of the cornet's kicks under the table and the glaring blunders the latter made in playing.

Liza brought in more fruit paste, three sorts of jam, and a special sort of soaked apples. From her position behind her mother's chair she followed the game, glancing up at the officers from time to time, especially at the pink nails and white hands of the count as he threw down the cards and picked up the tricks with such skill, grace, and confidence.

Again Anna Fyodorovna grew fluttered and completely

lost her head as she recklessly tried to outdo the others, bidding as high as seven, taking only four, and, on the demand of her brother, scribbling some unintelligible figures on the score sheet.

"Cheer up, Mama, you will win it all back," said Liza with a smile, trying to rescue her mother from the ridiculous position she had fallen into. "You'll take Uncle's cards and then he'll be in a hole."

"You might come to my aid, Lizochka," said Anna Fyodorovna, casting a frightened glance at her. "I don't know how . . ."

"I don't know how to play according to these rules either," said Liza, quickly calculating her mother's losses in her mind. "But you will lose everything at this rate, Mama. There won't even be enough left to buy Pimochka a frock," she added in jest.

"Indeed you can easily lose at least ten silver rubles in this way," said the cornet, gazing at Liza and longing to start a conversation with her.

"Why, aren't we playing with paper money?" asked Anna Fyodorovna, glancing round at the players.

"Perhaps," said the count, "but I for my part do not know how to calculate paper money. How do you . . . that is, what *is* this paper money?"

"Nobody plays with paper money nowadays," put in the uncle, who was winning.

The old lady had some fruit drinks brought in, she herself drank two glasses, grew red in the face, and seemed, so to speak, to have thrown up her hands in despair. She even neglected to tuck in a lock of gray hair that had escaped from under her cap. No doubt she felt that she had lost millions and was a ruined woman. Again and again the cornet kicked the count under the table. The count regularly wrote down all the old lady's losses.

At last the game was over. Despite all Anna Fyodorovna's efforts, at the expense of her conscience, to add something to her accounts, to pretend that she had made a mistake in her calculations, and that in general she could not calculate, and despite her horror at the enormity of

her losses, in the end the calculations showed that she had
lost nine hundred and twenty points. "Is that not nine rubles in paper money?" she asked several times, and she
was quite incapable of grasping the full extent of her losses
until her brother, to her horror, explained that she had
lost thirty-two rubles and a half in paper money and that
it must be paid without fail.

When the game was over the count got up without both-
ering to estimate his winnings and went to the window
near which Liza was laying out refreshments and putting
mushrooms on a plate for supper. Directly, and with perfect ease, he did what the cornet had been wanting to do
all evening and had been unable to: he began a conversation with Liza about the weather.

The cornet at that moment found himself in a most dis-
concerting position. When the count, and especially when
Liza, who had kept up Anna Fyodorovna's spirits, went
away, the old lady could no longer control her feelings.

"I am very sorry that we should have won your money,"
said Polozov for the sake of saying something. "It was not
very polite of us."

"And to have thought up those 'honors' and 'miseries' of
yours! I don't know how to play that way. How much did
you say it amounted to in paper money?" she asked.

"Thirty-two rubles; thirty-two and a half," said the old
cavalry officer, whose own winnings had put him in a jolly
mood. "Give me the money, sister; come, give it to me."

"It's the last time I shall ever be able to give you any. I
shall have none to give. I can never hope to win back so
much."

And Anna Fyodorovna hurried away with her rocking
walk and came back with nine paper rubles. It was only
on the insistence of the old man that she paid up in full.

Polozov nurtured a faint fear that Anna Fyodorovna
might launch a tirade against him if he spoke to her. And
so he quietly slipped away and joined the count and Liza,
who were standing and talking at the open window.

On the table laid for supper stood two wax candles.
Now and again their flames flickered in the fresh warm

breeze of the May night. It was light at the window that opened into the garden, but the light was entirely different from that inside the room. An almost full moon, which by this time had lost its golden tinge, was sailing over the high tips of the lime trees, pouring more and more light upon the diaphanous white clouds that kept flowing across it. Frogs were croaking in chorus down at the pond; through the trees could be glimpsed a bit of water, shimmering silver in the moonlight. Some little birds could be heard hopping about and ruffling their feathers in the fragrant lilac bush whose moist clusters of blossom nodded beside the window.

"What divine weather!" said the count, going over to Liza and sitting down on the low windowsill. "I suppose you often go for walks?"

"Yes," said Liza, for some reason feeling not the least discomfiture in talking with the count. "At seven in the morning I walk out to attend to my household duties, and I also take walks with Pimochka, the little girl Mama has adopted."

"It is such a pleasure to live in the country!" said the count, screwing his monocle into his eye and glancing now into the garden, now at Liza. "Do you ever go out to walk in the moonlight?"

"Not now. Three years ago Uncle and I used to go for walks every moonlit night, but then he was taken by a strange ailment—he could not sleep; he could never fall asleep when there was a full moon. His room—that one over there—opens directly into the garden and the window is low; the moon shines full on him."

"Strange," observed the count." "I thought that was your room?"

"I am sleeping there only for tonight. My room is the one you are sleeping in."

"Really? Dear me! I shall never forgive myself for inconveniencing you!" And the count dropped the monocle out of his eye as an indication of his sincerity. "Had I known our presence would cause you such inconvenience—"

"No inconvenience at all. On the contrary, I'm very glad.

Uncle's room is charming—very light and cheerful, and with a low window. I shall sit at it until I fall asleep, or perhaps I shall even climb out into the garden and take a stroll before I go to bed."

"What a sweet girl!" thought the count, screwing in his monocle again to get a better look at her and trying to touch her leg with his foot as he sat down on the window-sill. "And how cunningly she has let me know that I may see her at the window if I so desire." Indeed, so easy did his conquest over her seem that she lost much of the attraction she had held for him.

"What delight it must be," said he as he gazed ruminatively into the dark alley, "to spend a night such as this in a garden with a creature you adore."

Liza was somewhat embarrassed by these words and by another touch, as if by chance, of his leg against hers. Without thinking, she hastened to say something to cover her embarrassment. "Yes," she said, "it is delightful to walk in the moonlight." Feeling uncomfortable, she quickly tied up the mushroom jar and was about to walk away with it when the cornet came up and she had a sudden desire to find out what sort of person he was.

"What a beautiful night!" he said.

"They speak about nothing but the weather," thought Liza.

"And what a charming view!" went on the cornet. "But I suppose you have already grown weary of it," he added, due to a strange habit he had of always saying something unpleasant to people he liked very much.

"Why should you think so? One grows weary of eating the same things or wearing the same frock, but one never grows weary of a beautiful garden, especially when the moon rises even higher in the sky. From Uncle's room one gets a view of the entire pond. I shall see it tonight."

"I think there are no nightingales here, are there?" asked the count, greatly displeased that Polozov should have intruded at just this moment and kept him from making more definite arrangements for a rendezvous.

"No. There used to be, but last year a sportsman caught

one, and this year—last week, in fact—I heard one singing beautifully, but the constable rode by with bells on his
trap and frightened it away. The year before last Uncle
and I used to sit under the trees in the alley and listen to
them for hours at a stretch."

"What is this little chatterbox telling you?" said her uncle, coming up to them. "Would you not like something to
eat, gentlemen?"

After supper, during which the count, by praising the
food and displaying a good appetite, managed to somewhat improve Anna Fyodorovna's temper, the officers took
their leave and went to their room. The count shook the
uncle's hand, and, to the astonishment of Anna Fyodorovna, shook her hand, without kissing it, and even shook
Liza's, gazing straight into her eyes as he did so and giving one of his faint but pleasant smiles. Again his gaze
embarrassed her.

"He is good-looking," she thought, "but he thinks too
much of himself."

XIV

"Aren't you ashamed?" said Polozov when the officers
reached their room. "I did my best to make us lose and
kept kicking you under the table. You have no conscience
at all. The old woman was quite distressed."

The count burst out laughing.

"She's simply killing! How she did take it to heart!"

And he burst into another roar of laughter so catching
that even Johann, who was standing in front of them,
dropped his eyes and gave a furtive little smile.

"The son of the old friend of the family! Ha, ha, ha!" and
the count went on laughing.

"But really it wasn't nice, I even felt sorry for her," said
the cornet.

"Fiddlesticks! You're still so young! Did you expect me to
lose? Why should I? I, too, lost before I learnt how to play.
I can find good use for that ten rubles, my friend. A man

has to take a practical view of life if he doesn't want to join the fools."

Polozov grew silent. He wanted to withdraw into himself and think about Liza, whom he found to be a remarkably pure and lovely creature. He got undressed and lay down in the soft, clean bed that had been made for him.

"What nonsense—the honor and glory of life in the army!" he thought as he gazed at the window draped with a shawl through which the pale light of the moon was shining. "This is happiness—to live in some quiet retreat with a simple, clever, charming wife. This is true and lasting happiness."

But for some reason he did not confide his thoughts to his friend and did not so much as mention the country girl to him, although he was certain that the count, too, was thinking of her.

"Why aren't you undressing?" he asked the count, who was pacing the floor.

"Somehow I have no desire to sleep. Put out the light if you wish; I do not need it."

And he went on walking back and forth.

"Has no desire to sleep," repeated Polozov. The events of the evening had made him resent the count's influence over him more than ever, and had thrown him in a mood to resist it. "It is not hard to guess," said he mentally to Tourbin, "what thoughts are brewing in that sleek head of yours! I saw how taken you were by her! But you are incapable of understanding so simple and honest a creature. It's the Minnas you want, and a colonel's epaulettes. But here, let me ask him how he liked her."

But just as Polozov was about to turn over and address the count, he changed his mind. He felt that he would not only be unable to protest if the count's opinion of Liza turned out to be what he supposed, that he would even find himself acquiescing, so used was he to giving in to his influence, although with every passing day this was becoming more unjust and unbearable.

"Where are you going?" he asked when the count put on his cap and went to the door.

"Out to the stables. I want to make sure that everything is all right."

"Strange," thought the cornet, but he put out the candle and turned over, making an effort to drive away the absurdly jealous and antagonistic thoughts that his former friend inspired.

Meanwhile Anna Fyodorovna, having tenderly kissed and made the sign of the cross over her brother, her daughter, and her ward, as was her custom, had also withdrawn to her room. Long had it been since she had experienced so many keen sensations in a single day. She could not even say her prayers calmly, so disturbed was she by sad and vivid memories of the late count and of this young dandy who had so shamefully taken her money away from her. And yet she climbed into bed as usual after she had undressed and drunk the half a glass of kvass which was always left for her on the little table next to her bed. Her favorite cat crept softly into the room. Anna Fyodorovna called it over and began stroking it, listening to its purring, unable to fall asleep.

"It's the cat that keeps me awake," she thought, and pushed it away. The cat dropped softly on to the floor, then, curling up its fluffy tail, jumped up on the stove-bunk. At this point the serving maid who slept on the floor in her mistress's room brought her felt mat, spread it out, put out the candle, and lighted the icon lamp. Soon she was snoring away, but sleep refused to bring peace to Anna Fyodorovna's troubled soul. As soon as she closed her eyes the face of the hussar rose before her, and when she opened them all the objects in the room—the commode, the table, the white frocks hanging there, dimly lighted by the icon lamp—all of them seemed to represent him in strange forms. One minute she felt suffocated by the down quilt, the next she was annoyed by the striking of the clock or the snoring of the maid. She woke the girl up and ordered her to stop snoring. Thoughts of her daughter, of the old count and the young one, of the game of "preference," mingled oddly in her mind. Now she saw herself waltzing with the late count, saw her plump white shoul

ders, felt someone's lips pressed against them, then she saw
her daughter in the arms of the young count. Once more
Ustyushka began to snore. . . .

"Oh, no; people are not what they used to be. He was
ready to go through fire and water for my sake. And there
was good reason for it. But that one, you may be sure, is
sleeping like the dolt he is, gloating over his winnings, unwilling to bestir himself for lovemaking. But the professions
his father made to me on bended knee! 'What would you
have me do? Kill myself? I would gladly do it for your
sake.' And he would have, too, if I had wanted it."

Suddenly there was a patter of bare feet out in the hall,
and Liza, pale and trembling, with only a shawl thrown
over her dressing jacket, ran into the room and almost fell
on her mother's bed. . . .

After saying good night to her mother, Liza had gone
alone to her uncle's room. Having put on a white dressing
jacket and tied up her long hair in a kerchief, she put out
the candle, opened the window, and sat on a chair with
her legs tucked up under her, gazing pensively at the pond,
whose whole surface was now shimmering with silvery light.

All her usual interests and occupations suddenly appeared to her in an entirely new light: her old, capricious
mother, unquestioning love for whom had become part of
her very being, her kind but feeble uncle, the house servants who adored their young mistress, the milch cows and
the calves—all of them, and all of her natural surround-
ings, which had known the decline of so many autumns
and the renewal of so many springs, and in the midst of
which, loving and being loved, she had been reared—all
of this now seemed to be *nothing;* seemed to be wearisome and
unwanted. It was as if someone had whispered to her: "You
little fool! You little fool! For twenty years you've been
wasting your time waiting on others without knowing what
real life and happiness are!" Now, as she sat gazing into
the depths of the bright, still garden, these thoughts broke
upon her forcefully, more forcefully than ever before. What
had prompted them? Not at all a sudden love for the
count, as one might suppose. On the contrary, she did not

like him. She could more easily have fallen in love with the
cornet, but he was plain and taciturn. She had already
forgotten him. But it was with anger and resentment that
she remembered the count. "No, he is not the one," she
said to herself. Her ideal was someone wholly beautiful,
someone who, on a night like this, in a setting like this,
could be loved without violating the beauty all around—
an ideal that had never been cut down to fit coarse reality.

At first her life of solitude and the absence of people
who could interest her had preserved whole and undisturbed in her heart that great force of love that Providence
has implanted equally in the heart of each of us; now,
however, she had lived too long with the rueful joy of sens-
ing within herself the existence of this something (sometimes
stealing glimpses into the mysterious coffer of her heart to
rapturously contemplate the treasure it contained)—too
long to lavish it heedlessly now on the first chance comer.
God grant that she might enjoy this meager happiness to
the end of her days! Who could say but that it was the
best and the greatest joy? That it, alone, was the only true
and possible joy?

"Dear Father!" she murmured, "is it possible that youth
and happiness have passed me by . . . that I shall never
know them? Can it be true?" And she raised her eyes to
the high bright sky where fluffy white clouds were blotting
out the stars as they moved toward the moon. "If that top
cloud touches the moon it is true," she said to herself. A
foggy, smoky strip ran across the lower half of the bright
disc, and little by little the light shining on the grass, the
crowns of the lime trees, and the pond, grew dim, and the
black shadows of the trees grew indistinct. And as if in the
wake of the melancholy shadows darkening nature, a light
breeze passed over the leaves, wafting to the window the
fragrance of dewy leaves, moist earth, and lilac blossom.

"No, it is not true," she consoled herself. "And if a nightingale sings tonight, then all these sad thoughts are foolish
and there is no reason to despair," she thought. And for a
long time she sat on in silence, waiting for someone, while
the moon now came out of the clouds, making the scene

bright again, now went behind them, throwing the earth in shadow. She was just about to fall asleep when she heard a nightingale singing clearly down by the pond. The country girl opened her eyes. Once more, with new rapture, her soul was revived by a mysterious union with nature, which lay so bright and serene all about her. She leaned on both elbows. A sweet sadness pressed upon her heart and tears of a vast and pure love which yearned for fulfillment— good, comforting tears—filled her eyes. She folded her arms on the windowsill and laid her head upon them. Her favorite prayer rose of itself in her heart, and she drowsed off just as she was, her eyes still wet with tears.

She was roused by the touch of a hand. She woke up. The touch was light and pleasant. The clasp tightened upon her arm. Suddenly she realized where she was, gave a little cry, jumped up, and telling herself that it could not be the count who was standing there by the window, radiant in the moonlight, she ran out of the room.

XV

But it was the count. On hearing the girl's cry and the coughing of the night watchman as he came down the other side of the fence in response to it, he instantly ran through the dew-wet grass into the depths of the garden, feeling like a thief caught in the act. "What a fool I am!" he said to himself. "I frightened her. I should have been more cautious, and waked her up by speaking to her. What a clumsy beast I am!" He stopped and listened: the watchman had entered the garden through the gate and was dragging his stick along the sandy path. He must hide. He ran down to the pond. The frogs startled him by leaping up in alarm from under his very feet and flopping into the water. In spite of his wet feet he squatted down and went over in his mind all that he had done: how he had climbed over the fence, sought her window, and at last caught sight of her white shadow; how, fearful of the slightest rustle, he had approached her several times, only to withdraw; how at one minute he had been certain that she was waiting for him, that she was even vexed with him for keeping her waiting so long, and at the next he was sure she could not possibly have given such ready consent to this rendezvous; and how at last, assuming that the bashfulness of a provincial girl had led her to pretend to be asleep, he had gone up to her and seen clearly that she really was asleep; for some reason he had instantly run away, but a feeling of shame for his cowardice had made him come back and boldly put his hand upon her arm. The night watchman coughed again and the gate creaked as he went out of the garden. The window of the young girl's room was banged shut and inside shutters were fastened over it. The count found this very annoying. He would have given anything for the chance to begin all over again. Oh, he would not have behaved so foolishly a second time! "A charming girl! So fresh! Simply adorable! And I let her slip through my fingers! What a dunderhead I am!" By this time he had lost all desire to sleep, and with the firm step of one who has been sorely vexed, he set off down the alley of lime trees.

But even to him this night brought as its peace offering a tranquillizing sadness and longing for love. The clay path with bits of grass or dry stalks sprouting out of it here and there was mottled by pale moonlight that fell in direct rays through the thick foliage of the limes. Sometimes a twisted branch, lighted on one side only, gave the impression of being overgrown with white moss. The silvered leaves whispered together from time to time. The lights were put out in the house; all sounds died away; only the nightingale filled with song all this bright, silent, unencompassable space. "What a night! What a glorious night!" thought the count, drawing deep into his lungs the fresh and fragrant air of the garden. "But there's something amiss. I seem to be dissatisfied with myself and others, dissatisfied with life itself. What a dear sweet girl she is! Perhaps she really was offended. . . ." Here his musings took a new turn; now he saw himself in the garden with the country girl in the most odd and varied situations; then the country girl was supplanted by Minna. "What a fool I was! I ought to have simply seized her round the waist and kissed her!" And with this regret in mind, the count went back to his room.

The cornet had not yet fallen asleep. He immediately turned over in bed to face the count.

"Aren't you asleep?" asked the count.

"No."

"Shall I tell you what happened?"

"Well?"

"Perhaps I oughtn't to—but I shall. Here, move over."

And, shrugging off thoughts of his bungled opportunity, he sat down on his friend's bed with a lively smile on his face.

"Would you believe it? That young lady agreed to a rendezvous with me!"

"What are you saying!" cried Polozov, jumping up.

"Well, listen."

"How? When? I don't believe it!"

"While you were calculating your winnings at 'preference' she told me she would be waiting for me at the window, and that I could climb through it into her room. There's the advantage of being practical-minded! While you were making your calculations with the old lady, I was arranging my affairs. Why, you yourself heard her say she intended sitting at the window and gazing out at the pond tonight."

"But she meant nothing by it."

"That's it; I can't make up my mind whether she said it by chance or not. Perhaps she really did not have that in mind, but appearances are against her. The whole thing had an odd ending. I acted like a perfect fool," he added with a contemptuous smile.

"But how? Where have you been?"

The count told him what had happened, omitting nothing except his vacillations before going up to the window.

"I spoiled everything myself. I ought to have been bolder. She cried out and ran away."

"So she cried out and ran away," repeated the cornet, smiling awkwardly in response to the smile of this count whose influence over him had been so strong and had lasted so long.

"Yes. Well, now it's time to go to bed."

The cornet turned his back to the door again and lay in silence for ten minutes or so. It is hard to say what went on in his innermost soul during that time, but when he turned back again his face wore a look of pain and determination.

"Count Tourbin," he burst out.

"Are you delirious?" said the count serenely. "What is it, Cornet Polozov?"

"Count Tourbin, you're a cad!" cried Polozov, jumping out of bed.

XVI

The squadron left the next day. The officers did not see their hosts and did not seek them out to say good-bye. Nor did they speak to each other. They had agreed to hold a duel at their first halt, but Captain Shultz, a good comrade, an excellent horseman, a favorite among the hussars, and the man whom the count had chosen as his second, was able to arrange matters in such a way that not only was the duel averted, but not a soul in the regiment got wind of it. Tourbin and Polozov, while never resuming the close friendship that had been theirs, continued to use the intimate form of address when speaking to each other and sometimes met at dinners and parties.

1856

A HAPPY MARRIED LIFE

PART ONE.

I

We had been living alone in our village all winter—
Katya, Sonya and I—and were in mourning for my
mother, who had died in the autumn. Katya was an old
friend of the family, the governess who had brought us all
up, and whom I had loved ever since I could remember.
Sonya was my younger sister.

It was a sad and gloomy winter we spent in our old house
in Pokrovskoye. The weather was cold and windy and the
snow drifted up higher than the windows, which were
frosted over most of the time. We hardly left the house all
winter, and made no calls. Seldom did anyone come to see
us, and those who did brought us no joy. They all wore
sad faces and spoke softly, as though afraid of waking
someone; they never laughed, but only sighed and often
wept when they looked at me, and even more often when
they looked at little Sonya in her black frock. Death
seemed to linger in the house; sorrow and the ghost of
death hung in the air. Mama's room stood cold and empty.
Its locked door had a terrible fascination for me as I passed
it on my way to bed.

I was seventeen years old, and the very year she died,
Mother had intended to remove to the city to bring me out.
The loss of her was a great sorrow to me but I must admit
that underneath the sorrow I also felt that I was young,
and as people said, pretty, and here I was wasting a sec-

ond winter in solitude in the country. Toward the end of
the winter this melancholy born of loneliness and sheer
boredom grew on me to such an extent that I did not leave
my room; I never opened the piano or picked up a book.
When Katya tried to persuade me to busy myself with one
thing or another, I answered that I did not want to, or that
I could not, but in my heart, I asked myself: "Why should
I? Why do anything when the best part of my life is being
wasted? Why?" And the only answer was tears.

People said I had got thin and plain, but even that did
not interest me. What difference did it make? Who cared?
It seemed to me that my whole life would pass in this remote village, and in that hopeless boredom, which I had
neither the strength nor the desire to throw off. Towards
the end of the winter Katya began to fear for my health
and decided to take me abroad at all costs. But for that
we needed money, and we hardly knew what had been
left us after Mother's death. Every day we expected our
guardian, who was to come and settle our affairs. He arrived in March.

"Thank goodness!" Katya exclaimed one day when I was
roaming about the house like a shadow, doing nothing and
without a thought or a desire. "Sergei Mikhailich is back.
He has sent to ask about us, and wants to come for dinner.
You must shake off this mood of yours, Masha. What will
he think of you? He was always so fond of you."

Sergei Mikhailich was a near neighbor of ours and had
been a friend of my father's, though much younger. I was
happy over his arrival for it meant a change in our plans,
and would enable us to leave the village, but aside from
that I had loved and respected him from childhood. When
Katya told me to take myself in hand, she rightly guessed
that of all our friends I would have hated most to appear
to Sergei Mikhailich in an unfavorable light.

I had come to love him, as had all the others in the
house, from Katya and Sonya, who was his goddaughter,
down to the last coachman. But besides that, he held a
special place in my heart because of a word once dropped
by Mother while I was by. She said she would have liked

such a man to be my husband. This had seemed surprising
to me at the time and even unpleasant; my hero was an
entirely different sort of person. The man I dreamed of was
slim and spare, with a face that was pale and sad. Sergei
Mikhailich, on the other hand, was no longer young. He
was tall, heavily built and, it seemed to me, always jolly.
But in spite of that, what mother said had caught my imagination. Six years before, when I was only eleven, and he
used to play with me and call me his "little violet," I sometimes asked myself, almost in terror, what I would do if
he should want to marry me.

Sergei Mikhailich arrived before dinner, to which Katya
had added spinach sauce and a frosted cake. Through the
window I saw him drive up in a small sleigh, but as soon as
he rounded the corner of the house I ran into the parlor;
I thought I would pretend that I had not been expecting
him at all. But on hearing his heavy tread in the front hall,
his hearty voice and Katya running to meet him, I could
not hold back, and ran into the hall too. He was holding
Katya by the hand, talking in his big genial voice and
laughing. Seeing me, he stopped and gazed at me for several moments without bowing. It was awkward for me, and
I felt I was blushing.

"Ah! Can that be you?" he said in his bluff, outright way,
and came up to me with his arms open wide. "How you've
changed! How grown up you are! My violet has become a
rose!"

He took my small hand in his big one and gave it such
an honest, hard squeeze that he almost hurt me. I thought
he would kiss my hand and was about to lean over toward
him but he only squeezed it once more and his smiling gaze
met mine squarely.

I had not seen him for six years, and he had changed
greatly: he was older and darker and had grown side
whiskers which didn't become him at all. But his simple
manner was still there, and his open, honest face with its
large features, intelligent, shining eyes, and kind, almost
childlike smile.

In five minutes he had ceased to be a guest and was

perfectly at home with all of us, even the servants. The servants were especially glad to see him, as was apparent from their efforts to please.

He did not act at all as the neighbors had when they had come to see us after Mother's death and thought it necessary to keep silent and weep. On the contrary, he was talkative and gay and never said a word about our bereavement. His indifference seemed strange to me at first and even unseemly, since he was such a close friend. But then I realized that it was not indifference but sincerity, and I was grateful for it.

That evening we had tea in the parlor, with Katya pouring as she had in mother's time. Sonya and I sat down beside her. Old Grigory brought Sergei Mikhailich a pipe of Father's he had found, and he paced back and forth smoking just as in the old days.

"How many sad changes have come to this house," he said, pausing for a moment.

"Yes," Katya sighed. She put the lid on the samovar, and looked at him, on the verge of tears.

"I suppose you remember your father, don't you?" he said to me.

"Very little," I confessed.

"What a fine thing it would be for you if he could be with you now," he said softly, looking thoughtfully over my head.

"I thought a lot of your father," he said still more softly, and it seemed to me that his eyes were shining more than ever.

"And now God has taken her as well," Katya murmured, hastily putting the napkin on the teapot and taking out her handkerchief to wipe away her tears.

"Yes, sad changes have come to this house," he repeated, turning his head away. "Sonya, come and show me your toys," he added in a few moments, and went into the drawing room. I looked at Katya, my own eyes full of tears.

"What a nice friend!" she exclaimed.

And truly it gave me a warm and agreeable feeling to have the sympathy of this good man who was no kin to us.

In the drawing room we could hear Sergei Mikhailich romping with Sonya and making her squeal with laughter. I sent some tea in to him; then I heard him sit down at the piano and start drumming on the keys with Sonya's little fingers.

"Marya Alexandrovna!" he called. "Come and play something for us."

It was pleasant, the homely, comradely way in which he ordered me about. I went in to them.

"Here, take this," he said, opening my Beethoven at the *Adagio* from the Sonata *Quasi Una Fantasia*. "Let's see how you play," he added. And he took his glass of tea and withdrew to a corner away from the piano.

Somehow I felt that I could not refuse or begin with an apology that I played badly. So I obeyed without a word and played as well as I could, though I feared his criticism, knowing as I did that he appreciated and loved music. The *Adagio* was in the reminiscent mood of our conversation during tea, and it seemed to me I played it rather well.

But he would not let me finish the *Scherzo*. "No, you're not up to that," he said, coming over to me. "We won't have that, but the first wasn't bad. You seem to understand music."

Even such moderate praise made me blush with pleasure. It was such a novelty for me, and so pleasant that he, the friend and equal of my father, should speak to me so seriously, as with a grownup, not a child. Katya went upstairs to put Sonya to bed and we were left together in the drawing-room.

He began to talk to me about my father—how he had got to know him and what pleasant times they had had together back in the days when I was still interested only in books and toys. It was from his stories that I first saw my father clearly as a simple, lovable person quite different from what I had imagined. Then he asked me how I liked to spend my time, what I read, and what I intended to do, and gave me advice. He was no longer the gay playfellow who used to tease me and make toys for me, but a serious person, affectionate and direct, for whom I felt an involuntary respect and liking. It was pleasant to talk to him, but still I could not help feeling strained and nervous. I chose every word I said carefully because I wanted very badly to win his affection. So far, he had been fond of me because I was my father's daughter.

When Katya had put Sonya to bed she came back to us. She complained to him of my low spirits, which I had not mentioned.

"So she hasn't said a word to me about the most important thing," said Sergei Mikhailich, smiling and shaking his head reproachfully.

"What is there to say?" I answered. "It's all very tiresome and will soon pass away." At that moment it seemed to me that my melancholy had already passed, that indeed it had never existed.

"It's a bad thing not to be able to endure solitude," he said. "Are you really such an ordinary young lady?"

"Of course I am," I laughed,

"A pampered young lady, perhaps, who is keenly alive only when being admired, and wilts and finds no pleasure in life as soon as she is left alone. Everything for show and nothing for herself."

"You have a fine opinion of me," I said, just to say something.

"Yes, I have," he exclaimed, and then, after a pause: "You are not your father's daughter for nothing—there is something in you." And his kind, attentive glance again flattered me and filled me with glad confusion.

Only now did I notice that underneath the gayness that flitted across his face there was a look peculiar to him alone; at first it was just bright and sincere, but gradually it became more attentive and a little sad.

"You have no excuse for being bored, and you must not allow yourself to be," he said. "You appreciate music and have your books and studies. You have your whole life ahead of you, and now is the time to prepare yourself for it, so that you will have no regrets later on. Next year it will be too late."

He talked to me like a father or an uncle and I felt that

he was constantly making an effort to keep himself at my level. I resented his thinking he had to talk down to me, and yet it was pleasant to discover that I was the only one for whose sake he made an effort to be different.

The rest of the evening he talked with Katya about the affairs of the estate.

"Well, good-bye, my friends," he said, standing up. He came up to me and took me by the hand.

"When shall we see you again?" Katya asked.

"In the spring," he replied, still holding my hand.

"I'm going to Danilovka now" (our second village). "I'll find out how things are there, put what I can in order, and then go to Moscow on my own business. But we shall see much of each other this summer."

"Why are you going to be away so long?" I said, very much downcast. I had hoped to see him every day, and I was sorry and afraid that my melancholy would return. This must have been evident from my glance and voice.

"Keep yourself busy and don't allow yourself to mope." His voice seemed to me very cold and matter of fact. "In the spring I shall give you an examination," he added, re-leasing my hand and not looking at me.

In the front hall, while we were saying good-bye to him, he hurried into his coat, without so much as glancing my way.

"He need not try so hard," I thought. "Does he really think it gives me so much pleasure to have him notice me? He's a good man, a very good man, but that is all."

Still, that night, Katya and I could not sleep for a long time. We kept talking, not about him, but about how we would spend the summer and the following winter. The ter-rible question "Why?" no longer worried me. It seemed ob-vious that one must live so as to be happy, and I expected much happiness in the future. It was as though our gloomy old house in Pokrovskoye had suddenly become filled with life and light.

II

Spring came. My old melancholy was supplanted by the dreamy melancholy of confused hopes and desires that always come in the spring. I no longer lived as I had at the beginning of winter, but busied myself with Sonya, with music and reading. I often went out into the garden and wandered along the paths for hours at a time, or would sit alone on a bench thinking. Heaven only knows what I wanted or was hoping for. Sometimes I sat the whole night through by the window, especially when the moon was shining. Occasionally, unknown to Katya, I would slip out into the garden without a coat, and run through the dewy grass down to the pond; once I even went out into the fields, and another time walked from one end of our garden to the other at dead of night.

It is hard for me now to recall or understand the dreams that filled my mind in those days. And when I do recall them I can hardly believe they were really *mine*, so strange, so unreal were they.

At the end of May Sergei Mikhailich returned from his trip as he had promised. The first time he came to see us was in the evening, when we were not in the least expecting him. We were sitting on the verandah about to have tea. The garden was already in full leaf and the nightingales had moved into the untrimmed shrubs, where they would stay all summer. Here and there the lilacs were tinged with the violet or white of bursting buds. The leaves of the birches along the path were transparent in the evening sun. There was a fresh coolness on the shaded verandah, and later there would be a heavy dew on the grass. From the yard beyond the garden came the last sounds of the day's work and the lowing of the herd being driven home. Nikon, the half-wit, was driving along the path in front of the house with his barrel of water. He was watering the dahlias, and the cold stream from the watering can made dark circles in the upturned earth round the stems and their supports.

The table on the verandah where we were sitting was
laid with a snowy cloth. On it stood a freshly polished samovar, glittering and puffing out steam; there were also
plates of *kerndelki* and biscuits and a jug of cream. Katya
was rinsing the cups efficiently with her plump hands. I
was very hungry after my bathe, and, without waiting for
tea, had begun eating bread, dipping it into the thick
cream. I was wearing a blouse of unbleached linen with
loose sleeves, and my wet hair was tied up in a kerchief.
Katya was the first to see him.

"Sergei Mikhailich!" she exclaimed, "We were just talking about you."

I stood up to go in and dress, but he caught me in the
doorway.

"Why such ceremony out here in the country?" he said,
smiling, as he glanced at my head tied up in a kerchief.
"You aren't ashamed to show yourself to old Grigory, and
I am no more to you than he is."

But it struck me that he was looking at me quite differently than Grigory would have done, and I was ashamed.

"I'll be back in a minute," I said, leaving him.

"What's wrong with that blouse?" he called after me. "It
makes you look like a young peasant girl."

"How strangely he looked at me," I thought as I was
changing my dress upstairs. "Well, thank goodness he's
come—things won't be so dull now." After a glance in the
mirror I ran happily down the stairs and, without trying to
conceal my haste, went out on the verandah all out of
breath. He was sitting at the table telling Katya about our
affairs. He glanced at me, smiled, and went on talking.
According to him, our affairs were in an excellent state.
We would have to stay in the country only that summer;
then we could remove to St. Petersburg for Sonya's education, or go abroad.

"If you'd only go abroad with us!" said Katya. "Without
you, we'd be like babes in the wood."

"I should like to go round the world with you!" he said,
half serious, half joking.

"Do let's go round the world together!" I said. He smiled and shook his head.

"And what about my mother and my own affairs?" he asked. "But that is beside the point—tell me how you've been getting on. I hope you haven't been moping again?"

When I told him I had kept myself busy since he left, and had not become melancholy, and when Katya bore me out, he praised me, and was tender in word and look, as if he had some special right to be. And I felt that I must be utterly frank and sincere with him, must tell him every good thing I had done and admit everything that might have displeased him, as though he were my Father Confessor.

Since the evening was fine, we stayed on the verandah after the tea things had been cleared away. The conversation was so interesting that I did not notice the gradual cessation of all human sound in house and yard. The odor of the flowers grew stronger and the grass became drenched with dew. A nightingale in a lilac bush nearby began to warble, but stopped on hearing our voices. The starry sky seemed to have descended low upon us. I only noticed it had got dark when a bat flew in without a sound and fluttered about the white kerchief tied over my hair. I strained back against the wall and almost let out a scream, but the bat flew away as quickly and silently as it had come, disappearing in the dusk of the orchard.

"How I love your Pokrovskoye!" Sergei Mikhailich exclaimed during a break in the conversation. "I'd like to go on sitting here on your verandah for the rest of my life."

"Then do," said Katya.

"It would be nice," he murmured, "but life doesn't sit and wait."

"Why don't you get married?" Katya asked. "You'd make an excellent husband."

"Because I like to sit," he said, laughing. "No, Katerina Karlovna, you and I are past the marrying age. People stopped looking upon me as a possible suitor long ago. I did too, and I've felt finer ever since, truly I have."

It seemed to me that his tone was unnaturally sprightly.

"That's a fine thing to say!" Katya exclaimed. "He's all of thirty-six and his life's over!"

"All over," he agreed. "All I want to do is sit, but it takes something more than that to get married. She's the one you ought to ask," he added, nodding toward me. "It's people like her who should get married, and you and I will find pleasure in watching them."

I detected a note of sadness and of strain in his voice. He was silent for a moment; neither Katya nor I said anything.

"Why, just suppose," he went on, turning in his chair, "that I was to marry some seventeen-year-old girl, say Masha, here—I mean Marya Alexandrovna. That's a striking example. I'm very glad it comes out that way . . . that's the very best example."

I began to laugh; I did not understand why he was glad, or what it was that was "coming out that way."

"Well, cross your heart and tell me the truth," he joked, "wouldn't it be a misfortune for you if you were to tie yourself up to an old man who had had his day and only wanted to sit around, while all sorts of things, all sorts of wishes, were hiding in that little head of yours?"

I was embarrassed; I did not know what to answer.

"Of course I'm not making you a proposal," he said, laughing. "But I'm not the kind of husband you dream of when you roam about the garden in the evening by yourself, am I? And it . . . it would be a misfortune, wouldn't it?"

"Not a misfortune . . ." I began.

"But not a good thing either," he finished.

"No, but I might be mista—"

"There, you see," he interrupted again. "She's quite right, and I'm grateful to her for her frankness and for this talk we have had. For me, too, it would be a great misfortune," he added.

"What a queer person you are—you're just the same as you always were," said Katya, and she went into the house to have supper put on the table.

We both fell silent after Katya left, and there was silence

all about. A nightingale began to sing—not an evening song this time, impulsive and faltering, but a night song, calm and unhurried. The sound filled the whole garden, and then another nightingale answered from the ravine—the first time one had sung there that evening. The bird in the garden stopped singing for a moment as though listening, and then still louder and more intense came his trills. In that nocturnal world of theirs, so unknown to us, their songs resounded with magestic tranquillity.

The gardener went past on his way to bed in the greenhouse, the clump of his heavy boots growing fainter along the path. Twice there came a shrill whistle from the foot of the hill, then again all was silent. The leaves rustled slightly and the awning over the verandah stirred as a ripple of air laden with perfume came pouring over us.

It was awkward for me to keep silent after what had been said, but I did not know how to begin. I glanced at him—his eyes, shining in the half-light, were fixed on me.

"It's good to be alive," he murmured.

For some reason I sighed.

"What?" he said.

"Yes, it's good to be alive," I repeated.

Again we were silent, and again I felt awkward. I kept thinking I had hurt him by agreeing that he was old. I wanted to comfort him, but I did not know what to say.

"Well, good night," he said, rising. "Mother's expecting me to supper. I hardly saw her today."

"But I wanted to play you my new sonata," I objected.

"Another time." His answer seemed cold. "Good night."

Now I was sure I had offended him, and I was sorry. Katya and I walked around the house with him and stood looking after him as he rode down the drive. When the hoofbeats had died away I went back to the verandah, and again sat looking out into the garden—into the damp white mist laden with night sounds. I sat there for a long time dreaming, and my dream seemed to be real.

He came a second time, and a third, and the awkwardness that had arisen from our odd conversation completely disappeared. All summer long he came to see us two or

three times a week. I became so accustomed to his calls
that when he did not come for some time I missed him terribly. I thought he was behaving badly by deserting me
and would be angry with him. He treated me as if I were
a beloved younger comrade. He asked me questions, led
me to confide in him, offered me advice, encouraged me,
sometimes scolded me and checked my wrong impulses. But
in spite of all his efforts to treat me as an equal, I felt that
behind what I knew of him, there was a whole world I did
not know—a world into which he did not consider it necessary to admit me. It was this that attracted me to him most
and made me respect him. I knew from Katya and the
neighbors that besides taking care of his old mother with
whom he lived, managing his own estate and being our
guardian, he had public affairs of some sort that caused
him much trouble. Still I could never extract anything from
him as to what he thought of all this, or what his convictions, plans, and hopes were. No sooner did I turn the conversation to his affairs, than he would frown in a way he
had that seemed to say, "Come, what do you care for such
things?" and at once change the subject. At first I felt offended, but then I got so used to our talking only about
things concerning me, that I came to look on it as natural.

Another thing that I did not like at first, but which I later
found pleasant, was his absolute indifference, his seeming
contempt, even, for my appearance. He never hinted by
word or glance that I was pretty—on the contrary, he
wrinkled up his nose and laughed when I was called pretty
in his presence. He even liked to seek out defects in my
appearance, and to tease me about them. The fashionable
frocks Katya loved to deck me out in on special occasions
and the new ways she did my hair brought forth only gibes.
This hurt poor Katya, and embarrassed me terribly at first.
Katya, who had decided that I attracted him, could not for
the life of her understand how it was possible not to want
the woman one loved to look her best. For my part, I soon
realized what it was he wanted—he wanted to believe
that I was not coquettish. When I realized this, it was
not long before every shade of coquetry in my clothes,

my way of doing up my hair, and my manners, had disappeared completely. In its stead there now appeared a transparent coquetry of simplicity, for I could not as yet be truly simple. I knew that he loved me, though I had not asked myself whether it was as a child or as a woman, and I valued his love. I knew he considered me the best young lady in the world, and I could not help wanting him to be deceived. So I involuntarily encouraged it. But in deceiving him I improved myself. I felt how much better and more worthy it was to show him the beauties of my soul rather than of my body. The physical side—my hair, my hands and face, and my ways, good or bad as they might be, he seemed to know and appreciate at a glance and so well that there was nothing I could really add to his appreciation. But he did not know my soul because he loved it, and because it was still growing and developing, and it was here that I could and did deceive him. How easy it was for me to be with him when I finally realized this! My groundless embarrassment and constrained movements disappeared completely. I felt that no matter how he saw me, in full face or profile, sitting or standing, with my hair done high or low, he saw all of me, and appeared to be content with me as I was. I think that if he had departed from his habit and had suddenly told me, as others did, that I had a pretty face, I should not have been glad at all. But how glad and lighthearted I would feel when he gazed at me, after some remark of mine, and said in an earnest voice to which he tried to give a bantering tone:

"Yes, there *is* something in you. I must admit you're a fine girl!"

What was it that brought me these rewards, filling my heart with pride and joy? My saying that I was touched by old Grigory's love for his granddaughter; or my being moved to tears by some poem or novel I had read; or my preference of Mozart to Schulhoff. The flair I had for guessing everything that was good and ought to be loved, though I really had not the least idea of what was good or what ought to be loved, struck me as remarkable.

Sergei Mikhailich disapproved of many of my tastes and

habits, and it was enough for him to show by a glance or merely a movement of his brow that he did not approve of what I was about to say; enough for him to assume that rueful, slightly contemptuous expression of his, for me to fancy I did not really like what I had always liked. Sometimes, when he was about to give me advice, I would guess what he intended to say. Or again, looking me steadily in the eye, he would draw out of me the thought he desired. At that time none of my thoughts, none of my feelings were my own—they were all his, but had suddenly become mine. They had entered my life and illumined it. Without noticing it at all, I began to look at everything with different eyes —at Katya and Sonya and our servants, and at myself and my occupations. Before this I had read only because I was bored—now books became one of my greatest pleasures, and this only because we read books and talked about them together and he brought new ones to me.

Before this, the time I devoted to Sonya and the lessons I gave her had been a hard task that I forced myself to fulfill only from a sense of duty. Then one day he was present at a lesson, and I began to find pleasure in following Sonya's progress. Before this it had seemed impossible for me to learn an entire piece on the piano, but now, knowing that he would hear and, it might be, praise me, I played the same passage over forty times, so that poor Katya had to stuff cotton in her ears, and still it did not bore me. The old sonatas seemed to phrase themselves quite differently now—they came out much better. Even Katya, whom I knew and loved as my own self, changed in my eyes. It was only now that I realized she was by no means obliged to be the mother, friend and slave she was to us. I realized what a selfless, devoted and loving creature she was—realized how much I owed to her, and began to love her still more. He taught me to look on our peasants and household serfs, on the servants and girls in the house, quite differently than before. It may seem ridiculous, but until I was seventeen years old, these people among whom I had lived were strangers to me—more so even than people I had only read about. I had never stopped to think that they had their loves, their desires and their regrets, just as I did. The groves and fields I had known so long suddenly became new and beautiful to me. Sergei Mikhailich was right when he said there is only one real happiness in life—to live for others. It had seemed a strange thing to say then—I did not understand it; but without my realizing it, this conviction was already taking root in my heart. He revealed to me a whole world of joys around me, without changing anything in the course of my life, and without adding anything to each impression but himself. These things had surrounded me since my childhood, but they had been mute; no sooner did he come than they all began to speak and seek admission to my soul, filling it with happiness.

Often that summer I would go up to my room and lie down. Instead of the old longings and hopes for the future born of the springtide, I would be filled with the excitement of happiness in the present. I could not sleep, and would get up and sit on Katya's bed and tell her that I was completely happy, something which, I now realize as I look back on it, I need not have told her—she could see it for herself. And she used to tell me that she had everything she wanted, and that she too was very happy, and would kiss me. I believed her; I felt it was only right and just that everybody should be happy. But Katya could also sleep. She would sometimes even pretend to be angry, and drive me off her bed so that she could go to sleep. Then, for a long time, I would think over all the things that made me happy. Sometimes I would get up and say my prayers a second time. . . . I prayed in my own words, thanking God for all the happiness he had given me. There would not be a sound in our little room except Katya's even breathing and the ticking of the clock beside her, but even so I could not go to sleep; I would turn and twist and whisper my prayers and cross myself and kiss the cross hanging round my neck. The doors were closed and the windows shuttered, and some fly or mosquito would hover buzzing in one spot. And I never wanted to leave that room, never wanted the morning to come, never wanted this atmosphere of spiritual seclusion surrounding me to be dispelled.

I fancied that my dreams, my thoughts and prayers were living creatures here in the dusk with me, fluttering about my bed, hovering over me. And every thought was his thought, every feeling—his feeling. I did not realize then that this was love. I thought it was just a feeling that might come of itself at any time.

III

One day during harvest time Katya and I went out into the garden after dinner with Sonya. We sat down on our favorite bench in the shade of the limes above the ravine, from where we had a view of the woods and fields beyond. Sergei Mikhailich had not been to see us for three days and we were expecting him, the more so since our bailiff said he had told him he intended riding over to inspect our fields. Shortly after one o'clock we saw him coming through the rye on horseback, and Katya had some of his favorite peaches and cherries brought out. Then she glanced at me with a smile, lay down on the bench, and dozed off. I broke off a flat twisted twig of lime with succulent leaves and bark that was wet to the touch, and, waving it over Katya, continued to read, glancing every now and then at the road through the fields where he would appear. Sonya was building a house for her dolls against the roots of an old lime.

It was a hot and sultry day, with no wind. In the morning black thunderclouds had been piling up, threatening a shower. I had been nervous, as I always am before a thunderstorm. But after midday the clouds had withdrawn to the horizon and the sun sailed out into a clear sky. Now there came a rumble of thunder from one side and from time to time pale zigzags of lightning shot through the heavy clouds that merged with the dust of the fields on the horizon. It was clear that there would be no storm that day, at least in our vicinity. I sat there watching the patches of road that could be glimpsed beyond the garden. There was a constant movement of creaking carts crawling home piled high with sheaves, and of empty carts rattling along in the opposite direction with people in them bouncing about, their legs dangling, their shirts fluttering. The heavy dust was not carried away, nor did it settle; it hung low beyond the wattle fence and among the leaves in the orchard. Further away, from the rickyard, came the same sound of voices and the same creaking of wheels, and the same yellow sheaves were to be seen, first moving slowly along the fence, then flying up into the air as the oval stacks took shape before my eyes, like houses, with their pointed roofs and the muzhiks swarming over them. And in the dusty field before me carts were moving about, and I could again see the yellow sheaves, and hear the carts, the voices, and the songs. On one side the expanse of stubble with stripes of wormwood marking the boundary lines between the fields was spreading wider. Lower, and to the right, I could see the peasant women in their bright garments binding up the sheaves on the tousled mowed field; they were bent over, their arms moving steadily back and forth, and as they advanced the field became neat with the sheaves piled in orderly rows upon it. Summer seemed to be changing to autumn before my very eyes. It was hot and dusty everywhere except at this favorite spot of ours in the orchard. And through this dust and heat on all sides of us was the noise and talk and movement of the peasants working in the broiling sun.

Katya was snoring so sweetly on our cool bench under her white batiste handkerchief! The cherries were so juicy looking and shiny black on the plate! Our frocks were so fresh and clean! The water in the jug was so bright and cheerful as it played in the sunlight! I felt so blissful! "What is to be done about it?" thought I. "Is it my fault that I am so happy? But how shall I share my happiness? To whom can I give all of myself, all of my happiness?"

The sun had already sunk below the tops of the birches along the path and objects in the distance were becoming brighter and more distinct in its oblique rays; the dust was settling on the fields; the thunderclouds had completely scattered; in the rickyard beyond the village I could see the tops of three new stacks that the muzhiks had already

climbed off of; the carts had galloped past, evidently for
the last time, with people in them shouting; the women had
gone home singing at the top of their voices, with their
rakes across their shoulders and straw binders in their
girdles; but still Sergei Mikhailich did not come, though I
had seen him ride down the hill a long time before. Then
suddenly his figure appeared, coming from a direction I
had not in the least expected (he had come round by way
of the ravine). With a happy, smiling face, he was striding
quickly toward me, hat in hand. When he saw that Katya
was asleep he bit his lip, screwed up his eyes, and began
to tiptoe. I saw that he was in the mood of unaccountable
exuberance that I so loved in him and which we called a
"wild ecstasy." He was like a boy escaped from school; his
whole being breathed joy, happiness, and boyish energy.

"Hullo, little violet, how are you? Feeling fine?" he asked
in a whisper, as he squeezed my hand. "I'm feeling capital," he said in reply to my question. "I'm thirteen today
—I'd like to play hide-and-seek and climb trees."

"A 'wild ecstasy'?" I asked, looking into his laughing
eyes and aware that his mood was being communicated to
me.

"Yes," he answered, winking at me and trying not to
smile. "Only why hit Ekaterina Karlovna on the nose?"

I had gone on waving the lime twig while I was looking
at him and did not notice that I had knocked the handkerchief off Katya and was brushing her face with the leaves. I
laughed.

"She'll say she wasn't asleep," I whispered, as though to
keep from waking her, but really not for that reason—
simply for the pleasure of whispering to him.

He moved his lips in silent mockery, as though I were
whispering so softly he could not hear anything. Then, noticing the plate of cherries, he pretended to steal it and
took it over to Sonya under the lime, where he sat down
on her dolls. Sonya was angry at first, but he soon made
up with her by getting her to play with him, the game being to see who could gobble up cherries faster.

"I'll tell them to bring some more," I said, "or we can go and get some ourselves if you like."

He took the plate and put the dolls on it and we went off to the orchard with Sonya running after us, tugging at his coat to make him give back her dolls. He gave them to her, and then turned to me with a serious air.

"You really are a violet," he said, still speaking softly, though there was no danger now of waking anyone. "When I came up to you after all that dust and heat and work, I seemed to smell violets—not the fragrant garden sort, but the first little dark ones that smell of melting snow and spring grass."

"How is the harvesting getting on?" I asked to cover up the joyous confusion his words excited.

"Excellently. These people are excellent in everything they do. The more you know them, the more you love them."

"Yes," I said. "Before you came, I was watching the work from the garden, and suddenly I was ashamed that they were working while I—"

"Do not boast, my dear," he interrupted me, all at once becoming serious, but looking kindly into my eyes. "That is a sacred matter. Under no circumstances must you boast of such feelings."

"But you are the only person I have said it to."

"Yes, I know. Well, what about our cherries?"

The gate to the orchard was locked, and none of the gardeners was to be seen (he had sent them all to help with the harvesting). Sonya ran off to get the key, but instead of waiting for her, he climbed upon the wall, raised the netting and sprang down on the other side.

"Do you want some cherries?" he called. "Give me the plate."

"No, I want to pick them myself—I'll go for the key. Sonya will never find it."

But at the same time I wanted to see what he was doing in there—how he looked and behaved when he thought no one would see him. To tell the truth I simply did not want to lose sight of him for a moment. I ran round the wall through the nettles to the other side where it was lower. Standing on an empty tub so that the top of the wall did not quite reach my chest, I leaned over and looked inside. I glanced round at the gnarled old trees with the juicy black cherries hanging heavy under their broad, pointed leaves. I put my head under the netting and from under a knotty limb I saw Sergei Mikhailich. He must have thought I had gone and no one could see him. He had taken off his hat and was sitting in the crotch of an old tree, his eyes closed, kneading a piece of cherry-gum into a ball. Suddenly he shrugged his shoulders, opened his eyes, smiled, and murmured something. The word and the smile were so unlike him that I was ashamed to be spying upon him. It seemed to me he had said, "Masha." "It cannot be," I thought. Then he repeated it, "Darling Masha!"—more softly and more tenderly. This time I clearly heard those two words. My heart began to pound so hard and such an overpowering, almost forbidden joy came over me that I had to catch hold of the wall with both hands to keep from falling and giving myself away.

He heard me and, glancing round startled, dropped his eyes and blushed crimson like a girl. He wanted to say something to me but could not, and only stood there with flaming face. Still, he smiled as he looked at me. I smiled too. His whole face shone with happiness. He was no longer an oldish, family friend whom I looked up to and who taught me. He was my equal—a man who loved and feared me and whom I loved and feared. We said nothing, only looked at each other. But suddenly he frowned; the smile and the shine of his eyes disappeared and he spoke to me in his old fatherly tone again, and coldly, as though he had been doing something improper and now he had taken himself in hand and was advising me to do the same.

"Better get down—you'll fall," he said. "And smooth your hair—it's a sight."

"Why is he pretending? Why does he want to hurt me?" I thought in vexation. At that moment I was seized by an irresistible desire to embarrass him once more and to test my power over him.

"No, I want to pick some cherries myself," I said, and seizing hold of the nearest limb, jumped up on to the wall. Before he could give me a hand, I had jumped down into the orchard.

"What foolishness is this!" he exclaimed, blushing again and trying to conceal his confusion by pretending to be annoyed. "You might have hurt yourself. And how will you get out of here?"

He was more embarrassed than before, but now his embarrassment did not make me glad; it frightened me. It was my turn to be embarrassed. I blushed and avoided his eyes. In my confusion I began picking cherries with nothing to put them in. I scolded myself and regretted what I had done. I was afraid that I had disgraced myself in his eyes forever by this prank. We were both silent. Sonya came running with the key, and that delivered us from our awkward position. For a long time we said nothing to each other, we talked only to Sonya. When we got back to Katya, who assured us that she had not been asleep and had heard everything, I became more composed and he tried to assume his protective fatherly air again, but it proved difficult for him and did not deceive me.

A conversation we had had a few days before came back to me vividly. Katya had said that it was easier for a man to love and express his love than for a woman.

"A man can say he loves, but a woman can't," she said.

"But I think that a man, too, cannot and should not say that he loves," he had replied.

"Why not?" I asked.

"Because it will always be a lie. Is it a revelation for a man to say he is in love? As though as soon as he says it, something goes 'click'—and he loves. As though the saying of it ought to bring about a cataclysm, or have the effect of a salvo fired from a thousand guns. It seems to me," he went on, "that people who solemnly proclaim, 'I love you' are deceiving themselves, or what is worse, others."

"But how is a woman to know that a man loves her, if he doesn't tell her?" Katya asked.

"I cannot say," he answered. "Every person has his own

words. If there is feeling, it will be expressed. When I read novels, I always picture to myself what a puzzled expression there ought to be on the face of Lieutenant Strelsky, or of Alfred, when he says, 'I love you, Eleanora!' thinking that something unusual should happen, and nothing does—either to him or to her—their eyes and nose and all the rest remain just where they were."

I had felt then that there was something serious behind his joke—something concerning me—but Katya would not allow anyone to speak slightingly about the heroes of novels.

"Always paradoxes!" she said. "Now confess—have you never told a woman you loved her?"

"Never, and I have never got down on one knee," he answered, laughing, "and never will."

"Well, he doesn't have to tell me that he loves me," I thought now, recalling this conversation. "He loves me—I know it. And his efforts to feign indifference won't make me think otherwise."

All that evening he said little to me, but in every word he said to Katya and Sonya, in his every movement and glance, I read love, and read it indubitably. I was only vexed and sorry for him for thinking he must go on concealing what he felt and pretending to be cold when everything was already so clear, and when it would be so easy and simple to be unbelievably happy. But my jumping down into the orchard tormented me as though I had committed a crime. It seemed to me he had stopped respecting me, and was angry with me.

After dinner I went to the piano, and he came after me.

"Play something," he said, overtaking me in the parlor. "I haven't heard you for a long time."

"I wanted to . . . Sergei Mikhailich!" I said suddenly, looking him straight in the eye. "You're not angry with me?"

"Why should I be?"

"Because I didn't mind you after dinner," I said blushing.

He understood me, and shook his head, smiling. His glance said that he ought to scold me but lacked the heart.

"So everything's all right, and we're friends again?" I said, sitting down at the piano.

"I should think so!" he said.

The big, high-ceilinged drawing room was lighted only by the two candles on the piano, the rest of the room was in semidarkness. A clear, bright summer night looked in through the open windows. All was quiet except for the creaking of the floorboards in the dark parlor under Katya's feet, and the neighing and stamping of Sergei Mikhailich's horse under the window.

I could not see him, as he was sitting behind me, but I felt his presence everywhere in the shadowy room—in the music, and in my own self. My heart responded to his every glance, his every movement, though I could not see them. I played Mozart's "Sonata Fantasia" which he had brought to me, and which I had learned for him since his return. I was not thinking about my playing, but it seems I played well, and I felt that he was pleased. I felt the pleasure he was experiencing and, without looking at him, I felt his eyes upon me. Quite involuntarily, and while continuing unconsciously to move my fingers, I looked round at him. His head stood out against the background of the moonlit night. With chin propped in his hands, he sat staring at me with shining eyes. I smiled when I saw him and stopped playing. He also smiled, then reproachfully nodded for me to go on playing.

When I finished the piece the moon had risen high, and the feeble candlelight was supplemented by a different, silvery light that came through the window and fell on the floor. Katya said it was not at all like me to stop in the best place and that I had played badly. He said that on the contrary I had never played so well before, and began to wander through the rooms, going back and forth between the dark parlor and the drawing room, stopping every time to glance at me and smile. And I smiled; indeed, I wanted to laugh, so happy was I because of something that had happened—something that had happened only today, only now, this very moment. As soon as he went out I would put my arms round Katya (we were standing together by the piano) and begin to kiss her in my favorite spot under her soft chin. And as soon as he came back I would try to put on a serious face, but it was all I could do to keep from laughing.

"What has happened to her today?" Katya asked him.

He made no answer, only laughed at me—he knew what had happened.

"Just see what a night it is!" he called from the parlor, stopping before the open door of the balcony that looked out into the garden.

We went in to him. It really was a night such as I have never seen since. A full moon hung over the house behind us, out of sight, throwing the shadows of the roof and the pillars and the awning of the verandah obliquely, *en raccourci*, on the sandy path and the flower beds. All the rest was flooded with light, silvery with dew and moonbeams. The wide path through the flowers, with shadows of dahlias and their supports slanting across it on one side, swept away into the misty distance, bright and cold, its uneven gravel surface shimmering in the moonlight. Through the trees glimpsed the shiny roof of the greenhouse, and from the ravine a gathering mist was rising. Every twig of the lilac bushes, already shedding their leaves, was bright, and each dewy flower in the garden stood out distinctly. Light and shade were so intermingled in the alleys that the trees were like fantastic houses, swaying and transparent. To the right, the shadow of the house lay black, withdrawn, and fearsome. All the brighter seemed the bushy crown of the poplar that thrust up out of this shadow and for some strange reason hung in the bright light just above the house instead of sailing away into the deep blue of the sky.

"Let us go for a walk," I said.

Katya agreed but said I should put on my galoshes.

"I won't need them," I said. "Sergei Mikhailich will give me his arm."

As though that would prevent me from getting my feet wet! But they understood, and found nothing strange in my remark. He had never given me his arm before, but this evening I took it myself, and he did not find it strange. The three of us stepped down off the verandah, and the whole of this world—the sky, the garden, the air—was different from anything I had ever known.

When I looked ahead down the alley we were walking in, I felt it was impossible to go further in that direction—that the world of the possible ended here, that what was beyond must surely be locked up forever in its beauty. But as we advanced, the magic walls of beauty opened up to admit us, and there, too, it seemed, was the garden we knew so well, with its trees and paths and dry leaves. And we really *were* walking along the paths, stepping on the circles of light and shadow, and the dry leaves really *were* rustling underfoot and that really *was* a cool branch that brushed against my face. And it really *was* he walking with soft, measured step beside me, carefully supporting my arm, and it really *was* Katya walking beside me, her feet crunching in the sand. And it could only have been the moon in the sky that shone on us through the motionless branches.

But with every step, the magic walls again closed behind and before us, and I stopped believing we could go on; I stopped believing in all that was.

"Ugh! A toad!" Katya cried.

"Who could have said that, and why?" I wondered. But then I remembered it was Katya, and that she was afraid of toads, and looked down. A little toad leaped in front of me and stayed there, making a tiny black shadow on the bright sand of the path.

"Aren't you afraid?" he asked.

I glanced at him. There was a break in the line of trees at this spot and I could clearly see his face. How handsome it was, and how happy!

He said, "Aren't you afraid?" but I heard him say, "I love you, darling." His glance, his touch repeated, "I love you," and the light and the shadow and the air all repeated the words.

We went round the whole garden. Katya trotted along beside us, breathing heavily. She was tired and said it was time to go back. I was sorry for her. "Why doesn't she feel what we do?" I wondered. "Why aren't we all as young and as happy as this night and as he and I?"

We went back to the house, but he did not leave for a long time, though the cocks crowed and all the servants had gone to bed, and his horse, under the window, kept pawing the ground and snorting fretfully. Katya did not remind us of the hour, and we sat talking about the veriest trifles, not noticing the time until after two o'clock. The cocks had crowed the third time, and the dawn was at hand when he went away. He said good-bye the way he always did, and there was no particular significance in his words, but I knew that he was mine from that day, and that I would never lose him. As soon as I admitted to myself that I loved him I told Katya everything. She was glad and touched by my confidence, but she, poor dear, could sleep that night, while I paced the verandah for a long time and then went down into the garden where I walked along the paths we had walked together, recalling his every word and movement. I did not sleep the whole night and saw an early sunrise for the first time in my life. Such a night, such a morning, I have never seen since. "But why doesn't he simply say he loves me?" I wondered. "Why does he think of difficulties and call himself an old man, when it could all be so simple and beautiful? Why is he losing this golden time which may never come again? Let him say, 'I love you!' Let him say it, in words. Let him take my hand in his, bend his head over it and say, 'I love you!' Let him blush and drop his eyes before me, and then I shall tell him everything. Or I won't say anything—I'll put my arms round him, press close to him, and cry." But then the thought suddenly came to me: "What if I am mistaken and he doesn't love me?"

This thought frightened me. To what extremities might it not lead me! I remembered his and my embarrassment when I had jumped down off the orchard wall to him, and my heart grew heavy, my eyes brimmed with tears, and I began to pray. Then a strange, soothing thought—a hope—came to me. I decided to fast, to receive the Eucharist on my birthday, and on that same day become his betrothed.

I knew not why it should be so, but from that moment I believed and knew that it must be so. Day had already broken, and the servants were getting up when I went back to my room.

IV

It was the season of Uspensky, so no one was surprised by my resolution to fast.

He did not come to see us once the whole week, but I was not surprised or anxious and was not angry with him. On the contrary, I was glad he did not come and was expecting him only on my birthday. All that week I got up early every morning, and while they were putting in the horses, I would walk about the garden by myself, ruminating over my sins of the preceding day, and wondering how to spend the new day so that I should commit not a single sin and be completely content with it. It seemed easy to me at that time to be completely without sin. I thought that all one had to do was to try a little.

The trap would drive up and I would get in with Katya or one of the girls and we would ride three versts to the church. Each time as I went in I said to myself, "Blessed are they who enter with the fear of God in their hearts," and tried to mount the two grass-grown steps of the church porch with just that feeling. At that time there would be no more than a dozen pious women from among the peasants and household serfs in the church, and I tried to return their bows with humility. I myself went to the candle-box (feeling that this was very commendable) to get candles from the old soldier who was the elder and put them before the icons. Through the Holy Gates I could see the altar cloth my mother had embroidered. There on the iconostasis were the two wooden angels with stars on their heads that had seemed so big to me when I was a little girl, and the dove with the yellow halo which had always attracted my attention. Beyond the choir I could see the battered font in which so many children of our household serfs had been baptized, and in which I myself had been baptized. The old priest came out in a robe made of the pall that had covered my father's coffin, and read the service in the same voice in which he always read religious services at our house: Sonya's christening, my father's requiem and my mother's funeral. The same quavering voice of the sexton came from the choir; the same bent old woman, who, I remembered, was always in the church for every service, stood at the wall, her tear-filled eyes fixed on the icon, three fingers pressed to her lace kerchief as she crossed herself, her toothless mouth working all the while.

And all this was no longer curious to me, nor did I love it only for the memories it brought. It was something great and sacred in my eyes, and filled with the deepest significance. I listened attentively to every word of the prayers, trying to respond to them in spirit; I asked God to enlighten me whenever I did not understand and composed my own prayers whenever I did not hear. When prayers of repentance were read, I recalled my past, and that childish, innocent past seemed so black compared with my present condition of grace that I was horrified with myself. At the same time I felt that all would be forgiven, and that if I had committed even more sins, repentance would have been even sweeter. When at the end of the service the priest said, "The blessing of God be upon you," it seemed to communicate to me a feeling of physical well-being. It was as if light and warmth had entered my heart. After the service the priest came up to me and asked whether he should come to us to read Vespers, and at what time. I thanked him gratefully for the favor but said I would come to him myself.

"So you wish to trouble yourself to come here?" he asked, and I did not know how to answer so as not to sin through pride.

After Mass I always sent the horses home if I was without Katya and went back alone, humbly bowing low to everyone I met, and my eagerness to help, to advise, to sacrifice myself for someone else led me to help raise a load, or rock a baby, or step into the mud to allow others to pass.

One evening I heard the bailiff telling Katya that Semyon, one of our muzhiks, had come to ask for some boards to make a coffin for his daughter and a ruble for the funeral, and the bailiff said he had given them to him.

"Are they so poor, then?" I asked. "Very poor, miss— they cannot even buy salt," he answered. I felt a pang in my heart but it made me glad in a way. To deceive Katya I told her I was going for a walk, and then ran upstairs and took all my money (there was not much but I took all I had). Crossing myself, I slipped out on to the verandah and through the garden to the village. Semyon's hut was at the edge. No one noticed me go up to the window, put the money on the sill and knock on the pane. The door creaked as someone came out of the hut and called. Shaking with cold and fright, I ran home like a criminal.

Katya asked me where I had been, and what was the matter with me, but I did not even understand what she was saying and made no answer. Everything else suddenly seemed so paltry and mean. I shut myself up in my room and paced back and forth for a long time, unable to do anything, to collect my thoughts, or even to realize what I was experiencing. I thought about how happy Semyon's family would be, and how grateful they would be to the one who had left them the money, and I was sorry I had not given it to them with my own hands. I also wondered what Sergei Mikhailich would have said if he had known what I had done, and I rejoiced that no one would ever know. I was so filled with joy, and everybody, including myself, seemed so wicked, and I looked at myself and everyone else so meekly, that the thought of death came to me as a dream of happiness. I smiled and prayed and wept. How fervently, how passionately I loved everyone in the world at that moment, and myself, too!

Between services I read the Gospels, and they became more understandable to me. The story of that divine Life became simpler and more touching, and the depths of thought and love that I found in His teachings became more awe-inspiring and unfathomable. But then how plain and simple everything seemed to me when I laid the Book aside and again examined life around me, and pondered over it! It seemed so hard to live unrighteously, and so simple to love everyone and be loved. Everyone was so good and kind to me! Even Sonya, to whom I continued to give lessons, was quite different. She tried to understand and do what I wanted and not vex me. Everyone was to me as I was to them.

Thinking of the enemies of whom I must ask forgiveness before confession, I remembered only one outside our home —a certain young lady, a neighbor I had laughed at a year before in the presence of other guests, and who had for that reason stopped calling on us. I wrote her a letter, admitting my fault and asking her forgiveness. She answered my letter; she wrote that she forgave me, and asked to be forgiven herself. I wept with joy on reading those simple lines—at that time they seemed to me to be deeply touching.

My old nurse burst into tears when I asked her to forgive me. "Why are they all so good to me?" I asked myself. "What have I done to deserve such love?"

Then I would remember Sergei Mikhailich, and I would think about him for hours at a time. I could not help doing so, and considered it no sin. But I did not think of him as I had the night I discovered I was in love with him—I thought of him as I did of myself, involuntarily associating him with every thought of my future. The overpowering influence he wielded over me when I was in his presence completely disappeared at these times. I felt myself to be his equal, and from the heights of my spiritual exaltation, I understood him perfectly. What had seemed strange to me was clear at such moments, I realized why he had said that the only happiness was in living for others, and I agreed with him completely. I was sure we should be serenely happy together forever. I did not dream of trips abroad, nor of gaiety and brilliance, but of an entirely different life—a peaceful family life in the country, a life of constant self-sacrifice and love one for the other, in which there would always be the consciousness of a gentle and helpful Providence watching over everything.

I received the Eucharist on my birthday, as I had planned. My heart was so full of joy when I returned from church that day that I was afraid—afraid of any impression that might spoil my happiness. No sooner had we alighted from the trap at our porch than a familiar cabriolet rattled over the bridge, and I saw Sergei Mikhailich. He wished me many happy returns of the day and we went into the parlor together. Never had I been so calm and self-confident in his presence as I was that morning. I felt that there was a whole new world within me that he did not understand, and which was higher than his. I did not feel in the least embarrassed. He must have realized the cause of this for he was unusually gentle and very respectful to me. I went up to the piano, but he locked it and put the key in his pocket.

"Don't spoil your mood," he said. "The music in your soul at this moment is better than any other in the world."

I was grateful, and yet it was the least bit vexing that he should so easily and rightly have understood the things in my soul that ought to have been hidden from everyone. During dinner he said he had come to wish me a happy birthday and to say good-bye, as he was leaving for Moscow the next day. He looked at Katya when he said this but then glanced at me, and I perceived he was afraid there would be agitation painted on my face. But I was neither surprised nor upset, and did not even ask if he was going for long. I had known he would say this, and I had known he would not leave. How had I known? I cannot explain it even to myself, but on that day I had a feeling that I knew everything that ever had been or ever would be. I seemed to be living in a wonderful dream in which everything that happened had already happened long before, and I had known it long before; it would all happen again, and I knew how it would happen.

He wanted to leave directly after dinner, but Katya was tired after Mass and had gone to lie down and so he had to wait for her to wake so that he could bid farewell.

It was too sunny in the drawing room, so we went out on the verandah. As soon as we sat down I began quite calmly to speak about things that would decide the fate of my love. I began to speak the very moment we sat down, neither sooner nor later, and nothing had been said before this, no tone had been adopted, no subject broached, that might possibly hinder what I wanted to tell him. I do not know where I found such composure and determination, such exactness in my choice of words. It was as though it was not I who was speaking, but some voice within me, independent of my will. He was sitting opposite me leaning against the railing; he had pulled over a branch of lilac and was tearing off the leaves. When I began to speak, he let go the branch and leaned his head on one hand. His might have been the position of a person completely composed or greatly agitated.

"Why are you going away?" I asked slowly and deliberately, looking straight at him.

He did not answer at once. Then, dropping his eyes, he murmured, "Business."

I realized how difficult it was for him to lie to me, and particularly when I asked such a frank question.

"You know what today means to me," I said. "It is very important for a number of reasons. If I ask why you are leaving, it is not just an empty show of interest. You know without my saying it that I've become attached to you. I ask because I must know. Why are you leaving?"

"It is hard for me to tell you the real reason of my leaving," he answered. "This week I have thought a lot about you and about myself, and I have decided that I must go. You understand why, and if you think anything of me you will not press me to tell more." He rubbed his forehead and closed his eyes. "It is hard for me . . . but you understand."

My heart began to pound.

"I do not understand," I said. "I cannot understand, and so you must tell me . . . for my sake, for the sake of this day that means so much to me, tell me, I can bear to hear anything."

He shifted his position, glanced at me, and again pulled the branch over.

"Well," he said, then hesitated a moment before going on in a voice that he tried in vain to keep firm. "Though it is foolish and impossible to put in words, though it is painful for me, I shall try to explain." He winced as though from physical pain.

"Do," I said.

"Let us suppose," he said, "that there was a certain man —A, we shall call him—and he was old and had lived his life. And there was a certain woman—B, we shall call her —and she was young and happy and knew nothing about people or life. Because of family circumstances he loved her as a daughter and had no fear that he might come to love her in any other way."

He stopped. I waited for him to go on.

"But A had forgotten that B was so young—that life for her was still something to play with." Now he went on hurriedly and doggedly without looking at me. "He had forgotten that it would be easy to love her in a different way, but that this would only be play for her. He made a mistake and suddenly felt a different feeling, as painful as repentance, and he was afraid. He was afraid that their former friendship might be spoiled, and he decided to go away before this should happen." Saying this, he rubbed his eyes with a casual air and closed them again.

"Why was he afraid to love her in a different way?" I asked very softly, repressing my agitation and forcing my voice to be calm.

It must have sounded like a mockery, for there seemed to be a shade of hurt in his answer: "You are young; I am not. You want to play, but I need something else. Go on playing, but not with me, because I may think you are in earnest; that would hurt me and make you feel ashamed. . . . That was what A said," he added. "This is all nonsense, of course, but you realize why I am leaving. Let us not say anything more about it. Please!"

"No! No! We shall say something more about it," I exclaimed, and my voice was tremulous with tears. "Did he love her or not?"

He made no answer.

"If he did not love her, why did he play with her, as though she were a child?"

"Yes, yes, A was at fault," he interrupted hurriedly, "but that was the end of it, and they parted . . . as friends."

"But that is dreadful! Is there no other ending?" I barely murmured, frightened by what I was saying.

"Yes, there is," he said, removing his hand from his working face and looking straight at me. "There are two different endings. Only I pray you not to interrupt; listen calmly. Some say," he began, standing up and assuming a pained smile, "some say A lost his head, fell madly in love with B, and told her so . . . and she only laughed at him. To her it was a lark, to him it was a matter of life and death."

I started and was about to interrupt him and tell him not to dare speak for me, but he put his hand on mine and restrained me.

"Wait," he said, his voice trembling. "Others say she took pity on him. She imagined, poor thing, because of her inexperience, that she really could love him, and she agreed to be his wife. And he, fool that he was, believed—yes, he really believed—that his life would begin all over again. But soon she saw that she had deceived him and he had deceived her. . . . But we won't talk about it any more," he concluded, evidently unable to say more, and began silently to pace back and forth in front of me.

He had said, "We won't talk about it," but I saw that he was waiting in the greatest suspense for me to speak. I wanted to say something but was prevented by the lump in my throat. I glanced at him—he was pale and his lower lip was quivering. I began to feel sorry for him. I made an effort, and breaking through the silence that bound me, began to speak softly in an earnest voice which I feared might break any moment.

"And the third ending—" I said and stopped, but he remained silent. "The third ending is that he did not love her and hurt her deeply, and he went away thinking he had done right, and was even proud for some reason. It was a lark for you, not for me; I loved you from the very first. Yes, I loved you," I repeated, and as I said this my voice, which had been low and earnest, rose to a wild cry that frightened me.

He stood opposite me, very pale; his lip quivered more and more, and two tears rolled down his cheeks.

"That was too bad of you!" I almost shouted, choked by angry, unshed tears. "Why did you?" I demanded, and would have got up to leave him.

But he restrained me. His head went down on my knees; his lips kissed my trembling hands and they were wet with his tears. "Oh, God! If I had only known!" he murmured.

"Why did you? Why did you?" I kept repeating, but in my heart was happiness—a happiness that has gone forever, never to return.

Five minutes later Sonya ran upstairs to Katya, shouting for the whole house to hear that Masha was going to marry Sergei Mikhailich.

V

There was no reason for putting off our wedding, and neither he nor I wished to do so. True, Katya would have liked to go to Moscow to order a trousseau, and his mother would have liked to make Sergei Mikhailich buy a new carriage and new furniture before he got married, and to repaper the house, but we two insisted on all this being done afterward if it was really so indispensable, and in the meanwhile to get married two weeks after my birthday, quietly, with no trousseau, no bridesmaids or best man, no supper or champagne or any of the other conventional trappings of weddings. He told me how dissatisfied his mother was because the wedding would be without music, without a heap of trunks and the redoing of the whole house—not like *her* wedding which had cost thirty thou-

sand rubles. He told me she was going through the trunks
in the lumber room and consulting Maryushka in secret
about carpets, curtains and trays that were essential to our
happiness.

At our house Katya was doing the same with Kuzmin-
ishna, our old nurse. It was impossible to joke with her on
that score. She was firmly convinced that when we talked
together about our future life, we only indulged in endearments and occupied ourselves with trifles, as was to be expected of people in our position; our real happiness, however, depended on the correct cutting out and sewing up
of chemises, and the hemming of tablecloths and napkins.

Secret messages were sent back and forth several times
a day about the preparations being made; externally, relations between Katya and Tatyana Semyonovna, his mother, were of the tenderest, but a somewhat hostile and very
subtle diplomacy could already be felt.

Tatyana Semyonovna, whom I now came to know better,
was a prim, strict housewife—a gentlewoman of an age
that had passed. Sergei Mikhailich loved her, not only because it was his duty as a son to do so, but also because he
thought her the best, the kindest, and the most intelligent
and loving woman in the world. She had always been kind
to us, and especially to me, and was glad that her son was
marrying. Still, when I called on her as her son's fiancée, I
felt she wanted me to realize that her son might have made
a better match and I would do well to keep this ever in
mind. I understood her perfectly, and agreed with her.

Those last two weeks Sergei Mikhailich and I saw each
other every day. He would come to dinner and stay till
midnight. But though he said he could not live without me
(and I knew that he was speaking the truth), he never
spent a whole day in my company, and tried to busy himself with his affairs as before. Outwardly our relations remained unchanged: he still called me Marya Alexandrovna
and did not even kiss my hand, and far from seeking op-
portunities to be alone with me, he even avoided them. It
was as though he feared to give way to the excessive tenderness he felt and which he considered harmful. I do not

know whether it was he or I who had changed, but now I felt myself absolutely his equal. I no longer found in him what I had considered affected simplicity; now I was often delighted to see before me a dear child carried away by happiness, not a man inspiring me with respect and awe.

"So that's the sort of person he really is!" I thought. "He is exactly the same sort of person I am—no more." Now I felt that I knew him through and through—that I understood him completely. And all that I came to know in him was beautifully simple and suited to me. Even his plans of how we were to live together were the same as mine, only clearer and better expressed.

The weather was bad, and we spent most of the time indoors. The best, the most intimate of our talks, were held in the drawing room, in the corner between the piano and the window. The candlelight was reflected in the black windowpane, and now and then a raindrop would strike the shiny glass and slide down. There was the patter of rain on the roof, and the gurgle of rain in the spout, and the dampness of rain oozing through the window sash, and all of these things only made our corner the cozier, the brighter, the gayer.

"There's something I've been wanting to say to you for a long time," he began late one evening, when we were sitting by ourselves in our corner. "I kept thinking about it while you were playing."

"Don't say anything—I know everything without your telling me," I said.

He smiled. "Yes, that is true—we won't talk about it."

"No, tell me. What was it?"

"Very well, then. You remember my telling you about A and B?"

"How could I forget anything so foolish? It's a good thing everything turned out as it did—"

"Yes, a little bit more and I would have destroyed my happiness myself. But actually I wasn't telling the truth, and it bothers me. I should like to finish now what I began then."

"Oh, please don't."

"Have no fear," he said smiling. "I only want to explain myself. When I began to talk, I wanted to reason things out."

"Why reason?" I asked. "It is never of any use."

"No, it isn't. And I reasoned badly. When I arrived here this summer, I had convinced myself so thoroughly that after all my disappointments and mistakes in life, love for me was impossible and that nothing was left to me but the responsibility of living out my life, that for a long time I could not understand the nature of my feeling for you and what it would lead to. I hoped against hope, but one day I would think you were being coquettish; the next, I believed in your sincerity, and didn't know what to do. But after that night, you remember, when we walked in the garden, I was frightened. Then my present happiness seemed too great a thing to hope for—quite impossible in fact. What would have happened if I had let myself hope, and it had been in vain? Of course, I was thinking only about myself because I am a miserable egotist." He stopped and sat looking at me. "Still, what I said then wasn't all nonsense. I had reason to fear—I should have feared. I take so much from you and there is so little I can give you in return. You're still a child, just a bud beginning to open. You're in love for the first time, while I—"

"Tell me honestly whether—" I began, but then I was afraid to hear his answer. "No, say nothing," I added.

"Whether I have ever been in love before? Is that it?" he asked, catching my thought at once. "I can tell you that: no, I never have—never anything like what I feel now—" But here some painful memory seemed to flash through his mind. "But even so I must be sure that your heart belongs to me if I am to love you," he said sadly. "So wasn't it necessary for me to think well before I said that I loved you? What can I give you? Love, that's true."

"Is that little?" I asked, looking into his eyes.

"Too little, darling—for you it's too little," he answered. "You have youth and beauty. Often I am unable to sleep at night. I am too happy; I keep thinking of our life together. I have lived a long time and it seems to me I have found what is necessary for happiness—a quiet, secluded life here in the country, with an opportunity to do good to others— it's so easy to do good to those who are not used to it; then work that seems to be worthwhile, leisure, nature, books, music, the love of one's dear ones—that is my idea of happiness, and I cannot imagine anything finer. And to crown everything—a companion such as you; a family, perhaps—a man could not wish for anything more."

"Yes," I agreed.

"Especially a man like me, who is no longer young," he went on. "But not you. You have not lived yet—you may want to seek happiness in something else, and you may find it in something else. You think now that this is happiness because you love me."

"No, I have always loved a quiet family life, and that is all I have ever wanted," I said. "You have only said what I have always thought."

He smiled. "It only seems so to you, darling. It is not enough for you. You have youth and beauty," he repeated musingly.

I was vexed that he did not believe me and seemed to reproach me for my youth and beauty.

"Then why do you love me?" I said angrily. "Is it for my youth, or for me myself?"

"I don't know, but I do love you," he answered, looking at me with his attentive, compelling eyes.

I did not answer, but my gaze was drawn straight to his. An odd feeling suddenly came over me—at first I stopped seeing what was around me, then his face disappeared and only his eyes shone, close to my own; then his eyes were within me, and everything went black—I had to close my eyes tightly to shake off the feeling of delight and fear his gaze produced. . . .

The day before our wedding the weather cleared. The first autumn evening, clear and cold, came to replace the rains of summer. Everything was wet and cold and sunny, and for the first time the garden had an autumn look— spacious, bright, but bare looking. The sky was clear, cold and pale. I went to bed happy in the thought that on the morrow, our wedding day, the weather would be fine.

I woke with the sun, and I was a little surprised and frightened by the thought of what lay ahead. I went out into the garden. The sun had just risen and was pouring scattered light through the thinning yellow branches of the limes. The path was covered with rustling leaves. The wrinkled berries of the rowan bushes showed flaming red on the branches, where the few leaves remaining had been killed and twisted by the frost; the dahlias hung wilted and black. For the first time there was a silver bloom of frost on the pale green grass and on the trampled burdocks near the house. There was not a single cloud in the clear cold sky, nor could there have been.

"Can it really be today?" I asked myself, not believing my happiness. "Can it be that tomorrow I shall not wake up here, but in that strange house with the columns in Nikolskoye? Shall I never wait for him again, never go to meet him, never talk about him at night with Katya? Shall I never again sit at the piano here in the drawing room with him beside me? Or see him off and fear for his safety in the dark night?" But I remembered that yesterday he had said he had come for the last time, and that Katya had made me try on my wedding gown, and had said, "Till tomorrow." Then I believed for a moment, and then again began to doubt. "Can it really be that from today on I shall live there with his mother, without Nadezhda, old Grigory, or Katya? Shall I not kiss my old nurse at night and hear her say as she always does when she makes the sign of the cross over me, 'Good night, miss'? Shall I not teach Sonya any more, or play with her, or knock on her wall in the morning and hear her shrill laughter? Can it be that today I shall become a stranger to myself, and a new life will open up before me, bringing the realization of my hopes and dreams? Can this new life really be for good?"

I waited impatiently for Sergei Mikhailich; it was hard for me to be alone with my thoughts. He came early and only then did I begin to believe that from that day on I should be his wife; only then did the thought cease to frighten me.

Before dinner we went to church to attend a service for my father.

"If he were only alive now!" I thought, as we returned home, my hand on the arm of the man who had been his best friend. Bowing my head during the prayer till it touched the cold stone floor of the chapel, I had pictured my father so vividly, I had so fully believed that his soul understood mine and that he gave his blessing to my choice, that even now it seemed to me that his soul was hovering over us, and that I heard his blessing. Memories and hopes, joy and sadness mingled to produce a single solemn and pleasant emotion in tune with this still, fresh air, the silence, the bare fields, and the pale sky, that poured forth bright rays that were no longer strong enough to burn the cheek. It seemed to me that the man beside me understood and shared my emotion. He walked quietly, without speaking, and his face, at which I glanced now and then, expressed the same solemn feeling—partly joy, partly sadness—which was in my heart and in everything around.

Suddenly he turned to me, and I saw he was about to say something. The thought flashed through my mind: "Can it be he will speak of something other than what I am thinking about?" But he spoke of my father, without even uttering his name: "Once he said, 'Marry my Masha!' He was joking, of course."

"How happy he would be now!" I answered, squeezing his arm.

"Yes, you were only a child then," he went on, gazing into my eyes. "I used to kiss your eyes, but I loved them only because they were like his; I never thought they would be so dear to me for their own sake. I called you Masha then."

"Call me Masha now."

"I was just about to," he said. "I am only now beginning to think you are really mine," and his calm, happy gaze rested on me.

We kept on along the unbeaten track across the trampled stubble, and the only sounds were those of our steps and voices. To one side, across the ravine, brownish stubble stretched away to a bare grove in the distance, and along it a muzhik with a wooden plow was silently marking out a black strip that was growing wider and wider. A herd of horses browsing at the foot of the hill seemed quite close. On the other side, the field had been plowed and sown as far as the garden, behind which could be seen our house. Now that the frost had melted the earth was black, but here and there green strips of winter wheat were beginning to show. A coldish sun shone brightly over it all, and cobwebs were trailing over everything. They were flying in the air about us and catching in the stubble, already dry in the sun. They got in our eyes and hair and clung to our clothes. When we spoke, our voices hung in the still air as though we were completely alone in the world— alone under that blue dome where the sun stood throbbing and blazing, but was no longer hot.

I also wanted to call him by his nickname, but I found it hard. "Why are you walking so fast, Seryozha?" I said, and felt I was blushing.

He slowed his step and looked at me still more affectionately, his face happier than ever.

When we got home, Sergei Mikhailich's mother and the guests we had had to invite were waiting for us, and so it was not until after we left the church and got into the carriage to drive to Nikolskoye that I was alone with him again.

The church was almost empty. Out of the corner of my eye, I saw his mother standing very straight on a rug in the choir, Katya in a cap trimmed with purple ribbons and with tears on her cheeks, and two or three household serfs staring curiously at me. I did not look at him, but I felt his presence there beside me. I listened attentively to the words of the prayer and repeated them, but there was no response in my heart. I could not pray, and looked dully at the icons, at the candles, at the cross embroidered on the back of the priest's robe, at the iconostasis, and at the windows, but I understood nothing. I only felt that some ceremony was being performed over me. Then the priest turned to us with his cross in his hand. He congratulated us and recalled that he had christened me, and that now God had granted that he should marry me. Katya and Sergei Mikhailich's mother kissed us, and I heard Grigory calling for the carriage. I was astonished, then, and frightened that everything was already over, and nothing unusual, nothing corresponding to the rite performed over me, had taken place in my heart. He and I kissed, and the kiss was so strange, so foreign to our love! "And that's all," I thought.

We went out on to the porch, and the sound of the carriage wheels resounded under the arches of the portico, and there was a rush of fresh air in my face. He put on his hat and took my arm to help me into the carriage. From the window, I saw the frosty moon with a halo round it. He sat down beside me and shut the door. Something like a pain stabbed my heart. The assurance with which he did that seemed almost insulting. I heard Katya calling to me to cover my head, the wheels rattled over the stones and then on to the soft road, and we were off. I shrank into my corner and looked out of the window at the distant bright fields and at the road running away in the cold moonlight. I did not look at him, but I felt him there next to me. "And this is all I have received from this moment of which I had expected so much?" I thought, and it seemed somehow humiliating and insulting to sit there alone so near him. I turned to him, intending to say something, but no words would come; it was as though my feeling of tenderness for him had disappeared and had been replaced by a feeling of injury and fright.

"Until this very moment I have been unable to believe it is true," he said softly, in response to my glance.

"Yes, but for some reason I am frightened," I said.

"Do I frighten you, darling?" he asked and, taking my hand, bent his head down to it.

My hand lay lifeless in his, and my heart was cold.

"Yes," I murmured.

But as I said it, my heart beat stronger, my hand trembled and clutched his. A warm wave swept over me and

my eyes sought his in the half-light. All at once I felt that
I did not fear him—that this fright was love—a new love,
tenderer and stronger than before. I felt I was all his, and
I was happy because of his power over me.

PART TWO

VI

Days and weeks went by; finally two months of quiet country life had passed unnoticed, as it then seemed. At the
same time the love, excitement, and happiness of those two
months would have sufficed for a whole lifetime. His dreams
and mine as to how we should live in the country came out
entirely different, but not worse, from what we had expected. True, it was not that life of stern labor, self-
sacrifice, and doing for others, that I had pictured to myself when I was his fiancée. On the contrary, there was a
selfish feeling of love for each other and a desire to be
loved—an unreasoning, constant gaiety, and a forgetting
of everything else in the world. He sometimes went to his
study to busy himself with one thing or another. Sometimes he went to town on business or walked about the
estate. But I saw how hard it was for him to leave me. And
then he would admit to me that everything in the world
seemed so empty without me that he could not bear to
leave me. I felt the same. I read, put in time with my music,
my mother-in-law, and the school, but only because all
these occupations had something to do with him and would
win his approval. As soon as I began to do anything that
was not associated with thoughts of him, I lost interest completely, and it seemed very odd that there should be anything in the world but him. This may have been a petty,
selfish feeling, but it made me happy and elevated me
above the whole world. For me, nothing existed except him;
he was the most infallible person in the world. I lived only
for him and to be in his eyes the person he thought me.
And he thought me the finest and best woman in the world,
and endowed with all possible virtues—and I tried to be

this woman for the sake of the finest and best man in the world.

Once he came into the room while I was at my prayers. I glanced at him and went on praying. He sat down at the table so as not to disturb me and opened a book. But I felt him looking at me and glanced round. He smiled and I laughed outright. I could not go on.

"Have you said your prayers?" I asked.

"Yes, but I don't wish to disturb you. I'll go out."

"Have you really said your prayers?"

He made no answer and would have gone out, but I stopped him. "Please, dearest, just for me—say a prayer with me."

He got down on his knees beside me and began, clasping his hands awkwardly. His face was serious, and he kept stumbling over the words. Now and then he turned to me, seeking approval and help. When he finished I laughed and put my arms around him.

He blushed and began kissing my hands. "Always you! Always you! You make me feel ten years old again."

Our house was one of those old country houses where several generations of people had lived, loving and respecting one another. Everything called up family memories, which seemed to become mine as soon as I began to live there. Tatyana Semyonovna had furnished the house, and ran it in the old manner. It could hardly be said that all was elegant, but there was an abundance of everything, from servants to furniture and food, and everything was solid, clean and neat, and inspired respect. The furniture in the drawing room was arranged symmetrically, and there were portraits on the walls and homemade carpets and rugs on the floor. In the parlor there was an old piano, chiffoniers of two different styles, sofas, and small gilt, inlaid tables. The best furniture was in my room, which Tatyana Semyonovna had taken pains to furnish herself. There were pieces of different periods and styles, including an old pier glass which I was too shy to look into at first, but which later became a dear friend to me.

Tatyana Semyonovna never raised her voice, but everything in the house went like clockwork in spite of the many superfluous servants. But all these people in their soft heelless boots (Tatyana Semyonovna thought the creaking of soles and the pounding of heels the most unpleasant thing in the world)—all these people seemed to be proud of their posts. They quaked before their old mistress but looked on my husband and me with patronizing affection, and appeared to do their work with extraordinary pleasure. Regularly every Saturday the floors were scrubbed and the carpets beaten; on the first of every month prayers were held and the water blessed. On Tatyana Semyonovna's name day, and on that of her son (and for the first time that autumn, mine, also) feasts were held and the whole neighborhood invited. This had all been done as long as Tatyana Semyonovna could remember.

Her son did not interfere in the housekeeping; he occupied himself with the field work and the peasants, and at these matters he worked hard. He got up very early, even in winter, so that when I woke up he was already gone. He usually came home for lunch, which we had by ourselves, and almost always at such times, after his worries and exertions about the estate, he was in that particularly gay mood which we called a "wild ecstasy." I often demanded to know what he had been doing that morning, and he would tell me such nonsense that we almost died laughing. Sometimes I insisted on a serious account and he would give me one, trying to restrain a smile. I would gaze at his eyes and his moving lips and not understand a thing —it was enough for me to see him and hear his voice.

"Now what did I say?" he would ask. "Repeat it."

But I could not remember a thing. It seemed absurd that he should talk not about himself and me, but about something quite different. As though it mattered what happened in that outside world. It was only much later that I began to understand and take an interest in his affairs.

Tatyana Semyonovna never left her room till dinnertime; she had her tea alone and we exchanged morning greetings through envoys. In our own mad, happy world, a voice from her dignified, orderly corner sounded so odd that often I could not restrain myself, and laughed outright when her maid, standing with arms crossed, would solemnly report that Tatyana Semyonovna had bidden her inquire how we had slept after our walk, and say that for her part her side had pained her all night, and a stupid dog in the village had barked and disturbed her sleep. She had also bidden her ask how we found the biscuits today, and would have us know that it was not Taras who had done the baking but Nikolasha, for the first time, as a trial, and not at all badly it seemed to her, especially the *krendelki,* but he had almost burnt the toast.

Before dinner my husband and I were rarely together. I played the piano or read while he wrote or went out again. But at four o'clock we would all go into the parlor. *Maman* would sail out of her room, and the impoverished noblewomen and pious pilgrims, of whom there were always two or three in the house, would put in an appearance. Regularly every day my husband would give his arm to his mother to take her in to dinner, and she would demand that he give his other arm to me, and so every time we crowded through the door together and got in one another's way. *Maman* presided over dinner, and the conversation was very proper and sedate, even a little solemn. This solemnity, however, was relieved by the ordinary talk between me and my husband. Or sometimes arguments sprang up between mother and son, or they poked fun at one another. I liked to hear them arguing and bantering because it was in this that I felt most strongly the depth and tenderness of the love uniting them.

After dinner *maman* ensconced herself in a big armchair in the drawing room and ground tobacco into snuff, or cut the leaves of new books, while my husband read aloud or went into the parlor to play the piano. We read a lot together at that time, but music was our greatest, our favorite means of recreation. It stirred new strings in our hearts and seemed better to reveal us to each other. When I played his favorite pieces he would sit down on the far sofa where I could hardly see him; he was bashful about letting me see the impression music made upon him, and tried to conceal it. But often when he was not expecting it I would get up from the piano and go over to him, trying to catch on his face the traces of emotion, the heightened brightness, and the moisture of his eyes that he tried so hard to hide.

Maman often wanted to have a peep at us in the parlor but she was probably afraid of embarrassing us; she would walk through the room with what was meant to be a serious and indifferent expression on her face, but I knew she had no reason to go into her room and come out again so soon.

I poured evening tea in the drawing room, and again the whole household were there. This solemn gathering round the shining samovar, this passing round of cups and glasses, discomfited me for a long time. It seemed to me I was not worthy of the honor, that I was too young and frivolous to turn the cock of such a big samovar, put the glasses on Nikita's tray, and say, "For Pyotr Ivanich and Marya Minichna," and then ask, "More sugar?" And then I had to leave pieces of sugar for the nurse and the more privileged servants.

"Excellent, excellent!" my husband would often say. "Just like a real hostess," and that would confuse me still more.

After tea, *maman* would lay out her cards for "patience," or have Marya Minichna tell her fortune. Then she would kiss us both and make the sign of the cross over us, and we went to our room. We usually stayed up till midnight, and that was the best and most pleasant time of the whole day. He would tell me about his former life, or we would make plans, and sometimes we got into philosophical arguments. We tried to speak softly so as not to be heard upstairs—Tatyana Semyonovna demanded that we go to bed early. Sometimes, feeling hungry, we went to the pantry and got a cold supper under Nikita's patronage, which we ate in my boudoir.

We lived like strangers in this big old house where the rigid spirit of the past and of Tatyana Semyonovna reigned supreme. Not only she, but the old servants, the furniture, and even the curtains inspired me with respect and a certain awe—with a consciousness that this was not really our own place and that we must be very careful and attentive, he and I, while we lived there. When I recall it now I realize that much about the house—the unchanging order that laid a restraint on everyone, and the army of idle and inquisitive people everywhere—was stuffy and inconvenient. But at that time this restraint heightened our love.

Like me, he never allowed himself to show displeasure. On the contrary, he seemed to try not to see what was unpleasant. Every day after dinner Dmitry Sidorov, *maman's* footman, who liked to smoke, used to go into my husband's study while we were in the parlor and take tobacco from his drawer. It was amusing to see how Sergei Mikhailich would tiptoe up to me, winking, his finger at his lips, straining to keep back his laughter, and would have me look at Dmitry Sidorov, who never suspected he could be seen. When Dmitry went away without noticing us, happy in the confidence that everything had come out well, my husband would say I was a dear, and kiss me as he did on every possible occasion.

Sometimes his equanimity, his tolerance, and seeming indifference to everything, displeased me. I considered it weakness on his part, and was quite unaware that I was exactly the same. "As if he had no will of his own," I thought.

"Why, darling," he answered once when I told him I was surprised at his weakness, "how can I be displeased with anything when I am so happy? It's easier to give way oneself than to bend others—I became convinced of that long ago. There's no situation in which it is impossible to be happy. And we are so happy, you and I! I can't be angry; for me, now, nothing is bad—only pitiful or humorous. And most important of all, remember *le mieux est l'ennemi du bien*. Do you know, whenever the bell rings, or a letter comes, or even when I wake up in the morning, I am frightened—frightened because life goes on and things must change—and nothing could be better than it is just now."

I believed him, though I did not understand him. I was happy and it seemed to me that everything was just as it should be, just as it always is with everybody, and yet that somewhere there was another happiness—no greater, but different.

Two months passed in this way, winter came with its cold and snow, and in spite of the fact that my husband was with me I began to feel lonely. I began to feel that life was repeating itself—that there was nothing new in me or in him, and that we were returning to the old. He busied himself with his affairs without me more than before, and I fancied that there was a secret world within him to which he did not want to admit me. His perpetual composure irritated me. I did not love him less than before and was no less happy in his love, but my love had stopped where it was and did not grow, and a new feeling of unrest stole into my heart. It was not enough merely to go on loving after I had had the acute happiness of falling in love with him. I wanted more movement than this calm current of life afforded. I wanted danger and excitement, I wanted to sacrifice myself for my love. I had an abundance of energy for which there was no outlet in our quiet life. I had fits of melancholy which I tried to conceal from him, and moments of unrestrained tenderness and gaiety which frightened him.

He had noticed my condition before, and had proposed a visit to town, but I had been against it. I had asked him not to change our mode of life, not to spoil our happiness. And I really was happy, but I was tormented by the fact that my happiness cost me no trouble, no sacrifice of any kind, while the desire to labor and to sacrifice tormented me. I loved him and I saw that I was everything to him, but I wanted everyone to see our love; I wanted them to try to prevent me from loving him and to find all their efforts in vain. My mind and even my affections were occupied, but there was another feeling—a feeling of youth, a need for excitement which found no satisfaction in our quiet life.

Why had he said we could go to town whenever I liked? If he had not said that, I might have realized that the feeling tormenting me was folly and harmful. It was wrong of me not to realize that the opportunity to make the sacrifice I was yearning for lay in crushing this feeling. The thought that I could save myself from boredom simply by our removing to town kept occurring to me, but at the same time I would have been sorry and ashamed to tear him away from everything he loved, just for my sake.

The days dragged on; the snow drifted higher and higher round the house; we two were always together, never out of each other's sight. And in town, somewhere in the glitter and noise, crowds of people knew excitement, suffering, and joy, not giving a thought to us and our fleeting existence. The worst thing for me was the feeling that our habits were forcing our lives into a set form; that our love, instead of being free, was becoming subordinated to the cold, detached flow of time. In the morning we were gay, at dinner—respectful; in the evening—tender.

"Do good," I would say to myself. "It is a fine thing to do good and live honestly as he exhorts me to, but we shall have time for that later. There are other things I would do that must be done now, while I have the strength for them." Doing good was not what I wanted—I wanted excitement. I wanted love to order our life, and not life to order our love. I wanted to go to the edge of a precipice with him and say, "One step and I'll be over the brink; one moment and I'm lost." Then, pale as death, he would lift me in his strong arms, and, holding me for a moment over the precipice so that my heart stood still, would carry me away.

This frame of mind affected my health and upset my nerves. One morning I felt worse than usual and he came back from the office in a bad humor, which rarely happened with him. I at once noticed this and asked him what was wrong but he would not tell me—he said it was not worth talking about. Later I found out that the district police officer, who disliked my husband, had called in some of our muzhiks and made unlawful demands and threatened them. My husband had not been able to dismiss this as an amusing trifle, and so he had become irritable and did not want to talk to me. But I fancied it was because he thought me a child who was incapable of understanding what was worrying him. I turned away and was silent.

Marya Minichna was staying with us, and I sent for her asking her to tea.

After tea, which I finished quickly, I took Marya Minichna into the parlour and began to talk loudly to her about some trifle that did not interest me in the least. He paced up and down, glancing at me now and then. This had the effect of making me want to talk more, and even to laugh. Everything seemed funny to me—all I said, and all Marya Minichna said. Finally he went into his study without a word and shut the door. As soon as he had gone, my gaiety vanished so quickly that it disconcerted Marya Minichna, and she asked me what was wrong. I did not answer and sat down on the sofa, on the verge of tears.

"What is he worrying about?" I wondered. "Some nonsense that seems important to him, but which I would show him was only a trifle. But he thinks I would not understand —he humiliates me with his dignity and superiority and being always in the right. But I am in the right, too, when I am bored, and find my life empty, and want to live, want to move ahead. I want something new every day, every minute, but he wants to stand still and have me stand still with him. And how easy it would be for him! He would not have to take me to town; he would only have to be like me —simple, without inhibitions, without affectations. He advises me to be simple, but he isn't simple himself. That's what it is!"

I felt deeply hurt, and I was irritated with him. That frightened me and I went to him. He was sitting in his study writing. On hearing my step, he glanced up for a moment, quiet and composed, and then went on writing. I did not like his look and remained standing there at the desk instead of going over to him. I opened a book and began turning the leaves. He glanced up at me again.

"Are you out of sorts, Masha?" he asked.

I answered with a cold look which said, "Why ask? Why such civility?" He shook his head and smiled shyly and tenderly. And for the first time I did not smile in return.

"What happened today?" I asked. "Why wouldn't you tell me?"

"Nothing important. A little unpleasantness," he answered. "But I can tell you about it now. Two of our muzhiks went to town—"

I would not let him finish. "Why didn't you tell me when I asked you at tea?"

"I would have said something I'd have been sorry for. I was angry then."

"It was then I wanted to hear about it."

"Why?"

"Why do you think I can never be of any help to you?"

"Do I think that?" he said, throwing down his pen. "I think I couldn't live without you. You help me in everything, everything; you not only help me, you do everything. You little silly!" he laughed. "You're my whole life. Everything seems good to me only because you're here—because I need you."

"Yes, I know that—I'm a nice, dear child that has to be quieted," I said in a tone that made him look at me in surprise, as though seeing me for the first time. "I don't want quiet. There's enough of it in you—more than enough," I added.

"Well, then, it was this way," he began hurriedly, interrupting me, apparently afraid to let me finish. "What would you have done—"

"I don't want to hear about it now," I said. I really did want to, but I took pleasure in disturbing his composure. "I don't want to play at living—I want to live, just as you do."

A look of pain and strained attention appeared on his sensitive face.

"I want you to treat me as an equal. I want—"

But I could not finish—such sadness, such profound sadness came over him. He was silent a moment.

"But in what way do I not treat you as an equal?" he asked. "Is it because it is me and not you who must deal with the police officer and drunken muzhiks?"

"Not only that."

"Please understand me, darling," he went on. "I know that anxiety is always painful. I have lived enough to know that. I love you and so I cannot help wanting to spare you anxiety. My love for you is all of life to me, so do not deprive me of life."

"You're always right," I said without looking at him.

I was vexed that in his heart everything was again clear and calm, while in mine there was this vexation and something like contrition.

"Masha! What *is* the trouble?" he said. "The question is not which of us is right, but something quite different. Why are you angry with me? Don't say anything until you've thought it over, and then tell me everything. You are dissatisfied with me, and are probably right, only let me know exactly wherein I am at fault."

But how could I lay my whole heart open to him? The fact that he at once understood me, that again I was as a child to him, that I could do nothing he did not see and had not foreseen, excited me the more.

"I'm not angry with you," I said. "I'm simply bored and I don't want to be bored. But you say it should be that way and you must be right."

I looked at him as I said it. I had accomplished what I wanted—his composure was gone; his face expressed pain and alarm.

"Masha," he began in a low, agitated voice. "What we are doing now is serious—it's our fate that is being decided. I ask you not to answer, but to listen to me. Why do you want to torture me?"

But I interrupted him. "Whatever you say will be right. I know that, so you had better not say anything," I replied coldly, as if it were not I but some evil spirit speaking with my tongue.

"If you only knew what you are saying!" he exclaimed.

I burst out weeping, and felt better. He sat beside me and was silent. I was sorry for him and ashamed of myself and vexed because of what I had done. I did not look at him. I felt he must be gazing at me sternly or in bewilderment. I looked up: a gentle, tender glance was turned on me as though asking forgiveness. I took his hand and said:

"Forgive me. I didn't know what I was saying."

"No, but I did, and you were right."

"What?"

"We must go to St. Petersburg. There's nothing for us to do here."

"As you like," I said.

He put his arms round me and kissed me.

"Forgive me," he said. "I have been unfair to you."

That evening I played to him for a long time, and he walked about the room whispering something to himself. It was a habit of his to whisper to himself and I often asked him what he was saying. He always told me—usually he was reciting poetry or murmuring nonsense, but nonsense that showed me his frame of mind.

"What are you whispering today?" I asked.

He stopped, thought a moment, and then, with a smile, quoted two lines from Lermontov:

> But he, the mad one, seeks the storm,
> As though the storm could give him rest!

"He's more than a man—he knows everything!" I thought. "How could I help loving him?"

I stood up, took his arm, and began to walk with him, trying to keep in step.

"True?" he asked, smiling into my eyes.

"Yes," I murmured. And a mirthful mood came over both of us. Our eyes were laughing and we took longer and longer strides, walking more and more on our toes. We strode through all the rooms in this way, to the great indignation of Grigory and the astonishment of *maman* who was playing "patience" in the drawing room. When we got to the dining room we stopped, looked at each other, and burst out laughing.

Two weeks later, just before the holiday, we were in St. Petersburg.

VII

Our trip to St. Petersburg with a week in Moscow on the way—the road, the new towns, his and my relatives, our

settling down in new quarters—all that went by like a
dream. Everything was so different, so new and gay, so
warmly and brightly illumined by his presence and his love,
that our quiet country life seemed something remote and
insignificant. To my great astonishment, instead of the pride
and frigidity which I had expected to find among people of
fashion, everyone received me with such genuine kindliness
and cordiality, strangers as well as relatives, that it seemed
as if they had been thinking only of me—only waiting for
me so that they themselves would be made happy. It was
also unexpected for me to discover that my husband had
many acquaintances in the fashionable, and what seemed
to me the very best, circles—acquaintances he had never
mentioned. Often it seemed strange and unpleasant to hear
his sharp criticism of some of these people, who seemed to
me so kind. I could not understand why he treated them so
coldly, or why he tried to avoid many acquaintances whom
I thought we should feel flattered to know. I felt that the
more kind people one knew, the better, and they were all
kind.

Before we left the country, he had said, "Out here, you
see, we're little Croesuses, but there we shall be far from
rich, so we can only live in town till Easter and not go much
into society or we'll run into debt. And then, for you, I
wouldn't want . . ."

"Why society?" I had answered. "We'll only see our relatives and go to the theaters and hear some good music,
and come back to the country even before Easter."

But no sooner had we arrived in St. Petersburg than all
these plans were forgotten. I suddenly found myself in
such a new and fascinating world, and so many joys en-
gulfed me, so many new interests absorbed me, that I at
once, though unconsciously, renounced all my past and all
the plans made in that past.

"That was nothing—just a beginning—this is real life.
And what a lot more is ahead of me!" I thought. The res-
tiveness and ennui that had troubled me in the village disappeared like magic. My love for my husband became
calmer, and it never occurred to me to wonder if he loved

me less. I could not doubt his love—my every thought was at once understood, my every feeling shared, my every wish fulfilled. And his imperturbability seemed to have disappeared, or at least it no longer irritated me. And then I felt that besides his old love, he had here a new admiration for me. Often after a visit, the making of a new acquaintance, or an evening at our apartment, where I fulfilled the duties of hostess, inwardly quaking for fear of making a mistake, he would say, "Good girl! Don't let it frighten you—you're doing capitally." This made me very happy.

And then, soon after our arrival, he wrote a letter to his mother, and when he called me to add my bit to it, he tried to keep me from seeing what he had written, so of course I insisted on reading it.

"You would never know Masha," he wrote. "I don't know her myself. Where does she get such lovable, graceful poise and charm, even a kind of fashionable wit and graciousness, and it's all so unassuming, adorable and affable. Everybody is enraptured with her, myself included. I'd love her even more than I do if that were possible."

"So that's what I'm like!" I thought, and it made me so happy! I even seemed to love him more. My popularity with all our acquaintances was beyond anything I could have expected. I heard about it on all sides. At one house I had especially pleased an uncle; at another, an aunt was mad over me; some man would say there was no woman in St. Petersburg to compare with me; some woman would assure me I could be the most elegant woman in society if I wished to be. Princess D., in particular, an elderly woman of fashion and my husband's cousin, suddenly fell in love with me and flattered me more than anyone else, which quite turned my head. The first time she invited me to go to a ball and asked my husband if he objected, he turned to me, and with a barely concealed shy smile, asked me if I wanted to. I nodded and felt that I was blushing.

"You might think it was criminal to confess wanting to go," he said, smiling good-naturedly.

"But you said we couldn't go into society, and then you don't enjoy it," I answered with a pleading smile.

"We'll go, if you want to so badly," he said.

"But I don't think we ought to."

"But you want to? Badly?"

I made no answer.

"Society isn't bad, but worldly desires that remain unfulfilled *are* bad and ugly. We shall go—definitely," he said with resolution.

"To tell the truth," I admitted, "there's nothing in the world I should like better."

We went, and my pleasure was unbounded. At the ball, still more than before, I fancied I was the pivot round which everything was revolving—that it was for me the great hall was lit up, the music playing, and this crowd of people gathered. Everyone from the hairdresser and maid to the dancers and the old men walking about the hall seemed to be telling me or giving me to understand that they loved me. The general pronouncement about me at this ball as conveyed to me by my husband's cousin was that I was quite unlike any other woman—that there was something unusual about me, something rustic, simple, and charming. This success flattered me so much that I told my husband frankly that I should like to go to two or three balls that year. "So as to get my fill of them," I added hypocritically.

My husband consented willingly, and at first went about with me with evident enjoyment, rejoicing in my pleasure and apparently quite forgetting or retracting what he had said before. Later he became bored, and the life we led began to tire him. But that meant nothing to me, and if at times I did notice his serious, thoughtful glance turned questioningly upon me, I did not realize what it meant. I was so dazzled by what I took to be the love of all these new people, by the air of refinement, pleasure, and novelty that I breathed here for the first time; I was so suddenly released from the domination of his moral influence; I found it so pleasant to be considered in these circles not only his equal but his superior (a thing which enabled me to give him

more lavishly and voluntarily of my love), that I was unable
to understand what danger he could see for me in society
life. I experienced a feeling of pride and self-complacency
that was new to me when, on entering a ballroom, all eyes
were turned on me, while he, as though ashamed to acknowledge to everyone that I was his, hastened to leave
me and lose himself in the crowd of black evening jackets.

"Just wait!" I often thought as my eyes fell upon him—
lonely, disregarded, often showing signs of boredom—at
the end of the hall. "Just wait till we get home, and you'll
understand—you'll see for whom I've been trying to be
beautiful and charming, and who it is I love above all others." And it truly seemed to me that my success made me
glad only for his sake, only so that I could sacrifice it for
him. The only thing, I thought, that could be harmful for
me in society was the possibility of being attracted by someone I met, therefore causing my husband to be jealous. But
he had such faith in me, and all these young people seemed
so insignificant as compared with him, that I was not frightened by this danger. The attention of so many people gave
me pleasure, flattered me, and made me think there was a
certain merit in my loving my husband; it made my attitude
toward him more casual and self-confident.

"I noticed you were having a very lively chat with N. N.,"
I said one night on our way home from a ball, shaking my
finger at him. The woman I mentioned was very well known
in St. Petersburg, and he really had talked to her that evening. I said this to rouse him, as he was more than usually
silent and bored-looking.

"Why do you say such a thing? Can it be you speaking,
Masha?" he said, and he flinched as though from physical
pain. "How unlike you—and me. Leave such things to other
people. Such falseness may spoil our sincere relations, and
I still hope they'll be restored."

I was ashamed and kept silent.

"They will be restored, won't they, Masha? What do you
think?" he asked.

"They've never been spoiled, and never will be," I said,
and at the time it really seemed so to me.

"I sincerely hope so," he said. "But it is time we were returning to the country."

Only once did he speak to me in that way. The rest of the time I fancied he was as happy as I. And I was so gay and happy! "If he is bored at times," I reassured myself, "I was bored for his sake in the country; if our relations have changed a little, why, everything will be the same again as soon as we are alone with Tatyana Semyonovna again in Nikolskoye."

And so I hardly noticed the passing of the winter. Contrary to our plans, we even spent Easter in St. Petersburg. At the beginning of St. Timothy's week, when we were about to leave, and my husband, who had already bought presents and things for the house, and flowers to brighten our country life, was in an especially tender and happy mood, his cousin unexpectedly came and began to plead with us to postpone our departure till the Saturday, so that we could go to a rout at Countess R.'s. She said that Countess R. wanted me to come very much—that Prince M., who was then in St. Petersburg, had been wanting to make my acquaintance ever since the last ball and was going to the rout for that single purpose, and was saying I was the prettiest woman in Russia. The whole town would be there—in a word, I simply had to go.

My husband was talking with someone at the other end of the drawing room.

"So you'll go, *Marie?*" his cousin asked me.

"We intended leaving for the country the day after tomorrow," I began indecisively, glancing at my husband.

Our eyes met and he hurriedly looked away.

"I'll persuade him to stay," she said, "and we'll go on Saturday and turn everyone's head. Shall we?"

"It would upset our plans, and we've already packed," I answered, beginning to surrender.

"She'd better go and make her bow to the prince tonight," my husband said from the other end of the hall in a tone of restrained irritation I had never heard from him before.

"Dear me! he's jealous. I never noticed it before,"

laughed his cousin. "But don't you see, it isn't only for the prince, but for all of us that I am trying to persuade her, Sergei Mikhailich. If you'd only heard how Countess R. begged me to have her come!"

"It's for her to decide," my husband said coldly, and left the room.

I saw that he was more upset than usual; that tormented me, and I did not promise his cousin anything. As soon as she left I went to him. He was pacing up and down, deep in thought, and did not hear me tiptoe into the room.

"He's imagining our dear old home in Nikolskoye," I thought, looking at him, "our morning coffee in the bright sunny parlor, and his fields and muzhiks and the evenings in the drawing room, and our midnight suppers on the sly."

"No," I decided, "I would give up all the balls on earth and the flattery of all the princes on earth for the sake of his joyous bewilderment and gentle endearments." I wanted to tell him I would not go to the rout and did not even want to go, when he suddenly looked up and saw me.

He frowned, and his mild and pensive look changed. Again his glance expressed penetration, wisdom and patronizing superiority. He did not want to be an ordinary person in my eyes; he wanted to be a demigod—he wanted to keep himself on a pedestal before me.

"What is it, dear?" he asked carelessly, calmly turning round to me.

I made no answer. I was vexed that he was hiding from me—that he did not wish to show himself as I loved him.

"Do you want to go to the rout on Saturday?" he asked.

"I wanted to," I said, "but you are displeased . . and then everything is packed."

Never had he looked at me so coldly nor spoken so coldly. "I can wait until Tuesday and shall tell them to unpack," he said. "Go if you like, I beg you to. I shall not leave."

As usual when agitated, he began hurriedly pacing up and down, not looking at me.

"I don't understand you at all," I said, standing where I was and following him with my eyes. "You say you are al-

ways so calm (he had never said such a thing)—then why
do you speak so strangely to me? I'm willing to sacrifice
this pleasure for you, and here you demand that I go—
and in an ironical tone you have never used with me before."

"What would you have me do? You . . . *sacrifice* (he
stressed the word) . . . and so do I. What could be prettier? A contest as to who is more magnanimous. What other happy married life is there?"

This was the first time I had heard such bitter sarcasm
from him. But his sarcasm did not shame me—it offended
me, and the intensity of his emotion did not frighten me but
was communicated to me. Could it be he? He who had always been afraid of falseness in our relations; he who had
always been so simple and sincere—could it be he who was
saying this? And why? Just because I really wanted to sacrifice this pleasure for his sake—a pleasure in which I could
see no harm? just because a minute before I had understood him so well, and loved him so deeply? Our roles had
been reversed—now it was he who was avoiding simple
straightforward words, and I who was seeking them.

"You have changed very greatly," I sighed. "In what
way have I wronged you? It cannot be that rout—you must
be holding something else against me. Why this insincerity?
You used to be so wary of it. Tell me straight out what
you've got against me." "Now he'll have to say something,"
I thought, remembering complacently that there had been
nothing all winter that he could reproach me for.

I went to the middle of the room so he would have to
pass close to me, and looked at him. "He'll come up to me,
embrace me, and that will be the end of it," I thought, and
I was even sorry to lose the opportunity of showing him
how wrong he had been. But he stopped at the end of the
room and looked at me.

"Do you still fail to understand?" he asked.

"I do."

"Then, I shall explain. For the first time in my life I have
a feeling which I know is hateful, but which I cannot help

feeling. . . ." He paused, evidently startled by the harshness of his tone.

"What do you mean?" I asked with tears of indignation in my eyes.

"It is hateful that the prince thought you pretty, and that you, because of that, are running to meet him, forgetting your husband and yourself and your dignity as a woman, and that you do not want to understand what your husband must feel for you, even if you yourself have no sense of dignity. On the contrary, you come and tell your husband that you are making a sacrifice, in other words, 'it would be a pleasure for me to show myself to His Highness but I will sacrifice that pleasure for your sake.' "

The more he talked the angrier he got from the sound of his own voice, and his voice was harsh, savage, and biting. I had never seen him in such a state before, and had never expected to. The blood rushed to my face. I was frightened, but at the same time a feeling of undeserved shame and outraged pride rose within me, and I wanted to revenge myself on him.

"I have long expected this," I said. "Go on, go on!"

"I don't know what you expected," he went on. "I ought to have expected the worst, seeing you every day in the filth, idleness, and luxury of such stupid society, and now it has come. I let things go until today, when I was ashamed and hurt as never before; I was hurt when your friend plunged her filthy hands into my very heart and began to talk of jealousy—about my jealousy—and of whom? Of a man whom neither you nor I know. And you simply won't understand me and want to sacrifice yourself—and how? I'm ashamed of you—ashamed of seeing you humiliate yourself so. Sacrifice!" he repeated.

"So that's the right of a husband!" I thought. "To insult and humiliate a woman who is guilty of nothing at all. So that's the right of a husband! But I won't submit to it."

"No, I shan't sacrifice anything for you," I said, and I felt my nostrils dilate and the blood drain out of my face. "I'll go to the rout on Saturday—I shall certainly go."

"I hope you enjoy it, but all is over between you and

me," he shouted in uncontrollable fury. "I shall not allow
you to go on tormenting me. I was a fool," he began again,
but his lips quivered, and it was evidently only by a great
effort that he managed to keep himself from finishing what
he had begun to say.

I feared and hated him at that moment. There was much
I wanted to say to him to get revenge for all his insults,
but if I had opened my mouth I would have burst out weeping and lowered myself in his eyes. I left the room without
a word. But as soon as I could hear his footsteps no longer
I was frightened by what I had done. I was terrified to think
that the bond which had comprised all my happiness might
be broken forever.

"But will he have become calm enough to understand
me, if I go to him and silently offer him my hand and gaze
into his eyes? Will he understand my generosity? What if
he calls my grief hypocrisy? Or accepts my contrition in the
belief he is right, and forgives me with proud condescen-
sion? How could he—the man I loved so much—how could
he have insulted me so cruelly?"

I did not go to him. I went to my room, where I sat alone
for a long time and wept. I remembered with horror each
word we had said, replacing these words with others and
adding more—good words—and again remembering, with
horror and a feeling of insult, all that had been said. When
I left my room for tea that evening and met my husband
in the presence of S., who had called, I felt that a gulf had
opened up between us that would remain forever. S. asked
me when we were leaving.

"On Tuesday," my husband put in, giving me no time to
answer. "First we are going to the rout at Countess R.'s.
You are going, aren't you?" he asked, turning on me.

I was frightened at the indifference in his voice and
glanced at him. His eyes were fixed on me, and their expression was angry and sarcastic, his voice cold and hard.

"Yes," I answered.

In the evening, when we were alone, he came to me and
held out his hand.

"Please forget what I said to you," he murmured.

I took his hand. There was a tremulous smile on my lips, and my tears were beginning to overflow, but he drew back his hand, and, as though fearing a sentimental scene, sat down in an armchair at some distance. "Can it be he still considers himself in the right?" I wondered, and the explanation and the request not to go to the rout, which were on my tongue, remained unsaid.

"We'll have to write Mother that we've put off leaving," he said, "or she'll be worried."

"And when do you think of going?" I asked.

"On Tuesday after the rout."

"I hope you're not doing that for me," I said, looking him in the eye, but his eyes looked at me without saying anything, as though there was a veil over them. His face suddenly seemed to me old and unpleasant.

We went to the rout and the relations between us seemed to be friendly again, but they were quite different from what they had been before.

At the rout I was sitting between two women when the prince came up to me, so I had to stand up to talk to him. As I stood up I involuntarily sought out my husband with my eyes and I saw him look at me from the other end of the hall, then turn away. I suddenly felt so ashamed and hurt that I was painfully embarrassed, and the blood suffused my face and neck under the prince's glance. But I had to stand and listen to what he was saying as he eyed me from above. Our chat was short; there was no place he could sit beside me, and he probably sensed that I felt very ill at ease with him. We talked about the last ball, about where I lived in summer, and so on. On leaving me, he expressed a desire to make the acquaintance of my husband, and I saw them meet at the other end of the hall and begin talking. The prince must have said something about me, because in the midst of their conversation he glanced in my direction and smiled. My husband suddenly stiffened and flushed; he bowed low and turned away from the prince. I also blushed; I was ashamed of what the prince must think of me and, even more, of my husband. I fancied everyone had noticed my awkward shyness while talking to the prince, and also my husband's strange behavior. How could they explain it, or did they know of my conversation with my husband?

His cousin took me home and on the way we talked about him. I could not restrain myself and told her all about our quarrel over this ill-fated rout. She soothed me, saying it was a misunderstanding that would disappear without leaving a trace. She explained my husband's character as she understood it. She found that he had become very proud and unsociable. I agreed with her and it seemed to me that I myself had begun to understand him better, more unemotionally.

But when I found myself alone with my husband, this judgment of him lay on my conscience like a crime and I felt that the gulf dividing us had grown still wider.

VIII

From that day on our life and our relations changed completely. We no longer found such pleasure in each other's company. There were subjects we avoided, and it was easier for us to talk in the presence of a third person than alone. As soon as the conversation touched on life in the village, or on balls, little devils began to peep out of their holes, and we felt awkward when we looked at one another. We both seemed to be aware of the gulf that separated us and were afraid to approach it. I was convinced that he was proud and quick-tempered and that I must be careful not to offend him. He was convinced that I was unable to live without fashionable society, that I disliked country life, and that he must reconcile himself to my low taste. So we both avoided these topics and each falsely accused the other. We had long ceased to be perfect in each other's eyes. We made comparisons with others and secretly judged one another.

I fell ill before we left, and instead of going to Nikolskoye we took a cottage outside of town; from there Sergei Mikhailich went on to his mother without me. When he left me I was sufficiently recovered to travel with him, but he persuaded me to stay as if he feared for my health. I felt it was not my health he was worried about but that things would not go well with us in the country; I did not insist and remained behind.

I felt lonely without him, and my life was empty, but I was surprised to find that when he came back, his presence did not change life for me as it once had. The days of our early love, when I was depressed by every thought or impression that he did not share; when his every action, every word, seemed a model of perfection; when a glance into each other's eyes was enough to bring bright laughter to our lips—those days were gone; our relations changed so imperceptibly that we did not notice the vanishing of our old love. Each of us acquired his own interests and worries, and we did not attempt to share them. It even ceased to trouble us that each had his own world that had nothing to do with the other. We grew accustomed to this, and within a year or so we could look at each other without discomfiture. His fits of merriment in my company disappeared completely, as did his boyishness, his readiness to forgive everything, and also the indifference that had once exasperated me so. He no longer looked at me with the searching glance that used to embarrass and gladden me; we no longer said our prayers together or had those fits of wild ecstasy; we rarely saw one another as he was continually away on business and was not sorry or afraid to leave me alone. I was constantly in society, where I had no need of him.

We had no more scenes of disagreements. I tried to please him and he fulfilled all my wishes; we seemed to love each other.

When we were alone together, which did not often happen, I experienced no gladness, no agitation or confusion; it was as if I were alone with myself. I realized very well that he was my husband—not some stranger, but a good man, my husband, whom I knew as well as myself. I was convinced I knew everything he would do or say, and how he would look at me. If he did something else, or looked at me differently than I had expected, I fancied he had made a mistake. In a word, he was my husband, nothing more. I considered that was just as it should be, that husbands and wives were always like that, and we had always been like that.

When he went away, especially at first, I was lonely and afraid without him; I felt more strongly the need for his support. On his return I would throw my arms about him in joy, but two hours later I would have quite forgotten this gladness and be unable to find anything to talk to him about. Only during moments of quiet, restrained tenderness would I feel that something was wrong; my heart would grow heavy, and I seemed to read the same thing in his eyes. I was conscious of limits of tenderness beyond which he would not, and I could not, go. Sometimes this depressed me, but I was too busy to brood over it; I tried to drown the sadness arising from a vaguely perceived consciousness of change in the amusements always awaiting me.

Fashionable life, which had at first merely dazzled me with its glitter and flattery, soon captured me completely and became habitual. It laid its shackles on me and occupied the place in my heart that was longing for love. I forgot what solitude was and dared not think about my life. All my time was occupied, from late in the morning till late at night. I was never alone, even if I did not go out. All this neither amused nor bored me any more; I assumed that I must go on living this way forever.

Three years went by, and our relations remained the same. It was as if they had become congealed, set in a mold, and could not grow better or worse. During those three years two important events occurred in our family, but neither changed my life. These were the birth of my first child, and the death of Tatyana Semyonovna. At first mother love took such strong hold of me and caused me such unexpected rapture that I thought a new life would begin for me. In two months, however, when I again began to appear in society, this feeling dwindled away till it became only habit and a formal fulfillment of my duty. My husband, on the contrary, became, with the birth of our son, the quiet and contented stay-at-home he had been before, and transferred his former tenderness and gaiety to the baby. Often when I went into the nursery in my ball-gown to make the sign of the cross over the child, I would find my husband there, and I noticed what seemed a re-proachful and searching look turned on me, and would be ashamed. I would suddenly be conscience stricken at my indifference to the child, and would ask myself if I was really worse than other women. "But what can I do?" I won-dered. "I love my son, but I cannot sit beside him all day long—it would bore me. And I won't pretend—not for any-thing."

The death of Sergei Mikhailich's mother was a great sor-row for him. He said it was hard for him to live in Nikol-skoye now that she was gone. As for me, I found life in the country more pleasant and peaceful without her, though I grieved over her death and sympathized with my husband. All those three years we lived in town most of the time. I went to the country once for two months, and in the third year we went abroad.

We spent the summer at a watering place. I was then twenty-one. Our affairs were, as I thought, flourishing; I de-manded nothing more from family life than it gave me. Ev-eryone I knew seemed to love me; my health was good; my gowns were the finest at the spa; I knew I was pretty; the weather was excellent; I was surrounded by an atmos-phere of beauty and elegance; and I was enjoying myself greatly. I was not as lighthearted as I had been at Nikol-skoye, when I felt happy just in being myself, when I felt that I deserved to be happy, and that however great my happiness, it ought to be still greater; when I thirsted for more and more happiness. That had been a different hap-piness, but this summer, too, I was content. There was noth-ing I feared; my life seemed full and my conscience at rest.

Of all the young men that season, there was not one I found more interesting than another or even than old Prince K., our Ambassador, who paid court to me. One was young-er, another older; one was a blond Englishman, another a Frenchman with a little beard; they were all alike to me, and all of them necessary. Only one of them, Marquis D.,

an Italian, attracted me more than the others because of
the boldness with which he expressed his admiration of me.
He never missed an opportunity to be with me, to dance or
ride with me, to be in the casino with me, and to tell me
how pretty I was.

Several times I saw him from our window standing in
front of our house, and often the unpleasant stare of his
shining eyes made me blush and turn round. He was young,
handsome, and elegant, but the most important thing was
that his smile and his forehead reminded me of my husband. This resemblance astonished me, especially since, in
place of Sergei Mikhailich's charming expression of kindliness and composure, there was something coarse and bru-
tal about him—in his lips, his glance, his long chin. I believed then that he loved me passionately and sometimes
thought of him with proud compassion. I would have liked
to soothe him and coax him over to a tone of half-friendly
reserved confidence, but he sharply rejected these overtures
and continued to disconcert me with the unspoken passion
which was ready to pour from his lips at any moment. I
feared this man, though I did not admit it to myself, and
often thought of him against my will. My husband was ac-
quainted with him and was even more cold and haughty
with him than with our other acquaintances, to whom he
was only his wife's husband.

Toward the end of the season I fell ill and could not
leave the house for two weeks. When I went out one evening to hear the music (my first appearance since my recovery) I learned of the arrival of Lady S., a celebrated
beauty, who had long been expected here. I was joyfully
greeted and was at once the center of a circle of acquaintances, but a larger company gathered round the new
beauty. People could talk of nothing but her beauty. They
pointed her out to me, and I saw she really was charming,
but I was unpleasantly struck by her look of self-complacency and said as much. That day everything seemed tedi-
ous to me that had once been so gay.

The next day Lady S. arranged a trip to the castle but
I declined to go. Practically no one stayed with me and

everything changed completely in my eyes. Everyone and everything seemed stupid and tiresome. I wanted to weep; I wanted only to finish my cure and go back to Russia. My heart was heavy, but I would not admit it even to myself. I pleaded weakness and stopped appearing in society; only in the mornings did I sometimes go out to drink the waters, or to take a drive in the surrounding country with L. M., a Russian lady of my acquaintance. My husband was in Heidelberg at the time waiting for me to finish my cure so that we could return to Russia. He came to see me occasionally.

One day Lady S. took everyone off on a hunting expedition, and after dinner L. M. and I rode out to the castle. We got to talking seriously in a way we never had before as we rode slowly along. The highway wound between ancient chestnut trees, through which we caught glimpses of the pretty, carefully tended countryside around Baden illumined by the setting sun. Though I had known L. M. for a long time, I had never before realized she was a kind and intelligent woman in whom I could confide and whom it was pleasant to have as a friend.

We talked about our families, about our children, and about the frivolity of life at the spa. We wished we were back in Russia, in the country, and a sad but pleasant feeling of nostalgia came over us and remained with us as we entered the castle.

It was cool and shady inside the walls, and from above, where the sunlight played on the ruins, came the sound of footsteps and voices. The Baden landscape was framed in the doorway—charming, but cold-looking to a Russian. We sat down to rest and gazed silently at the sunset.

The voices became more distinct and I thought I heard someone utter my name. I began to listen and heard every word. The voices were familiar: it was Marquis D. and a friend of his whom I also knew—a Frenchman. They were talking about me and Lady S. The Frenchman was comparing the two of us and analyzing our types of beauty. He said nothing offensive, but the blood rushed to my face as I heard what he was saying. He discussed our good points in detail: I already had a baby, while Lady S. was only nineteen; my hair was thicker, but Lady S.'s figure was more graceful; Lady S. was distinguished, while "your friend is so-so—just one of those little Russian princesses that are beginning to come here so often." He concluded with the remark that I had done wisely by not trying to compete with Lady S. and that I was now dead and buried as far as Baden was concerned.

"I'm sorry for her," he said, adding with a sardonic, cruel laugh, "if only she doesn't decide to find consolation in you."

"If she goes away, I'll follow her," came a harsh voice with an Italian accent.

"Happy mortal! He can still love!" the Frenchman laughed.

"Love!" the voice echoed, and then, after a pause: "I can't help loving. That's what life is for—the only thing worth doing is to turn life into a romance. And my romances never break off in the middle. I intend to push this one to an end, too."

"Bonne chance, mon ami," said the Frenchman.

We heard no more because they went round the corner, and the sound of their steps came to us from the other side. They went down the stairs and in a few minutes came out of a side door, and were greatly taken aback on seeing us. I blushed when Marquis D. came up to me, and was horrified when he offered me his arm as we came out of the castle. But I could not refuse and we set out for the carriage behind L. M. and his friend. I was indignant at what the Frenchman had said, although I admitted in my heart of hearts that he had only said what I myself had already guessed. It was the coarse way in which the marquis had spoken that astonished and shocked me. There was something distressing in his feeling no timidity in my presence, though he must have known we had overheard them. I was filled with loathing at having him so close to me. Without looking at him, without answering him, trying to hold his arm in such a way as not to feel him, I hurried after L. M. and the Frenchman. The marquis was saying something about the wonderful view, about the unexpected pleasure of meeting me, and other things in this vein, but I did not listen to him. I was thinking about my husband and my son, and about Russia. I felt ashamed, I regretted something, wanted something, and was in a hurry to get back to my little room in *Hôtel de Bade* so that, alone and undisturbed, I could think things over. But L. M. was walking slowly and it was still a long way to the carriage, and my escort seemed to be intentionally slowing his steps as if wanting to detain me. "It cannot be!" I thought, and I tried to go faster. But he was actually holding me back; he even squeezed my hand. L. M. went round a bend in the road and we were quite alone. I was frightened.

"Pardon me," I said coldly, and tried to free my hand, but the lace of my sleeve caught on the button of his jacket. He leaned over, his breast close to mine, and began to free the lace, and his bare fingers touched my hand. Some new feeling—perhaps horror, perhaps pleasure—caused little shudders to run up and down my spine. I glanced at him, trying to put all the contempt I felt for him in a cold glance but instead my glance expressed fright and agitation. His moist and burning eyes were close to my very face, devouring me, my neck and breast; both his hands fondled my arm; his open lips murmured something—said that he loved me, that I was everything to him. His lips came nearer, and his hot hands pressed mine tighter. Fire coursed through my veins, and everything went black; I trembled, and the words with which I wanted to stop him stuck in my throat.

Suddenly I felt his lips on my cheek, and, cold and trembling I stopped and looked at him. Powerless to speak or move—horrified—I waited for something, wanted something. This lasted but a moment, but it was a terrible moment. I saw him so completely; I read his face so well— that low forehead so like my husband's showing from under the brim of his straw hat; that handsome straight nose with the dilated nostrils; his long waxed moustache and his beard, his smooth-shaven cheeks and tanned neck. I hated him; I feared him; he was alien to me; but at the same time what agitation and passion this alien, hateful person aroused in me! What an irresistible desire I had to give myself up to the kisses of that coarse, handsome mouth, to the embraces of those hands with the fine veins and the rings on the fingers. How I wanted to throw myself headlong into the slough of forbidden pleasures that had suddenly opened up before me and was drawing me on!

"I am so miserable!" I thought. "What matter if more misfortunes gather round me?"

He put one arm round me and bent over me. "What matter if still more shame and sin be poured upon my head!"

"Je vous aime," he whispered in a voice so like my husband's. I remembered my husband and baby as creatures once dear to me, but now ceasing to exist for me. Suddenly I heard L. M. calling me from round the bend. I came to myself, tore my arm free, and, without looking at him, ran to her.

We got into the carriage, and only then did I steal a glance at him. He had taken off his hat and was smiling and saying something. He could not have known the unspeakable aversion I felt for him at that moment. My life seemed so unhappy, my future so hopeless, my past so black! L. M. was talking to me, but I did not grasp what she was saying. It seemed to me she was only talking because she was sorry for me, and to conceal the contempt she felt for me. I felt this contempt and insulting pity in her every word and glance. My cheek burned with shame where he had kissed me, and the thought of my husband and child was unbearable.

Alone in my room I had intended thinking about my position, but I was afraid to be alone. Without finishing the tea they brought me I began packing—in hot haste—without stopping to think why—and left for Heidelberg and my husband by the evening train.

When I got into the empty carriage with my maid and the train started, and the fresh air blew on me from the window, I began to revive and take a clearer view of my past and my future. I saw all my married life from the time we removed to St. Petersburg in a new light, and my conscience troubled me. Our life in the country when we were just married and the plans we had then made came back to me vividly for the first time, and for the first time I asked myself what pleasure *he* had had all this time, and I had a guilty feeling. "But why did he not stop me?" I asked myself. "Why this hypocrisy? Why did he avoid an explanation? Why humiliate me? Why did he not exercise the power of his love over me? Or did he not love me?" But however great his fault may have been, the kiss of that other man was on my cheek, and I felt it there. The nearer we got to Heidelberg, the more clearly I saw my husband, and the more terrified I became by the prospect of seeing him. "I shall tell him everything," I thought. "I shall shed tears of repentance and he will forgive me." But I myself did not know what this "everything" was, nor did I believe that he would forgive me.

But no sooner had I entered the room and seen his calm yet surprised face, than I realized I had nothing to say to him, nothing to confess, nothing to ask forgiveness for. My unspoken sorrow and repentance must remain locked up within me.

"What made you come?" he said. "I thought of coming to you tomorrow." Then, glancing more closely into my face, he seemed to be frightened. "What is the matter? Has anything happened?" he asked.

"Nothing," I replied, hardly able to keep back my tears. "I've come for good. I'm ready to go back to Russia—even tomorrow, if you wish."

For rather a long moment he was silent and studied me attentively.

"But tell me what has happened," he repeated.

I blushed and dropped my eyes. An expression of rage and insult flashed over his face. Frightened by the thoughts that must have passed through his mind, I said with a power of dissimulation of which I had not known myself capable:

"Nothing has happened—I simply got bored and depressed and began thinking about our life, and about you. I have been treating you badly for so long! Why do you take me to places where you have no desire to go? I have been at fault so long," I repeated, and again tears came to my eyes. "Let us go back to the country forever."

"Ah, my dear! Spare me a scene," he said coldly. "I am glad you want to go back to the country because we have not much money, but as for staying there, that is only a dream. I know you would never be able to stand it. Have some tea now—that's the best thing," and he stood up to ring for the servant.

I imagined what he must think of me, and I was outraged by the terrible thought I had ascribed to him when I caught the hesitant and, it seemed, ashamed glance he turned on me. No! He could not and did not care to understand me. I said I would go and look at the child and left him. I wanted to be alone and weep, weep, weep. . . .

IX

The house in Nikolskoye, empty and long unheated, again came to life but what had once lived in it was dead. *Maman* was no longer there, and we were alone together, but now we had no need of this solitude, and it weighed heavily on us. The winter dragged by. I was ill and recovered only after the birth of my second son. My relations with my husband continued to be as coldly friendly as they had been in town, but here in the country, every board in the floor, every wall, every piece of furniture reminded me of what he had once been to me and what I had lost. It was as though some unforgiven injury stood between us—as though he was punishing me for something and pretending to be unaware of it. There was nothing I could ask forgiveness for, no reason to plead for mercy: his only punishment was that of not giving up to me his whole being, his whole soul, as before. But he gave it to no one and nothing—it was as though it no longer existed. Sometimes the thought occurred to me that he was pretending in order to torment me, and that the old feeling was still alive in him, and I tried to evoke it. But he avoided confidences, seemed to suspect me of dissimulation, and feared all show of emotion as something ludicrous. His glance and his voice said:

"I know everything, absolutely everything—I even know what you want to say. I know you will say one thing and do another." At first I was offended by his fear of being confidential with me, but then I grew accustomed to the thought that it was not fear, but reluctance that kept him from being confidential with me. I myself could not have suddenly told him I loved him, or asked him to say his prayers with me, or called him to listen to me while I played. Certain rules of propriety governed our conduct toward one another. Each of us lived his own life. He had his affairs in which there was no need for me to participate, and in which I now had no desire to do so. I had my idleness, which no longer offended him or made him sad. The children were still too small to bring us together.

But spring came and Katya and Sonya arrived in the country for the summer. Our house in Nikolskoye was being made over, and so we removed to Pokrovskoye. It was the same old house with its verandah, the extension table and piano in the bright drawing room, my old room with the white curtains at the windows and my girlish dreams that I seemed to have left behind and forgotten. There were two little beds there—one was my old bed where at night I made the sign of the cross over Kokosha, who lay sprawling there, his chubby arms outspread; the other was a tiny bed where Vanya's little face peeped out of the swaddling cloths. After making the sign of the cross over them, I would stop in the middle of the silent room, and suddenly old forgotten visions of my youth would come swarming from the corners, the walls, the curtains. I heard the old songs of my girlhood. What had become of my dreams? Of those dear, sweet songs? Everything I had hardly dared hope for had come true. My vague, confused dreams had become reality, and reality had become a life that was grim, difficult, and cheerless. And everything here had remained the same—I could see the same garden through the window, the same lawn, the same path, the same bench there by the ravine, the same nightingales singing from the pond, the same lilacs in full bloom, and the same moon over the house. And at the same time everything had changed so terribly, so unbelievably! Everything that might have been so near and dear was so cold and remote!

As in the old days, I now sit with Katya in the parlor talking softly about him. But Katya has become wrinkled and sallow, her eyes no longer shine with joy and hope, but speak of sad sympathy and regret. We do not go into raptures over him as we used to; we sit in judgment upon him. We no longer wonder why we are so happy, and no longer want to tell the whole world what we think. We sit whispering to one another like conspirators, and a hundred times we ask one another why things have changed so sadly. And he is still the same as he was, only the line between his brows is deeper, and he is grayer about the temples, and his deep and searching glance is always hidden from me. And I am still the same, but there is no love in me, nor desire to love. I have no need for work, and no satisfaction with myself. How remote, how impossible seems my old religious ecstasy, and my old love for him, my old fullness of life. I no longer understand what once seemed so clear and right: the happiness of living for others. Why for others, when I have no desire to live even for myself?

I completely dropped my music on removing to St. Petersburg, but now the old piano and the old music again attract me.

One day I was unwell and stayed home alone. Katya and Sonya had gone with him to Nikolskoye to see how the building was getting on. The table was laid for tea; I went downstairs and sat down at the piano while waiting for them. I opened Beethoven at the Sonata *Quasi Una Fantasia* and began to play. There was no one to see or hear; the windows into the garden were open, and the familiar, sadly solemn sounds filled the room. I finished the first movement, and quite unconsciously, by sheer force of habit, glanced into the corner where he used to sit listening to me. He was not there; his chair stood in its corner, where it had long stood undisturbed; through the window I saw a lilac bush standing out against the sunset, and the cool evening air came in through the open windows. I put my elbows on the piano, my face in my hands, and began to think. I sat there for a long time, thinking painfully of the past that had gone never to return, and thinking timidly of the future. But I saw nothing before me. I seemed to want nothing and to hope for nothing. "Can I have lived out my life?" I wondered, and lifting my head, played again so as to forget and not think, and again it was the same Andante. "Dear God," I breathed, "forgive me if I am at fault, and give back to me all that was so beautiful; or teach me what to do—how to go on living."

I heard the sound of wheels in the grass, and familiar cautious footsteps in front of the porch and on the verandah, and then they were still. But the sound of those familiar steps no longer aroused the old feeling. When I finished playing the steps sounded behind me, and a hand was laid on my shoulder.

"How nice it is to hear that sonata," he said.

I did not answer.

"Have you had tea?"

I shook my head, not looking at him, so as not to betray the traces of emotion on my face.

"They'll be here in a minute—the horse was frisky, so they got out and are coming by the short cut," he said.

"We'll wait for them," I said and went out on to the verandah, hoping he would follow me; but he only asked about the children and went to them. Again his presence, his kind, unaffected voice, told me I was wrong in thinking I had lost something. What more could I want? He was gentle and kind, a good husband, a good father—could I ask for more? I went out on to the verandah and sat down under the awning on the very bench I had been sitting on when he had told me he loved me. The sun had gone down and dusk was gathering; a dark cloud hung over the house and the garden, and only beyond the trees was there a clear strip of sky tinted with the dying sunset and set with the evening star that had just come out. The shadow of the cloud lay over everything and everything was waiting for a light spring shower. The wind died down and not a leaf, not a blade of grass was stirring; the fragrance of the lilacs

and the bird cherry was so strong that the whole air seemed
to be in bloom; it filled the garden and the verandah, coming in waves, now weaker, now stronger. One wanted to
close one's eyes and see nothing, hear nothing, only drink
in this sweet fragrance. The dahlias and the roses, not yet
in bloom, seemed to be slowly climbing their black trellises.
The frogs were croaking loudly and shrilly in the ravine, as
though for the last time before the rain that would drive
them into the water. One high thin voice rose above all this
clamor. The nightingales were calling to one another anxiously as they flitted from place to place. Again this spring
a nightingale had thought of making its abode in the bush
under the window, but when I went out I heard its voice
coming from the lane; it gave one warble and then fell silent, also waiting.

In vain I tried to reassure myself: I, too, was waiting for
something and was filled with regret.

He came downstairs and sat down beside me.

"I'm afraid our girls will get a wetting," he said.

"Yes," I murmured, and again we were silent for a long
time.

There was no wind, and the clouds settled lower and
lower; all became stiller and more fragrant. Suddenly a
raindrop fell on the canvas awning and seemed to bounce
off. Another fell on the gravel of the path. A few large
drops splashed on the broad leaves of the burdocks, and
then a fresh rain began, gathering in strength. The nightingales and the frogs grew silent all at once; only the one
shrill voice still rose in the air, though it seemed further
away because of the rain, and some bird, evidently hidden in the dry leaves near the verandah, regularly emitted
two monotonous notes. He got up and would have gone in.

"Where are you going?" I asked, detaining him. "It's so
pleasant here."

"I must send them an umbrella and their galoshes," he
answered.

"They won't need them—it will be over in a minute."

He agreed with me, and we stayed there together by
the railing of the verandah. I leaned my arm against the

wet, slippery rail and thrust my head out from under the canvas. The cool rain fitfully sprinkled my hair and neck. The little cloud above got thinner and lighter as it emptied itself over us, and the even drumming of the rain gave way to sparse drops falling from the sky and the leaves. Again the frogs below set up their croaking, again the nightingales took heart and began to call to each other. It grew lighter all about us.

"Isn't it wonderful?" he said, sitting down on the railing and stroking my wet hair.

This simple caress was like a reproach to me and I wanted to weep.

"What more does a man need?" he asked. "I'm so contented now—I want nothing else; I am absolutely happy!"

"That is not what you used to say about happiness," I thought to myself. "You used to say no matter how great your happiness, you still wanted something else. And now you are calm and contented, while my heart is full of unspoken repentance and unshed tears." But aloud, I said:

"I am satisfied, too, but such contentment makes me sad. Everything within me is so confused, so incomplete. I am always wanting something, even though everything here is so beautiful and full of repose. Doesn't Nature ever waken in you a sort of melancholy pleasure, as though you wanted the impossible, and were sorry for something that was gone?"

He took his hand off my head and was silent a moment.

"It used to be that way, especially in spring," he said, as though remembering something. "I, too, could not sleep at night, waiting and hoping for something—those were beautiful nights! But then everything was ahead of me, and now everything is behind; now I am satisfied with what I have and am well content." He finished so carelessly and confidently that though it hurt me to hear him, I believed he was speaking the truth.

"And there is nothing you want?" I asked.

"Nothing impossible," he replied, guessing what I felt. "You are getting your head wet," he added, and again ran his hand over my hair, caressing me as though I were a

child. "You are envious of the leaves and the grass for being wet by the rain—you would like to be the leaves and
the grass and the rain. But I am satisfied merely to look at
them, as at everything else that is young and beautiful and
happy."

"And there is nothing in the past that you regret?" I
went on asking, feeling heavier and heavier at heart.

He considered a moment. I could see he was anxious to
be utterly sincere.

"No," he said curtly.

"That is not true! Not true!" I exclaimed, and turning,
looked into his eyes. "Do you not regret what we have
lost?"

"No," he repeated. "I am grateful for the past, not sorry."

"But do you not wish it would return?" I insisted.

He turned away and gazed out into the garden.

"I no more wish for that than I wish for wings," he said.
"It is impossible."

"And do you never find fault with the past? Never reproach yourself or me?"

"Never. Everything was for the best."

"Listen," I said, touching his hand to make him look at
me. "Why did you never tell me you wanted me to live as
you saw fit? Why did you give me a freedom I did not know
how to use? Why did you stop teaching me? If you had
wanted to—if you had guided me, nothing would have
happened, nothing." And my voice rose in cold irritation
and reproach, not with the old love.

"What would not have happened?" he asked in astonishment, turning round to me. "Nothing has happened as it is.
Everything is good—very good," he added with a smile.

"Can it be," I wondered, "that he does not understand
me, or what is worse, does not want to understand me?"
and tears filled my eyes.

"It wouldn't have happened that I must always be punished by your indifference, even contempt, though you have
nothing to blame me for," I burst out. "It would not have

happened that you've taken everything away from me that I held dear, though I am completely innocent."

"Why, what are you saying, darling?" he said as though not understanding me.

"Don't interrupt, let me say everything. You have taken away from me your confidence, your love, your respect, and after what once was, I no longer believe you love me. Wait, I must say everything that has been tormenting me so long," I said when he attempted to speak again. "Is it my fault that I did not know life, and you allowed me to learn it all alone? Is it my fault that now, when I do understand what I want, when for almost a year I have been trying in every way to come back to you, you repulse me, as though you did not know what I wanted? And you do it in a way that is beyond reproach, making me the only one who is guilty and unhappy. Yes, you want to throw me back into a life that may bring disaster to you and to me."

What makes you think that?" he asked, frankly astonished and alarmed.

"Was it not you who said only yesterday that I would never be able to stay here? And are you not constantly saying that in winter we shall have to go back to that St. Petersburg I hate? Instead of helping me, you never confide in me, never speak a sincere and tender word. And then when I fall completely, you will reproach me and be glad that I have fallen."

"Wait," he said sternly and coldly. "It is wrong of you to say what you are saying now. It only shows you are ill disposed toward me, and that you do not—"

"Do not love you? Say it! Say it!" I finished, and burst out weeping. I sat down on the bench and covered my face with my handkerchief.

"And that is how he understands me!" I thought, trying to hold back the sobs that smothered me. "Our love is gone, gone," some voice kept telling me. He did not come to me, did not try to comfort me. He was offended by what I had said. His voice was calm and cold.

"I do not know what you are reproaching me with," he began. "If it is that I do not love you as I used to—"

"Used to!" I murmured into my handkerchief, and the bitter tears flowed still faster.

"—then it is time that is at fault, and ourselves. Every time has its own form of love." He paused. "Shall I tell you the whole truth? If you insist on being candid . . . Just as that year, when I first came to know you, I could not sleep nights for thinking of you and creating a love that grew and grew in my heart, so in St. Petersburg and abroad, there were terrible nights when I could not sleep as I broke and destroyed the love that had tormented me. I did not destroy it, I only destroyed what tormented me; I found peace, and I still love you, but in another way."

"You call it love, but it is torture," I murmured. "Why did you let me live in society, if you found it so harmful that you stopped loving me on its account?"

"Not society's, dear."

"Why did you not use your power over me?" I went on. "Why did you not tie me up—kill me? It would have been better than to have deprived me of everything that made me happy. I would have been content and not ashamed."

Again I began to sob and covered my face.

At that moment Katya and Sonya, wet and excited, came up on the verandah, laughing and talking loudly, but on seeing us they withdrew without a word.

We sat in silence for a long time after they had left. I cried myself out and felt easier. I glanced at him. He was sitting with his head in his hands, and wanted to say something in answer to my glance, but he only sighed heavily and again buried his head in this hands.

I went up to him and pulled away his hand. He turned a pensive gaze on me.

"Yes," he said, as though continuing his thoughts. "All of us, but especially you women, must live through the superficiality of life so as to discover real life. And none of us can profit by another's experience. You were far from having lived through that charming superficiality, and I allowed you to go through it alone, feeling I had no right to restrain you, though my own time for such things had long passed."

"Why did you stay with me and live through it with me if you loved me?" I asked.

"Because however you wished to, you could not have taken my word for it. You had to see for yourself, and you did."

"You weighed things too much and loved too little," I said.

Again we were silent.

"What you just said was cruel, but it was the truth," he said and, getting up abruptly, began pacing the verandah. "Yes, it was the truth. It was my fault," he added, stopping in front of me. "Either I should not have allowed myself to love you, or I should have loved you more simply."

"Let us forget everything," I said timidly.

"No, what is done cannot be undone—can never, never be undone," and his voice became tenderer as he said it.

"Everything has been undone," I said, putting my hand on his shoulder.

He took it and pressed it.

"I was not telling the truth when I said I had no regrets. I do regret the past. I grieve over the love that is dead and can never be revived. Whose fault is it? I don't know. Love remains, but it is not what it once was. The place for love is left, but love itself has undergone some illness—it has no strength or energy left. There are memories and gratitude, but . . ."

"Don't say that," I interrupted. "Everything will be as it used to be. It can be, can't it? I asked looking into his eyes. But his eyes were clear and serene and did not look deeply into mine.

And as I spoke I realized that what I was pleading for was impossible. He smiled calmly, kindly, with what seemed to me an old man's smile.

"How young you are, while I am so old!" he said. "I have no longer within me what you seek for—why deceive myself?" he added, continuing to smile.

I stood silently beside him and my heart was more at ease.

"We won't try to bring back what is gone," he resumed.

"We won't lie to ourselves. And if there is no longer the old anxiety and the old excitement, let us be thankful for that! We have nothing to seek, nothing to disturb us. We have had no small share of happiness. Now it is time for us to stand aside and make way for him," he said, pointing to Vanya in the arms of the nurse, who had stopped with him in the doorway. "That is so, my dear," he finished, and, bending over, kissed me on the head. And the kiss was not that of a lover, but of an old friend.

And from the garden, stronger and sweeter rose the fragrance of the night, and more solemn became the sounds and the silence, and more intense the light of the stars. I looked at him, and all at once my heart felt easier, as though an aching nerve had been removed. I clearly and calmly realized that the love of that time had gone forever, and that it was not only impossible to revive it, it would have been painful and constraining to do so. And had it really been so wonderful—that time that seemed to me to have been bliss? How long ago, how very long ago, it had been!

"We are forgetting tea," he said, and we went into the parlor together. In the doorway we again met the nurse with Vanya in her arms. I took the baby, covered his naked pink feet, pressed him to me, and kissed him, barely touching him with my lips. He spread his tiny wrinkled fingers as if in sleep, and opened his hazy eyes as if looking for something or remembering something. Suddenly these eyes fixed themselves on me, and a spark flashed in them; his full lips gathered and opened in a smile. "Mine, all mine!" I thought, and with a happy tension in all my limbs pressed him to my breast, and could hardly keep myself from hurting him. And I began to kiss his cold little feet, his belly and hands, and his little head, covered with down. My husband came up to me. I quickly covered the baby's face, then again uncovered it.

"Ivan Sergeich!" said my husband, touching him under the chin with his finger. But I again quickly covered Ivan Sergeich. No one but me should look at him long. I glanced at my husband, and his eyes were smiling as he looked at me, and for the first time in a long while I felt glad and light at heart as I gazed into them.

That day ended my romance with my husband; my old love remained a dear memory of what would never return, but a new feeling of love for my children and for the father of my children provided the beginning of another happy life, but an entirely different one, and this life has not ended to this day.

1859

YARDSTICK

(A STORY ABOUT A HORSE)

I

The light rose higher and higher, the sunrise spread wider, the opaque silvery dew glistened whiter, the sickle of the moon grew fainter, the forest—noisier, people began to stir, and in the horse yard of the manor house the snorting and shuffling in the straw became more insistent and there were even shrill whinnyings as the horses pushed each other angrily about and bickered over something.

"Whoa, there! Plenty of time! Ye ain't starved yet!" said the old herdsman as he opened the creaking gate. "Back!" he shouted, waving his arm, as a mare made a lunge for the gate.

Herdsman Nester was wearing a Cossack jacket held in by a leather belt from which hung various instruments; his whip was thrown across his shoulder, and his bread, wrapped in a towel, was thrust into his belt. He was carrying a saddle and a bridle.

The horses were neither frightened nor offended by the herdsman's mocking tone, they pretended not to care and turned unconcernedly away from the gate—all but an old bay mare with a shaggy mane, who folded back her ears and swiftly turned her back on him. At that a young mare standing behind her, who really ought not to have taken any notice, gave a whinny and kicked up her hind legs at the first horse that came near her.

"Ho-ho!" cried the herdsman in a louder and more menacing tone as he made for a far corner of the yard.

Of all the horses in the enclosure (there were about a hundred of them), the one who showed the least impatience was a piebald gelding standing alone under an overhanging roof and gazing about with half-closed eyes as he licked the oak post of the shed. It is hard to say just what the taste of this post was, but the piebald gelding looked very grave and pensive as he licked it.

"Up to mischief, eh?" said the herdsman in the same tone as he came up to him and put down the saddle and glossy saddlecloth on a manure pile.

The piebald gelding stopped licking and stood staring at Nester without moving a muscle. The horse did not laugh, did not frown, did not lose his temper, but in a few seconds a shudder passed over his belly, he gave a deep sigh, and turned away. The herdsman encircled his neck with his arm and put on the bridle.

"What are you sighing for?" asked Nester.

The gelding gave a whisk of his tail, as much as to say, "Oh, nothing in particular, Nester." The herdsman put on the saddle and saddlecloth, the gelding laid back his ears to show his disapproval, but he was only called a fool for it. When the girth was tightened, the gelding blew himself up to stop it, but a fist thrust into his mouth and a knee-kick in the belly knocked the breath out of him. And yet when Nester pulled on the strap with his teeth, the gelding dared to lay back his ears again and even glance round at him. He knew it would do no good, but he wanted Nester to know he disapproved and had no intention of hiding his disapproval. Once saddled, he relaxed his swollen right leg and set to chewing on his bit, although he ought to have known by this time that nothing could be more tasteless than a bit.

When Nester had put his foot in the short stirrup and mounted, he unwound his whip, pulled his coat out from under his knees, struck the pose in the saddle peculiar to coachmen, fox hunters, and herdsmen, and pulled on the reins. The gelding lifted his head as a mark of readiness to go wherever he was told, but did not stir. He knew that before they set out his rider would bellow a string of orders to Vaska, the other herdsman, and to the horses as well. And sure enough, Nester began to shout.

"Vaska!" he called. "Hi, Vaska! Have you let out the mares? Where are you, you rascal? Asleep? Open the gates! Let the mares out first!" and other things of the same nature.

The gates creaked. Vaska, cross and sleepy, was standing at the gatepost holding one horse by the bridle as he let the others out. The horses passed through one after another, stepping cautiously over the straw and sniffing at it: fillies, yearling stallions, suckling colts, mares heavy with young, who, solicitous of their great bellies, went through the gates in single file. The young mares pushed ahead in twos and threes, thrusting their heads over one another's backs and tripping over their feet in their hurry, for which they were sworn at by the herdsmen. The suckling colts darted between the legs of even strange mares, and whinnied shrilly in response to the neighing of their elders.

A frisky young mare tossed her head up and down as soon as she was out of the gates, kicked up her hind legs, and let out little cries, but she did not dare to rush ahead of old dappled Zhuldyba, who, as always, walked at the head of the other horses with a slow, heavy, dignified tread, her big belly swinging from side to side.

A few minutes later the enclosure, that had just been so lively and crowded, was empty. The posts holding up the roof-shelters looked sad and lonely and there was nothing else to be seen but crumpled, dung-covered straw. The piebald gelding was used to this scene, and yet it seemed to have a depressing effect on him. He swung his head slowly up and down as if nodding to someone, sighed as deeply as the girth permitted, and dragged his stiff and crooked legs in the wake of the herd, carrying old Nester on his bony back.

"As soon as we reach the road he is sure to strike a light and smoke that old pipe of his with the brass trimmings

and the chain," he thought to himself. "And very glad I
am, for it is pleasant to catch the fragrance of his pipe
early in the morning, while the dew is still on the grass;
the smell of it reminds me of many pleasant things. The only objection I have is that as soon as the old man has a
pipe between his teeth he puts on airs, fancies himself a
great person, and sits sidewise—and always on the side
that hurts me. But the devil with him! It's not the first time I
have had to sacrifice myself for the sake of another's enjoyment. Horse that I am, I've even come to take a certain
satisfaction in it. Let him put on airs, poor fellow; he only
does it when he's alone and nobody sees him. Let him sit
sidewise if it gives him pleasure," reflected the gelding as
he walked down the middle of the road, stepping cautiously on his shaky legs.

II

Having driven the herd to the riverbank where the horses
were to graze, Nester climbed down and unsaddled the
gelding. Slowly the horses made their way toward the fresh
water meadows that were drenched in dew and veiled in
the mist rising from the earth and the encircling arm of the
river.

As soon as the bridle was removed Nester scratched the
gelding under the chin, at which the horse closed his eyes
to express pleasure and gratitude. "He loves it, the old
ninny," muttered Nester. But the gelding did not love it at
all; it was only a delicacy of feeling that made him pretend to, and to nod his head in acquiescence. But suddenly,
without warning or reason (unless, perhaps, Nester felt that
too much familiarity might lower his importance in the gelding's eyes), the old man pushed the horse's head away and
swung out with the bridle, striking the gelding painfully on
his skinny leg with the buckle, and then without a word he
walked over to a stump on a mound where he usually sat.

Such behavior could not but vex the gelding, but he gave
no sign of it. He merely turned and made his way down to
the river, slowly swinging his stringy tail, sniffing the air,

and browsing for the sake of appearances. The young mares, yearlings, and sucklings, rejoicing in the fine morning, were cutting capers all around him, but he paid no attention to them. Knowing that the best thing for one's health, especially at his age, was to have a good drink on an empty stomach and only then to take one's breakfast, he selected the most sloping and expansive spot on the riverbank, wet his hoofs and fetlocks, poked his muzzle into the water, and began to suck it up with his ragged lips, expanding his sides and switching his streaked and scanty tail that had gone bald where it joined the spine.

A mischievous bay mare who was always teasing the old gelding and causing him annoyance, came through the water toward him as if on some business, but really to stir up the water where he was drinking. But by this time the gelding had drunk his fill, and, as if unaware of the mare's ill intentions, he calmly drew one foot out of the mud after another, shook his head, withdrew to a safe distance from the young folk, and began his breakfast. He ate for three hours on end, scarcely lifting his head, flinging out his legs in odd postures so as to trample down as little grass as possible. When he had eaten so much that his belly hung from his sharp protruding ribs like a stuffed sack, he balanced himself on his four aching legs in a way that would cause as little pain as possible, especially in his right foreleg, the weakest of all, and fell asleep.

Sometimes old age is majestic, sometimes repulsive, sometimes pathetic. Sometimes it is both majestic and repulsive. The piebald gelding's old age was of that sort.

The gelding was a big horse—at least five and a half feet tall. He was almost black with cream-colored spots. That is, he had been once, but now the spots had become a dirty brown. He had three color spots on him in all: one slanting up one side of his nose, covering the top of his head and half his neck. His long mane, matted with burrs, was white in some places, brown in others. The second spot extended along his right side and took in half his belly. The third was on his crupper and spread over the upper part of his tail and half his flanks. The rest of his tail was streaked and whitish. His big bony head, with deep hollows around the eye sockets and a dark and pendant lower lip that had been torn in some fray, hung low and heavy at the end of a scrawny neck that seemed carved of wood. His pendant lower lip gave glimpses of a blackish tongue lolling in the side of his mouth, and some stumps of yellow teeth. His ears, one of which had a rip in it, flopped over most of the time, but occasionally he would twitch them to scare off a too persistent fly. A remnant of forelock hung down behind one ear; his bare forehead was sunken and furrowed, and his dewlaps hung like empty bags. The knotted veins on his head and neck shook and trembled at every touch of a fly. The expression of his face was sternly patient, profound, and long-suffering. His forelegs were bowed at the knee, both hoofs were swollen, and there was a lump the size of a fist near the knee of his spotted right foreleg. His hind legs were in better shape, but the nap had once got rubbed off his flanks and had never grown back. His legs looked too long for his skinny body. His ribs, though well rounded, were so exposed and protruding that the skin seemed to have grown fast to the hollows between them. His withers and back bore the scars of many a beating and there was a fresh sore, swollen and festering, on his hindquarters. The black tail stump, ridged with vertebrae, hung down long and almost bald. On the bay crupper near his tail there was a sore the size of a hand with white hairs growing out of it (perhaps from an insect sting), and on his shoulder blade there was the scar of another sore. His hocks and tail were stained by chronic diarrhea. The short hair of his hide stood up like bristles. Yet, despite the repulsive senility of this gelding, one could not help thinking, and an expert was sure to say, that he had been a fine horse in his day.

Indeed, an expert would say there was only one stock in Russia that could produce such broad bones, such large knee-pans, such fine hoofs, such slender legs, such a graceful neck, and, most important of all, such a fine head, with its large, black, radiant eyes, its aristocratic knotting of veins on face and neck, its refinement of hide and hair.

There really was something majestic about the horse, even in the terrible combination of repulsive decrepitude (enhanced by the piebald coloring) and serene self-confidence of look and manner, characteristic of those who are aware of their strength and beauty.

Like a living ruin the horse stood alone in the dew-drenched meadow, while not far away could be heard the stamping and snorting, the neighing and youthful whinnying of the scattered herd.

III

The sun had already climbed above the forest and was shining brightly on the meadow and the curve of the river. The dew had shrunk into drops as it dried; here and there above the swamp and forest the dissolving mist hovered like thin smoke. Clouds came billowing up, but there was still no wind. In the fields across the river the rye stood in short green pipelike bristles, and the air was fragrant with verdure and blossom. A cuckoo called hoarsely from out of the forest, and Nester, sprawled on his back, was counting the number of years of life left to him. Larks soared over the rye fields and water meadows. A belated hare found itself caught among the herd; it scurried to a safe distance and sat down under a bush, alert to danger. Vaska drowsed off with his head buried in the grass; the mares circled widely round him and scattered over the lower half of the slope. The older ones, snorting, left a bright trail in the dew as they sought grazing spots where no one would disturb them, and having found them, nibbled at the succulent grass. The whole herd moved imperceptibly in the same direction. And again dignified old Zhuldyba, taking the lead, showed the others the way. Young Mushka, who had foaled for the first time, lifted her tail, giggled and snorted at her little mauve colt who, with trembling knees, kept sidling up to her. Brown Swallow, still single, with a hide as smooth and glossy as satin, dropped her head until her silky black forelock covered her brow and eyes as she played with the grass, biting it off, throwing it up into the air, and striking it with her dew-wet fetlock as it came down. One of the older colts, no doubt imagining it was playing a game, had already run twenty-six times round its mother, while she, used to the ways of her son by now, went on calmly cropping grass, merely darting a glance at him every once in a while with her big black eyes. One of the smallest of the colts, a black one with a large head and a forelock that lent it a look of surprise by standing straight up between its ears, and with a tail that was still twisted to one side as it had been in the womb, stood stock-still with its ears cocked and its eyes fixed on the playful colt, whether in envy or disapproval it would be hard to say. Some of the young were poking their mothers' bellies impatiently with their muzzles, seeking the nipple, others went loping away at a quick, ungainly gait in defiance of their mothers' calls and in exactly the opposite direction, as if they were looking for something, and then, still for no good reason, stopping suddenly and giving piercing cries; still others were sprawling on the ground, or learning to crop grass, or scratching behind their ears with their hind legs. Two mares who had not yet foaled had withdrawn from the others and were browsing together, walking with difficulty. The others clearly had respect for their state and none of the colts dared to go near and disturb them. If some frisky young thing ventured near them, a twitch of the ear or the tail was sufficient to point out to him the impropriety of his conduct.

The yearling stallions and fillies put on the airs of grown-ups; rarely did they allow themselves to leap into the air or join the gay youngsters. With great dignity they munched the grass, curving down their clipped swanlike necks and waving their little whiskbrooms as if they, too, had tails. Like their elders, they would sometimes lie down and roll over or scratch one another's backs. Gayest of all were the two- and three-year-old fillies and the virgin mares. They almost always formed a separate group of spirited maidens who were forever stamping their feet, snorting, whinnying, and neighing. They would come together, put their heads on each other's shoulders, sniff each other, leap

into the air, and sometimes, with a snort and a flourish of
their tails, parade in front of each other coquettishly, in a
half-trot, half-amble.

The most beautiful and impish of these gay maidens was
the bay mare. Whatever she did, the others did too. Wherever she went the whole flock of pretty maidens followed.
She was in particularly high spirits this morning. Her gay
mood had come upon her just as it comes upon humans.
After playing her prank on the old gelding at the river, she
had rushed along the water's edge, pretended to be frightened by something, let out a snort, and dashed at top speed
into the meadow, so that Vaska had to gallop after her and
the others who had followed her. When she had eaten a
little, she rolled over on the ground, then set to teasing the
old mares by racing under their very noses; then she
chased one of the colts away from its mother and ran after
it as if to bite it. The mother was terrified and the colt whinnied plaintively, but the bay mare did not so much as touch
it, she only gave it a fright for the entertainment of her girl
friends, who watched with delight. Then she had the bright
idea of turning the head of a gray plowhorse that was being driven by a muzhik in a rye field on the far side of the
river. She stopped, threw up her head proudly, shook herself, and gave a sweetly tender, long-drawn whinny. There
was spirit and feeling and a certain sadness in this whinny.
And there was also desire, and the promise of love, and the
longing for it.

A corncrake deep in the reeds was hopping about and
calling passionately for a mate; a cuckoo and a quail were
singing of love; even the flowers were sending sweet-smell-
ing dust down the wind to each other.

"I am young and beautiful and strong," whinnied the
mare. "And yet I have not yet been allowed to taste the
sweetness of love; more than that, no lover, not a single
one, has yet set eyes on me."

And this meaningful whinny spread sadly and youthfully
down the slope and over the fields and reached the ears of
the distant gray horse. He pricked up his ears and came to
a standstill. The muzhik kicked him with his bast shoe, but

the gray horse was so enchanted by the silvery sound that he stood still and whinnied in response. The muzhik grew angry, pulled on the reins, and gave him another kick in the belly, so hard this time that he broke off in the middle of his call and moved on. But a sweet sadness had come over the gray horse, and the sound of his passionate whinny and of the muzhik's angry protest were carried from the distant rye field to the herd of horses on the other bank.

If the mere sound of the mare's voice could so enchant the gray horse that he forgot his duty, what would he have felt had he seen all the beauty of her, as she called to him, standing with ears pricked up, nostrils dilated, sucking in the air and straining forward, trembling in every limb of her young and beautiful body.

But the mare did not give herself up to her feelings for long. When the answering voice died away she whinnied once more, then, dropping her head, pawed the ground and rushed off to tease and annoy the piebald gelding. He was the constant brunt of the young folks' jesting and joking, and suffered more at their hands than at human ones.

Yet he had never done harm to either. Human beings still had need of him, but why should the colts torture him so?

IV

He was old, they were young; he was skinny, they were sleek; he was sad, they were gay. In a word, he was a strange, alien, utterly different being, and so not to be pitied. Horses pity only themselves, with rare exceptions made for those of their kind whom they imagine to be like themselves. But surely the piebald gelding could not be blamed for being old and skinny and ugly? One would not suppose so. But according to the other horses he was to blame, and only those were blameless who were young and strong and happy, those who had everything before them, those whose muscles quivered and tails stood upright at the slightest provocation. Perhaps the piebald gelding realized this and in his more rational moments admitted that he was to blame for having lived out his life, and was willing to pay the penalty. But he was a mere horse after all, and as he looked at these young folk who tortured him for nothing but what each of them would have to face as their lives came to an end, he could not help feeling sad, indignant, and offended. There was an aristocratic sentiment behind the heartlessness of the horses. Each of them had a pedigree tracing back to the famous Smetanka, whereas nobody knew from whom the old piebald descended. He was a nobody who had been bought three years before at the horse market for eighty rubles.

The bay mare walked up to him in the most nonchalant way and gave him a push. He expected nothing better, and without so much as opening his eyes he put down his ears and bared his teeth. The mare turned her back on him and made as if to kick him. He opened his eyes and walked away. No longer sleepy, he took to browsing. Again the mare and her friends sauntered over to him. A silly bald-headed two-year-old filly, who always aped everything the bay mare did, walked beside her and, like all imitators, overdid what she was imitating. The bay mare usually approached him as if she were going about her own affairs, passing under his very nose without so much as looking at him, so that he could never tell whether he had a right to get angry or not, and that was most amusing. She did this now, but her bald-headed friend, who was feeling very playful, struck the gelding full force with her chest. Again he bared his teeth, let out a cry, and with an asperity hardly to be expected from him, set out after her and bit her in the flank. The bald-headed filly struck him with her hind-quarters, hitting him painfully on his bare ribs. The old horse snorted and was about to set out after her, but thought better of it and, sighing deeply, walked away.

Apparently all the young folk in the herd resolved to get revenge for the daring attack the gelding had made on the bald-headed filly, for they did not even give him a chance to eat for the rest of the day, so persistently did they plague him. Several times the herdsman drove them away from him and was quite at a loss to explain their be-

havior. The gelding was so frightfully offended that he himself went up to Nester when it was time to drive the herd
home, and he felt much happier and more secure when he
was saddled and the herdsman was on his back.

Who can say what thoughts came into his mind as he
carried the old herdsman home? Perhaps he brooded sadly over the heartlessness of youth, or perhaps, in the way
of the old, he forgave his offenders, holding them in proud
and silent contempt. Whatever his ruminations, he kept
them to himself until they reached the horse yard.

That evening some neighbors paid Nester a call. As he
drove the herd past the huts belonging to the manor house
servants he noticed a horse and cart tied to the post of his
hut. He was in such a hurry to reach home that as soon as
the herd was in the enclosure he let the gelding go, shouting to Vaska that he was to unsaddle him. Then he locked
the gate and went to join his friends.

An extraordinary event took place in the enclosure that
night, due perhaps to the insult meted out to the bald filly,
Smetanka's great-granddaughter (and therefore to the
aristocratic feelings of the entire herd) by the "mangy nag"
bought at the horse market and knowing neither father
nor mother; or perhaps to the fantastic appearance the
gelding presented to the other horses in his high saddle
without any rider. All the horses, young and old alike, ran
with bared teeth after the gelding, chasing him to and
fro, thumping his hollow sides with their hoofs, forcing loud
groans from him. When the gelding could stand it no longer he came to a halt in the middle of the enclosure, his face
expressing the feeble fury of impotent old age, an expression supplanted by one of despair. He dropped his ears
and suddenly did something that made all the horses stop
dead in their tracks. Vyazopurikha, the eldest mare, sniffed
the gelding and drew a deep sigh. The gelding, too, drew
a deep sigh. . . .

v

In the middle of the moonlit enclosure stood the tall figure of the gelding with the high saddle on his back. The other horses stood silent and motionless around him as if amazed by something he had just told them. And indeed they were.

This is what it was.

* * * * * * * * * * * * * *

FIRST NIGHT

"I am the son of Gracious-the-First and Baba. According to my pedigree my name is Muzhik-the-First. But, though my pedigree name is Muzhik-the-First, I have always been called Yardstick, a name people gave me because of my long stride, the like of which was not to be found in all Russia. No horse in the world has more thoroughbred blood flowing through his veins than mine. I would never have told you this—why should I?—you would not have recognized me any more than Vyazopurikha did, who lived with me in Khrenovo in my youth and has just discovered who I am; you would not believe me now if it were not for the witness of Vyazopurikha, and I would never have told you—I have no need to be pitied by a set of horses—but you made me. Yes, I am that Yardstick whom the connoisseurs of horse-flesh are searching for everywhere and cannot find, that same Yardstick whom the count himself knew and banished from the stud because I outran his beloved Swan.

* * * * * * * * * * * * * *

"I was born without knowing what *piebald* meant. I thought I was just a horse. I remember that the first remarks made on my coloring deeply shocked my mother and me. I was born at night, it seems, and by morning, after my mother had licked me clean, I could stand on my legs. I remember wanting something, and everything seemed very astonishing and yet very simple. Our stalls were in a long warm corridor with grating on the doors through which we could see everything. Mother offered me her teats, but I was still so innocent that I poked my muzzle now into her foreleg, now into her breast. Suddenly mother glanced through the grating, put a leg over me, and drew back.

The groom for that day was staring at us through the grating.

" 'Just see, Baba has foaled,' he said, and pushed back the bolt. He walked over the fresh straw and put his arms about me.

" 'Come and look, Taras,' he called. 'He's as piebald as a magpie.'

"I darted away from him and fell on my knees.

" 'Hi! you little devil!' he said.

"Mother was uneasy but made no effort to protect me; she merely heaved a deep sigh and turned away. The other grooms came in and looked at me. One of them went to tell the keeper of the stables. All of them laughed at my coloring and gave me all sorts of funny names. Neither my mother nor I understood the meaning of them. Up to this time there had never been a piebald horse among us or our relatives. We had no idea that there could be anything blameworthy in a horse's coloring. Even then everyone praised me for my strength and handsome form.

" 'Just see what a lively little fellow he is!' said the groom. 'There's no holding him.'

"In a little while the keeper came in; he showed astonishment and even seemed distressed.

" 'Where did such a little monster come from?' he said. 'The general won't keep him in the stud. Damn it all, Baba, you've done me a fine turn!' he said, turning to my mother. 'You might better have given us a bald colt than this piebald clown!'

"My mother said nothing; she only heaved another sigh, as was her habit in such circumstances.

" 'Who the devil does he take after? Just like a muzhik,' he went on. 'He can't be left in the stud, he'll disgrace us, and yet he's a fine horse—very fine,' he said, and everyone who looked at me said the same.

"A few days later the general himself came to see me, and he, too, was horrified, and upbraided me and my mother for the color of my hide.

" 'And yet he's a fine horse—very fine,' said everyone who laid eyes on me.

"We lived in the mare stables until spring, each to himself, the colts with their mothers; but when the snow on the shed roofs began to melt in the heat of the sun we were occasionally allowed to go out with our mothers into the large enclosure strewn with fresh straw. Here for the first time I made the acquaintance of my relatives, near and distant. I saw all the most famous mares of that time come out of separate doors with their colts. Among them were old Golanka; and Mushka, Smetanka's daughter; and Krasnukha; and Dobrokhotikha, the saddle horse—all the celebrities of the day. They gathered there with their offspring, walked about in the sun, rolled in the straw, and sniffed each other, just as common horses do. To this day I remember the sight of that enclosure filled with beauties. You must find it strange and hard to believe that I, too, was once young and frisky, but I was. It was there I met Vyazopurikha, then a yearling—a very kind, gay, and spirited horse. And yet I must say, meaning no offense, that although you look upon her as a rare thoroughbred, in those days she was considered one of the least of the herd. She herself will confirm this.

"My piebaldness, so detested by humans, was found very pleasing by the horses. They all surrounded me, admired me, and played with me. I began to forget what people said about my coloring and felt happy. But soon I was to experience my first sorrow, and it was caused by my mother.

"When the thaw set in and the sparrows twittered under the roofs and the air was filled with the scents of spring, my mother's attitude toward me changed. Indeed, everything about her changed: she raced and capered about the enclosure in a manner unbecoming to one of her age; or she fell into a brown study and began to whinny; or she bit and kicked the other mares; or she sniffed me and snorted contemptuously, or she stood in the sun with her head over the shoulder of her cousin Kupchikha and scratched her back long and pensively, pushing me unceremoniously away from her teats.

"One day the keeper came and had them put a bridle

on her and lead her away. She neighed, I answered and ran after her. But she did not so much as look at me. Groom Taras seized me in his arms and held me as the door was locked behind her. I struggled and threw the groom down in the straw, but the door was locked and I could only hear my mother's whinnying growing fainter and fainter. And in her whinnying I heard not a call to me, but something quite different. As I learned later, another voice, a deep and powerful voice, answered her; it was the voice of Dobry, who was being led by two grooms to a rendezvous with my mother. I was so heartbroken I didn't even notice Taras leave our stall. I felt that I had lost the love of my mother forever. 'And all because I am piebald,' I thought as I recalled the remarks people had made about my coloring, and such anger rose within me that I began to beat the walls of the stall with my head and knees, and went on beating them until I broke out in a sweat and stood still exhausted.

"In a short while my mother came back. I heard her come trotting at an unusual pace down the corridor. The door was opened to her and I scarcely recognized her, so young and pretty had she become. She sniffed me, snorted, and began to laugh. Everything about her indicated she no longer loved me. She told me how handsome Dobry was and how deeply she loved him. Again and again she was taken to meet him, and the relations between her and myself grew colder and colder.

"Soon we were let out to grass. This brought me new joys that somewhat compensated for the loss of my mother's love. I acquired friends and comrades, and together we learned to crop grass, to neigh like grownup horses, and to gallop in circles round our mothers. Those were happy days. Everything was forgiven me, everyone loved me, admired me, and was indulgent with me.

"But this did not last long. Soon a terrible thing happened." The gelding drew a deep sigh and walked away.

Dawn had come. The gates creaked and Nester came in. The horses dispersed. The herdsman tightened the saddle on the gelding and drove the herd to pasture.

VI
THE SECOND NIGHT

As soon as the horses were driven home in the evening they again gathered about the piebald gelding.

"In August I was taken away from my mother," he went on. "I suffered no particular grief. I saw that my mother was about to give birth to my younger brother (the famous Usan) and I no longer meant to her what I once had. I was not jealous. I felt my love for her cooling. Furthermore, I knew that on leaving my mother I would be put in the colt stables where we would live together in twos and threes, and every day we would all be taken out for an airing. I was put in a stall with Darling. Darling was a saddle horse who later became the Emperor's mount and was painted by artists and modeled by sculptors. At that time he was an ordinary colt with a soft, glossy hide, a swanlike neck, and legs as thin and straight as harp strings. He was always jolly, good-natured, and gracious, and he loved to frisk, lick his comrades, and play tricks on horses and men. He and I became great friends, and our friendship lasted all through our youth. At that time he was gay and frivolous. He had already begun to fall in love and flirt with the fillies, and he laughed at my innocence. To my grief, my sense of self-respect led me to copy his ways. Very soon I was in love. This early infatuation was the cause of an enormous change in my life.

"Yes, I fell in love. Vyazopurikha was one year older than I was and she and I were fast friends. But toward the end of autumn I noticed that she began to be shy of me. . . . I shall not attempt to tell the whole sad story of my first love; she herself remembers the mad passion I had for her which ended in the most important change in my life. The herdsmen drove her away from me and beat me mercilessly. One evening they took me into a special stall. I cried all night long, as if I foresaw what was to happen on the next day.

"In the morning the general, the stable keeper, the

grooms, the herdsmen came down the corridor to my stall and a dreadful row began. The general shouted at the keeper, the keeper defended himself by saying he had given orders not to let me out but the grooms had disobeyed him. The general said he would give everyone a thrashing and the colt must be castrated. The keeper said all his orders would be carried out. Everything quieted down and they went away. I understood nothing but could see they intended doing something to me.

*   *   *   *   *   *   *   *   *   *   *   *   *   *

"On the next day I stopped whinnying forever. I became what I am now. The whole world changed for me. I no longer took any joy in anything, I withdrew into myself and gave myself up to reflection. At first nothing could rouse me. I even refused to eat and drink and walk, let alone play with my comrades. Later on I sometimes felt an urge to leap up, to canter and whinny, but then I would ask myself the dreadful question: 'Why? What for?' and all the life would go out of me.

"One evening I was taken out for a walk as the herd was driven back from the fields. In the distance I saw a cloud of dust enveloping the vague forms of our mares. I heard their gay laughter and stamping. Despite the cutting of the rope into my neck as the groom pulled on it, I halted and gazed at the approaching herd as one gazes at a happiness that is irrevocably lost. As they drew near I recognized one after another—all my old friends, so handsome, majestic, sleek, and healthy. A few of them glanced in my direction. The groom kept jerking on the rope, but the pain was as nothing. Forgetting myself, I neighed in the old way and cantered toward them. But my neighing sounded sad, comical, incongruous. None of my old friends laughed, but I noticed that many of them turned their backs on me for the sake of propriety. Evidently they found the sight of me repulsive, pathetic, shameful, and above all—ridiculous. My thin, stringy neck must have looked comical, and my big head too (I had lost a lot of weight), and my long, awkward legs, and the silly trotting gait with which I circled round the groom as I had done in the old days. No one answered my neighing, everyone turned away from me. And suddenly I understood everything, I saw that I had become a stranger to them forever. How I got back to the stable I don't know, so great was my grief.

"Even before this I had shown an inclination to be grave and reflective; now I became wholly so. My piebaldness, exciting in people such an incomprehensible contempt, my strange and unexpected misfortune, the peculiar position I found myself in on the stud farm, a position I was aware of but could in no way account for, forced me to withdraw into myself. I brooded over the injustice of human beings, who blamed me for being piebald; I brooded over the fickleness of maternal love, and the love of women in general, depending as it does on purely physical factors; most of all I brooded over the whims of that particular variety of animal called man, who plays such an important role in our lives—whims giving rise to that peculiar position of mine on the farm that I was aware of but could not explain. The following incident was a complete revelation to me of the human qualities from which it sprang.

"It happened during the winter holidays. I had been given no food or drink all day long. As I learned later, this was because the groom was drunk. On that day the keeper looked into my stall, and on seeing I had not been fed he addressed a string of abuse to the absent groom and went away. When the groom and his friend brought hay to our stall on the next day I noticed he was particularly pale and depressed, and there was something about his long back that attracted my attention and roused my sympathy. He tossed the hay through the grating angrily. I poked my head out and wanted to lay it on his shoulder, but he gave me a punch in the nose that sent me flying back. This was followed by a kick in the belly.

" 'Nothing would have happened if it hadn't been for this mangy devil!' he said.

" 'Why?' asked another groom.

" 'He don't go round checking up on the count's colts, but he looks in on *his own* twice a day.'

" 'Why, have they given piebald to him?' asked another.

" 'The devil knows whether they gave it him or sold it him. The count's colts can die of starvation for all he cares, but how did I dare starve *his property!* "Lie down!" says he, and he lays on the switch. A fine Christian, him! Thinks more of beasts than humans. Anyone can see he's a godless man. Counted the strokes himself, the brute. The general never gave a man such a flogging—plowed up my whole back, he did. No soul on him.'

"I understood very well what he said about Christianity and floggings, but at that time I had not the slightest conception of what the words *his own, his property* meant. I could see they implied some sort of connection between me and the keeper. At that time I had no idea what this connection was. It was not until some time later, when I had been separated from the other horses, that I understood. At that time I could not possibly understand how *I* could be called the property of a man. The words *my horse,* referring to me, a living horse, sounded as strange as if he had said *my earth, my air, my water.*

"And yet these words made an enormous impression on me. I pondered them all the time, and it was only after experiencing the most varied relations with human beings that I at last comprehended the meaning people attach to these odd words. The meaning is as follows: people are guided in life not by deeds, but by words. It is not the chance to do or not do something that they enjoy, it is the chance to apply certain conventional words to objects. Among the words to which they attach most importance are *my* and *mine,* which they apply to all sorts of creatures and objects, even to land, people, and horses. They have agreed among themselves that only one person shall have the right to apply the word *my* to a given object. And the one who wins the right to apply this word to the largest number of objects in this game they play is considered the happiest of men. Why this should be I cannot imagine, but so it is. For a long time I tried to discover some direct advantage in it, but I could not.

"For instance, many of the people who called me their property did not ride me; I was ridden by quite different people. And it was not they who fed me, but quite different people. And it was not they who did me kind services, but quite different people—coachmen, grooms, and the like. And so, as a result of wide observation, I came to the conclusion that in respect to all things, not only to us horses, the conception of *my,* and *mine,* is founded on nothing but the low and bestial human instinct which they themselves call the instinct (or the right) of private property. A man says '*my* house,' although he does not live in it, he only builds it and keeps it up. A tradesman says '*my* cloth shop,' although he does not wear clothes of the finest cloth in his own shop. There are people who call a certain piece of land theirs, and yet they have never seen or put foot on that land. There are even people who call other people theirs, and yet they have never even seen those people, and the only connection they have with them is that they do them harm. There are men who call certain women *their* women, *their wives,* although these women live with other men. And people's aim in life is not to do as much good as they can, but to call as many things *theirs* as they can. Herein, I am convinced, lies the main difference between us and human beings. Human activities, at least the activities of all those humans with whom I have had any contact, are guided by words, while ours are guided by deeds, and this alone, to say nothing of all the other advantages we have over human beings, is sufficient to allow us to say that we stand one rung higher in the ladder of living creatures than human beings.

"Well, this right to call me *my* horse was given to the keeper of the stables, and for that reason he flogged the groom. I was overwhelmed by this discovery, as well as by the thoughts and attitudes my coloring evoked in people. All this, added to the melancholy resulting from my mother's unfaithfulness, made of me the grave and reflective gelding I now am.

"I was thrice unfortunate: I was piebald, I was a gelding, and instead of belonging only to God and myself, as is natural for every living creature, people imagined that I belonged to the stable keeper.

"There were many consequences of their imagining such a thing about me. The first of them was that I was kept apart from the other horses, was fed better, was exercised more often, and was broken in earlier. It was in my third year that a bridle was put on me for the first time. Well do I remember the day when that very keeper who imagined I was his property came with a crowd of grooms to hitch me up, supposing that I would resist and become unmanageable. They cut my lip; they tied me with ropes as they forced me between the shafts; they put a wide cross of leather straps on my back and fastened it to the shafts to keep me from kicking; and all the while I was filled with the single desire to show my love for and longing to work.

"They were amazed on seeing me step out like an old horse. They began to drive me and I began practicing trotting. I made such excellent progress that at the end of three months the general and many others praised my gait. But strange as it may seem, precisely because they imagined I belonged to the keeper rather than to myself, my gait had an entirely different meaning for them.

"My brother colts were taken to races, had their records kept, people came to see them, they were hitched to gilded sulkies and had expensive horse cloths thrown over their backs. I was hitched to the keeper's common cart and driven on his business to Chesmenka and other hamlets. And this was all because I was piebald, and because in their opinion I belonged to the keeper rather than to the count.

"Tomorrow, if we are still alive, I shall tell you what grave consequences the keeper's assumption that I was his property held for me."

All the next day the horses treated Yardstick with the greatest deference. But Nester was as rough with him as ever. The muzhik's gray plow horse made its way to the herd and whinnied, and again the bay mare flirted with him.

VII
THE THIRD NIGHT

A new moon was born and the light of its slender crescent fell on Yardstick standing in the middle of the enclosure with the other horses crowding round him.

"The most surprising result of my belonging not to the count or to God, but to the keeper," went on the piebald gelding, "was that my fast gait, a horse's greatest virtue, became the cause of my banishment.

"One day as Swan was being exercised, the keeper, who was returning from Chesmenka, drove me up to the track. Swan passed us by. He was going well, but showing off, and lacked the technique I had developed of lifting one hoof the instant the other touched the ground, so that not a single movement should be wasted and every effort should serve to impel the body forward. Swan, as I have said, passed us by. I made for the track and the keeper did not stop me. 'Why not let the piebald have a try?' he cried, and when Swan came up to us the next time he let me go. Swan had already got up speed and so I was left behind on the first round, but on the second I began to gain ground, I caught the sulky up, came abreast, held my own, outstripped him. I was given a second try. The same thing happened. I was faster. And that terrified everybody. It was decided I must be sold in some distant place where no one would get wind of me. 'There will be a fine row if the count hears of it!' was what they said.

"And so I was sold to a horse dealer as a center horse. The dealer did not keep me long. I was bought by a hussar who had been sent for remounts. All this was so cruel and unjust that I was glad when I was taken away from Khrenovo, taken away forever from all that had been so near and dear to me. Too painful was it for me to remain among my former comrades. For them—love, honor, freedom; for me—work and humiliation, humiliation and work to the end of my days. Why, oh why? Simply because I was piebald, and for that reason had been made somebody else's property."

Yardstick had no chance to go on with his story that night. Something happened that caused great excitement among the horses. Kupchikha, the mare who had not yet foaled, had been listening attentively to the story, but all of a sudden she turned and went slowly off to the shed, where she began to groan so loudly that all the horses turned their heads. They saw her lie down, scramble to her feet, lie down again. The old mares understood what was the matter with her, but the young colts were so alarmed that they abandoned the gelding and gathered round her.

By morning there was another colt standing shakily on its legs. Nester called to the groom, who led the mare and her colt into the stable, and he drove the herd away without her.

VIII
THE FOURTH NIGHT

That evening, when the gates were closed and everything was still, the piebald gelding resumed his story.

"I saw a great deal of men and horses as I passed from hand to hand. I was held longest by two masters: one was a prince, an officer in the hussars; the other was an old woman who lived near the church of St. Nicholas the Miracle Worker.

"The best days of my life were spent with the hussar. Even though he was the cause of my ruin, even though he never in his life loved anybody or anything, I loved him, and loved him just because of this. I loved him because he was handsome, rich, and happy, and therefore loved nobody. You can understand this; it is the most exalted feeling we horses have. His coldness, his cruelty, my utter dependence upon him, lent particular strength to my love for him. 'Beat me, drive me to death,' I used to think in those good old days, 'I will only be the happier for it.'

"He bought me for eight hundred rubles from the horse dealer to whom the keeper had sold me. He bought me because nobody had any piebald horses. Those were the best days of my life. He had a mistress. I knew this because I took him to her every day and sometimes took them riding together. His mistress was handsome, and so was he, and so was his coachman, and I loved them for it. I was supremely happy.

"This is how my days passed: in the morning the groom came to tend to me—not the coachman, but the groom. The groom was a lively young lad of peasant stock. He would open the door to let out the steam from our bodies and throw out the dung, then he would take off our horse cloths and begin to scrape me with a currycomb, letting the scrapings fall in whitish rows on the floorboards, all scratched and indented by my hoofs. I would bite at his arm playfully and stamp my feet. When my turn came he would lead me to a tub of cold water and gaze admiringly at his work, at my legs, straight as arrows and ending in broad hoofs, and at my glossy back and crupper, smooth enough to slide on. Then some hay would be thrown over the high grating and oats poured into the oaken manger. At last Feofan, the head coachman, would come in.

"The coachman resembled his master. Neither one feared or loved anyone but himself, and for that reason both were loved by all. Feofan wore a red blouse, plush trousers, and a sleeveless coat. I used to enjoy having him come into the stable on holidays in his sleeveless coat, his hair and whiskers shining with oil, and cry out, 'Forgotten me, you beast?' and give me a poke in the flank with the handle of a pitchfork, not painfully, just in fun. I knew it was just in fun and would flatten my ears and gnash my teeth.

"We had a black colt who worked in a pair. At night I was hitched up with him. This Polkan had no sense of humor and was a spiteful devil. Our stalls were next to each other, and sometimes we would bite each other through the bars, not the least in fun. Feofan was not afraid of him. He would walk straight up to him and roar as if he meant to kill him, but no—he would just walk past and come back with the halter. Once Polkan and I broke into a gallop along Kuznetsky Street. Neither the master nor the coachman were frightened, they just laughed and shouted at the people and held us in and guided us so skillfully that not a soul was hurt.

"I gave half my life and all my best qualities to them. They allowed me to drink too much and ruin my legs, but even so, those were the best days of my life.

"At twelve o'clock they came to harness me, grease my hoofs, wet my mane and forelock, and put me between the shafts.

"Ours was a wicker sleigh lined with velvet, the harness had little silver buckles on it, and the reins were of silk, as was the netting. The harness was such that when all the belts and straps were in place and fastened you could not tell where the harness stopped and the horse began. 1 was usually hitched up in the shed. Feofan, with a backside broader than his shoulders, would come in holding his red girdle under one arm, put his foot in the stirrup, make some jest, hang up the whip just for the looks of it, for he never used it on me, and say, 'Off we go!' And I would go prancing out of the gates, and the cook who had come out with a bucket of swill would stop in the doorway, and the muzhiks bringing firewood into the yard would stand agape.

"Outside the gates we would drive on a little way before we came to a halt. Then the lackeys and the other coachmen would gather about us and fall to gossiping. There at the entrance we would wait, all of us, sometimes for as long as three hours, occasionally taking a little run, only to come back and go on waiting.

"At last there would be a noise in the entranceway and gray-haired, potbellied Tikhon would run out in a frock coat crying, 'Drive up!' In those days they did not have the foolish habit of crying, 'Forward!' as if I didn't know whether to go forward or backward. Feofan would click his tongue. We would drive up, and the prince, in helmet and greatcoat, with a gray beaver collar hiding his handsome, ruddy, black-browed face that never should have been hidden, would hurry out with a casual air, as if there were nothing extraordinary about the sleigh, the horse, and Feofan, who arched his back and held his arms outstretched in an attitude one would think he could not possibly hold for long—the prince, I say, would come out with a clatter of spurs and saber and brass heels, stepping over the carpet as if he were in too great a hurry to notice me and Feofan and all the things that everyone but he were staring at in awe and admiration. Feofan clicked his tongue, I pulled at the traces and moved at a decent walk over to the mounting block. There I cast a sidelong glance at the prince and tossed my thoroughbred head with its silky forelock. If the prince was in a good humor he would make some witty remark to Feofan, Feofan would turn his handsome head ever so slightly as he answered him, and, without lowering his arms, would make a scarcely perceptible movement of the reins that I alone understood, and off I would go, clop, clop, clop, widening my pace with every step, trembling in every muscle of my body, kicking the snow and mud back on to the dashboard. In those days there was not that other foolish habit of calling out 'Ekh!' as if the coachman had a pain in his belly; in those days they called out, 'Watch out!' and Feofan called out 'Watch out!' and the people scattered, cleared the way and stood craning their necks to see the handsome gelding and the handsome coachman and the handsome prince go by.

"I loved to outstrip a trotter. If Feofan and I caught sight of a harness worthy our effort we would fly after it swift as the wind, gradually coming closer and closer until I was splashing mud on the back of the other sleigh, then running abreast of the passenger and snorting over his head, then running abreast of the horse's yoke, then running so far ahead that I could not see my rival and could only hear the sound of him growing fainter and fainter behind me. The prince and Feofan and I did not utter a sound, pretending to be so intent on our own business that we took no notice of the second-rate horses drawing those we passed on the way. I loved to outstrip other horses, but I also loved to catch sight of a good trotter coming toward me: a single instant, a swish, a glance, and it was past, and again we were flying on alone, each in its own direction."

The gates creaked and the voices of Nester and Vaska were heard.

THE FIFTH NIGHT

The weather was changing. The sky had been sullen since morning and there had been no dew, but the air was warm and the mosquitoes were pestering. As soon as the herd was back in the enclosure the horses gathered round the piebald gelding and he concluded his story.

"Soon my happy life came to an end. It had lasted only two years. At the end of the second winter I experienced the greatest joy I had ever known, and soon after that the greatest sorrow.

"During Shrovetide I took the prince to the races. Atlasny and Bychok were racing. I do not know what my master talked about in the betting booth, but when he came out he ordered Feofan to drive me on to the track. I remember being driven on and made to race with Atlasny. Atlasny was drawing a sulky, I, a town sleigh. At the turn I passed him and was met by a roar of laughter and cheers.

"A whole crowd surged after me when I was led away. Some five horse-lovers offered the prince thousands for me. He only laughed, displaying his fine white teeth.

" 'Oh, no,' he said, 'he is not a horse but a friend; I wouldn't sell him for a mountain of gold. Good-day, gentlemen,' and he opened the door of the sleigh and got in.

" 'To Ostozhenka Street!' That was the address of his mistress. Off we went.

"And that was the last happy day I knew.

"We reached her house. He called her 'his,' but she loved another and had gone off with him. This he was told on reaching her flat. It was five o'clock, and without taking me out of the harness he set off after her. And a thing was done to me that had never been done before: I was lashed with the whip and made to gallop. For the first time I made a misstep; I was ashamed and wished to redeem myself, but suddenly I heard the prince shout at the top of his lungs, 'Run, damn you!' and the whip whistled through the

air and struck me and I galloped ahead, striking my legs
against the metal dashboard. When we had gone twenty-
five versts we caught her up.

"I brought him home, but I could not stop trembling all
night long and could eat nothing. In the morning they gave
me some water. I drank it, but from then on I was a different horse. I fell ill, they tortured and mutilated me—'gave
me treatments,' as people call it. My hoofs came off, I broke
out in sores, my legs went crooked, my chest caved in, I
became languid in spirit and weak in body.

"They sold me to a horse dealer. He fed me carrots and
something else and made me out to be something I no
longer was, so as to fool the ignorant. I no longer had
strength or a fast gait. The horse dealer further tortured
me by coming into my stall whenever a customer appeared
and thrashing me with the whip and frightening me out of
my wits. Then he would wipe off the marks of the whip and
lead me out.

"An old woman bought me. She was always driving me
to the church of St. Nicholas the Miracle Worker, and she
flogged her coachman. The coachman used to come to my
stall and cry. That is how I discovered that tears have a
pleasant salty taste. Then the old woman died. Her stew-
ard sold me to a shopkeeper, and while with him I ate too
much wheat and my ailments increased. He sold me to a
peasant. I pulled his plow and ate almost nothing at all.
Again I fell ill.

"I was bartered to a gypsy. He treated me abominably
and at last sold me to the bailiff here. And here I am."

No one made a sound. It began to rain.

IX

As the herd was being driven home the following evening,
they came upon the master, who had a visitor with him.
Zhuldyba had seen them first as she approached the house
—two male figures: one of them was the young master in a
straw hat, the other was a tall, fat man in military uniform.
The old mare looked askance at them and sidled past. The

others, being young, felt shy and uneasy, especially when the master and his guest walked straight into the midst of them and began pointing out things to each other and talking.

"I bought that one, the dappled gray, from Voycikov," said the master.

"Whose is that young black with the white socks? She's a beauty," said the guest.

They looked over a number of the horses, running after them and making them stand still. They noticed the bay mare.

"She's of the Khrenovo saddle-horse stock," said the master.

They could not examine all the horses on the go. The master called Nester and the old man drove his spurs into the sides of the piebald gelding and came trotting up. The gelding put forth an effort, though he limped on one leg, and it was clear he would not have murmured had he been ordered to run at top speed to the end of the earth. He would have liked to have galloped, and made an attempt to with his good leg.

"You'll not find a better mare than her in the whole of Russia, take my word for it," said the master, pointing to one of the horses. The guest said something complimentary. The master ran here and there excitedly, showing off the animals and giving the history and pedigree of each of them. The guest seemed to be bored, but he invented questions to give the appearance of being interested.

"Yes? Ah," he said absentmindedly.

"Just look at this," said the master, unconscious of his guest's boredom. "Look at these legs. She cost me a pretty sum, but her three-year-old son is trotting already."

"A good trotter?" asked the guest.

They talked about one horse after another until they had discussed them all and there was nothing else to say. There was a pause.

"Well, shall we go?"

"Let's."

They went through the gate. The guest was glad the

demonstration was over and they could go home, where
they could eat and drink and smoke. He seemed to be in
better spirits. As they passed Nester on his piebald mount
waiting for further orders, the guest struck the gelding on
the crupper with his big fleshy hand.

"Here's a beauty for you!" he said. "I had a piebald
horse once myself, remember my telling you?"

Since the remark did not concern his own horses, the
master did not listen, he just went on gazing at his herd.

Suddenly he was startled by a weak, senile, absurd attempt at a neigh in his very ear. It was the gelding neighing, but he broke off in confusion without finishing. Neither
the guest nor the master paid any attention to him and
went on home.

Yardstick had recognized the fat man as his beloved master, the once rich and handsome Prince Serpukhovskoi.

                                    x

*   *   *   *   *   *   *   *   *   *   *   *   *   *

The rain kept on coming down in a drizzle. It was dismal
in the enclosure, but not in the big house. A luxurious tea
was being served in a luxurious drawing room. At the table
sat the host, the hostess, and their guest.

The hostess was pregnant, as could be seen from her
swollen belly, the erectness with which she sat behind the
samovar, her plumpness, and especially from her large
eyes, which had a meek and solemn expression and seemed
to be turned inward upon herself.

The host was holding a box of extra quality ten-year-old
cigars that nobody but he owned, or so he boasted to his
guest. The host was a handsome man of about five-and-
twenty—fresh-looking, well-brushed, well-groomed. At
home he wore a loose woolen suit tailored in London. Massive gold trinkets hung from his watch chain. His cuff links,
too, were of massive gold set with turquoise. His beard
was clipped à la Napoleon III, with little mouse tails sticking out on either side of his upper lip, waxed and twisted
as neatly as if done in Paris. The hostess was wearing a

gauzy silk gown patterned with bunches of flowers, and there were big twisted gold pins in her thick brown hair—very beautiful hair, even if it was not all her own. She had many expensive rings and bracelets on her arms and hands. The samovar was of silver, the tea service of the finest china. A footman, magnificent in tails, white waistcoat, and neckerchief, was standing at the door like a statue, waiting for orders. The furniture was carved and twisted and ornate, the wallpaper dark and floral. Near the table lay the most purebred of greyhounds with a silver chain round its neck that clinked from time to time. The dog had been given an extraordinary English name which neither its master nor mistress could pronounce since neither of them knew English. An inlaid grand piano stood among plants in one corner. All the furnishings had the air of being new, rare, and expensive. That would have been all very well if they had not also borne the stamp of luxury, ostentation, and the absence of intellectual interests.

The host was mad on racehorses. He was a strong and healthy man of sanguine disposition, a type of person that never dies out, one who rides about in sable coats, tosses expensive bouquets to actresses, drinks the most expensive wines of the newest brands in the most expensive hotels, offers prizes in his own name, and keeps the most expensive mistresses.

His guest, Nikita Serpukhovskoi, was a man over forty—tall, fat, and bald, with a large mustache and side-whiskers. He must have been very handsome in his youth; now he had the appearance of one who has gone to pieces physically, morally, and financially.

He was so deeply in debt that he had had to go into the government service to keep out of jail. At present he was on his way to a provincial town where he had been put in charge of horse breeding. It was only through the efforts of influential relatives that he had got even this post. He was wearing a military tunic and blue trousers. The tunic and trousers were such as only the rich wear, so was his linen, and his watch had been made in England. His boots had extraordinary soles almost an inch thick.

Nikita Serpukhovskoi had gone through a fortune of two million rubles, and was now a hundred and twenty thousand rubles in debt. A fortune of such a size gives a man a reputation that enables him to get money on credit and go on living almost in luxury for another ten years. These ten years had expired and the reputation had evaporated, and now Nikita's life had become a burden. He began to drink —that is, wine had begun to make him drunk, a thing that had never happened to him before. As for drinking, he had never really begun or ended. His fallen state was evident most of all from the uneasiness of his glance (his eyes had begun to wander) and the hesitancy in his voice and movements. This uneasiness was the more striking in that one could easily see it was new to him, that never before had he feared anyone or anything, and that it was only his recent vicissitudes that had thrown him into a state of apprehension quite incompatible with his nature. The host and hostess both noticed this and exchanged glances indicating that they understood each other's thoughts and would put off a discussion of the man until they were in bed; for the present they would put up with poor Nikita and even be nice to him. Nikita felt humiliated by the happiness of his host; it forced upon him recollections of his irretrievable past and made him envious.

"Do you mind our smoking, Mary?" he asked, addressing the lady in that peculiar, that elusive tone that comes of great experience—a polite and friendly tone, but not entirely respectful—the tone in which the sophisticated address their friends' mistresses in distinction to their wives. Not that he wished to offend her—on the contrary, he wished to enter into the good graces of her and the host, even though he himself would hardly have admitted it. It was just that he was used to adopting this tone with such women. He knew that she herself would have been surprised, even offended, if he had treated her as a lady. And besides, he had to keep in reserve the accepted tone of esteem for use when speaking to the real wife of his equal. He always addressed kept women with respect, not because he shared the so-called convictions expressed in the magazines (he never read such trash) as to the worth of every human being regardless of his station, the false-ness of marriage, and all the rest, but because all decent people treated them in that way and he was eminently de-cent, even if fallen.

He took a cigar. The host tactlessly picked up a handful of cigars and offered them to him.

"Here, take these, you'll see how good they are."

Nikita pushed away the cigars and an expression of in-sult and injury flashed into his eyes.

"Thank you." He took out his cigar case. "Try mine."

The hostess was more sensitive. Noticing what had hap-pened, she hastened to say, "I'm terribly fond of cigars. I think I would be tempted to smoke myself if everybody about me were not always smoking." And she gave one of her pretty, kindly smiles. He half smiled in response; two of his teeth were missing.

"No, take this," insisted the unfeeling host. "Those others are weaker. Fritz, *bringen Sie noch eine Kasten*," he said, *"dort zwei."*

The German footman brought in a fresh box.

"Which do you like better? Strong ones? These are capi-tal. Take them all," he went on insisting. His delight at be-ing able to show off his rare possessions made him oblivious of everything else. Serpukhovskoi lighted up and hastened to resume the conversation they had begun.

"What were you saying you paid for Atlasny?" he asked.

"A lot. At least five thousand, but the horse was worth it. You ought to see his offspring!"

"Racers?"

"Every one. This year his son took three prizes: in Tula, Moscow, and St. Petersburg, running against Voyeikov's Vo-ronoi. If that rascal of a jockey had not made four blunders he would have left him behind the flag."

"He's a little raw yet. Too much Dutch blood in him if you want my opinion," said Serpukhovskoi.

"And what about the mares? I'll show them to you to-morrow. I paid three thousand for Dobrinya and two for Laskovaya."

And again the host began boasting of his riches. The hostess could see that this was painful for Serpukhovskoi and that he was only pretending to listen.

"Will you have some more tea?" she asked.

"No," said the host, and went on talking. She got up, but the host stopped her, put his arms round her and kissed her.

Serpukhovskoi was about to smile as he watched them— smile in an unnatural way for their benefit, but when the host got up, put his arm about her waist and saw her to the door, his expression suddenly changed. He gave a deep sigh and a look of despair came over his puffy face. There was even a shade of angry resentment in it.

XI

The host came back smiling and sat down opposite Nikita. They did not speak for a while.

"You were saying you bought him from Voyeikov?" Serpukhovskoi remarked in an offhand way.

"Yes, Atlasny. I wanted to buy a mare from Dubovitsky but there was nothing worth having."

"He's ruined," said Serpukhovskoi, then suddenly stopped and glanced about him. He remembered that he owed this "ruined" gentleman twenty thousand rubles. If people spoke of Dubovitsky as ruined, what must they say about him? He was silent.

Again there was a long pause. The host went over in his mind all the things he might boast about to his guest. Serpukhovskoi wondered what he could say to show he did not consider himself ruined. But the minds of both of them worked sluggishly, in spite of the bracing cigars.

"When is he going to offer me a drink?" thought Serpukhovskoi.

"We'd better be having a drink, otherwise I'll die of boredom," thought the host.

"Do you intend staying here long?" asked Serpukhovskoi.

"Another month. What about a little supper, eh? Is it ready, Fritz?"

They went into the dining room. Under a chandelier stood a table with candelabra on it and laid with all sorts of fine things: siphons, bottles with dolls stuck into the corks, vodka, decanters filled with remarkable wines, plates filled with remarkable food. They drank, ate, drank again, ate again, and at last began to talk. Serpukhovskoi grew red in the face and spoke without reserve.

They talked about women. They talked about the women they had lived with—gypsy women, French women, dancers.

"And so you left Matier?" asked the host. Matier was the woman who had brought about Serpukhovskoi's ruin.

"Not I; she left me. Ah, the things a man has to live through! Nowadays I'm happy to get my hands on a thousand rubles and I count it a pleasure to be going away from everybody. I can't live in Moscow any more. Oh, when I think of it!"

The host was bored with Serpukhovskoi's talk. He wanted to talk about himself, he wanted to boast. And Serpukhovskoi wanted to talk about himself, about his brilliant past. The host poured him out a glass of wine and waited for him to finish so that he could tell him how he had arranged his stud farm in a way nobody had ever thought of before, and that Mary loved him not just for his money, but with her whole heart.

"I was just going to tell you that on my farm—" he began, but Serpukhovskoi interrupted.

"I can truly say that there was a time when I loved life and knew how to live," he said. "You were just talking about riding; tell me this, what was the fastest horse you ever drove?"

The host jumped at the chance to talk about his stud farm, but before he had scarcely begun Serpukhovskoi interrupted again.

"Oh yes," he said, "you owners of farms are interested only in becoming famous, not in enjoying yourselves, not in having a good time. I was never like that. Remember my telling you today that I once had a piebald trotter, spotted just like that horse your herdsman was riding? There was a horse for you! You wouldn't believe it. That was way back in '42, I had just come to Moscow. I go to the horse dealer and see a piebald gelding. Good points. Price? One thousand. I liked him, bought him, began driving him. You nor I nor anybody else has ever had or ever will have a horse his equal! Couldn't be matched for speed or strength or beauty! You were just a boy then, you wouldn't have known him, but you must have heard of him. All Moscow had."

"Yes, I seem to have heard of him," said the host reluctantly. "But I wanted to tell you about my—"

"Of course you did. I bought him just like that, without any papers or pedigree or recommendation. Voyeikov and I traced his line. He was Yardstick, son of Gracious the First. A stride this long. The Khrenovo stud farm sold him to the stable keeper because he was piebald, and the keeper castrated him and sold him to a horse dealer. There never was a horse his like! Ah, those were the days! Youth, my lost youth!" he sighed, quoting a gypsy song. He was getting drunk. "Yes, those were the days. I was five-and-twenty, I had eighty thousand a year, not a single gray hair, all my teeth, and each like a pearl. I was successful in everything I turned my hand to, and now—everything is over."

"In those days horses didn't have the speed they have now," said the host, taking advantage of the pause. "If you'd like to know, my first horses began to run without—"

"Your horses! Why, they were a lot faster in those days."

"What do you mean, faster?"

"Just that—faster. I remember once driving Yardstick out to the races in Moscow. I didn't enter any horses of my own. I never liked racehorses, only kept thoroughbreds: General, Sholet, Mohammed. I drove the piebald out. I had a capital coachman, too. Loved the fellow. Drank himself to death. Well, I got to the racing grounds. 'When are you going to go in for racehorses, Serpukhovskoi?' they asked me. 'What do I want with racehorses? This piebald nag of mine will outrun your blessed racehorses,' I said. 'Not on your life, he won't,' they said. 'A thousand rubles on it,' I said. We shook hands on it. Raced them. Mine came in first by five seconds and I won the thousand rubles. But that

was nothing. Once I did a hundred versts in three hours
with a troika of thoroughbreds. It was the talk of Moscow."

Serpukhovskoi lied so steadily and skillfully that the host
could not get a word in edgewise and sat opposite him
with a crestfallen expression on his face, finding his only
diversion in pouring out wine for himself and his guest.

It began to get light. Still they sat on. The host was unspeakably bored. He got up.

"Well, time to turn in," said Serpukhovskoi and, struggling to his feet and puffing out his cheeks, he staggered
off to his room.

The host was lying beside his mistress.

"He's simply impossible. He got drunk and told nothing
but lies."

"And he tried to flirt with me."

"I'm afraid he'll ask me for a loan."

Serpukhovskoi lay puffing away, fully dressed, on top of
the bed.

"I seem to have been telling lies," he thought. "What of
it? Good wine, but he's a pig. Like a merchant. And I'm a
pig," he said to himself and burst out laughing. "First I kept
them, now they are keeping me. The Winkler woman's
keeping me—I take money from her. Serves him right, he
deserves it. But I'd better get undressed. Can't get these
boots off."

"Hey!" he shouted, but the man who served him had
gone to bed long before.

He sat up, took off his tunic and waistcoat and managed
to kick off his trousers, but he could not take off his boots—
his soft paunch was in the way. One of the boots was off at
last, but no puffing and pulling could get the other off.
And so he flopped down with this boot still on and began
to snore, filling the room with the smell of tobacco, wine,
and nasty old age.

XII

There were many things Yardstick could have recalled that

night, but he was distracted by Vaska, who threw a horse
cloth over him and galloped away and kept him tied all
night outside of a public house next to a horse belonging to
a peasant. The two horses licked each other. In the morning
they rode back to the herd and Yardstick began scratching
himself.

"Why should I itch so?" he thought to himself.

Five days passed. They called the veterinary surgeon.

"He's got scab," said the surgeon gleefully. "Sell him to
the gypsies."

"What for? Cut his throat or anything you like so long
as he's out of the way this very day."

The morning was clear and quiet. The herd had gone to
pasture. Yardstick had been left behind. A strange-looking
man came up to him—thin, dark, dirty, with stains all over
his coat. He was the flayer. He took hold of the halter without glancing at Yardstick and led him away. Yardstick went
quietly, without glancing back, dragging his legs as usual,
stumbling in the straw with his hind ones. When they were
out the gate he turned in the direction of the well, but the
flayer pulled him back, saying:

"What's the use?"

The flayer and Vaska, who was walking behind, took
him to a ravine behind the brick shed and stopped as if
there were something extraordinary about this most ordinary of spots, and there the flayer, after handing the halter
to Vaska, took off his coat, rolled up his sleeves, took a
knife and whetstone out of his boot top, and began sharp-
ening the blade. The gelding reached for the halter rope
so that he could while the time away by chewing on it, but
it was too far away, and so he just heaved a sigh and
closed his eyes. His lip hung down, revealing his stumps of
yellow teeth, and he began to drowse to the sound of the
whetting of the knife. The only thing that annoyed him was
the twitching of his relaxed sore leg with the swelling on it.
Suddenly he felt someone take him by the jaw and jerk his
head up. He opened his eyes. He saw two dogs standing in
front of him. One was sniffing the air in the direction of
the flayer, the other was sitting and staring at the gelding

as if expecting something of him. The gelding looked at them and began to rub his cheek against the arm that was holding him.

"They are going to give me a cure," he thought. "Well, let them."

And sure enough, he felt them doing something to his throat. There was a stab of pain; he started, kicked out with his legs, then checked himself and waited to see what would happen next. A warm liquid began to stream down over his neck and breast. He drew in so deep a breath that his sides swelled out, and instantly he felt much better. The whole burden of his life fell away from him. He closed his eyes and let his head drop. Nobody held it up. He dropped his neck, his legs began to tremble, and his body tottered. He was less frightened than surprised. Everything was so different. In his surprise he tried to dart forward, to leap upward, but his legs got twisted and he began to fall over on his side. In trying to catch himself he plunged forward on his left side. The flayer waited and held off the dogs until the convulsions were over, and then, coming closer, he took hold of one leg and turned the horse over on his back, asking Vaska to hold him while he flayed him.

"A good horse in its day," said Vaska.

"And a fine hide if it had a little more flesh on it," said the flayer.

The herd came back up the hill in the evening, and those on the left side could see some dogs busy at a red object lying on the ground, and some crows and kites flying above it. One dog seized the object in two paws and tore at it with its teeth, shaking its head until a piece came off with a crunching sound.

The bay mare stood still, stretched out her neck, and sniffed the air for a long time. The others could hardly make her come away.

At dawn some wolf cubs whimpered playfully in the thick underbrush of the ravine cutting through the old forest. There were five of them, four almost of a size, and a small-

er one with a head bigger than its body. A thin and
scrawny mother wolf came out of the bushes, dragging her
bursting belly with the teats hanging down to the ground,
and sat down opposite the cubs, who formed into a semi-
circle. She went up to the smallest one, bent her forelegs,
lowered her head, opened her jaws, made a few convul-
sive movements of her belly, and threw up a big piece of
horsemeat. The bigger cubs rushed at it, but the mother
chased them back and gave the whole piece to the little
one. The little one growled as if in rage, seized on the
piece, held it between its paws, and began to tear it apart.
In the same way the mother threw up a second piece, a
third piece, and so on until all five had food; only then
did she lie down near them and rest.

Within a week's time nothing remained near the brick
shed but a big skull and two femurs; everything else had
disappeared. A muzhik collecting bones for the summer
took away even the skull and femurs and ground them up
for his needs.

The dead body of Serpukhovskoi that went about eating
and drinking was committed to earth much later. Of no use
to anyone was his skin, flesh, and bones. And just as his
dead body walking about on the earth had been a burden
for twenty years, so the committing of this body to earth
was nothing but a bother to those to whom the task fell.

For a long time nobody had any need of him, had found
him only a nuisance, and yet the dead who bury the dead
considered it necessary to clothe his bloated, decaying
body in a fine uniform and good boots and lay it in a fine
new coffin with new tassels at all four corners and put
this new coffin in another lead coffin and take it to Moscow, where other older human bones were dug up so that
in precisely that spot his decaying, worm-ridden body in its
new uniform and polished boots could be buried in earth.

1886

THE DEATH OF
IVAN ILYICH

Funeral

I

In the large building of the Law Courts, during an intermission in the hearing of the Melvinsky case, members of the court gathered with the public prosecutor in the office of Ivan Yegorovich Shebek, and the talk centered on the Krasov case. Fyodor Vasilyevich hotly denied that it was within the jurisdiction of the courts, but Ivan Yegorovich was not to be moved. Pyotr Ivanovich, who had taken no part in the argument from the very beginning, was reading the newspaper that had just been delivered.

"Gentlemen!" he said. "Ivan Ilyich is dead."

"Not really!"

"Here, read this," he said to Fyodor Vasilyevich, handing him the fresh issue, still smelling of printer's ink.

Inside a black border was written: "Praskovya Fyodorovna Golovina is grieved to inform relatives and friends that her beloved husband, Ivan Ilyich Golovin, Member of the Court of Justice, passed away on the 4th of February, 1882. The funeral will be held on Thursday at one o'clock."

Ivan Ilyich had been a colleague of the gentlemen gathered there, and all of them had liked him. He had been ill for many weeks and it was said that his disease was incurable. His post had been reserved for him, but it was rumored that in the event of his death Alexeyev might be appointed in his place, and either Vinnikov or Shtabel would succeed to Alexeyev. And so on learning of the death of Ivan Ilyich the first thought that entered the mind

of each of the gentlemen in the office was the changes
and promotions affecting their own positions or those of
their friends that would result.

"I am sure to be appointed in place of Shtabel or Vinnikov," thought Fyodor Vasilyevich. "The post was promised to me long ago, and the promotion will mean a salary
increase of 800 rubles in addition to grants for office ex-
penses."

"I must put in an application to have my brother-in-law
transferred from Kaluga," thought Pyotr Ivanovich. "My
wife will be happy. Now she won't be able to accuse me of
never doing anything for her family."

"I was sure he would never get over it," said Pyotr Ivanovich out loud. "What a pity!"

"Just what was the matter with him?"

"The doctors could not decide. That is, they did decide,
but each for himself. The last time I saw him I thought he
looked better."

"I haven't been there since the holidays. I kept meaning
to go."

"Do you think he was a man of means?"

"His wife had a little something, but nothing to speak of,
it seems."

"Well, now we can't get out of calling. They live so deucedly far away."

"From you. Everything's far away from you."

"He just can't forgive me for living over the river," said
Pyotr Ivanovich, smiling at Shebek. This led to a discussion
of relative distances in the town, and then they went back
into the courtroom.

In addition to speculations as to possible changes and
promotions which the news of this death gave rise to, the
very fact of the death of one they had known so well made
each of them rejoice that it was his friend rather than himself who had died.

"Fancy that: he is dead, but I am not," was the thought
or the feeling of each one of them. The more intimate acquaintances, the so-called friends of Ivan Ilyich, involuntarily added to themselves that now they had to carry out

the wearisome duty imposed by decorum of attending the funeral and then paying the widow a call of condolence.

None had been such close friends as Fyodor Vasilyevich and Pyotr Ivanovich. Pyotr Ivanovich had been a fellow student of Ivan Ilyich's, and besides this he considered himself to be under certain obligations to him. At dinner that evening he told his wife the news of the death of Ivan Ilyich and informed her of the chances of having her brother transferred to their circuit now, and then, without lying down for his usual rest, he put on his frock coat and set out for the house of Ivan Ilyich.

A carriage and two cabs were standing at the entrance when he got there. Downstairs in the entry, next to the hat-stand, a coffin lid decorated with tassels and highly polished gilt braid stood propped against the wall. Two women dressed in black were taking off their coats. He knew one of them, the sister of Ivan Ilyich; the other was a stranger. Schwartz, a friend of Pyotr Ivanovich's, had just started down the stairs, but on catching sight of him he stopped and gave him a wink, as if to say, "Ivan Ilyich has certainly bungled things; it's quite different with you and me."

As always, there was a certain elegant solemnity about Schwartz, with his English side whiskers and his lean figure in a frock coat; and this solemnity, always in such striking contrast with the playfulness of his character, had on the present occasion a peculiar piquancy. That, at least, is what Pyotr Ivanovich thought.

Pyotr Ivanovich stepped aside to let the ladies go first, and then slowly followed them up the stairs. Schwartz checked his steps and waited for him at the top. Pyotr Ivanovich guessed why: he no doubt wanted to settle where they should meet to play whist that evening. The ladies went in to see the widow, and Schwartz, his lips set in a serious line and his eyes glinting playfully, made a movement of his brows to point out to Pyotr Ivanovich the room in which the deceased lay.

Pyotr Ivanovich went in wondering, as one always does wonder, what he was expected to do. He knew it never did any harm to cross oneself on such occasions. He was not

quite sure whether he ought to bow or not, and so he did
something halfway in between: on entering the room he
crossed himself and made a little movement that might be
taken for a bow. To whatever extent this was possible, he
simultaneously glanced about the room at the same time.
Two young men, probably nephews, one of them a student,
were crossing themselves as they went out. An old woman
was standing motionless. A woman with her eyebrows
raised in an odd way was whispering something to her. A
deacon in a frock coat—a spirited, resolute man—was
reading something in a loud voice and in a tone that
brooked no contradiction; Gerasim, the pantry boy, passed
in front of Pyotr Ivanovich with a light step as he sprinkled
something on the floor. On seeing this, Pyotr Ivanovich instantly became conscious of a faint odor of decay. The last
time he had called on Ivan Ilyich he had seen this boy in
his room; he had been watching at the sick man's bedside,
and Ivan Ilyich had been particularly attached to him.
Pyotr Ivanovich kept crossing himself and bowing slightly in
a direction between the coffin and the deacon, facing the
icons on the table in the corner. When he felt he was in
danger of overdoing the crossing, he stopped and gazed at
the dead man.

The body, like all dead bodies, gave the appearance of
being particularly heavy as it lay, in the manner of the
dead, with its stiffened limbs sunk among the cushions of
the coffin and its head permanently bent forward on the
pillow, displaying, as dead bodies always do, its yellow,
waxlike forehead, the shiny spots on its sunken temples,
and the protruding nose that seemed to be pressing down
on the upper lip. Ivan Ilyich had changed greatly. He had
grown much thinner since Pyotr Ivanovich had last seen
him, and yet, like all dead men, his face had assumed an
expression of greater beauty—or rather, of greater significance—than it had worn in life. The expression seemed to
say that what had to be done was done, and done properly. Furthermore, the expression seemed to be a reproach,
or a reminder to the living. Pyotr Ivanovich found this reminder uncalled for; at any rate it had nothing to do with

him. He began to feel uncomfortable, and so he crossed himself hurriedly—hardly within the bounds of decency, he felt—and went out.

In the next room he found Schwartz waiting for him, his feet planted wide apart, his hands playing with the top hat he held behind his back. One glance at this playful, well groomed, elegant figure was enough to revive Pyotr Ivanovich's spirits. Pyotr Ivanovich realized that he, Schwartz, stood above all this and refused to become a prey to mournful influences. His whole appearance seemed to say: "The incident of the funeral of Ivan Ilyich can in no wise be considered sufficient grounds for calling off our usual gathering, i.e., nothing is to interfere with our meeting this evening and opening up a new pack of cards, even though Ivan Ilyich's footman will be placing four candles round the coffin at that very time. In general there is no reason to suppose that this incident can keep us from enjoying ourselves this evening." And he really whispered all this into Pyotr Ivanovich's ear as he passed through the room.

But Pyotr Ivanovich was not destined to play cards that evening. Praskovya Fyodorovna, a fat, shortish woman, much wider toward the base than at the shoulders despite all her efforts to achieve the opposite, dressed all in black with a lace scarf over her head and with eyebrows raised in the same odd manner as the woman standing at the coffin, came out of her sanctuary in the company of some other ladies whom she showed to the door of the room where the body lay and said, "A service is about to begin; come in."

Schwartz, with a vague sort of bow, stopped without either accepting or rejecting the invitation. On recognizing Pyotr Ivanovich, Praskovya Fyodorovna gave a sigh and came straight up to him, taking his hand and saying, "I know you were a true friend of Ivan Ilyich's. . . ." Then she looked at him in expectation of a fitting response. Just as Pyotr Ivanovich had known he was expected to cross himself in there, he knew he was expected to press her hand, sigh, and say, "I assure you. . . ." That is just what he did, and having done it felt he had achieved the desired effect. He was touched and so was she.

"Come here before it begins, I want to speak to you," said the widow. "Give me your arm."

Pyotr Ivanovich gave her his arm and they withdrew into the inner rooms, passing Schwartz, who gave Pyotr Ivanovich a rueful wink which seemed to say:

"There's your card game for you! Don't mind if we find someone else to take your place. And when you are free you can make a fifth."

Pyotr Ivanovich sighed more deeply and sorrowfully, and Praskovya Fyodorovna squeezed his fingers gratefully. On entering her drawing room done in pink cretonne and lighted by a dim lamp, they sat down at a table—she on the sofa, Pyotr Ivanovich on a low ottoman with broken springs that careened when he sat on it. Praskovya Fyodorovna wanted to warn him against using it but she felt it would not be in keeping with the present situation. As he sat down on the ottoman Pyotr Ivanovich recalled how, when Ivan Ilyich had been decorating this drawing room, he had consulted him as to the pink cretonne with green leaves. In passing the table to sit on the sofa (the room was crowded with furniture and bric-a-brac) the widow caught the lace of her black scarf on some carving. Pyotr Ivanovich half rose to detach it, and as he did so the released springs gave him a little push. The widow disentangled the lace herself and Pyotr Ivanovich resumed his seat, thus suppressing the recalcitrant springs. But the widow had not quite disentangled the lace, and Pyotr Ivanovich again half rose, and again the ottoman upsurged and even gave a little click. When this was over she took out a white batiste handkerchief and began to weep. But Pyotr Ivanovich's spirits had been chilled by the episode with the lace and the struggle with the ottoman, and so he just sat and scowled. The strain of the situation was broken by the entrance of Sokolov, Ivan Ilyich's manservant, who announced that the place in the cemetery selected by Praskovya Fyodorovna would cost 200 rubles. She stopped weeping to cast upon Pyotr Ivanovich a martyr's glance and tell him in French how hard this was for her. Pyotr Ivanovich gave a sigh expressing his sympathy.

"Smoke if you wish," she said in a magnanimous yet stricken tone, and turned to discuss with Sokolov the price of the grave. As he lighted up, Pyotr Ivanovich noticed that she made detailed inquiries into the cost of various grave plots and made an astute choice. When this matter was settled she discussed the question of hiring choristers. Then Sokolov went out.

"I see to everything myself," she added to Pyotr Ivanovich, pushing aside the albums lying on the table. Noticing that the ashes of his cigarette were in danger of falling upon the table, she quickly handed him an ashtray, saying, "It would be mere pretense if I said I was unable in my grief to attend to practical affairs. On the contrary, if anything is able to . . . er . . . not console, but distract me, it is the doing of things for his sake." Again she took out her handkerchief as if about to weep, but, with a sudden effort, she took herself in hand, gave a little toss of her head, and spoke calmly.

"There is a business matter I wish to consult you about."

Pyotr Ivanovich bowed without allowing the springs, which gave new signs of revolt, to have their way.

"The last few days he suffered horribly."

"Did he?" asked Pyotr Ivanovich.

"Simply horribly! He screamed incessantly, not for minutes, but for hours. He screamed for three days running, without stopping for breath. It was unspeakable. I don't know how I ever endured it; he could be heard three rooms away. If you ever knew what I went through!"

"Do you mean he was conscious right up to the last?" asked Pyotr Ivanovich.

"Yes," she whispered. "To the very last. He took leave of us only fifteen minutes before he died, and asked us to take Volodya away."

Despite a disagreeable awareness of his own and this woman's hypocrisy, Pyotr Ivanovich was deeply shaken by the thought of the sufferings of one he had known so well, first as a gay and carefree schoolboy, then as a grown man, his colleague. Once more he saw that forehead, and that nose pressing down on the upper lip, and fear for himself took possession of him.

"Three days of horrible suffering and death. Why, at any moment the same thing might happen to me," he thought, and for a brief second he was gripped by fear. But instantly, he himself could not have said why, the usual thought came to his aid that death had visited not him, but Ivan Ilyich, and that such a thing could not and should not happen to him. Such thoughts would only lead him into a state of depression, a thing that was to be avoided, as the face of Schwartz had so eloquently told him. By following this line of reasoning, Pyotr Ivanovich recovered his composure and even displayed genuine interest as he inquired into the details of the death of Ivan Ilyich, as if death were a mishap that could happen only to Ivan Ilyich—never to himself.

It was only after a detailed account of the truly horrible physical suffering of Ivan Ilyich (Pyotr Ivanovich learned of the tortures of Ivan Ilyich in the light of their effect on the nerves of Praskovya Fyodorovna) that the widow found it possible to proceed to matters of business.

"Ah, Pyotr Ivanovich, how hard it is for me, how terribly, terribly hard!" and again she fell to weeping.

Pyotr Ivanovich gave another sigh and waited for her to blow her nose. When she had blown her nose he said, "I assure you . . ." and again she began to speak and now got down to the business she had wanted to consult him about. She asked him how, in connection with her husband's death, she could get a grant of money from the government. She made out to be asking him about a pension, but he could see that she knew of matters that even he was ignorant of, and knew them down to the last detail; she knew exactly the amount of money this death entitled her to, but she wanted to find out if there were not some means by which she could increase it. Pyotr Ivanovich tried to think of how this might be done, but after considering the matter for some minutes and showing his sympathy by upbraiding the government for its stinginess, he said he was afraid it was impossible to get more. At this she drew a deep sigh and apparently gave herself up to thoughts of how she could bring the interview to a close. He divined this, put out his cigarette, got up, shook her hand, and went out into the hall.

In the dining room where the clock hung that Ivan Ilyich had been so happy to have added to his collection of bric-a-brac, Pyotr Ivanovich found the priest and a few other acquaintances who had come to the funeral, and he also saw the pretty daughter of Ivan Ilyich. She was dressed all in black, which made her slender waist seem slenderer than ever. She wore a gloomy, determined, almost angry look. She bowed to Pyotr Ivanovich as if he were to blame for something. Behind her stood a young man who looked just as disgruntled as she did. Pyotr Ivanovich knew him—he was a rich young man, an examining magistrate, who was said to be the young lady's fiancé. Pyotr Ivanovich gave a melancholy bow and was about to return to the room where the body lay when Ivan Ilyich's son, a gymnasium student who greatly resembled his father, came down the staircase. The lad might have been the young Ivan Ilyich whom Pyotr Ivanovich had known as a law student. His eyes were red from crying and were like the eyes of most scrubby little boys of thirteen or fourteen. On catching sight of Pyotr Ivanovich he frowned shamefacedly. Pyotr Ivanovich nodded to him and went into the room where the corpse was lying. The service began. Candles, groans, incense, tears, sobs. Pyotr Ivanovich stood with drawn brows, staring at the legs of the people in front of him. Not once did he glance at the body or at anything that might cause him to fall prey to depressing influences, and he was one of the first to leave the room. There was nobody out in the hall. Gerasim, the pantry boy, ran quickly down the stairs and rummaged with strong hands through the mountain of wraps until he found Pyotr Ivanovich's coat and held it for him.

"Well, Gerasim," said Pyotr Ivanovich in order to say something, "are you sorry?"

"It's the Lord's will, sir. We'll all die some day," said Gerasim, revealing an unbroken line of strong white peasant teeth as he grinned; then, like a man in a rush of extra work, he opened the door, shouted to the coachman, helped Pyotr Ivanovich into the carriage, and leaped back up the steps as if impatient to find something else to do.

Pyotr Ivanovich found it particularly pleasant to breathe in the fresh air after the smell of incense, the corpse, and carbolic acid.

"Where to?" asked the coachman.

"It isn't late yet. I'll drop in to see Fyodor Vasilyevich."

And off he went. He found them just finishing the first rubber, so that it was convenient for him to make a fifth for the next.

Youth   II

The story of the life of Ivan Ilyich is simple, ordinary, and appalling.

Ivan Ilyich died at the age of 45, a member of the Judicial Council. He was the son of an official who, in various ministries and departments, made for himself the sort of career which brings men at last to a post from which, even though it is clear they are incapable of doing anything of true importance, it is impossible to dismiss them because of their long term of service and high rank, and therefore they hold fictitious offices and receive by no means fictitious salaries of from six to ten thousand on which they live to a ripe old age.

Such was Privy Councillor Ilya Yefimovich Golovin, superfluous member of various superfluous institutions.

He had three sons, of whom Ivan Ilyich was the second. The eldest made for himself a career similar to his father's only in a different ministry, and soon he would reach the age of service at which salaries are paid by inertia. The third son was a failure. He had made a bad reputation for himself in various positions and was now working for the Railway Department. His father and brothers, and especially their wives, avoided meeting him and even forgot about his existence whenever possible. Their sister was married to Baron Greff, the same sort of St. Petersburg official as his father-in-law. Ivan Ilyich was *le phénix de la famille*,

as they were fond of saying. He was not so cold and punc-
tilious as his elder brother and not so reckless as his younger. He was something in between—a clever, lively, attractive man. Both he and his younger brother had attended
the school of jurisprudence. The younger never finished for
he was expelled when he reached the fifth course. Ivan
Ilyich finished very creditably. As a law student he had
been exactly what he continued to be all his life: capable,
cheerful, sociable, good-natured, and strict in carrying out
whatever he considered his duty, and he considered all
things his duty that were designated as such by men in high
position. Neither as a child nor as a grown man had he
been a toady, but from earliest youth he had been drawn
to those who stood above him, as a moth is drawn to the
flame; he had adopted their manners and views, and had
established friendly relations with them. All the enthusiasms
of childhood and youth passed away without leaving a
trace; he had at one time indulged his vanity and sensuality, and, in the last years of his student days, he had played
with liberalism, but all within the judicious limits dictated by
his instincts.

During his student days he had done things which, at
the time, he had looked upon as loathsome and had made
him disgusted with himself, but later, seeing that the same
things were done by men of high standing without any
scruples, he forgot all about them. While not regarding
them as good, he was not haunted by memories of his sins.

On completing the law course and receiving money from
his father for his outfit, Ivan Ilyich ordered some suits made
at Sharmer's, pinned on his lapel a medallion bearing the
inscription *respice finem,* took leave of the head of the
school, dined in state with his friends at Donon's, and then,
with fashionable new bags, suits, linen, shaving and toilet
articles, all ordered and purchased at the finest shops, left
for a provincial town to occupy the post his father had se-
cured for him as Secretary on Special Commissions for the
governor of the province.

In the provincial town Ivan Ilyich immediately made his
life as easy and pleasant as it had been during his student

days. He worked, he saw to his career, and at the same
time indulged in pleasant and well-bred forms of recreation. Occasionally he traveled into the countryside on as-
signments for his chief, on which occasions he preserved
his dignity when dealing with those below as well as above
him, and he fulfilled the duties entrusted to him (having to
do mostly with dissenters) with an incorruptibility of which
he was justly proud. When engaged in official duties he
was, in spite of his youth and love of amusement, exceedingly reserved, official in his manner, and even strict. But
in society he was jovial and witty, always good-humored,
courteous, and, as his chief and his chief's wife, whose
house he frequented, said, a *bon enfant*.

Here in the provinces he formed a connection with one of
the ladies who threw themselves at the stylish young advo-
cate; there was also a milliner; there were drinking parties
with visiting officers and after-supper calls at a house on a
distant street. There were services rendered to his chief and
even to the wife of his chief. But all of this was done in a
tone of such elevated good breeding that it could hardly
be called by a bad name; it was all excused by the French
saying: *il faut que jeunesse se passe:* it was done with clean
hands, in a clean shirt, with French words, and, what was
most important, in high society, which meant with the approval of those in high position.

Ivan Ilyich held this position for five years, and at the
end of this time there came a change in the law. New
courts were instituted and new men were needed.

Ivan Ilyich was one of those new men.

He was offered a post as examining magistrate and he
accepted the offer, even though it meant going to a different gubernia, breaking his present connections, and making new ones. Ivan Ilyich was given a farewell party, his
friends had a group photograph made for him, they presented him with a silver cigarette case, and off he went to
his new appointment.

As an examining magistrate Ivan Ilyich was just as
comme il faut and well-bred, displayed just as great a talent for separating his public duties from his private ones

and for inspiring general respect as he had when carrying out special commissions for the governor. He found the post of magistrate much more interesting and pleasant than his former one. It had, of course, been very gratifying in his former post to stride with an easy swing in his trim uniform from Sharmer's, straight past the anxious clients and clerks sitting in the waiting room and throwing him envious glances, and go into the office of his chief to sit with him over a glass of tea and a cigarette. But there had been few people directly under him—only the district police superintendents and the dissenters he met when sent into the countryside on commissions. And he enjoyed nothing better than to treat such people with civility, to discuss matters in an almost comradely way with them, making them feel that he, who had it in his power to crush them, actually dealt with them in a friendly, unpretentious manner. But there had been few such people. Now, as examining magistrate, he felt that all, all without exception, including the most important and self-satisfied—all were in his power, and he had but to write down certain words on a sheet of paper with an official heading and even the most important and self-satisfied would be brought before him as witnesses or even as prisoners, and if Ivan Ilyich did not deign to invite them to sit down, they would have to stand before him as they answered his questions. Ivan Ilyich never took advantage of his power; on the contrary, he tried to use it graciously. But the awareness of this power and his right to be gracious constituted for him the main interest and attraction of his new post. In the actual fulfillment of his duties, that is, when examining, Ivan Ilyich quickly mastered the art of eliminating all circumstances for which he, as examining magistrate, was not directly responsible, and of devising written forms of expression for even the most complicated cases that registered only their external aspects, completely divesting them of his personal opinion, and yet observing, above everything else, all the formalities. This work was new, and he was one of the first to give practical application to the reforms in judicial procedure introduced in 1864.

On arriving in the new town as examining magistrate, Ivan Ilyich formed new contacts, made new acquaintances, assumed a new line of conduct, and adopted a new tone. This time he held himself dignifiedly aloof from the local authorities, choosing his friends from among the best law circles and the wealthy gentry, and he adopted a tone of moderate liberalism and social-mindedness, allowing himself to mildly criticize the government. And while taking as many pains with his clothes as ever, he stopped shaving his chin and allowed his beard to grow as it liked.

Here in the new town Ivan Ilyich's life became just as pleasant as it had been in the old. The group that set itself against the governor's circle proved to be very friendly and interesting; his income was bigger, and a new diversion was added by Ivan Ilyich's learning to play whist. In general he had a knack for playing cards good-humoredly and making quick and subtle decisions, so that as a general rule he won.

When he had been living in this town for two years Ivan Ilyich met his future wife. Praskovya Fyodorovna Mikhel was the brightest, cleverest, most brilliant and attractive young lady of the set in which Ivan Ilyich moved. To the amusements and diversions bringing him relief from his duties as examining magistrate, Ivan Ilyich now added a light flirtation with Praskovya Fyodorovna.

As secretary on special commissions, Ivan Ilyich had danced as a rule; as examining magistrate, he danced as an exception. He danced to show that, although he was an executor of the new legal code and a lawyer of the fifth rank, in matters of dancing, too, he was above the average. And so he occasionally danced at the end of an evening with Praskovya Fyodorovna, and it was mostly during these dances that he conquered her. She fell in love with him. Ivan Ilyich had no clear, definite intention of getting married, but when this girl fell in love with him he faced the question. "Why," said he to himself, "should I not get married?"

Praskovya Fyodorovna came of a good family and was attractive; she also had a little money. Ivan Ilyich could

have counted on making a better match, but this was not a
bad one. He had his salary; she—her income, which he
hoped would amount to as much again. He would acquire
worthwhile in-laws. She was a sweet, pretty, well-bred
young woman. To have said that Ivan Ilyich married her
because he loved her and she sympathized with all his
views of life would have been just as erroneous as to have
said that he married her because the people of his set approved of the match. Ivan Ilyich married her because of
both of these considerations: in acquiring this particular
wife he did what brought him pleasure as well as doing
what those in high position considered it proper for him to
do.

Ivan Ilyich got married.

The actual process of getting married and the first period
of married life, with its conjugal caresses, new furniture,
new dishes, new linen—the period up to his wife's first
pregnancy—passed very well; so well, in fact, that Ivan
Ilyich began to think that marriage was in no way a hindrance to the pleasant, easygoing, diverting, well-bred life
approved of by society; that it even intensified this life. But
during the first months of his wife's pregnancy he was confronted by something new, unexpected, disagreeable, unseemly, and hard to bear; something he could not possibly
have foreseen and could do nothing to abolish.

For no reason at all, simply *de gaîté de cœur* as he said
to himself, she began to spoil the pleasantness and the decorum of their living: for no reason at all she began to be
jealous of him and demand that he pay her more attention,
to find fault with everything he did and make coarse, indecent scenes.

At first Ivan Ilyich hoped to free himself from the unpleasantness of the situation by preserving the same well-
bred and easygoing attitude that had brought him his early
success. He tried ignoring his wife's fits of bad temper and
went on living in a pleasant, easygoing way: he invited his
friends for cards and he himself went to the club or to his
friends' houses. But on one occasion his wife upbraided
him in such coarse language and thereafter upbraided him

so furiously every time he failed to do what she told him to (having apparently firmly resolved not to let up until he succumbed to her rule, which meant until he sat home and moped as she did) that Ivan Ilyich was appalled. He realized that being married—at least to this wife—did not necessarily augment the pleasures and proprieties of life, but, on the contrary, threatened them, and that therefore he must guard himself against these threats. And Ivan Ilyich set about finding a means of doing this. Since his work was the only thing that impressed Praskovya Fyodorovna, Ivan Ilyich began to use his work and the obligations it entailed as a means of combating his wife and preserving his independence.

With the birth of the baby, bringing troubles with feeding, and real and fancied illnesses of baby and mother (which Ivan Ilyich was expected to sympathize with, but which he had no understanding of), the necessity of fencing off for himself a world outside of the family grew more urgent. The more irritable and exacting his wife became, the more deliberately he transferred the center of gravity of his life to his office. He grew more attached to his work and more ambitious than ever.

Very soon, only one year after his marriage, Ivan Ilyich realized that conjugal life, while offering certain conveniences, was actually a very complicated and difficult matter, and that in order to perform one's duty in this respect, which meant putting up a decent front to win the approbation of society, one must work out definite principles, just as one must do in respect to one's profession.

And Ivan Ilyich worked out these principles. Of married life he demanded only the conveniences of dinners at home, of wife, and bed, and, most important, the preserving of good form, for upon this depended social approbation. He wanted to find pleasure in family life. If he got it, he was grateful; if he was rebuffed and heard nothing but grumbling and complaints, he instantly retired to his fenced-off world of business and found his pleasure there.

Ivan Ilyich won approval by his diligent service, and in three years he was promoted to assistant public prosecutor.

His new duties, the importance of them, his right to bring people to trial and put them in prison, his public speaking and the success it brought him—all of these things increased the attraction his work held for him.

Other children were born. His wife grew more querulous and ill-tempered, but the principles of family life that Ivan Ilyich had adopted made him almost immune to her grumbling.

After serving for seven years in this town Ivan Ilyich was made public prosecutor of a different gubernia. They moved, they were short of money, and his wife disliked the new town. Though his salary was bigger, the cost of living was higher. In addition, two of their children died, making family life more disagreeable than ever for Ivan Ilyich.

Praskovya Fyodorovna blamed her husband for every misfortune that befell them in the new town. Almost every subject of conversation between husband and wife, especially the education of their children, brought up questions on which they had quarreled at one time or another, and these past quarrels always threatened to break out afresh. There were rare periods of being in love, but they never lasted for long. They were mere islands on which the couple rested briefly before setting out again upon the sea of secret hostility expressed in complete aloofness. This aloofness would have distressed Ivan Ilyich if he had supposed it should not exist, but he had by this time come to look upon it as not only normal but desirable, a relationship he consciously sought to achieve. He aimed to free himself more and more from all the upsets of family life and to keep them from becoming harmful or indecorous. He achieved this by spending less and less time at home, and by securing the peace when he had to be there by inviting outsiders. The most important thing in his life was his work. The world of his official duties formed the one real interest of his life, and this interest absorbed him completely. The consciousness of his power, his right to ruin anyone he desired to ruin, the weightiness of even his appearance as he entered the court and spoke to his subordinates, his popularity with those above and below him, the skill with which he handled his cases, and his own appreciation of this skill —all these things brought him joy, and, together with his talks with his colleagues, the dinners he attended, and the whist he played, made his life a full one. And so, on the whole, Ivan Ilyich's life was just what he considered it ought to be—pleasant and decorous.

This continued for another seven years. His daughter was now sixteen years old, one more child had died, one son remained—a schoolboy who was the cause of much dissension. Ivan Ilyich wanted him to be sent to the school of jurisprudence, and just for spite Praskovya Fyodorovna had insisted on his going to the gymnasium. The girl studied at home and was making good progress; the boy, too, was rather a good student.

Best Days III

In this way Ivan Ilyich spent seventeen years of his married life. He was already an experienced public prosecutor who had declined several good offers in expectation of a better one, when something occurred that upset the even tenor of his life. Ivan Ilyich had set his heart on being appointed presiding judge in a university town, but in some way Goppe managed to step in ahead of him and get the appointment. Ivan Ilyich was greatly upset, made accusations, quarreled with Goppe and his immediate superiors. Their attitude chilled toward him, and when the next appointments were made he was again passed over.

This happened in 1880. It turned out to be the most unpleasant year of Ivan Ilyich's life. On the one hand, his income was insufficient to support his family; on the other, he was being slighted, and what seemed to him to be the most flagrant and heartless injustice was accepted by others as quite ordinary. Even his father did not consider it his duty to help him. Ivan Ilyich felt that everyone had abandoned him, whereas they felt it was quite normal, and even fortunate, that he should be drawing a salary of 3,500 rubles. He alone knew that, what with the snubs he had received, the incessant nagging of his wife, and the debts he had accumulated by living beyond his means, things for him were far from normal.

That summer, with the purpose of cutting expenses, he and his wife went to live in the country with his wife's brother during his holiday. There in the country with nothing to do for the first time in his life, Ivan Ilyich was more than bored; he was so unspeakably miserable that he decided he must do something, must take decisive measures.

After a sleepless night, which he spent walking back and forth on the verandah, he resolved to go to St. Petersburg and try to get himself transferred to a different ministry, thereby punishing those who had failed to appreciate him.

On the next day, despite the protests of his wife and brother-in-law, he set out for St. Petersburg. He had only one purpose in going: to secure himself a post that would pay five thousand rubles. He did not care in what ministry or department it might be or what sort of work it required. He only wanted a post paying five thousand in any administrative organization—the banks, the railways, the Empress Maria's institutions, even the customs duties. The only essential was that it pay five thousand and enable him to stop working for a ministry that did not appreciate him.

And this trip was crowned by amazing and unexpected success. When his train arrived at Kursk, a friend of his by the name of F. S. Ilyin got into his first-class carriage and told him of a telegram that had just been received by the governor of Kursk saying that an important change was about to take place in the ministry: Ivan Semyonovich was to be appointed in place of Pyotr Ivanovich.

The proposed change, in addition to the significance it had for Russia, was of particular significance for Ivan Ilyich, since in advancing a new man, Pyotr Petrovich, and apparently, his friend Zakhar Ivanovich, circumstances were made propitious for Ivan Ilyich. Zakhar Ivanovich was a friend and fellow student of Ivan Ilyich's.

In Moscow the news was confirmed, and on reaching St. Petersburg Ivan Ilyich looked up Zakhar Ivanovich, who promised to procure him a post without fail in the same Ministry of Law in which he served.

A week later he sent the following wire to his wife:
*Zakhar appointed Miller's place stop I get appointment
after first report.*

Thanks to this change Ivan Ilyich unexpectedly received
an appointment in his ministry that raised him two ranks
above his colleagues, gave him a salary of five thousand,
with three thousand five hundred to cover the expenses attending his change of residence. He forgot the resentment
he had harbored against his opponents and the ministry,
and was entirely happy.

Ivan Ilyich returned to the country more cheerful and
content than he had been for many a day. Praskovya Fyodorovna's spirits rose too, and peace reigned for the time
being. Ivan Ilyich described how cordially he had been received in St. Petersburg, and how all those who had been
his enemies were disgraced and now fawned upon him, and
envied him his new position and especially the favor in
which he was held in St. Petersburg.

Praskovya Fyodorovna listened attentively, pretended to
believe everything he said, and opposed him in nothing,
giving herself up wholly to making plans of how they would
live in the new town to which they were to move. And Ivan
Ilyich was happy to see that her plans coincided with his,
that they were in agreement, and that after this little upset
his life was once more to become pleasant and decorous,
which he felt was in the natural course of things.

Ivan Ilyich had come back for only a brief stay. On the
10th of September he had to take over his duties, and furthermore he had to settle himself in the new place, move all
his possessions from the provincial town, buy many new
things and order many others. In a word, he had to set
himself up in the manner he had resolved upon in his mind,
and Praskovya Fyodorovna had resolved upon in her soul.

Now that everything was settled so favorably and he
and his wife were in agreement, and, moreover, saw little
of each other, they became more friendly than they had
been since the first days of their married life. Ivan Ilyich
had at first thought of taking his family with him at once,
but on the insistence of his sister-in-law and brother-in-law,

who suddenly became very solicitous and amiable toward
Ivan Ilyich and his family, he set out alone.

Ivan Ilyich set out alone, and the happy frame of mind
evoked by his success and the harmonious relations with his
wife, the one augmenting the other, remained with him all
the time. He found a charming flat, exactly what he and
his wife had dreamed of. Large, high-ceilinged drawing
rooms in the old style, an enormous and convenient study,
rooms for his wife and daughter, a room for his son to be
tutored in—all as if purposely planned for them. Ivan Ilyich
himself undertook the furnishing and decorating, selecting
wallpaper and upholstery and buying furniture, mostly old
pieces, which seemed to him to be particularly *comme il
faut,* and everything grew and grew until his future home
approached the ideal he had set for himself. When the
work was only half done the result exceeded his expectations. He could see in his mind's eye how handsome and
correct, without a shade of vulgarity, the flat would look
when ready. He fell asleep at night with a vision in his mind
of the finished reception room. As he glanced into the unfinished drawing room he could see the fireplace, the
screen, the *étagère,* the chairs placed at random here and
there, the walls hung with fine china plates, the bronzes in
their places. He found pleasure in thinking of how he would
delight his wife and daughter, who also had a taste for
such things. They could not dream of what was in store
for them. He was particularly fortunate in making cheap
purchases of old furniture, which added elegance to the
general impression. In his letters he intentionally described
things as being worse than they were so as to heighten
the final effect. He was so taken up by these activities that
even his new official duties, which were of the sort he most
enjoyed, absorbed him less than he had expected. During
court sessions he would sometimes become abstracted, his
mind wandering to a consideration of whether the cross-
piece at the top of the hangings should be plain or draped.
So taken up was he by all this that he himself often lent the
workmen a hand, moving furniture here and there and
hanging portieres. One day, when he had climbed a ladder

to show a workman how he wanted the draperies hung, he slipped and almost fell, but so strong and agile was he that he saved himself, escaping with nothing but a bad bruise from striking his side against the window frame. He had a pain in his side for a little while, but it soon went away. All this time Ivan Ilyich felt particularly well and cheerful. He wrote: "I feel fifteen years younger." He expected to finish everything in September, but the work dragged on until the middle of October. The results, however, were ravishing. He was not the only one who thought so; everyone who saw the flat agreed.

As a matter of fact it was just what is achieved by all people who are not really rich, but who wish to resemble the rich, and end up by only resembling one another: hangings, ebony, flowers, carpets, and bronzes, everything dark and highly polished—precisely what a certain class of people create so as to make themselves like all other people of this particular class. And his flat was so very like other people's that it made no impression. But he felt it to be very exceptional. When he went to the station to meet his family and brought them back to the brightly lighted flat, and a footman wearing a white necktie opened the door into the flower-bedecked entrance hall, from which they went into the drawing room, then into his study, and when they gasped with delight—when all this happened he was extremely happy, he showed them over the whole place, doted on their praises, and beamed with satisfaction. During tea that evening, when Praskovya Fyodorovna asked him how he had fallen, he laughed and gave an amusing demonstration of how he had slipped, and how he had given the workman a fright.

"It's a good thing I studied gymnastics. Another man would have had a bad fall, but I got off with just a little bump here on my side; it still hurts when I touch it, but it's going away. Nothing but a bruise."

And they began to live in their new place, which, as is always the case when a house gets lived in, lacked but one room to make it perfect; and on their new income, which, as is always true, needed but the least little bit more—five hundred rubles—to make it sufficient for all their needs. But on the whole, everything was fine. Everything was especially fine at the beginning, before the flat was quite complete, when there were still things that had to be bought or ordered or mended or shifted from one place to another. True, little misunderstandings did occasionally crop up, but both husband and wife were so pleased and there was so much to keep them occupied, that these misunderstandings were always straightened out before they developed into real quarrels. When the flat was complete, life became rather dull and something seemed to be missing, but by this time they were making acquaintances and developing habits that kept them busy.

Ivan Ilyich spent his mornings in court and returned home to dinner; at first he was in the best of spirits, although he suffered a little because of the house (every spot on the tablecloth or the upholstery, every loose cord on the hangings, was a cause of irritation to him—after all, he had spent so much effort in arranging things that the least sign of destruction caused him pain). But on the whole the life of Ivan Ilyich became just what, according to his faith, it ought to be: easy, pleasant, and decorous. He got up at nine, had his coffee, read the paper, then put on his official uniform and went to court. There the yoke that was his daily work had been made ready for him and he easily slipped into it. Petitioners, inquiries sent to the office, the office itself, sittings—public and preliminary. One had to be able to delete from these matters all that, being fresh and vital, would impede official business; one must have no relations with people except official ones; the very cause of these relations must be official, and the relations themselves must be purely official. For instance, a man comes in to make inquiries about something. Ivan Ilyich could not possibly have any dealings with such a man outside of his official position, but if this man bears some relation to him as a member of the court (a relation that can be expressed on a sheet of paper bearing an official heading) then within the limits of this relationship Ivan Ilyich will do everything for him, absolutely everything within his power, and will even treat him with respect—that semblance of human, even friendly, relations. But the minute official relations end, all others end likewise. Ivan Ilyich had an extraordinary gift for isolating official relations, keeping them quite separate from real life, and so highly had he developed it, thanks to his talent and experience, that he had reached a stage of virtuosity at which he could allow himself to occasionally mix human and official relations, as if in fun. He could allow himself to do this because he had the strength of will to again isolate the official and discard the human if necessity demanded. Ivan Ilyich did this not only easily, pleasantly, and with decorum; he did it with virtuosity. In between times he smoked, had tea, talked a little about politics, a little about professional matters, a little about cards, and a lot about appointments. At last, tired, but with the satisfaction of a virtuoso who has given a superb performance, in his case on one of the first violins of the orchestra, he would return home. At home his wife and daughter would be either going out for the evening or entertaining; his son would be at school or preparing his lessons with a tutor, diligently studying all that is taught at the gymnasium. Everything was fine. After dinner, if there were no guests, Ivan Ilyich would sometimes read a book that was the talk of the day, then he would sit down to work, examining documents, looking up laws, studying testimony and bringing it in line with the law. He found this neither dull nor entertaining. It was dull if it meant giving up a card game, but if there was no game on, it was better than sitting alone or with his wife. Ivan Ilyich's greatest pleasure was to give little dinner parties to which he invited ladies and gentlemen of good social position, and the manner in which they spent the evening together was as much like the manner in which these people were used to spending their evenings as his drawing room was like their drawing rooms.

Once they even held an evening party with dancing. Ivan Ilyich was in the gayest of spirits and everything went off capitally except that he had a nasty row with his wife over the bonbons and pastries. Praskovya Fyodorovna had made up her mind about the refreshments, but Ivan Ilyich insisted that they be ordered from the most expensive confectioner; he ordered a great many pastries and the quarrel arose because many of them were left over and the bill came to forty-five rubles. How serious and unpleasant the quarrel was may be judged by the fact that Praskovya Fyodorovna called him "a fool" and "spineless" and he clutched his head and made inward utterances about getting a divorce. But the party itself was jolly. All the best people came and Ivan Ilyich danced with Princess Trufonova, sister to the Trufonova who founded the charitable institution called "Take My Yoke Upon Thee." The joy he derived from his official labors lay in the gratification of his ambition; the joy he derived from social life lay in the gratification of his vanity; but the most genuine joy of all was that he derived from playing cards. He confessed that no matter what happened, however great the disappointments he suffered, there was one joy that shone through all like a bright little candle, and that was the joy of sitting down with some good players, with partners who did not shout, to a four-hand game of "vint" (it is too painful in a five-hand game to be the one who has to sit by and watch, even though you pretend not to mind in the least), then to have supper and drink a glass of wine. Ivan Ilyich always went to bed in a particularly good humor after a game of cards, especially if he had won a little something (big winnings made him feel uncomfortable).

And so their life went on. They moved in the best circles, their house was frequented by people of importance and by the young folk.

Husband, wife, and daughter were in complete accord as to who should form their set, and without consulting each other they showed equal skill in shaking off all sorts of undesirable friends and relatives, whom they considered blots on their scutcheon, and who insisted on coming to pay their respects in the drawing room with the Japanese plates on the walls. Soon these undesirable creatures stopped coming, and the Golovins were left with friends from only the best society. Liza was courted by promising young men, and the young examining magistrate Petrishchev, son of Dmitry Ivanovich and sole heir to his estate, courted her with such zeal that Ivan Ilyich spoke of it to Praskovya Fyodorovna and suggested having a sleighing party or getting up some theatricals for them.

That is how they lived. Everything went on without change from day to day, and everything was fine.

IV

All of them were well. Sometimes Ivan Ilyich complained of a strange taste in his mouth and something wrong with his left side, but this could hardly be called an illness.

But the something wrong grew worse, and although it was not yet real pain, it was a feeling of pressure in his side which threw him into a constant stage of depression. The state of depression deepened and began to spoil the pleasure of the easy and decorous life that the Golovin family had recaptured. Husband and wife began to quarrel more often, and soon the ease and pleasure of living disappeared and the decorum was preserved with difficulty. Rows took place more frequently. Once more there were only islands, and those few, on which the husband and wife could find themselves together without an explosion occurring.

And now Praskovya Fyodorovna could say with justice that her husband had a trying disposition. With the exaggeration characteristic of her, she said he had always had such a trying disposition and that only one with her angelic disposition could have stood it for twenty years. It was true that he was now the one who began the arguments. He usually found fault just before sitting down to dinner, or when the soup was being served. Either the dishes were soiled, or the food was bad, or his son put his elbow on the table, or his daughter's hair was not combed properly. And he blamed Praskovya Fyodorovna for everything. At first Praskovya Fyodorovna fought back and said horrid things to him, but on two occasions he was thrown into such a wild fury at the very outset of dinner that she realized it was the sickness brought on by eating that accounted for his bad temper, and so she controlled herself and did not answer him back; she merely tried to get through dinner as quickly as possible. Praskovya Fyodorovna took great credit to herself for exercising such self-control. Having decided that her husband had an impossible disposition and had made her life a misery, she began to pity herself. And the more she pitied herself, the more she hated her husband. She began to hope he would die, but she could not really hope for such a thing because then there would be no income. This set her against him the more. Her sense of injury was heightened by the realization that even his death could not save her. She was irritated by this, and she concealed her irritation, and her suppressed irritation aggravated her irritation.

After a scene in which Ivan Ilyich had been particularly unjust in his accusations, so unjust, in fact, that during the reconciliation he had confessed to being irritable but had said it was due to his illness, she had told him that if he was ill he must take measures to cure his illness, and insisted on his consulting a celebrated physician.

He did. The visit was just what he had expected it to be, just what it always is: the waiting, the physician's important mien (so familiar to him, for it was the same mien he himself assumed on entering the court), the tapping, the listening, the questions requiring answers that were obviously superfluous since they were all known beforehand, the significant look insinuating that all would be well if he just put himself in the doctor's hands, for the doctor unquestionably knew just what had to be done—one and the same approach to every patient, no matter who he was. Everything was just as it was in court. The doctor assumed the same air of importance in dealing with his patients that he himself assumed in dealing with the prosecuted.

The doctor said: this-and-that indicates that this-and-that is wrong with you, but if an analysis of this-and-that does not confirm our diagnosis, we must suspect you of having this-and-that. If we assume you have this-and-that, then . . . and so on. There was only one question Ivan Ilyich wanted answered: was his condition dangerous or not? But the doctor ignored that question as irrelevant. From the doctor's point of view, such a question was unworthy of consideration. One had only to weigh possibilities: floating kidneys, chronic catarrh, or an ailment of the caecum. There was no question of the life of Ivan Ilyich—nothing but a contest between floating kidneys and the caecum. In the presence of Ivan Ilyich the doctor gave a brilliant solution of the problem in favor of the caecum, with the reservation that the analysis of his water might supply new information necessitating a reconsideration of the case. This was exactly what Ivan Ilyich had done a thousand times, and in just as brilliant a manner, in the presence of the prisoner in the dock. And now the doctor made a brilliant résumé, glancing triumphantly, even jovially, over his glasses at the prisoner. From the doctor's résumé Ivan Ilyich concluded that things were bad with him, but that it mattered nothing to the doctor, nor indeed to anyone else. Ivan Ilyich was painfully shocked by this conclusion, which roused in him a strong feeling of self-pity, and an equally strong feeling of self-pity, and an equally strong feeling of resentment against the doctor for being so indifferent to a matter of such vast importance. But he made no protest, he simply got up, put the fee on the writing table, and said with a sigh:

"I suppose you are used to having your patients ask you foolish questions, but, in general, would you call my illness dangerous or not?"

The doctor shot him a severe look over his glasses, as if to say, "If you do not restrict yourself to the questions allowed, prisoner, I shall be compelled to have you put out of court."

"I have already told you all that I considered necessary and proper," said the doctor. "Anything further will be revealed by the analysis." And the doctor bowed him out.

Ivan Ilyich went out slowly, sat down glumly in his sleigh, and rode home. All the way home he kept going over in his mind what the doctor had said, trying to translate all those vague and confusing scientific terms into plain lan-

guage and find in them the answer to his question: "Bad—
very bad, or not yet too bad?" And he fancied that the es-
sence of all the doctor had said was that things were very
bad. Now everything Ivan Ilyich set eyes on looked dismal:
the cab drivers looked dismal, the houses looked dismal,
the passersby, the shops everything looked dismal. His
pain—that dull, aching pain that did not let up for a second—assumed a new and graver significance in the light
of the doctor's obscure remarks. And he concentrated his
attention on it with a new sense of alarm.

He reached home and told his wife what had happened.
She listened, but in the middle of the story his daughter
came in with her hat on. She and her mother were going
out. She forced herself to sit and listen to his dull account
for a while, but not for long, and his wife, too, did not hear
him out.

"Well, I'm very glad," said his wife. "See that you take
your medicine regularly now. Give me your prescription,
I'll send Gerasim to the apothecary's." And she went out to
change her clothes.

He held his breath as long as she was in the room, then
he gave a deep sigh.

"Oh, well," he said, "maybe things aren't really so bad
after all."

He began to take medicine and to follow all the doctor's
instructions, which were changed after the analysis of his
water. But there was some sort of misunderstanding about
the analysis, or about what should have followed from the
analysis; it was impossible to appeal to the celebrity about
such a trifling matter, but somehow things were not turning
out as he had said they should. Either the doctor had forgotten something, or had lied to the patient, or had concealed something from him.

However, Ivan Ilyich followed his instructions explicitly,
and at first the very following of them brought some relief.

After his visit to the doctor Ivan Ilyich's main occupation
became the explicit following of the doctor's instructions
about hygiene and the taking of medicine and the register-

ing of any change in his pain and in the functioning of his organism. Ivan Ilyich's main interest in life became human ailments and human health. Whenever anyone spoke in his presence of someone who was ill or who had died or was recuperating, especially from an illness that resembled his own, he would listen intently, trying to hide his nervousness, would ask questions and make mental comparisons with his own state.

The pain did not subside, but Ivan Ilyich forced himself to think he was feeling better. And he succeeded in deceiving himself as long as everything went well, but as soon as he had a row with his wife, or unpleasantness at the office, or bad luck at cards, he was made acutely conscious of his illness. Formerly he had bravely withstood misfortune, confident that he would overcome it, he had put up resistance, certain that he would be successful, would at last have his "grand slam." Now every mishap knocked the ground out from under his feet and threw him into a state of despair. He said to himself: here I was, just beginning to get better, the medicine was just beginning to take effect, and this accursed mishap or misfortune had to come along. . . . And he fumed against the misfortune, or against the people who were killing him by bringing him misfortune, and he felt that his fuming was killing him, but there was nothing he could do about it. Surely he ought to have realized that the anger he vented on people and circumstances only aggravated his illness, and for that reason he ought not to have paid any attention to chance disturbances. But his reasoning took just the opposite direction: he said that what he needed was peace, and was on his guard against anything that disturbed his peace, and the slightest violation made him furious. He made things worse by reading medical books and consulting doctors. He grew worse so gradually that it was easy for him to deceive himself by comparing one day with the next—the difference was almost imperceptible. But when he sought the advice of doctors he felt that he was not only growing worse, but doing it very rapidly. And in spite of this he kept on consulting doctors.

That very month he visited another celebrated physician. This celebrity said practically the same thing as the first, although he posed the problem a bit differently. The advice of this celebrity only increased Ivan Ilyich's doubts and fears. A friend of a friend of his—an excellent doctor—gave an entirely different diagnosis, and while he promised that Ivan Ilyich would get well, his questions and suppositions only confused him the more and increased his doubts. A homeopath gave still another diagnosis and prescribed another medicine, and for one week Ivan Ilyich took this medicine without letting anyone know. When the week passed without bringing relief, destroying his faith in this as well as other means of treatment, he became more depressed than ever.

Once a woman of his acquaintance told of cures that had been worked by icons. Ivan Ilyich found himself listening attentively and believing in the possibility of such cures. This incident frightened him. "Have I really become such an imbecile?" he asked himself. "Nonsense! What I must do is to stop being so nervous, choose one doctor and keep strictly to the course of treatment he prescribes. That is what I shall do. Enough. I will stop thinking about myself and strictly carry out the doctor's orders until summer, and then we shall see. No more vacillating!"

It was easy to make this decision, but impossible to carry it out. The pain in his side wore him down, it seemed to be getting worse, it gave him no rest, the taste in his mouth became more peculiar, he felt that he had a disgustingly bad breath, he lost his appetite and grew weaker. There was no deceiving himself: something dreadful was happening to Ivan Ilyich, something novel, something of such great moment that nothing of greater moment had ever happened to him. And he alone was aware of this; the people about him either did not understand or did not care to understand, and went on thinking that everything in the world was just as it had always been. It was this that tortured him more than anything else. The people in his house —especially his wife and daughter, who were going through the height of the social season—saw nothing, un-

derstood nothing, and were annoyed with him for being so
downcast and exacting, as if it were his fault. No matter
how hard they tried to hide it, he saw that they looked
upon him as a nuisance, and that his wife had adopted a
certain attitude toward his illness that she clung to despite
anything he said or did. This was her attitude: "You see,"
she said to her friends, "Ivan Ilyich, like all kindhearted
people, is incapable of carrying out doctors' orders to the
letter. Today he takes his drops and eats what he is told;
tomorrow, if I don't keep an eye on him, he forgets to take
his medicine and eats sturgeon (which is forbidden), and
sits up playing cards till one o'clock in the morning."

"When have I ever done such a thing?" Ivan Ilyich once
asked her in vexation. "Only once, at Pyotr Ivanovich's."

"And last night with Shebek."

"That doesn't count; I couldn't sleep for the pain."

"It doesn't matter, if you keep that up you'll never get
well and just go on torturing us."

Judging by what Praskovya Fyodorovna said to her
friends and to Ivan Ilyich himself, her attitude toward her
husband's illness was that he himself was responsible for
it, and that the whole thing was just another means of causing her trouble. Ivan Ilyich felt that this attitude was not
intentional, but that did not make it any the easier for him.

At work, too, Ivan Ilyich noticed, or at least thought he
noticed, a strange attitude toward him: at times he felt that
his colleagues were stealing glances at him as at one who
was about to vacate a post; at other times his friends would
chaff him amiably about his fancied illness, as if that fearful, that horrible, that unheard-of something that was growing inside of him and gnawing at his vitals night and day,
irresistibly dragging him off somewhere, was a highly ap-
propriate subject for a joke. He became especially irritated
with Schwartz, whose liveliness, playfulness, and quality of
being always *comme il faut* reminded Ivan Ilyich of himself
ten years earlier.

His friends came to play cards with him. They sat down
at the table, shuffled and dealt the new cards, he arranged
his hand, putting all the diamonds together—seven in all.

His partner said, "No trumps," and put down two diamonds. What else could he wish for? He ought to have felt delighted—a "grand slam."

But suddenly Ivan Ilyich is aware of that gnawing pain and that taste in his mouth, and he feels it is madness under the circumstances to take pleasure in a "grand slam." He sees how his partner, Mikhail Mikhailovich, strikes the table with a meaty hand and indulgently refuses to pick up his tricks, pushing them toward Ivan Ilyich, so that he may have the pleasure of taking them in without exerting himself by stretching out his hand very far. "Does he suppose I am too weak to stretch out my hand?" thinks Ivan Ilyich, forgetting what is trump and trumping his partner's card, thereby missing a "grand slam" by three. The worst of all is that he can see how upset Mikhail Mikhailovich is, and yet he does not care. And it is dreadful to think why he does not care.

Everyone can see how bad he feels, and they say to him, "We can stop if you're tired. Take a little rest." Rest? Why, he is not tired in the least, he will finish the rubber. They are all glum and silent. Ivan Ilyich knows that he is responsible for the gloom but is unable to disperse it. They have supper and the guests go home, leaving Ivan Ilyich alone with the knowledge that his life is poisoned and that he is poisoning the lives of others, and that instead of growing weaker, the poison is penetrating deeper and deeper into his being.

And it is with this knowledge, and the physical pain, and the sense of horror as well, that he must lie in bed, often kept awake by pain the greater part of the night. And in the morning he must get up again, dress himself, go to court, talk, and write, and if he did not go to court he would have to spend the same twenty-four hours at home, every one of them a torture. And he has to go on living like this, on the brink of doom, all by himself, without a single person to understand and pity him.

V

One month, then another went by this way. Just before
the new year his brother-in-law came to pay them a visit.
Ivan Ilyich was at court when he arrived. Praskovya Fyodorovna was out shopping. On coming home Ivan Ilyich
found his brother-in-law, a hale and hearty man, in his
study unpacking his bag. He raised his head on hearing
Ivan Ilyich's step and stared at him a moment in silence.
This stare revealed everything to Ivan Ilyich. His brother-in-
law opened his mouth to gasp, but checked himself. And
this confirmed everything.

"Why, have I changed?"

"Y-yes, you have."

After that, try as he might, Ivan Ilyich could not get his
brother-in-law to make a single comment on his appearance. Ivan Ilyich locked the door and examined himself in
the looking glass, first in profile, then full-face. He picked
up a photograph he had had taken with his wife and compared it with what he saw in the looking glass. The difference was terrible. He bared his arm to the elbow and examined it, then he pulled down his sleeve, sank down on an
ottoman, and gave himself up to thoughts blacker than
night.

"I mustn't, I mustn't," he said to himself. He jumped up,
went to his writing table, opened his notes on a case, and
tried to read, but could not. He opened the door and went
into the reception room. The door into the drawing room
was ajar. He tiptoed over to it and listened.

"Oh, you're exaggerating," said Praskovya Fyodorovna.

"Exaggerating? Can't you see for yourself? He's like a
dead man. Look at his eyes. No life in them. What's the
matter with him?"

"Nobody knows. Nikolayev" (another doctor) "said
something, but I can't tell. . . . Leshchetitsky" (the celebrated doctor) "said just the opposite."

Ivan Ilyich walked away, went to his own room, lay down
and fell to thinking: "Kidneys. A floating kidney." He re-

called all that the doctors had told him, how the kidney had come loose and how it was floating about. And in his imagination he caught the kidney and fixed it in place. It was so easy, it seemed. "Yes, I must go and see Pyotr Ivanovich" (the friend who had a doctor friend). He rang, ordered the carriage, and made ready to go and see him.

"Where are you going, *Jean?*" asked his wife in a particularly mournful and unusually kindly tone.

The unusual kindliness of her tone annoyed him. He gave her a black look.

"I've got to go and see Pyotr Ivanovich."

He went to his friend's who had the doctor friend, and together they went to see the doctor. The doctor was at home and he had a long talk with him.

Everything became clear to Ivan Ilyich as soon as he found out all about the anatomical and physiological changes that, according to the doctor, were taking place inside of him.

There was something, the smallest of somethings, in the caecum. It could be remedied. The functioning of one organ had to be strengthened, of another had to be weakened, the something had to be absorbed, and everything would be all right.

Ivan Ilyich was a little late for dinner. After dinner he sat talking cheerfully for some time and could not make himself go and work in his study. At last he went to his study and sat down to work. He read through some cases, concentrated on his work, but in the back of his mind he was constantly aware of some pressing and private matter that he had put off, but which he would attend to as soon as he was through. When he finished he remembered what the private matter was: ruminations on his caecum. But he did not give himself up to them; instead he went into the drawing room for tea. There were guests who were talking and playing the piano and singing. Among them was the examining magistrate, a desirable fiancé for his daughter. Praskovya Fyodorovna observed that Ivan Ilyich was the gayest of the party, but not for a minute did he forget that he had put off important ruminations on his caecum. At

eleven o'clock he took leave of everyone and retired to
his room. Ever since his illness he had been sleeping alone
in a little room adjoining his study. He went in, undressed,
and took up a novel by Zola, but instead of reading he
gave himself up to his thoughts. He fancied that the longed-
for cure of his caecum had been effected. Absorption, ejec-
tion, and a restoration of normal functioning. "Of course,"
he said to himself, "all we must do is assist nature." This
reminded him of his medicine; he raised himself, took it, and
lay on his back, feeling what a beneficial effect the medicine had, how it eased his pain. "Only I must take it regularly and avoid all bad influences. I feel better already,
ever so much better." He poked his side. It was not painful
to the touch. "I don't feel anything at all, I am really much
better." He put out the candle and lay on his side. His
caecum was improving, was absorbing. Suddenly he felt the
old familiar gnawing pain—quiet, serious, insistent. And the
same bad taste in his mouth. His heart sank, he felt dizzy.
"My God, my God!" he muttered. "Again, again, and it
will never stop." And suddenly he saw things in an entirely
different light. "The caecum. Kidneys," he said to himself.
"It isn't a matter of caecum and kidneys, it is a matter of
life . . . and death. Yes, once there was life, and now
it is passing away, passing away, and there is nothing I can
do to stop it. Why should I deceive myself? Is it not clear to
everyone except me that I am dying, that it is merely a
question of weeks, days, even hours? There was light, now
there is darkness. I was here, I am going there. Where?"
He broke out in a cold sweat and he had difficulty in
breathing. He could hear nothing but the beating of his
heart.

"I will no longer exist. What will exist? Nothing. Where
will I be when I cease to exist? Is this really death? Oh, I
don't want to die!" He jumped up to light the candle, he
felt for it with trembling hands, he dropped the candle
and candlestick on the floor, and fell back on the pillow
again. "What does it matter? It's all the same," he said to
himself as he stared into the darkness with wide-open eyes.
"Death. Yes, death. And they don't know it and don't want

to know it, and have no pity. They are playing." (He heard the distant trilling of a woman's voice and the piano accompaniment coming through the closed door.) "It's all the same to them now, but soon they will die too. The fools. I shall go first, then they; it will come to them, too. Now they are rejoicing, the beasts." His resentment fairly choked him. He was horribly, unspeakably miserable. It was inconceivable that everyone, always, should be doomed to this horror. He raised himself.

"Something is wrong; I must calm myself and think it through from the beginning." And he began to think. "The beginning of my illness. I struck my side, but I was just the same then, and the following day; it only ached a little, but then it got worse, and then I started going to see doctors, and then I felt downcast, depressed, and then more doctors; and all the while I was moving closer and closer to the edge of the precipice. My strength gave out. Closer and closer. And here I am a wreck, no life in my eyes. Death. And I still think about my caecum. I think of mending my intestines, and all the time it is death. But is it, really?" And again he was seized by terror; he gasped, bent down, felt for the matches, and knocked his elbow against the bedside table. It was in the way and it hurt him and he became angry with it and struck it a second time harder and knocked it over. In desperation, gasping for breath, he fell on his back and waited for death to come that very moment.

The guests were going home. Praskovya Fyodorovna, who was seeing them off, heard the table fall and came into the room.

"What's the matter?"

"Nothing. I accidentally knocked it over."

She went out and came back with a candle. He lay there with his eyes fixed on her, breathing loudly and quickly, like a man who has had a long run.

"What is it, *Jean?*"

"N-nothing. I knocked it . . . over." ("Why should I tell her? She won't understand," he thought.)

And she did not understand. She picked up the table,

lighted the candle, and hurried away. She had to see her guests off.

When she came back he was still lying on his back staring at the ceiling.

"What is it, are you worse?"

"Yes."

She shook her head and sat down.

"I'm wondering, *Jean*, if we shouldn't send for Leshchetitsky?"

Sending for the celebrity meant spending a lot of money again. He gave a sardonic smile and said no. She sat down for a little while, then went over to him and kissed him on the forehead.

He hated her with his whole heart when she kissed him, and it cost him a great effort to keep from pushing her away.

"Good night. God willing, you'll fall asleep."

"Yes."

Ivan's 3rd mo. VI illness

Ivan Ilyich saw that he was dying, and he was in a constant state of despair. In his heart of hearts he knew he was dying, and it was not simply that he could not get used to the idea; he could not grasp it, could not possibly grasp it.

All his life he had regarded the syllogism he had learned while studying Kiesewetter's *Logics:* "Caius is a man, men are mortal, and therefore Caius is mortal," as being true only in respect to Caius, not to himself. Caius was a man, a man in the abstract sense, and so the syllogism applied to him; but Ivan Ilyich was not Caius, and not a man in the abstract sense; he had always been quite, quite different from all other men. He had been little Vanya to his mama and papa, to his brothers Mitya and Volodya, to the coachman and the nursemaid and to his toys, and to Katya; Vanya, who had lived through all the joys and sorrows and ecstasies of childhood, boyhood, and youth. Had Caius ever known the leathery smell of a football that Vanya had loved so dearly? Had Caius ever kissed his mother's hand

with such feeling, or so loved the rustle of her silk skirts?
Had Caius ever made a row over the buns at school? Or
ever been so in love? Or presided so brilliantly over a court
session?

Caius was indeed mortal, and it was only right and proper that he should die, but he, Vanya, Ivan Ilyich, with all
his thoughts and feelings—it was quite a different matter
with him. And it could not be right and proper that he
should die. The thought was too horrifying.

That was what he felt.

"If I were doomed to die like Caius I would have known
of it, some inner voice would have told me. But I have never
been aware of anything of the sort; I have always known,
and so have all of my friends, that I was not of the same
stuff as Caius. And now, lo and behold!" he said to himself.
"But it cannot be. It cannot be. It cannot be, and yet it is.
How is it possible? How is one to understand it?"

He could not understand it and tried to drive the thought
away as being false, misleading, and unwholesome, and
he tried to evoke true, wholesome thoughts to take its place.
But the thought was more than a thought, it was reality itself, and it kept coming back and confronting him.

One by one he summoned up other thoughts to take its
place in the hope of finding support in them. He tried to
recover a former way of thinking that had protected him
from thoughts of death. But, strange as it may seem, the
things that had once screened, hidden, obliterated the consciousness of death, were now unable to do so. Ivan Ilyich
had spent most of his time of late trying to recover a former
way of thinking that had screened death from him. He
would, for instance, say to himself, "I must lose myself in
work; after all, that was once my whole life." And he would
go to court, driving all his doubts out of his mind. He would
enter into conversation with his friends, and take his seat
among them as he always had, casting a vague and pon-
derous glance over the people gathered in the courtroom
as he sat down, grasping the arms of his oaken chair with
his thin hands, bending toward his neighbor, shifting the
papers about, whispering, then suddenly straightening up

and raising his eyes to pronounce the well-known words with which proceedings were opened. But in the very middle of a court sitting that pain in his side, irrespective of the stage proceedings had reached, would begin its gnawing proceedings. Ivan Ilyich would pay it brief attention, then try to drive it out of his mind, but it went right on with its work, and came and stood facing him, staring him straight in the eye, and he was confounded, and the light went out of his eyes, and once more he asked himself, "Is *It* the only truth?" And his colleagues and subordinates saw with surprise and grief that he, who had always been such a brilliant and subtle judge, was getting muddled and making mistakes. He would give a toss of his head and try to pull himself together and somehow carry proceedings through to the end, and return home, sadly aware that legal proceedings could no longer hide from him that which he wished to hide; that no legal proceedings could enable him to escape from *It*. And the worst thing of all was that *It* demanded all his attention without asking him to do anything but just stare at *It*, stare it straight in the eye, doing nothing but suffer unspeakable torment.

To escape this horrible state of mind Ivan Ilyich sought other comforts, other screens, and he found other screens, and for a while they seemed to bring relief, but very soon they collapsed, or rather grew transparent, as if *It* had the power of penetrating all things and nothing in the world could shut it out.

Sometimes in those latter days he would go into the drawing room, that he had taken such pains to furnish, into the very drawing room where he had fallen, and for which, as he would think with a bitter smile, he had sacrificed his life, for he was certain that his illness had begun with his fall. He went into that drawing room and saw a deep scratch on his polished table. He looked for the cause of the damage and discovered it in the twisted clasp of an album with bronze trimmings. He picked up the album, a costly one that he himself had filled with loving care, and grew indignant at the carelessness of his daughter and her friends: here the clasp was twisted, inside the photographs were upside down. He painstakingly put the pictures in order and straightened the clasp.

Then he had the idea of transferring the whole *établissement* with the album on it to another corner of the room, where the plants were. He called the footman. His wife came to help him, they disagreed, she objected to the change, he argued and grew angry. But that was all very well, because it helped him to forget about *It*; *It* was pushed out of sight.

But when he began to move the table himself his wife said, "Don't. Let the servants do it, you'll hurt yourself again," and suddenly *It* stepped out from behind the screen. *It* flashed across his sight. He hoped *It* would disappear again, but he involuntarily became conscious of the pain in his side—the something was still there, was still gnawing, and he could not forget *It* and *It* was staring at him very clearly from behind the plants. And so what was the use of all this fuss?

"Can it be true that here, on these hangings, as at the storming of a bastion, I lost my life? Not really! How ghastly! How absurd! It cannot be. It cannot be . . . but it is."

He went into his study, lay down, and once more found himself alone with *It*. Face to face with *It*, and there was nothing he could do about it. Nothing but contemplate *It* and feel his blood running cold.

VII   Day + Nite

It is hard to say how it came about that, in the third month of Ivan Ilyich's illness, his wife, his daughter, his son, the servants, his friends, the doctors, and especially he himself knew that the only interest he held for others any more lay in how soon he would leave his post vacant, free the living from the constraint of his presence, and himself from his sufferings. It is hard to say because it came about slowly, imperceptibly, step by step.

He slept less and less. They gave him doses of opium and began morphine injections. But this brought no relief. At first the dull misery of his half-conscious state was a relief in the sense that it was something novel, but soon it became just as great, if not greater suffering than the unalleviated pain.

Special foods were prepared for him according to the doctor's instructions, but he found all of them more and more unpalatable, more and more revolting.

And special arrangements were made for his bowel movements. This was a daily torture—a torture because of the uncleanliness, the unseemliness, and the stench, and because another person had to assist at the operation. But this disagreeable business brought Ivan Ilyich one comfort: Gerasim, the pantry boy, always came to carry out the chamberpot.

Gerasim was a fresh, clean peasant lad who was flourishing on town food. He was always bright and cheerful. At first it embarrassed Ivan Ilyich to see this clean lad in his Russian clothes performing such a disgusting task. Once, on getting up off the pot, he collapsed into an armchair, too weak to draw on his trousers, and lay back staring in horror at his naked calves with the flaccid muscles hanging upon them.

At that moment Gerasim came in with his light, vigorous stride, emanating an odor of fresh wintry air and the tar his stout boots were rubbed with. He was wearing a clean homespun apron and a clean cotton shirt with the sleeves rolled up, baring his strong young arms. Without looking at Ivan Ilyich (afraid, perhaps, to taunt him with the joy of life radiating from his own face) he went over to the pot.

"Gerasim," said Ivan Ilyich feebly.

Gerasim gave a little start, fearing he had done something amiss, and with a quick movement turned his fresh, simple, good-natured young face, which was showing the first signs of a beard, to the sick man.

"What is it, sir?"

"You must find this very disagreeable. Forgive me. I can't do it myself."

"What are you saying, sir!" and Gerasim's eyes and

teeth flashed in a smile. "Why shouldn't I help you? You're sick."

And with strong able hands he did his usual task, walking out of the room with a light step. Five minutes later he came back with just as light a step.

Ivan Ilyich was still lying in the armchair.

"Gerasim," he said when the lad had put down the clean pot. "Please help me, come here." Gerasim went up to him. "Lift me up. I can't get up myself and I've sent Dmitry out."

Gerasim bent down. With strong hands and a touch that was as light as his step, he picked him up gently, deftly, and held him with one hand while he pulled up his trousers with the other. He was about to put him in the chair again, when Ivan Ilyich asked him to help him to the sofa.

"Thank you. How capable you are . . . how well you do everything."

Gerasim smiled again and was about to go out, but Ivan Ilyich was so glad to have him near that he did not let him go.

"Here, bring over that chair if you don't mind. No, that one, to put under my feet. I feel better when my feet are up."

Gerasim carried over the chair, dropped it with one swift movement almost to the floor, then checked the movement and set it down noiselessly and put Ivan Ilyich's feet up on it. It seemed to Ivan Ilyich that he felt better when Gerasim lifted his feet up.

"I feel better with my feet up," said Ivan Ilyich. "Bring the pillow and pull it under them."

Gerasim did what he was asked. He lifted up the sick man's feet again and put the pillow under them. Again Ivan Ilyich felt better while Gerasim held his feet up. When he let them down he felt worse.

"Gerasim," he said, "are you busy at present?"

"No indeed, sir," said Gerasim, who had learnt from the townsfolk how to address his betters.

"What else have you to do?"

"Why, nothing else. I've done everything except chop some wood for tomorrow."

"Could you hold my feet up high like that for a little while?"

"Indeed I could, sir." Gerasim held his feet up high and Ivan Ilyich fancied that he felt no pain at all in that position.

"And what about the wood?"

"Don't trouble yourself about that, sir. I'll have time for that."

Ivan Ilyich had Gerasim sit down and hold his feet and talk to him. And strange as it may seem, he fancied he really did feel better while Gerasim was holding his feet.

After that Ivan Ilyich would send for Gerasim from time to time and have him put his feet up on his shoulders, and he loved to talk to the lad. Gerasim did everything willingly, easily, simply, and with such good humor that Ivan Ilyich was touched. The health, strength, and cheerfulness of everyone but Gerasim irritated Ivan Ilyich. Gerasim's health and cheerfulness, on the contrary, soothed rather than irritated him.

Ivan Ilyich suffered most of all from the lie—the lie adopted by everyone for some reason, which said that he was only ill and not dying, and that everything would be all right if he just kept quiet and did what the doctors told him to. He knew perfectly well that no matter what was done, nothing would change except that his sufferings would increase and he would die. He was tortured by this lie, tortured by no one's wanting to acknowledge the lie, by his knowing the truth and everyone else's knowing the truth, and yet pressing this lie upon him because of the horror of his position, forcing him to become a party to the lie. This lie, the lie forced upon him on the eve of his death, the lie degrading the solemn, awesome act of his dying to the level of their social calls, portieres, and oysters for supper, was an unspeakable torture to Ivan Ilyich. And, strangely enough, time and again when they went through the forms with him, he came within a hair's breadth of shouting out, "Stop your lying! You know and I know that I am about to die. You might at least stop lying!" But he never had the courage to do it. He could see that the dread, the fearsome act of his dying had been degraded by those about him to the level of a chance unpleasantness, a sort of breach of etiquette (they behaved toward him as they might to a man who gave off a foul odor on entering a drawing room), a violation of that "decorum" to which he had been a bondslave all his life. He saw that no one felt sorry for him because no one cared to understand his position. The only person who understood and who felt sorry for him was Gerasim. And for that reason the only person Ivan Ilyich cared to be with was Gerasim. He was quite content when Gerasim sat with him sometimes the whole night through, holding his feet and refusing to go to bed, saying, "Don't trouble yourself about that, Ivan Ilyich; I'll sleep later"; or when he would say to him, "Why should I not serve you, now that you are ill?" Gerasim was the only one who did not lie; everything he did showed that he was the only one who understood the true state of affairs and saw no need of hiding it. He simply felt sorry for his poor wasting master. Once when Ivan Ilyich sent him away he said to him quite frankly, "We'll all die some day. Why should I not help you now?" And in saying this he said that he did not find waiting on Ivan Ilyich irksome because he was doing it for a dying man, and he hoped that someone would do the same for him when his time came.

Next to the lie and all it entailed, the most painful thing for Ivan Ilyich was that no one felt sorry for him as he would have liked them to. There were moments when, after long suffering, the thing he most wanted, even though he was ashamed to admit it, was to be fondled pityingly, like a sick child. He wanted to be petted, kissed, cried over, as sick children are kissed and comforted. He knew that he was an important member of the law court and that his beard was turning gray and that therefore such a thing was impossible. But that was what he wanted. There was something approaching this in his relations with Gerasim, and that was why he found comfort in Gerasim. Ivan Ilyich wanted to cry, wanted to be petted and wept over, but here comes Shebek to see him, his colleague Shebek, also a member of the law court, and instead of crying and seeking comfort, Ivan Ilyich puts on a grave, profound look and, from sheer inertia, gives his opinion of the importance of the decisions of the Court of Appeal and stubbornly defends it.

Nothing did so much to poison the last days of Ivan Ilyich as this lie within him and all around him.

a day   VIII

Morning had come. The only evidence that morning had come was that Gerasim went out and Pyotr, the footman, came in, put out the candles, drew back the hangings over one of the windows, and began to tidy up the room quietly. Morning or night, Friday or Sunday, made no difference, it was all the same—the same gnawing, racking pain that did not let up for a moment; the same consciousness that life was irrevocably passing away but was not yet gone and that abhorrent death, the only reality, was slowly and implacably creeping up on him; and then—the lie. What thought could there be of days, weeks, hours?

"Will you have tea, sir?"

("The man must have order: in the morning the family takes tea," thought Ivan Ilyich.)

"No," he said.

"Perhaps you would like to shift to the sofa, sir?"

("He must tidy up the room and I am in the way, I am messing up the room, creating disorder," thought Ivan Ilyich.)

"No. Leave me alone," he said.

The footman busied himself a little longer. Ivan Ilyich held out his hand. Pyotr came over solicitously.

"What is it, sir?"

"My watch."

Pyotr picked up the watch that was lying within Ivan Ilyich's reach and handed it to him.

"Half past eight. Are the others up?"

"Not yet, sir. Vasily Ivanovich" (the son) "has gone to school and Praskovya Fyodorovna left orders to call her if you asked for her. Shall I call her, sir?"

"Don't bother." ("Perhaps I should have some tea?" he

thought.) "Bring me some tea."

Pyotr made for the door. Ivan Ilyich was frightened by the prospect of being left alone. ("What can I do to keep him? Ah, yes; my medicine.")

"Pyotr, give me my medicine." ("Why not? It really might help.") He took a spoonful. ("No, it cannot help. Nonsense. Self-deception," he decided as soon as he again became conscious of that familiar sweetish, hopeless taste in his mouth. "I don't believe in it any more. But why, oh why must I suffer this pain? If it would only let up for a minute!") He gave a groan. Pyotr came back.

"No, go. Bring me some tea."

Pyotr went out. Left alone, Ivan Ilyich moaned less from pain, however agonizing it was, than from misery. "The same thing on and on, the same endless days and nights. If only it would come quickly! If only *what* would come quickly? Death, darkness. No, no! Anything is better than death!"

When Pyotr came back with the breakfast tray Ivan Ilyich looked at him in perplexity for some time, unable to comprehend who he was and what he wanted. Pyotr was disconcerted by this look. His disconcertment brought Ivan Ilyich to his senses.

"Oh, yes," said he. "Tea. Good. Put it down. Only help me wash myself, and give me a clean shirt."

And Ivan Ilyich began to wash himself. Resting now and again, he washed his hands and face, brushed his teeth, combed his hair, and looked at himself in the mirror. He was horrified, especially horrified to see how his limp hair clung to his pale forehead. When his shirt was being changed he knew he would be even more horrified if he looked at his body, and so he did not look at it. At last everything was done. He put on a dressing gown, threw a rug over his legs, and sat down in an armchair to have his tea. For a single moment he had felt refreshed, but as soon as he began to drink tea he again became conscious of his pain and the taste in his mouth. He forced himself to drink it and then lay down, stretching out his legs. He lay down and told Pyotr to go away.

The same thing all over again. One moment the glimmer of a drop of hope, the next a raging sea of despair, and always this pain, this pain, this misery, on and on. The misery is unbearable when he is alone, he wishes to call someone, but he knows beforehand that it will only be worse. "If they'd only give me morphine again, so that I could forget. I must tell the doctor to think of something. This is impossible, impossible."

One hour, another hour passed in this way. The bell in the entrance hall rang. Perhaps the doctor. Yes, it was the doctor—fresh, fat, energetic, cheerful, wearing an expression that said, "Come, now; something has frightened you, but we'll have it all straight in a trice." The doctor knew that this expression was inappropriate here, but he had put it on once and for all and could no more change it than he could change the frock coat he had donned in the morning before he had set out on his round of calls.

The doctor rubbed his hands together vigorously, comfortingly.

"I'm chilled. Dreadfully cold out. Wait a minute until I warm up," he said in a tone suggesting that it was necessary only to wait a minute until he warmed up and then he would put everything right.

"Well, how are you feeling?"

Ivan Ilyich was sure the doctor would have liked to say, "How's our tummy?" but felt it would be a little too waggish and changed it to "How did you spend the night?"

Ivan Ilyich looked at the doctor in a way that said, "Will you never feel ashamed of lying?" But the doctor did not wish to understand.

"In the same ghastly way," said Ivan Ilyich. "The pain never stops and never lessens. If only you would give me something!"

"Come, come, all you patients are the same. Well, now, I seem to have warmed up. Even Praskovya Fyodorovna, strict as she is, could not find fault with my temperature now. Well, good morning," and the doctor shook hands with him.

Throwing off all his playfulness, the doctor put on a serious face and began examining his patient, taking his pulse, his temperature, sounding his chest, listening to his heart.

Ivan Ilyich knew very definitely and without question that this was all nonsense, empty deception, but when the doctor got down on his knees in front of him and leaned over, placing his ear now lower, now higher, and went through all sorts of contortions with the gravest mien in the world, Ivan Ilyich fell under his spell, just as he had fallen under the spell of lawyers' speeches, even though he knew very well they were lying and even knew why they were lying.

The doctor was still on his knees on the sofa tapping his chest when a rustle of silk came from the doorway and Praskovya Fyodorovna was heard remonstrating with Pyotr for not having told her of the doctor's arrival.

She came in and kissed her husband and instantly began to explain that she had been up for a long time and it was just because of some misunderstanding that she had not been in the sick man's room when the doctor arrived.

Ivan Ilyich looked at her, he took in every detail of her person, and he resented her whiteness, her plumpness, the cleanliness of her arms and neck, the luster of her hair and the shine of her eyes, so full of life. He hated her with every fiber of his being. Every time she touched him he felt an upsurge of hatred.

Her attitude toward him and his illness had not changed. Just as the doctor had developed an attitude toward his patients that he could not change, so she had developed an attitude toward him—that he was doing what he ought not to do and so he himself was to blame for his condition and her only recourse was to reprove him lovingly for it—and she could not change this attitude.

"He simply will not listen! He does not take his medicine regularly. And the worst thing is that he insists on lying in a position that surely must be bad for him—with his feet up in the air."

And she told how he made Gerasim hold up his feet.

The doctor gave a fond, condescending smile: "What is to be done about it? These patients of ours are always thinking of absurd tricks, but we have to forgive them."

When he had finished his examination the doctor glanced at his watch, and then Praskovya Fyodorovna announced to Ivan Ilyich that he could like it or not, but she had asked a great celebrity to come and see him today and he and Mikhail Danilovich (that was the name of the ordinary doctor) would examine him together and hold a consultation.

"No protesting, if you please. I am doing this for my own sake," she said ironically, letting him know that she was doing it for his sake and had just said this to deprive him of the right to protest. He frowned and said nothing. He was aware that he was caught in such a web of lies that it was impossible to distinguish the true from the false. Everything she did for him was done entirely for her own sake, and she told him she was doing for her own sake what she actually was doing for her own sake, representing it as something so incredible that he would take it as meaning just the opposite.

True enough, at half past eleven the celebrated doctor arrived. Again there were soundings and weighty talk in his presence and in the other room about kidneys and caecums, and questions and answers uttered with as grave a mien as if instead of the real question of life and death, which was the only one confronting Ivan Ilyich now, there had arisen a question of kidneys and caecums that were not behaving themselves and were therefore being taken in hand by Mikhail Danilovich and the celebrity and made to toe the line.

The celebrated doctor took leave of him with a grave but not hopeless look. And when Ivan Ilyich raised eyes glistening with fear and hope and timidly asked him whether there was any chance of recovery, he replied that he could not say for sure, but there was a chance. So touching was the gleam of hope in Ivan Ilyich's eyes as they followed the doctor to the door that Praskovya Fyodorovna broke down as she went out of the study to give the celebrity his fee.

The doctor's encouragement caused his spirits to rise, but not for long. Again the same room, the same pictures, hangings, wallpaper, bric-a-brac, and the same aching, suffering body. Ivan Ilyich began to groan. They gave him an injection and he fell into a state of oblivion.

When he roused it was twilight. They brought him his dinner. He forced himself to take some broth. Again everything the same; again the coming of night.

After dinner, at seven o'clock, Praskovya Fyodorovna came into the room in evening dress, with her full bosom laced up and traces of powder on her face. In the morning she had reminded him that they were going to the theater. Sarah Bernhardt had come to town and they had taken a box at his own insistence. He had forgotten all about it and was hurt by the sight of her elaborate toilette. But he hid his feelings on remembering that he himself had insisted on their taking the box because he felt that the aesthetic enjoyment would have educational value for the children.

Praskovya Fyodorovna came in looking pleased with herself, yet with a slightly guilty air. She sat down and asked how he was feeling, merely, as he could see, for the sake of asking and not because she wanted to find out anything, for there was nothing to find out, and then she said what it was needful to say: that she would not think of going if it were not that the box was taken and that Ellen and their daughter and Petrishchev (the examining magistrate who was their daughter's fiancé) were going and she could not let them go unchaperoned, but that she would much prefer sitting at home with him, and would he please be sure to do everything the doctor had told him to while she was away.

"And Fyodor Petrovich" (the fiancé) "wants to see you. May he come in? And Liza, too."

"Let them."

His daughter came in all dressed up, with much of her young body naked, making a show of it, while his body was causing him such torture. She was strong and healthy, evidently very much in love, and annoyed that his illness and suffering and death should cast a shadow upon her happiness.

Fyodor Petrovich came in wearing evening clothes and with his hair curled *à la Capoul*, his long, sinewy neck encircled by a stiff white collar, his chest covered by an expanse of white shirtfront, his strong calves sheathed in narrow black trousers, one hand encased in a white glove, the other holding an opera hat.

Behind him Ivan Ilyich's son, the schoolboy, slipped in unnoticed, all decked out in a new uniform, poor chap, and with gloves on his hands and those dreadful dark circles under his eyes that Ivan Ilyich knew the meaning of.

He had always felt sorry for his son. And now there was something dreadful for him in the boy's frightened, pitying glance. Ivan Ilyich felt that Vasya was the only one besides Gerasim who understood and pitied him.

They all sat down and asked him again how he felt. A pause. Liza asked her mother about the opera glasses. This brought on a little tiff between mother and daughter as to which of them had mislaid them. Very unpleasant.

Fyodor Petrovich asked Ivan Ilyich if he had ever seen Sarah Bernhardt. At first Ivan Ilyich did not understand the question, then he said:

"No. Have you?"

"Yes. In *Adrienne Lecouvreur*."

Praskovya Fyodorovna said that she was particularly enchanting in something-or-other. The daughter objected. There began a discussion of the charm and naturalness of her acting, in which they said the same things that are always said on the subject.

In the middle of the conversation Fyodor Petrovich glanced at Ivan Ilyich and stopped talking. The others also glanced at him and stopped talking. Ivan Ilyich was staring in front of him with glittering eyes, unable to hide his resentment. Something had to be done, but nothing could be done. The silence had to be broken, but nobody dared to break it. They all began to fear that something might expose the lie that was being supported for decency's sake, and things would suddenly be seen in their true light. Liza was the first to pluck up courage. She broke the silence. She did it with the intention of hiding what everyone was feeling, but instead she gave it utterance.

"Well, *if we are going,* we must go," she said, glancing at her watch, which had been a present from her father, and smiling significantly but scarcely perceptibly at her young man about something that only they two were aware of. Then she got up with a rustle of silk.

They all got up, said good-bye, and went away.

Ivan Ilyich fancied he felt better when they were gone: at least the lie was gone, too—it had departed with them. But the pain remained. The same old pain, the same old fear that made nothing harder, nothing easier. And it kept growing worse.

Again the time dragged on, minute by minute, hour by hour, just the same, without end, yet with the horror of the certain end growing upon him.

"Yes, send up Gerasim," he said in reply to Pyotr's question.

IX

It was late when his wife returned. She tiptoed into the room but he heard her. He opened his eyes and quickly closed them again. She wanted to send Gerasim out and sit beside him herself, but he opened his eyes and said:

"No, go away."

"Are you suffering very much?"

"It doesn't matter."

"Take some opium."

He consented and drank it. She went out.

Until three in the morning he was in a semiconscious state of torture. He fancied they were torturing him by trying to push him into a narrow black sack, and that they kept pushing him in deeper and deeper but could not push him to the bottom. And this dreadful business was causing him suffering. He was afraid, yet he wanted to get into the sack, and he simultaneously resisted and tried to get in. Suddenly he broke loose and fell and woke up. Gerasim was still sitting on the foot of the bed, drowsing quietly, patiently. And Ivan Ilyich was lying with his emaciated stockinged feet on the lad's shoulders. The candle was still burning behind the shade, and the pain was still with him.

"Go to bed, Gerasim," he whispered.

"That's all right, sir. I shall stay a while."

"No, go away."

He lowered his legs and turned over on his side with his hand under his cheek and began to pity himself. He waited until Gerasim had gone into the next room, and then, letting himself go, cried like a baby. He cried because of his helplessness, because of his dreadful loneliness, because of the heartlessness of people and of God, and because of the absence of God.

"Why hast Thou done all this? Why didst Thou bring me into the world? What, oh what have I done that Thou shouldst torture me so?"

He did not expect an answer, and he cried because there was not and could not be any answer. The pain began again, but he did not stir, did not call anyone. He merely said to himself, "Very well, hit me again. Harder! But what for? What have I ever done to Thee?"

Then he grew quiet and not only stopped crying, but stopped breathing as well and was all attention: he seemed to be listening not to the speaking voice, but to the voice of his soul, to the stream of thought flowing through him.

"What do you want?" was the first concept sufficiently lucid to be expressed in words. "What do you want? What do you want?" he repeated to himself. "Not to suffer. To live," he replied.

And once more he was all attention, such strained attention that even his pain could not distract him.

"Live? Live how?" asked the voice of his soul.

"Live as I lived before; a good, pleasant life."

"And was your life so good and pleasant before?" asked the voice. And he began to go over in his mind the best moments of his pleasant life. But, strange as it may seem, all the best moments of his pleasant life no longer seemed to be what he had considered them. All, except the earliest memories of his childhood. In his childhood there had been something really pleasant, something worth living for, if it could have been brought back again. But the person who had experienced this pleasantness was no more. He seemed to be calling up memories of someone else.

As soon as his memories involved the person who turned out to be the present Ivan Ilyich, all that had once seemed joyful dissolved under his fixed attention and turned into something worthless and even disgusting.

The further away he went from his childhood and the closer he came to the present, the more worthless and dubious became his joy. This began with the school of jurisprudence. He had known things that were genuinely good there: he had known gaiety, friendship, and hope. But these good things grew more rare as he reached the higher classes. Later, during his first years of service as secretary to the governor, he had again known some good things; most of them had been connected with being in love. Then his life had grown complicated and the good things had decreased. Later on there was even less of the good, and the further he went, the less there was.

His marriage—such a chance marriage, and the disillusionment, and the odor of his wife's breath, and the sensuality, and the pretense! And that lifeless profession of his, and the worry over money—year after year, one year, two, ten, twenty, without any change. And the longer it lasted, the more lifeless everything became. "As if I had been going steadily downhill, while I fancied I was going uphill. Yes, that is how it was. In the opinion of my fellows I was going uphill, but only to the extent that life itself was crumbling away under my feet. And now here I am, dying.

"What is happening? Why? Incredible. Incredible that my life should have been so disgusting and meaningless. But even if it was so disgusting and meaningless, why must I die, and die in such agony? Something must be wrong.

"Perhaps I did not live as I ought to have?" was an idea that came into his mind. "But it cannot be that I did not live as I ought to have, for I did everything as it ought to have been done," he said to himself, and instantly drove away this one answer to the whole problem of life and death, considering it utterly impossible.

"What do you want now? To live? To live how?

"As if you were in court, and the usher was crying out, 'The Judge is coming!' The Judge is coming, the Judge is coming!" he repeated to himself. "Here he is, the Judge. But I am not to blame!" he cried out indignantly. "What am I to blame for?" And he stopped crying, and, turning his face to the wall, went on thinking of the same thing over and over: "Why, for what reason, must I go through all this horror?"

But think as he might, he could find no answer. And whenever the thought occurred to him (as it often did) that all of this was because he had not lived as he ought to have, he instantly drove away so preposterous a thought by recalling how correctly he had lived.

X

Two more weeks went by. Ivan Ilyich no longer got up off the sofa. He lay on the sofa because he did not want to lie in bed. And as he lay there, mostly with his face to the wall, he suffered all alone the same inexplicable suffering, and pondered all alone the same inexplicable questions: "What is it? Can it really be death?" And the inner voice answered, "Yes, it really is." "But why this suffering?" And the inner voice answered, "For no reason at all." That was as far as it went—nothing but this.

Ever since the very beginning of his illness, since the day he first went to the doctor, Ivan Ilyich's life had become divided between two opposite moods that kept alternating one with the other: one a mood of despair and the anticipation of a dreadful and incomprehensible death; the other a mood of hope, which led him to take a lively interest in observing the functions of his body. Now he saw before him a kidney or a caecum that was temporarily refusing to perform its duty; now he saw nothing but death, dreadful and unfathomable, from which there was no escape.

These two moods had alternated from the very beginning of his illness; but the further the illness progressed, the more fantastic and unlikely appeared his speculations on his kidneys and the more actual his consciousness of approaching death.

The mere remembrance of what he had been three months earlier and what he was now, the remembrance of how steadily he had been going downhill, was sufficient to destroy all possibility of hope.

During the last days of the solitude in which he lived, lying on the sofa with his face to the wall, of his solitude in the midst of the populous town, among all his many friends and relatives, a solitude that could not possibly have been more complete at the bottom of the sea or in the bowels of the earth—during the last days of that dreadful solitude Ivan Ilyich lived only in the past. One by one pictures of bygone days passed through his mind. They always began with something from the immediate past and went back to times more remote, to his childhood, and lingered there. If he recalled the plum jam he had been offered in the morning, he was sure to recall the sticky, wrinkled French prunes of his childhood, their peculiar taste, and the strong flow of saliva caused by the sucking of their stones, and this memory of a taste brought a whole train of recollections of that time in its wake: nursemaids, his brother, his toys. "I mustn't think of them . . . it is too painful," Ivan Ilyich said to himself, and switched his thoughts to the present. The button on the back of the sofa and the fold in the morocco. "Morocco is expensive and does not wear well; I quarreled with my wife over it. That time when we ripped Papa's briefcase the morocco was different, and so was the row we had, and we were punished for it and Mama brought us pastries." And again his thoughts centered on his childhood, and again he found them painful and tried to drive them away by thinking of something else.

And simultaneously with this train of memories, others pressed themselves upon him—memories of how his illness had begun and developed. And he felt that the further back he went into the past, the more vital his life had been. There had been more goodness in his life earlier, and more vitality. The one merged with the other. "Just as my sufferings are growing worse and worse, so my whole life has grown worse and worse," he thought. There was only one bright spot, and that was back at the very beginning of life. After that things grew blacker and blacker, faster and faster. "In inverse ratio to the square of the distance separating me from death," thought Ivan Ilyich. And the metaphor of a stone falling with increasing velocity flashed into his mind. Life, a series of increasing sufferings, is falling faster and faster toward its goal, which is unspeakable suffering. "I am falling. . . ." He started, shuddered, tried to resist; but he now knew there could be no resisting. And again, weary from contemplating, but unable to turn his eyes away from that which rose up in front of them, he stared at the back of the sofa and waited—waited for that fearful fall, the final shock, the destruction. "There is no resisting," he said to himself. "If I could only understand why it should be so!" But that, too, was impossible. "It might make some sense if I had not lived as I ought to have. But such an admission is impossible," he said to himself, remembering all the correctness, the decorum, the propriety of his life. "I cannot admit such a thing," he said to himself, drawing his lips apart as if someone could see his smile and be deceived by it. "There is no sense to it. Agony. Death. Why?"

XI

Another fortnight passed in this way. During that time the event he and his wife had hoped for occurred. Petrishchev made a formal proposal. It happened in the evening. The next morning Praskovya Fyodorovna came to her husband's room, going over in her mind how she would announce the proposal to him, but during the night Ivan Ilyich had undergone a change for the worse. Praskovya Fyodorovna found him on the same sofa, but in a different position. He was lying on his face, groaning and staring before him with a fixed gaze.

She began to speak to him about his medicine. He turned his eyes upon her. She did not finish what she was saying, so great was the hatred—the hatred of her—that she read in his eyes.

"For God's sake, let me die in peace," he said.

She made as if to go out, but at that moment their daughter came in and went over to say good morning to him. He looked at her just as he had looked at his wife, and when she asked him how he felt he answered dryly that they would soon be rid of him. Both of them were silent, sat down for a moment, then went out.

"Why are we to blame?" Liza asked her mother. "You might think it was our fault. I feel sorry for Papa but why should he torture us so?"

The doctor came at the usual time. Ivan Ilyich answered "Yes" and "No" without taking his glowering eyes off him, and toward the end he said:

"You know perfectly well that nothing can help; leave me alone."

"We can lessen your suffering," said the doctor.

"No, you can't even do that; leave me alone."

The doctor went into the drawing room and told Praskovya Fyodorovna that his condition was very bad and there was only one thing, opium, that could relieve his suffering, which must be dreadful.

The doctor said his physical suffering must be dreadful, and so it was; but more dreadful than his physical suffering was his moral suffering; in this lay his real torment.

His moral suffering came from having, that night, gazed at the sleepy, good-humored, broad face of Gerasim and thought: "What if all my life, all my mature life, really has not been what it ought to have been?"

He was struck by the thought that what had formerly seemed to him utterly impossible (that his life had been spent not as it ought to have been) might be true. He was struck by the thought that those scarcely perceptible impulses to struggle against what people in high position considered good, scarcely perceptible impulses which he had always suppressed, might be the real thing, and all the rest might be aside from the real thing. His official duties, his manner of living, his family, his social and professional interests—all of these might be aside from the real thing. He attempted a defense of these things, but suddenly he became aware of the worthlessness of what he was defending. There was nothing to defend.

"If that is the case," he said to himself, "and I am taking leave of life with the realization that I have squandered all that was given to me, and that it is too late to do anything about it—what then?" He lay on his face and began reviewing his life from an entirely different point of view.

When, in the morning, he saw first the footman, then his wife, then his daughter, and at last the doctor, their every movement, their every word, confirmed the dreadful truth revealed to him in the night. In them he saw himself, saw all that had formed his life, and saw clearly that all of this was aside from the real thing, that it was all a dreadful and enormous deception hiding the truths of life and death. This realization increased his physical sufferings, multiplied them tenfold. He moaned and tossed and clutched at his clothes. His clothes seemed to be squeezing him, suffocating him, and he hated them.

He was given a big dose of opium that made him forget, but at dinnertime it all began again. He drove everyone out and lay tossing on the bed.

His wife came to him and said:

"*Jean,* dear, do this for me." (For me?) "It cannot do you any harm and it often helps. It doesn't mean anything. And even well people sometimes—"

He looked at her wide-eyed.

"What? Take the sacrament? Why? I don't want to. And yet . . ."

She began to cry.

"Won't you, dear? I'll send for our priest, he is such a good man."

"Very well. Excellent," he said.

When the priest came and had heard his confession, the heart of Ivan Ilyich was softened, he seemed to be relieved of his doubts, and this brought him relief from his sufferings, and for a moment he had hope. Again he began to think of his caecum and the possibility of curing it. There were tears in his eyes as he took the sacrament.

When they laid him down again after the sacrament he

felt better for a moment, and he was filled once more with the hope of recovery.

He thought of the operation the doctor had suggested performing. "I want to live, to live," he said to himself. His wife came in to congratulate him; she said the usual things, and then added:

"You really do feel better, don't you?"

"Yes," he said without looking at her.

Her dress, her figure, the expression of her face, the sound of her voice—everything said to him: "Aside from the real thing. Everything that has been and still is your life is a lie and a deception hiding the reality of life and death from you." And the minute this thought came to him, hatred rose within him; and with the hatred, agonizing physical suffering; and with the suffering, the realization of his imminent and inevitable end. New sensations put in an appearance: something inside of him began to twist and snap and choke the breath out of him.

The expression of his face when he pronounced that "yes" was terrible. And having pronounced it, looking her straight in the eye, he flung himself down on his face with a swiftness incredible in anyone as weak as he was, and shrieked:

"Go away! Go away! Leave me alone!"

XII

From that moment there began three days of such terrible and uninterrupted shrieking that even two rooms away one could not hear it without shuddering. The moment he had replied to his wife's question he had understood that all was over, that there was no hope, that the end, the very end, was at hand, that all his doubts remained doubts and would never be answered.

"Ah! Ah! Ah!" he shrieked in different tones. He had begun by shouting, "I don't wa-a-nt to!" and had gone on shouting that "Ah!"

Throughout those three days, which for him were timeless, he struggled in that black sack that some invisible and irresistible force was pushing him into. He struggled as one who is condemned to death and knows there is no hope of escape, struggles in the arms of the executioner. And he realized that with every minute, despite the desperateness of his struggle, he was coming closer and closer to that which terrified him. He felt that his torture was caused by his being pushed into that black hole, but even more by his being unable to crawl into it himself. He was prevented from crawling into it by the belief that his life had been a good one. This defense of the life he had lived was the hindrance that kept him from moving ahead, and it caused him more torture than anything else.

Suddenly some force struck him in the chest and the side and cut off his breath; he plunged straight into the hole, and there, at the end of the hole, he found a glimmer of light. He had the sensation he had once experienced while riding in a railway carriage, when he had thought he was moving forward and was actually moving backward and suddenly became aware of the true direction.

"Yes, it is all aside from the real thing," he said to himself. "But that is all right. I can still make it the real thing. But what *is* the real thing?" he asked himself, and suddenly grew quiet.

This took place at the end of the third day, an hour before his death. Just then his son crept into his room and up to his bed. The dying man was still screaming wildly and throwing his arms about. One hand fell on the head of his son. The boy seized it, pressed it to his lips, and began to cry. It was just at this moment that Ivan Ilyich plunged into the hole and saw the light, and it was revealed to him that his life had not been what it ought to have been, but he could still mend matters. "What is the real thing?" he asked himself, and grew quiet, listening. It was then he realized that someone was kissing his hand. He opened his eyes and looked at his son. He was filled with pity for him. His wife came in. He glanced at her. She stood looking at him with her mouth hanging open, with the tears unwiped on her nose and cheeks, with an expression of despair on her face. He was filled with pity for her.

"I am torturing them," he thought. "They feel sorry for me, but things will be better for them when I am gone." He wanted to tell them this, but lacked the strength. "But what is the use of speaking? I must do something," he thought. He turned to his wife and indicated his son with his eyes.

"Take him away," he said. "Poor boy . . . and you . . ." He wanted to add, "Forgive," and it came out, "Forget," but he had not the strength to correct himself; he merely gave a little wave of his hand, knowing that the one who was to understand would understand.

And presently it became clear to him that all he had been tortured by and been unable to throw off, was now falling away of itself, falling away on two sides, ten sides, all sides at once. He felt sorry for them, he must do something to ease their pain. He must relieve them and himself of the suffering. "How good and how simple!" he thought. "And the pain?" he asked himself. "How am I to dispose of it? Here, where are you, pain?"

He felt for the pain.

"Ah, here it is. What of it? Let it be."

"And death? Where is death?"

He searched for his accustomed terror of death and could not find it. Where was death? What was death? There was no fear because there was no death.

There was light instead of death.

"So that is it!" he suddenly said out loud. "What happiness!"

All of this took place in an instant, but the significance of that instant was lasting. For those present his death agony continued for another two hours. Something rattled in his throat; his emaciated body twitched. But gradually the wheezing and the rattling ceased.

"All is over," someone said.

He heard these words and repeated them in his soul.

"Death is over," he said to himself. "There is no more death."

He drew in a deep breath, broke off in the middle of it, stretched out his limbs, and died.

1886

THE KREUTZER SONATA

". . . But I say unto you That whosoever look-
eth on a woman to lust after her hath committed
adultery with her already in his heart."

Math. 5:28.

"His disciples say unto him, if the case of the
man be so with his wife, it is not good to marry.
But he said unto them, All men cannot receive this
saying, save they to whom it is given. For there
are some eunuchs, which were so born from their
mother's womb: and there are some eunuchs,
which were made eunuchs by men: and there be
eunuchs, which have made themselves eunuchs
for the kingdom of heaven's sake. He that is able
to receive it, let him receive it."

Math. 19:10,11,12.

I

It was early spring. We had been traveling for almost
two days. Passengers who were going short distances
kept entering and leaving the carriage, but three, like myself, had been traveling since the train set out. One of them
was an unattractive middle-aged woman with a haggard
look, who smoked cigarettes and wore a mannish coat and
hat; another was an acquaintance of hers, a loquacious
man of about forty, with tidy new luggage; the third was a
gentleman who held himself aloof. He was of middle height,
his movements were impulsive, he was not yet old but his
curly hair had turned prematurely gray, and his eyes had

an unusual shine to them and kept darting quickly from one object to another. He was wearing an astrakhan cap and an old coat with an astrakhan collar that had evidently been made by an expensive tailor. When he unfastened his coat one caught a glimpse of a Russian jacket and a Russian blouse with an embroidered collar. A peculiarity of this gentleman lay in his making odd sounds from time to time that resembled the clearing of one's throat or the breaking out into a laugh that was instantly stifled.

Throughout the journey this gentleman painstakingly avoided all talk and contact with other passengers. He made curt, brusque answers whenever spoken to and spent his time reading, gazing out of the window, smoking, or rummaging for food in his old sack and then having tea or a snack.

Fancying that he was oppressed by his solitude I made several attempts to talk to him, but each time our eyes met (and this occurred frequently, since we were sitting opposite each other) he turned away and either picked up a book or looked out of the window.

During a prolonged stop at a big station on the evening of the second day, this nervous gentleman went out for boiling water and made himself some tea. The man with the tidy luggage (a lawyer, as I learned later) and his friend, the woman who smoked and was wearing a mannish coat, went to have tea in the station restaurant.

During the absence of the lady and gentleman several new passengers entered our carriage, among them a tall, clean-shaven, wrinkled old man, apparently a merchant, in a fur-lined coat and a cloth cap with an enormous visor. The merchant took a seat opposite the place where the lawyer and the woman had been sitting and instantly entered into conversation with a young man who had the appearance of being a shop assistant and had also just entered the carriage.

I was sitting obliquely opposite, and since the train was standing still, caught snatches of their conversation when people were not passing to and fro. The merchant announced that he was on his way to his country house, only one station away; then they launched into the usual discussion of trade and prices, which led them to the usual observations on the Moscow market and the Nizhni-Novgorod fair. The shop assistant began to describe the debaucheries at the fair of some rich tradesman whom they both knew, but the old man interrupted by telling him about the debaucheries in Kunavino in which he himself had taken part.

He was evidently proud of having taken part in them, and with a gloating look on his face told how he and that same acquaintance had done something when they were both drunk that had to be described in a whisper; the shop assistant burst out into a roar of laughter that filled the whole carriage, and the old man laughed too, revealing two long yellow teeth.

Not expecting to hear anything of interest, I got up with the intention of taking a walk on the station platform until the train left. In the doorway I met the lawyer and the woman, who were holding an animated conversation.

"No time for a walk," the sociable lawyer said to me. "The second bell will ring any moment now."

And true enough, before I had gone the length of the train the last bell rang. I returned to find the lawyer and the woman talking as animatedly as ever. The old merchant was sitting in silence across from them, staring fixedly in front of him and showing his disapproval by giving a chew on his two teeth from time to time.

"And so she simply announced to her husband," the lawyer was saying with a smile as I walked past, "that she could not and would not live with him any more because—"

But the rest was lost. Other passengers came in after me, then the conductor, then an artisan ran past, and for some time there was so much noise and confusion that I could not hear what was being said.

When things quieted down and the lawyer's voice was carried to me again, his account of a particular case had led to a discussion of a general situation. The lawyer was saying that the question of divorce was occupying public opinion in Europe, and that cases of divorce were becoming more and more common in Russia. On noticing that his was the only voice to be heard, he turned to the old man.

"It was not like that in the old days, was it?" he said with a pleasant smile.

The old man was just about to answer when the train started up and he took off his cap, crossed himself, and began to say a prayer under his breath. The lawyer courteously turned his eyes away and waited for him to finish. When the old man had finished praying and had crossed himself three times, he put his cap on very straight, pulled it down tightly, settled himself in his seat, and began to speak.

"There were such cases in the old days, but they were fewer," he said. "But it is only to be expected these days. People are getting too much education."

The train went clattering over some switches as it gathered speed, making it hard for me to hear, and since I found the matter interesting, I took a seat closer to the speakers.

My neighbor, the nervous gentleman with the glittering eyes, also seemed to find it interesting, for, without leaving his seat, he strained forward to listen.

"Is it wrong to get an education?" the woman said with a faint smile. "Do you think it is better to get married as people used to, with the bride and bridegroom never even seeing each other before the wedding?" she went on, replying, in the manner of many women, not to what the other person had said, but to what she thought he had said. "They married whoever came along without knowing whether they loved each other or ever could love each other, and then suffered tortures for the rest of their lives. Do you think that was better?" she said, obviously appealing to me and the lawyer rather than to the old man.

"It's a great deal of education they're getting these days," repeated the merchant, looking contemptuously at the woman and letting her question go unanswered.

"And what connection do you find between education and unhappy marriages?" asked the lawyer with a faint smile.

The merchant was about to reply when the woman interrupted.

"Oh no, those times have gone forever," she said.

"Wait, let him tell us what he thinks," put in the lawyer.

"Education brings a lot of foolishness with it," said the old man decisively.

"They make people marry who do not love each other, and then are amazed to find them unhappy together," said the woman hurriedly, glancing at me and the lawyer and even the shop assistant, who had got up and was standing leaning on the back of the seat and listening with a smile on his face. "It is only animals that can be mated at their master's will; human beings have their own tastes and preferences," she said, evidently wishing to be cutting to the old man.

"What you are saying is not right, my woman," said the old man. "Animals are beasts; human beings have the law to go by."

"And how do you propose that a person is to live with one he doesn't love?" said the woman, anxious to air ideas which she seemed to consider novel.

"Formerly no such distinctions were made," said the old man weightily. "That's a newfangled idea. You never used to hear her say, 'I'll up and leave you.' Even the peasants have caught on to the new style. 'Here,' she says, 'take your shirts and breeches; I'm going off with Vanya—his hair is curlier.' And there you are. It's fear that should rule a woman's heart."

The shop assistant looked from the lawyer to me, and from me to the woman, suppressing a smile and ready to either approve or laugh at the merchant's views, depending on how they were received.

"Fear of what?" asked the woman.

"What? Of her husband, that's what."

"Well, my good man, the time for that is past," said the woman testily.

"No, my good woman, that time will never be past. Eve was made out of the rib of the man, and so she will remain to the end of time," said the old man so sternly and with such a convincing shake of his head that the shop assistant instantly decided he had won the victory and gave a loud guffaw.

"It's only you men who think like that," said the woman, with a look that said she had not given in. "You've taken all the freedom for yourselves and want to keep us women in jail. You give yourselves the right to do anything you like."

"Nobody gives us the right, but there's no increase in the household from what a man does, while a woman's a creature to be handled with care," went on the old man in the same impressive tone.

This tone seemed to convince his listeners; the woman felt that her cause was damaged, but even so she did not surrender.

"But surely you must admit that a woman is a human being too and has feelings just as a man has. What is she to do if she does not love her husband?"

"Doesn't love him?" repeated the merchant grimly, drawing down his brows and lips. "She must learn to love him!"

This unexpected answer particularly tickled the shop assistant and he let out a cry of approbation.

"She must do nothing of the kind," said the woman. "If she doesn't love him, she cannot be forced to."

"And what if a wife is not true to her husband?" asked the lawyer.

"That is not to be allowed," said the old man. "One has to keep a sharp eye out for that."

"But if it happens, what then? After all, it does happen."

"Perhaps it does among some people, but not among our class," said the old man.

No one said a word. The shop assistant shifted his feet, moved closer, smiled, and began to speak, as if anxious not to be left out of the conversation.

"There was a scandal in my employer's family once. And very hard it was to place the blame. The son's wife turned out to be a loose woman. She began her tricks. He was an able, respectable young man. First she had an affair with the bookkeeper. He tried to bring her round by talking to her. Did no good. She was very nasty. Began stealing his money. He beat her. Only made her worse. She had an affair with one of the unbaptized—that is, with a Jew, if you don't mind my saying so. What was left for him to do? He left her. Lives as a bachelor to this day, and she walks the streets."

"He was a fool," said the old man. "If he had given her no rope from the very first and if he had drawn her up short as he ought to have, she would no doubt be living with him to this day. It's wrong to let them have their own way from the very beginning. 'Don't trust a horse in the pasture or a wife in the home!'"

Just then the conductor came to collect the tickets for the next station. The old man handed him his.

"Yes, the fair sex has to be taken in hand from the very outset, otherwise everything is lost."

"And what about the tale you told a while back about the way you married men carried on at the fair in Kunavino?" I could not resist saying.

"That's a different matter," said the merchant, and shut up like a clam.

When the whistle blew the old man got up, dragged his sack out from under the seat, folded his greatcoat round him, lifted his cap, and went out.

II

As soon as he was gone, several voices spoke simultaneously.

"A man of the old school," said the shop assistant.

"A patriarchal despot," said the woman. "What primitive ideas he has about women and marriage!"

"Hm, we're way behind European views on marriage," said the lawyer

"The main thing that such people fail to understand," said the woman, "is that a marriage without love is no marriage at all, that only love sanctifies marriage, and that the only true marriage is that sanctified by love."

The shop assistant smiled as he listened, trying to memorize as many of these clever observations as he could for future use.

In the middle of what the woman was saying I heard something behind me that sounded like a stifled laugh or sob, and turning round saw my neighbor, the lonely gray-haired gentleman with the glittering eyes. We had not noticed that during our conversation he had drawn closer, evidently interested in what we were saying. He was standing leaning on the back of the seat and seemed to be very much agitated. His face was red and the muscles of his cheeks were twitching.

"Just what is that love . . . that love . . . that love that sanctifies marriage?" he stuttered.

Seeing his agitation, the woman answered him gently and seriously.

"True love. If such love exists between a man and woman, then marriage is possible," she said.

"Yes, but how are we to understand what true love is?" said the gentleman with the glittering eyes hesitantly, with a self-conscious smile.

"Everyone knows what true love is," said the woman, evidently anxious to end the conversation.

"Not I," said the gentleman. "It is necessary to define what you have in mind."

"That's simple enough," said the woman, but she stopped and considered. "Love? Love is the preferring of one person to all others," she said.

"A preference lasting how long? A month? Two days? Half an hour?" said the gray-haired gentleman with a laugh.

"But wait, perhaps you are thinking of something quite different."

"No, I am thinking of the same thing."

"She means to say," put in the lawyer, "that marriage should spring, first of all, from devotion—love, if you wish —and that only if this exists can marriage be looked upon as something . . . er . . . sacred, so to speak. Further, that any marriage which is not founded on this mutual de-

votion—love, if you wish—does not carry any moral obligations. Have I understood you correctly?" he said, turning
to the woman.

The woman nodded.

"And then . . ." said the lawyer, but he was cut short
by the gentleman, whose eyes were now burning like coals
and whose agitation had reached such a pitch that he
could no longer restrain himself.

"That is precisely what I am talking about—the preferring of one man or woman to all others, but what I am asking is—for how long?"

"For how long? For very long, sometimes for a whole
lifetime," said the woman with a shrug of her shoulders.

"But that only happens in novels, never in life. In life
this preference for one person lasts in rare cases for years,
more often for a few months, sometimes for mere weeks or
days or hours," he said, obviously aware that he was shocking everyone by his opinion and pleased to be doing so.

"What are you saying! Nothing of the sort. But listen—"
the three of us protested in one voice. Even the shop assistant let out a grunt of disapproval.

"Oh, yes, I know," cried the gray-haired gentleman in a
voice that drowned us all out. "You are speaking about
what is thought to exist. I am speaking about what actually
does exist! Every man experiences what you call love whenever he sees a beautiful woman."

"But it is dreadful, what you say! After all, there is a
feeling between people that is called love and which lasts
not months and years, but a lifetime."

"No, no, there is no such thing! If we admit the possibility
of a man's preferring a certain woman all his life, it is more
than probable that the woman prefers someone else. That
is the situation as it is and always has been," he said, taking out a cigarette and lighting up.

"But it is possible for the feeling to be mutual," said the
lawyer.

"No, it is not," the other retorted. "It is no more possible
than for two peas, selected beforehand, to fall next to each
other when a whole wagon is being loaded with peas. Be-

sides, in the case of a man and woman it is not so much the law of probability as the state of exhaustion that determines things. To love one man or one woman all one's life —why, that would be the same as to expect a single candle to burn a lifetime," he said, drawing greedily on his cigarette.

"But you are speaking only of carnal love. Do you not admit of love based on a unity of ideas, on spiritual affinity?" asked the woman.

"Spiritual affinity! Unity of ideas!" he echoed, again making the sound I had noticed. "In that case, there is no reason for sleeping together (forgive my bluntness). Who ever heard of unity of ideas leading people to sleep together?" he said with a nervous laugh.

"But wait," said the lawyer. "Facts contradict your contention. We see that conjugal relations exist, that all mankind, or at least the majority, live in this way, and that many live a faithful married life to the end of their days."

The gray-haired gentleman laughed again

"First you say that marriage is based on love, and when I express my doubt as to the existence of any but carnal love, you prove the existence of love by pointing to the existence of marriage. These days marriage is nothing but deception!"

"Oh, no; I protest," said the lawyer. "The only thing I said was that marriages exist and have always existed."

"True. But on what basis do they exist? They exist and always have existed among people who see something holy in marriage, a holiness that involves duties for which they are answerable to God. Among such people they exist, but not among people of our class. Among us, people get married without seeing in marriage anything but copulation, and therefore their marriages turn out to be either violence or deception. Deception is the lesser of the two evils. The husband and wife deceive others into thinking they are living in monogamy, when actually they are living in polygamy. That is foul, but tolerable. But when, as is usually the case, the husband and wife take upon themselves the obligation of living together all their lives, and after the first month hate each other and long to separate and still go on living together, it results in that unspeakable torture that drives people to drink, to commit suicide, to kill and poison themselves and each other," he said with growing agitation, speaking faster and faster, as if afraid somebody might put in a word. When he finished there was an awkward silence.

"Oh, yes; unquestionably there are critical moments in married life," said the lawyer, hoping thereby to put an end to this excited, unseemly talk.

"I see you have recognized me?" said the gray-haired gentleman softly and with a semblance of composure.

"No, I have not had the pleasure of—"

"Hardly a pleasure. I am Pozdnyshev, the one who went through the critical moment you mentioned and killed his wife in doing so," he said, casting a swift glance at each of us.

Finding nothing to say, we all sat silent.

"It doesn't matter," he said, making that strange sound again. "But I must beg your pardon. I . . . er . . . do not wish to embarrass you."

"Come, I say . . ." put in the lawyer, not knowing himself what he meant by that "I say."

Ignoring him, Pozdnyshev turned quickly and sat down. The lawyer and the woman whispered together. I, who sat next to Pozdnyshev, said nothing. It was too dark to read and so I closed my eyes and pretended to fall asleep. In this way we traveled in silence as far as the next station.

There the lawyer and the woman changed to another carriage, as they had arranged with the conductor to do. The shop assistant lay down on the bench and fell asleep. Pozdnyshev smoked endless cigarettes and drank the tea he had made while the train was at the station.

When I opened my eyes and glanced at him, he suddenly addressed himself to me in an irritated, determined tone.

"Perhaps you find it disagreeable to be in my company now that you know who I am? If so, I will leave you."

"Oh, not at all."

"In that case, perhaps you will have some? But it's very strong," he said as he poured me out some tea.

"Talk, talk . . . and nothing but lies," he said.

"What are you referring to?" I asked.

"The same thing: that love of theirs, and what it really is. Are you very tired?"

"Not at all."

"Then if you like I shall tell you how I was led to do what I did by that same love."

"If you don't find it too painful."

"I find it more painful to say nothing. Drink your tea. Or is it too strong?"

The tea was indeed like beer, but I drank a glass. Just then the conductor passed by. My companion followed him with burning eyes and waited until he was gone to begin his story.

III

"Well, then, I shall tell you. Are you sure you want me to?"

I repeated that I did. He waited a minute, rubbed his face with his hands, and began.

"If I am to tell it at all, I must begin from the very beginning; I must tell you why I got married and what I was like before my marriage.

"Before my marriage I lived like everyone else—everyone, that is, of our class. I am a landlord with a master's degree from the university, and I was a Marshal of Nobility. Before my marriage I lived like everyone else—which means I lived a life of profligacy, and like all the people of our class I was sure that in living such a life I was doing the right thing. I considered myself a good sort, quite a decent fellow. I was not a seducer, had no depraved tastes, and did not make this the main interest of my life as many men of my age did; I indulged my lust in a dignified, decorous way, merely for the sake of my health. I avoided women who might become an encumbrance by having babies or forming too strong an attachment. As a matter of fact there may have been babies and strong attachments, but I shut my eyes to them. And I not only looked upon this as highly moral; I was even proud of it."

He stopped and made the sound he seemed to be in the habit of making whenever a new thought occurred to him.

"And that is the most foul thing of all," he cried. "Depravity does not lie in the physical act; there is nothing depraved about the physical act; depravity—true depravity —lies in the shaking off of all moral responsibility in respect to the woman with whom you enter into physical relations. And I counted it a feather in my cap that I was able to shake off this moral responsibility. I remember the pangs of conscience I once suffered because I had forgotten to pay a woman who, having fallen in love with me, gave herself to me. I regained my equanimity only when I had sent her the money, thereby releasing myself from all moral responsibility in respect to her. Do not shake your head as if you agreed with me," he suddenly shouted. "I know better. You, you, all of you—you are all the same, unless you are some rare exception. At your best you hold the same views as I held. But what of it? Forgive me," he said. "I cannot help it; it is so dreadful, dreadful, dreadful."

"What is so dreadful?" I asked.

"That abyss of error in which we live so far as women and our relations to them are concerned. No, I cannot speak calmly on this subject, and not so much because that 'critical moment' as that gentleman called it occurred in my life, as because ever since it occurred my eyes have been opened and I have seen things in an entirely different light. Everything inside out, inside out!"

He lighted a cigarette, leaned over with his elbows on his knees, and resumed. I could not see his face in the darkness, but I could hear his earnest, pleasant voice speaking above the rattle of the railway carriage.

IV

"Yes, it was only after suffering as I suffered, only because of that, that I realized wherein lie the roots of the evil, realized how things ought to be, and beheld all the horror of things as they are.

"And now allow me to tell you how and when everything began that led me to that critical moment. It began when I was in my sixteenth year. It happened when I was still a gymnasium student and my elder brother was in the first year of the university. I was still a virgin, but, like all the unfortunate children of our class, I was not innocent. For two years I had been under the demoralizing influence of other boys. I was already tortured by women—not some particular woman, but women in general, as something sweetly tantalizing—every woman, and the nakedness of woman. I was not pure in my solitude. I suffered the tortures that ninety-nine percent of our boys suffer. I was horrified, I suffered, I prayed, I succumbed. I sinned in fact and in fancy, but I had not yet taken the final step. I was ruining myself, but I had not yet laid a hand on any other creature. But one evening a friend of my brother's, a student, a jolly fellow, one of those 'good fellows,' who teach others to drink and play cards and are really rogues of the first order—this friend of my brother's suggested after a drinking party that we go 'there.' We went. My brother was also a virgin and had his fall on that same night. I, a fifteen-year-old boy, sullied myself and was party to the sullying of a woman without comprehending what I was doing. Never had I heard from my elders that what I was doing was wrong. And no one hears it today. True, the ten commandments tell us it is wrong, but the only reason we have to know the ten commandments is so that we can give the correct answer to the priest when we take our examinations in Bible Study, and even so the knowledge is not very important, much less important than knowing the use of 'ut' in conditional clauses.

"And so not a single one of my elders whose opinion I valued had ever told me that what I was doing was wrong. On the contrary, I heard people whom I respected say it was right. I heard that my struggles and tortures would be eased after I had done it. I heard this and I read it, I heard my elders say it was good for the health; I heard my companions say it was the right thing and the smart thing to do. And so on the whole I could see nothing bad in it. The danger of infection? This had all been foreseen. A solicitous government had taken measures in this respect. It saw to it that brothels were under surveillance so that schoolboys might indulge their lust in safety. It paid doctors a salary to see to this. And that was only natural. Since it assumed that profligacy was good for the health, it had to create conditions insuring a nice, clean sort of profligacy. I have known mothers who saw to these matters for their sons. Science itself sends young men to brothels."

"Science?" I said.

"Are not doctors scientists? Priests of science. Who is it depraves our youth by asserting that their health demands it? They do. And then they set about with grave faces to cure syphilis!"

"Why shouldn't they cure syphilis?"

"Because if one-tenth of the effort which is expended on the curing of syphilis were devoted to the wiping out of profligacy, syphilis would have disappeared long ago. But our efforts are expended not on the wiping out of profligacy, but on the encouraging of it, on making it safe. But that is not the point. The point is that I, like nine-tenths (if not more) of the youth not only of my class but of all classes including the peasantry, sinned not because there was some particular woman whose charms I could not resist. No, there was no woman who seduced me. I sinned because of the society in which I lived; I sinned because some of the people around me looked upon my sin as a proper measure for insuring my health, and others looked upon it as a natural form of amusement for a young man, and found it not only pardonable, but even quite innocent. I myself did not regard it as a sin; I simply began to indulge in what was partly a pleasure, partly the satisfying of a need characteristic (or so I was told) of a certain age; I began to indulge my lust as I had earlier begun to smoke and drink. And yet there was something touching and exceptional about this first fall. I remember that at the time, before I had even gone out of the room, a great sadness came over me and I wanted to weep—to weep for my lost innocence, to weep for a relationship with women that was gone forever. Yes, a natural, simple relationship was gone forever. From that time on it was not and could not be pure. I became what is called a lecher. And to be a lecher means to be in a physical state corresponding to that of a drunkard, a smoker, or a dope addict. Just as a drunkard, a smoker, or a dope addict is not a normal person, so a man who has taken several women for the sake of his pleasure is not a normal person, is a person spoiled for all time, is a lecher. And just as a drunkard or a dope addict can be recognized by his face and behavior, so a lecher can be recognized. A lecher can resist, can struggle against his vice, but never again can he know a pure, bright, simple relation to women—a brotherly relation. A lecher can instantly be recognized by the way in which he looks at a young woman. And I became a lecher and have remained one, and that is what brought about my ruin."

V

"Things went on in this way for some time, during which I took up new aspects of the same experience. Good God! The remembrance of all my bestiality fills me with horror! I remember myself as one whom my comrades laughed at for my so-called innocence. And the gilded youth! The officers! The Parisians! I remember all of these gentlemen and myself—thirty-year-old profligates, guilty of hundreds of the most dreadful and various crimes against women. I remember how we thirty-year-old profligates strutted about, well-scrubbed and clean-shaven, in spotless linen, scented, in frock coats and uniforms, in drawing rooms and ballrooms—so handsome—very symbols of purity!

"Just consider for a moment how things ought to be and how they are. When such a gentleman comes to see my sister or daughter, I, who know what sort of life he leads, ought to go up to him, draw him aside, and say quietly, 'Listen, my dear fellow, I know the sort of life you lead, where and with whom you spend your nights. This is no place for you. There are pure and innocent girls here. Go away.' That is how it ought to be. But actually when such a gentleman turns up and begins to dance with my daughter or sister, putting his arm round her waist, we rejoice if he is a gentleman with means and connections. He may yet favor my daughter with his attentions after his night at Rigolbouche! It makes no difference even if he is tainted or diseased. Nowadays they know how to cure such things. Why, I know several girls from well-known families whose parents were delighted to give them in marriage to syphilitics! How vile! How loathsome! Surely the time will come when this vileness and deception will be exposed."

He made his odd sound several times and set to drinking tea. It was fearfully strong and there was no water with which to dilute it. I definitely felt the effects of the two glasses I had drunk. He must have felt them too, for he grew more and more excited. His voice became more expressive and singsong. He kept shifting his position, now taking off his hat, now putting it on, and odd changes of expression crossed his face in the half-shadow in which we were sitting.

"And so that is how I lived to the age of thirty, without relinquishing for a moment my intention of marrying and settling down to the most pure and elevated family life, and with this purpose in mind I kept my eye out for a suitable girl," he went on. "At the same time that I was wallowing in the muck of fornication, I was looking for a girl whose purity would make her worthy of being my wife. I turned down many of them just because they were not pure enough for me. At last I found one whom I considered worthy. She was one of two daughters of a landlord from Penza who had once been very wealthy but had lost most of his money.

"One night as we were returning home in the moonlight after spending the day boating, and I was sitting beside her gazing with admiration at her graceful form encased in a tight woolen jersey, and at her curly hair, I suddenly decided that she was the one. That evening I fancied she understood all my thoughts and feelings, and that they

were on the most elevated plane. As a matter of fact it was
only that the jersey and the curls were most becoming to
her and that after being so close to her all day long I wanted to be even closer.

"It is astonishing how complete can be the illusion that
beauty is good. A beautiful woman may talk rot and you
listen and fancy she is saying clever things instead of rot.
She says and does vile things and you find them charming.
And if by any chance she says pretty things instead of rot
and vileness, you are instantly convinced that she is a very
paragon of goodness and wisdom.

"I returned home in a state of rapture, convinced that
she was moral perfection itself, and that therefore she was
worthy to become my wife. On the next day I proposed to
her.

"But just see the falseness of it all! Of a thousand men
who get married (unfortunately men not only from our class
but from the lower classes as well), hardly one can be
found who has not been previously married at least ten
times, and perhaps a hundred or a thousand, like Don
Juan. True, I have heard and observed that nowadays
there are pure men who know and feel that this is a great
and profound act and not a trifling matter. May God give
them His blessing! But in my day there was not one of that
sort in ten thousand. And everybody knows this and pretends not to know it. All the novels give detailed de-
scriptions of the hero's feelings, of the flowers and pools
beside which he strolls, but in describing the great love the
handsome hero feels for some young lady, they say nothing
about how he spent his time previously—nothing of the
brothels, the parlormaids, the cooks, the wives of other
men. And whenever such indecent novels are written, they
are not given into the hands of those who most need to
read them and learn about such things, that is, into the
hands of innocent young ladies. At first their elders would
have the young ladies believe there is no such thing as the
licentiousness making up half the life of our towns and even
our villages: later they become so accustomed to this pretense that in the end they themselves, like the English, come

to believe sincerely that they are a people of high moral principles living in a highly moral world. And the young ladies, poor things, believe this very seriously. My unfortunate wife was just such a young lady. I remember showing her my diary when I was already her fiancé; from this diary she could get a glimpse of my past, she could at least learn what I most wanted her to know—about my latest affair. Others might have told her about it and that is why I felt it expedient to tell her myself. I remember her horror and despair and bewilderment when she found out and understood. I could see she wanted to break off ties with me then and there. Oh, if she only had!"

He made that sound again, stopped talking, and took a swallow of tea.

VI

"But no! Better as it was, better as it was!" he cried. "It served me right! But that is aside from the story. What I wanted to say was that the unfortunate girls are the only ones who are deceived. Their mothers know everything, especially those mothers who have learned from their own husbands. They pretend to believe in the pureness of men, but they behave just the opposite. They know what bait to use in catching men for themselves and their daughters.

"It is only we men who do not know, and we do not know because we do not wish to know; the women know very well that the most exalted and poetic so-called love is inspired not by moral virtues, but by physical proximity, by coiffures, by the color and cut of a frock. Ask an experienced cocotte who has set her cap for a certain gentleman, which risk she would rather take: that of being accused in his presence of cruelty, deception, even of depravity, or of appearing before him in an ugly, ill-fitting gown. She is sure to choose the first. She knows that we men are just lying when we talk of elevated feelings; what we want is the body, and therefore we will forgive her her sins, but never an ugly, ill-fitting, tasteless gown. A cocotte is consciously aware of this, but any innocent young girl knows it intuitively, as an animal knows it.

"That accounts for those loathsome jerseys, those bustles on their behinds, those bare shoulders and arms and almost bare bosoms. Women, especially those who get their knowledge from men, know only too well that talk on elevated themes is mere talk, and that what a man really wants is the body and whatever adds to the seductiveness of the body, and so this is what they offer him. If we could view the life of the upper classes in its true light, not through the prism of a habitual attitude that has become second nature to us, we would see that it is a veritable brothel. You disagree? Here, I shall prove it to you," he said, not giving me a chance to speak. "You say the women of our class have other interests than the women in a brothel, but I say you are wrong and will prove that you are wrong. If people have different aims in life, if their inner lives are different, the outer forms of their lives will be different too. But look at the unfortunate women whom we despise and then at young ladies from the very highest society: the same toilettes, the same fashions, the same perfumes, the same bare arms, shoulders and bosoms, the same exaggerated behinds, the same passion for precious stones and expensive, glittering ornaments, the same amusements —dancing, music, and singing. All the same means of enticing men are used by one as by the other. No difference at all. To make a very strict distinction between them we can only say that short-term prostitutes are usually despised whereas long-term prostitutes are esteemed."

VII

"And so I was ensnared by the jerseys, curls, and bustles. It was easy to catch me because I was brought up in those special conditions that, like hothouses for cucumbers, cultivate the love tendency in young folk. The superabundance of stimulating food and drink that we consume, combined with complete physical idleness, is nothing less than a systematic stimulation of lust. That is a fact, whether it

astonishes you or not. I myself failed to realize it until late-
ly. But now I do realize it, and that is why I become so upset on seeing that others do not understand and talk the
same sort of claptrap as that woman who was here.

"This spring some peasants were working on a railway
not far from me. The usual diet of a young peasant is
bread, kvass, and onions: it keeps him alive, cheerful, and
busy at easy field work. He goes to work on the railway,
and his daily fare becomes porridge and a pound of
meat. But he expends this meat on a sixteen-hour working
day wheeling a barrow weighing thirty poods. His fare is
just right for him. And what about us, eating as much as
two pounds of meat, poultry, and other caloric dainties and
drinks—how do we expend it all? On sensual excesses. If
we really expend it, everything is all right for the safety
valve is open. But if it is closed, as mine was from time to
time, it results in a sensual excitement that, passing through
the prism of our artificial life, finds expression in an over-
refined sort of love, sometimes even platonic love. And I
fell in love like everyone else. And my love had all the
attributes: rapture, adoration, poetry. . . . As a matter of
fact this love of mine was created on the one hand by her
mother and dressmaker, and on the other by the excess
food which I consumed, living as I did a life of idleness. If,
on the one hand, there had been no boating, no dressmaker emphasizing her waistline and other points, if my future wife had been wearing a shapeless dressing gown and
sitting at home, and if, on the other hand, I had been living
in the normal conditions of a man who consumes only as
much food as is required by the work he does, and if my
safety valve had been open (it happened to be closed at
the time) I would not have fallen in love and there would
have been no consequences."

VIII

"But it so happened that everything coincided: my physical state, her toilette, and the boating. Twenty times before things had not clicked but this time they did. Like fall-

ing into a trap. I am not joking. In our day marriages are set beforehand, like traps. What is the natural thing? A girl comes of age, she must be married off. A very simple thing, it seems, if the girl is not a monstrosity and there are men who wish to get married. That is how it was done in the old days. A girl came of age and her parents found a husband for her. That is how it was and still is done among all peoples—Chinese, Indians, Mohammedans, and our own peasants. That is how it is done among at least ninety-nine percent of the people of the world. But one percent of the people, profligate creatures like us, have decided that this is wrong and have thought of a new system. And what is the new system? The new system consists in having the girls sit down while the men walk up and down in front of them as at a fair, making their choice. The girls sit there and say to themselves, not daring to say it out loud, 'Here, take me! Me! Not her, but me! Look what fine shoulders and . . . er . . . other things I have!' And we men walk up and down and gaze at them and are very much pleased to have this show put on for our benefit. We gaze, and if we are not careful—snap!—we are caught!"

"And how else could it be?" I asked. "Would you have the women do the proposing?"

"I don't know how else, but if there is supposed to be equality, let there be real equality. And if the making of matches by parents is considered degrading, this is a thousand times more so. In the first case the rights and chances are at least even, whereas in this case the woman is either a slave sold on the market, or a bait put in a trap. But if you dared to suggest to a girl (or her mother) that the only thing she was occupied with was the catching of a husband —my God, what offense would be taken! And yet that actually is the only thing she does, and there is nothing else for her to do. It is an awful thing to see young and innocent creatures occupied in this way. And again, if it were all done in the open, but no, it is all underhand. 'Ah, *The Origin of the Species!* How very interesting! My Liza dotes on painting! And you intend going to the exhibition too? How edifying! And sleigh rides, and the play, and symphony concerts? How marvelous! My Liza is mad about music. How is it you do not share her views? And boating! . . .' And all the while her one thought is: 'Take me, me, or my Liza! No, me! Just for a try!' Ugh! The falseness! The horror!" And, saying this, he drank the last of the tea and set about putting away the glasses.

IX

"You are perhaps aware," he began again as he put the tea and sugar in his sack, "that all of this springs from the domination of woman—a source of untold trouble in this world."

"What do you mean by the domination of woman?" I said. "The law gives the advantage to man."

"Yes, yes, that is just it," he interrupted. "That is just what I wanted to tell you; it is that that explains the extraordinary phenomenon of woman dominating, even though she has been reduced to the lowest stage of humiliation. The one is compensation for the other, just as the Jews find compensation for the oppression they suffer in the power their money gives them. 'So, you would like us to be nothing but moneychangers, would you? Very well, then a moneychangers we shall wield power over you,' say the Jews. 'Ah, you would like us to be nothing but sensual creatures? Very well, as sensual creatures we shall make you our slaves,' say the women. A woman's lack of rights does not lie in her not having the right to vote or become a judge—the exercising of these functions is no right at all. It lies in her not being the equal of the man in sexual life, in not having the right to give herself to a man or refuse to give herself to him as she likes, in not having the right to choose a man as she likes instead of being chosen by him.

"You say this is an outrage. Very well. Then the man should not have this right either. At present the woman is deprived of a right which a man enjoys. And so to compensate for the loss of this right she acts on the man's sensibilities, subjugates him through acting on his sensibilities to such an extent that his choosing is a mere formality. It is she who does the real choosing. Once she has found this means of achieving her end, she takes advantage of it to wield a dreadful power over all people."

"Wherein lies this dreadful power?" I asked.

"Wherein? In everything, everywhere. Go through the shops of any large town. Millions of hands—more than can be counted—have labored over the things displayed there, and just see! Can anything for men's use be found in nine-tenths of these shops? All the luxuries of life are demanded and consumed by women. Count the factories. The enormous majority of them are engaged in making useless ornaments, carriages, furniture, and knicknacks for women. Millions of people, generations of slaves, wear themselves out at this cruel factory labor to satisfy the whims of women. Women, like queens, have forced nine-tenths of the human race to labor for them as their slaves. And all because they have been humiliated and deprived of equal rights with man. And so they wreak vengeance by acting on our sensibilities, by catching us in their trap. Yes, it is all because of this. Women have made of themselves so effective an instrument for working on men's sensibilities that men are unable to preserve their equanimity in their presence. As soon as a man finds himself with a woman he becomes stupefied, as by a narcotic. Formerly I cringed and felt uncomfortable when I saw a woman all decked out in a ballgown. Now I feel terrified, for I see in her something dangerous, something without the law, and I have an impulse to call for help, for the police, to demand that this danger be taken away and locked up.

"Laughing?" he shouted at me. "There is nothing to laugh at. I am certain that the time will come, and perhaps soon, when people will understand this and be amazed that there could have existed a society permitting anything as disturbing to the peace as the ornamenting of the female body with the direct intent of exciting the sensibilities. Why, it is just the same as if we set traps along the paths upon which men walked. Even worse! Why is it that gambling is forbidden, but the dressing up of women in prostitutical finery

meant to excite man's feelings is not forbidden? That is a
thousand times more dangerous!"

X

"And so, as I say, I was caught. I was what they call 'in
love.' I not only found that she was the acme of perfection,
I found that I, too, during my engagement, was the acme of
perfection. After all, the blackguard does not exist who
cannot find someone who in some respect is worse than he
is and therefore gives him some reason to be proud and
pleased with himself. So it was with me. I was not marrying
for money, greed was not a motive with me as it was with
most of my acquaintances, who married either for money
or connections; I was rich and she was poor. That was one
thing. Another was that others married with the intention of
continuing to live the same sort of polygamous lives as they
were accustomed to living, but I had made the firm resolve
to be strictly monogamous after my marriage, and this
made me unspeakably proud of myself. Yes, I was a loathsome pig who fancied himself a saint.

"My engagement did not last long. I cannot recall that
time without blushing with shame. We assume that it is a
period of spiritual and not sensual love, but if it is spiritual
love, spiritual communion, then our words, our talks, our
conversations ought to reflect this spiritual communion. But
this was not the case. Whenever we were left alone it was
very difficult to talk at all, it required a sort of Sisyphean
effort. It would take me a long time to think of something
to say. I would say it, fall silent, and try to think of something else to say. There was nothing to talk about. Everything that could be said about our future lives together,
about our plans and arrangements, had been said. What
else was there? If we had been animals, we would have
known that we were not expected to talk; but as humans
we were expected to talk and there was nothing to talk
about, because that which occupied our thoughts was not a
fitting subject for conversation. And in addition to all this,
that disgusting tradition—chocolates, the stuffing of our-

selves with sweetmeats, and all those loathsome preparations for the wedding—getting ready the apartment, the
bedroom, the bedding, dressing gowns, linen, the ward-
robe. Don't you see that under the patriarchal system defended by that old man, the dowry, the bedding, the feather beds—all of these things were details attending the
mystery. But nowadays, when hardly one man out of ten
preparing to get married believes in the mystery, or even
that what he is about to do carries with it any obligations,
when hardly one man out of a hundred can be found who
has not already been married before his marriage, and
hardly one out of fifty who is not ready to deceive his wife
at the first opportunity, when the majority of those getting
married look upon the church ceremony as merely the condition laid down for the coming into ownership of a certain
woman—when you think of all this, the dreadful significance of all these preparations becomes clear. It turns out
that they are an end in themselves. It turns out to be a sort
of sale: an innocent girl is sold to a dissolute man and the
sale is attended by fitting rites."

XI

"That is how everyone gets married, and that is how I got
married and set out on the much-sung honeymoon. How
vulgar the very name!" he muttered viciously "In Paris I
once went to an exhibition of various monstrosities, where
I saw a bearded woman and a dog that was half fish. It
turned out that the bearded woman was just a man dressed
up in woman's clothes and the dog had been put into a
seal's hide and made to swim in a bathtub. There was nothing of interest to be seen, but when I was going out the
barker pointed to me and said to the public: 'Here, ask this
gentleman whether or not it is worth seeing! Get your tickets! Get your tickets! One franc only!' I was ashamed to
say the show was not worth seeing, and this was evidently
what the barker counted on. I suppose that is how it is with
those who have had the disgusting experience of a honeymoon; they are ashamed to disillusion others. I, too, re-

frained from disillusioning others, but now I see no reason for hiding the truth. I even consider it my duty to tell the truth. My honeymoon was embarrassing, shameful, loathsome, pathetic, and above all else—boring. Unspeakably boring. It was something similar to the time when I learned to smoke, when I drooled and wanted to throw up, but swallowed down my droolings and pretended to be enjoying myself. The enjoyment of smoking comes later, if it comes at all, and so it is with this: the couple must train themselves to this vice if they are to get any pleasure out of it."

"Vice, you say?" I put in. "But you are speaking of the most natural human function."

"Natural?" said he. "Natural? No, I must say that I have come to the opposite conclusion—that it is against nature, that it is highly unnatural. Ask children. Ask innocent young girls. When my sister was very young she married a dissolute man twice her age. I remember how surprised we were on the night of her wedding to have her come running out, pale and in tears, crying that she wouldn't—not for anything, not for anything! That she could not even find words to describe what he wanted of her!

"And you call it natural! There are things that are natural. There are things that are pleasant and delightful and without shame from the very beginning. But not this. This is loathsome and shameful and painful. No, it is not natural! And I am convinced that an innocent girl always hates it."

"But how," said I, "is the human race to be perpetuated?"

"How is the human race to be perpetuated?" echoed he in a voice of irony, as if he had been expecting this usual and shameful question. "It is possible to preach birth control so that English lords may have enough to gorge themselves on; it is possible to preach birth control so that one may enjoy oneself without unpleasant consequences; but the minute one opens one's mouth to preach birth control in the name of morality—oh, what a din is raised! How is the human race to be perpetuated if a dozen or two individuals resolve that they have had enough of being pigs? But I beg your pardon. That light annoys me, do you mind if I put something over it?" he said, pointing to the lamp.

I said it made no difference to me, and he climbed up on the bench in his impulsive way and pulled the curtain over the light.

"And yet," said I, "if everyone were to adopt your ideas, the human race would become extinct."

His answer was instantly forthcoming.

"You are worried about the perpetuation of the human race?" he said, once more taking a seat opposite me, spreading his legs far apart and leaning down to put his elbows on his knees. "Why should it be perpetuated, the human race?" he asked.

"Why do you ask? Otherwise you and I would not exist."

"And why should we exist?"

"To live."

"And why should we live? If there is no aim in life, if life is an end in itself, then there is nothing to live for. And if this is true, then Schopenhauer and Hartmann and the Buddhists are perfectly right. But if there is an aim in life, then it is clear that life should come to an end when this aim is reached. That is the only conclusion," he said with agitation, evidently placing great store in this idea. "That is the only conclusion. Observe this: if the aim of human life is goodness, kindness, love; if the aim of human life is what is told us in the prophecies, that all people are to be united by love, that the sword is to be exchanged for the plowshare, and all the rest, then what is it that prevents us from achieving this aim? Our passions. And of all the passions, the strongest, the most vicious and persistent, is sexual, carnal love, and therefore if the passions are subdued, especially this, the most powerful of them, carnal love, then the prophecies will be fulfilled and mankind will be united into one, the aim of human life will be achieved, and there will no longer be anything to live for. As long as mankind exists it is inspired by the ideal, and certainly not the ideal of pigs and rabbits, which is to have as many offspring as possible, nor the ideal of monkeys and Parisians, which is to get the most refined enjoyment out of sexual indulgence. It is the ideal of goodness achieved through continence and purity. Man always has and always will strive to attain this. But see what comes of it.

"This is what comes of it: carnal love, it appears, is a safety valve. The present generation has not achieved the aim of mankind, and it has not achieved it only because of its passions, the strongest of which is sex. The sex passion exists, it produces a new generation, the new generation is presented with the opportunity of achieving the aim. But the new generation does not achieve the aim either, and so the opportunity is passed on to the next generation, and to the next, and to the next, until the aim is achieved, until the prophecies are fulfilled, until all mankind is united into one. How could it be otherwise? Let us imagine that God created human beings for the achievement of a certain aim, but created them either mortal and without the sex instinct, or immortal. If he created them mortal but without the sex instinct, what would be the result? They would live without achieving their aim and then die, and for the achievement of the aim God would have to create new people. If He created them immortal, then it is possible (although it is harder for one and the same people to correct their errors than for new people to correct the errors of their forebears and approach perfection)—it is possible, I say, that after many thousands of years they would achieve their aim. But what would be the use of these immortals then? What could be done with them? No, things are better as they are. But perhaps you object to such a statement of the case? Perhaps you are a supporter of the theory of evolution? The result is the same. The highest form of animal life—human beings—must unite like a swarm of bees in order to survive the struggle with other animals; they must not give themselves up to unlimited reproduction. Like the bees, they must develop sexless individuals, that is, must aspire to chastity rather than to the indulging of the sex instinct as is done in our society." He paused a moment. "The end of the human race? But can anyone, no matter what his views, doubt the inevitability of that? It is as certain as death. All sacred teachings foretell the end of the world, and all scientific teachings do the same. Is it, then, so strange if moral teachings point to the same end?"

For a long time after this he was silent. He drank more tea, finished smoking his cigarette, took a new supply out of his sack, and put them in his old, stained cigarette case.

"I understand your idea," I said. "The Shakers have a similar one."

"And they are right," he said. "The sex passion, in whatever form it is presented, is an evil, a dreadful evil, which is to be combated and not encouraged as it is with us. The words of the Bible, that anyone who looks upon a woman with lust has already committed adultery with her, apply not only to other men's wives, but also, and primarily, to our own wives."

XII

"In our world, everything is just the opposite. If a man practices abstinence while a bachelor, as soon as he gets married he considers abstinence no longer necessary. After all, those trips taken after the wedding, that seclusion into which the young people withdraw with the sanction of their parents—it is nothing but the sanction of profligacy. But moral laws inflict their own punishment if violated. Hard as I tried to turn our holiday into a honeymoon, I did not succeed. From beginning to end it was shameful, disgusting, and boring. But soon it became even more trying. Very soon. On the third, or perhaps the fourth day I found my wife depressed. I asked her the reason and began to pet her, thinking that must be what she wanted, but she pushed my arm away and began to cry. Why? She could not tell me. But she was unhappy, she was miserable. Probably her strained nerves told her the truth as to how loathsome our relations were, but she could not express it. I pressed her, she muttered something about missing her mother. I felt it was not the truth. I began to coax her, ignoring what she had said about her mother. I did not understand that she was simply miserable and used her mother as an excuse. But she took offense with me for having ignored her mother, as if I had not believed her. She said she was sure I did not love her. I accused her of being capricious, and suddenly her face changed completely; the expression of misery was supplanted by one of irritation, and in the most biting terms she began to accuse me of selfishness and cruelty. I looked at her. Her whole face expressed utter frigidity and hostility, almost hatred of me. I remember how shocked I was 'How is this?' I thought. 'Instead of love, a union of souls—this. Impossible! She is not herself.' I tried to mollify her, but I found myself confronted by such an implacable wall of cold, caustic hostility, that before I knew it I myself had flown into a rage and we said a lot of nasty things to each other. That first quarrel made a dreadful impression on me. I call it a quarrel, but it was not really a quarrel; it was merely a revelation of the great gulf that lay between us. Our love was exhausted as soon as our desire was satisfied, and now we stood facing each other in our true relationship, which was of two completely alien and completely selfish individuals who only wanted to get the greatest amount of satisfaction out of each other.

"I have called what happened a quarrel, but it was not a quarrel; it was merely the exposure of our true relationship brought about by the cessation of sensual desire. I did not realize that this attitude of cold hostility was the normal relationship between us, and I did not realize it because soon this attitude of hostility was hidden from sight by a new wave of sensuality, of being in love.

"I thought we had quarreled and made it up, and that we would never do such a thing again. But in this first month of honeymooning we soon reached another period of surfeit when we no longer needed each other, and this brought on another quarrel. I found the second quarrel more painful than the first. 'And so our first quarrel was not an accident after all,' I thought. 'It was only what was to be expected and will surely be repeated.' I found the second quarrel particularly shocking because it arose from the most trivial of causes—something about money, of which I was never sparing and could not possibly have begrudged my wife. I only remember that she twisted something I had said into meaning that my money gave me power over her and that I alone had the right to dispose of my money, or something equally vile and stupid and unworthy of either of us. I became angry and accused her of showing a lack of tact, she answered me back, and again we were off. In her words, in the expression of her face and eyes, I again saw that cold, cruel hostility that had shocked me so the first time. I remember having quarreled with my brother, my friends, even my father, but never had there been that peculiarly poisonous malevolence that I saw here.

"With the passage of time, however, this mutual hatred was again screened by the state of being in love, that is to say by sensuality, and again I consoled myself with the thought that these two quarrels had been mistakes that could be righted. But then there came the third and the fourth, and I realized once and for all that they were not accidents, that they could not have been avoided then and could not be avoided in the future, and the prospect horrified me. I was further tormented by the thought that it was only *my* marriage that had turned out so badly, so differently from my expectations, and that other marriages were successful. I was not then aware that this is everyone's fate, and that everyone thinks, just as I then thought, that his misfortune is an exception and hides this exceptional and shameful misfortune not only from others, but even from himself, refusing to admit it.

"Our hostility began as soon as we were married and went on and on, growing deeper and more relentless. From the very first week I felt in my heart that I was *caught,* that this was not at all what I had expected, and that marriage, instead of being a great happiness, was a great misfortune. But I, like everyone else, did not want to admit it (I would never have admitted it if it had not been for the outcome) and I hid the truth not only from others, but from myself as well. When I think back over it I am amazed that for so long a time I could have failed to see things as they really were. The very fact that our quarrels began with matters so trivial that we could not even remember them afterward should have made everything clear to me. Our reason was given no opportunity to invent weighty motives, to support the perpetual state of hostility we found ourselves in. But even more shocking were the sham motives for our reconciliations. Sometimes there were words, explanations, even tears, but at other times—how loathsome the recollection! —after having said the most cruel things to each other, we would steal shy glances, smile, kiss, embrace. Ugh, how low! How could I possibly have failed to see the vileness of it all?"

XIII

Two passengers entered and took their places in the far end of the carriage. He stopped talking until they had settled themselves, then resumed, not for a moment having lost his train of thought.

"The most loathsome thing about it," he began, "is that love is supposed to be something ideal, something elevated, whereas actually it is something so vile and bestial that even to talk or think of it is vile and shameful. And nature had her reasons for making it vile and shameful. Once it is vile and shameful it ought to be accepted as such, but instead people pretend that what is vile and shameful is beautiful and elevated. What were the first signs of my love? My indulgence in animal excess without the least shame, with even a sense of pride in being able to indulge myself in excess, and in doing so I showed not the least regard for her spiritual or even her physical welfare. I could not understand why we were so cross with each other, but the reason is clear: this crossness was nothing other than the protest made by our human nature against being subjected to the animal nature.

"I was amazed by our hatred for each other. But nothing else could have been expected. It was the mutual hatred of two parties to a crime—to the instigation and perpetration of a crime. For was it not a crime indeed when she, poor thing, became pregnant the very first month and still our animal relations went on? Do you think this is all irrelevant to the story? You are wrong. It is all part of the story of how I killed my wife. At the trial they asked me how I killed her and what I killed her with. Fools! They thought I killed her on the 5th of October with a knife. It was not then that I killed her, it was much earlier. And I did it in just the same way as all the others are doing it— all, all!"

"What do you mean?" I asked.

"That is the amazing thing—nobody wants to admit the plain and simple truth, a truth that the doctors ought to know and preach but about which they keep silent. Men and women are made just like animals in that an indulgence in carnal love is followed by pregnancy, the feeding of the offspring, a physical state during which physical love is harmful for both mother and child. There is an equal number of men and women. What does that indicate? I think it is clear. It does not require great wisdom to draw the conclusion drawn by animals, namely—abstinence. But it is not drawn. Scientists are clever enough to have discovered a lot of useless things such as leucocytes that swim about in the blood, but they are not clever enough to have discovered this. I, at least, have not heard them mention it.

"And so there are only two ways out for the woman: one is to mutilate herself by destroying at once or by degrees her ability to be a woman that is, a mother, so that her husband may take his pleasure whenever he likes; the other is hardly a way out, it is simply the coarse and direct violation of laws of nature that is committed by all of our so-called upright families. It means that a woman, despite her nature, must be an expectant mother and a nursing mother and her husband's mistress at one and the same time, an imposition that not a single animal will submit to. And she has not the strength for it. That is why women of our class become nervous and hysterical, and women of the peasant class become *klikushi*.* Observe that young girls, innocent young girls are never *klikushi;* only women, and women who have husbands. That is true of our people. It is just as true of Europeans. All the hospitals are filled with women who have been made hysterical by violating

Klikushi—the folk name for brawling, hysterical peasant women.—*Tr.*

laws of nature. But *klikushi* and Charcot's patients are women who have become completely deranged; the world is full of women who have not yet reached that stage.

"How awe-inspiring is the woman's act of bearing the fruit of her womb and nursing the child she has borne! It is our successors she creates, those who are to prolong the human race. And what is it that breaks in upon this sacred act? The very thought is horrifying! And yet they talk of emancipation, of the rights of women! It is as if cannibals who were fattening their victims for the slaughter assured them at the same time that they were concerned about their rights and freedom."

I found his ideas new and shocking.

"But what is to be done?" I said. "If what you say is true, then a man can make love to his wife only once in two years; but men—"

"Men cannot live without it," he broke in. "Again the respected priests of science have convinced everyone of this. I would like to hear what these savants would say if they were forced to carry out the functions of the women who they claim are so necessary to men. Impress upon a man that vodka, tobacco, and opium are essential to him, and they will become essential. It is as if God had created things all wrong because He did not know what was essential and did not consult the savants. As you see, things do not dovetail. The men have decided that they cannot live without satisfying their lust, but here comes childbirth and nursing to interfere with the satisfying of their lust. What is to be done? Appeal to the savants. They will arrange everything. And they do. Oh, when will the doctors and their lies be exposed? It is high time! It has reached the point at which people go mad and shoot themselves all on account of this. And how could it be otherwise? Animals seem to know that offspring are for the purpose of perpetuating their kind, and they observe laws in respect to this. Only man does not know and does not care to know. The only thing he wants is to enjoy himself as much as possible. And who is he? Man, the King of the Universe. Just think—animals copulate only when it is possible to create offspring, whereas the filthy King of the Universe copulates whenever he can, and only for pleasure. What is more, he tries to identify this with the most exalted feeling—love. And in the name of this love—that is, this vileness—he sacrifices half of the human race. For the sake of his own pleasure he makes an enemy of woman, who ought to be his helpmate in leading mankind to a recognition of goodness and truth. Tell me this: who prevents mankind from moving ahead? Woman. And why is she what she is? Only because of this. Yes, yes," he repeated over and over again as he rummaged for a cigarette, then began to smoke, evidently trying to compose himself.

XIV

"So that was the bestial sort of life I lived," he went on in the same tone. "The worst thing about it was that, living such a life, I fancied that because I did not allow myself to be seduced by other women and remained faithful to my wife I was a man of moral principle, a man without fault, and that if we quarreled, she, or rather her character, was to blame.

"But she was not to blame. She was no different from all other women, at least the majority of them. She had been brought up in the way demanded by the position of woman in our society, in the way all women from the privileged classes are brought up, in the only way it is natural for them to be brought up. We hear much talk about the modern education of women. Empty words. The education of women is exactly what it ought to be so long as our attitude to women remains what it is (and not what we pretend it is).

"The education of women will always correspond with men's attitude toward them. We all know how men look upon women. *'Wein, Weiber, und Gesang'*—that is what the poets sing. Take the whole of poetry, the whole of painting and sculpture, beginning with the appearance of love lyrics and naked Venuses—everywhere woman is looked upon as a means of enjoyment, at court balls as

well as on Trubnaya Square or Grachevka Street. And note
the devil's cunning: if it were nothing but pleasure and enjoyment, we would accept it as such—pleasure and enjoyment. Woman is a sweet morsel and nothing else. But no,
the knights were the first who professed to worship woman
as something above them (worshiped her and yet looked
upon her as a means of enjoyment). Today men profess to
respect her. Some men give up their chairs to her and pick
up her handkerchiefs, others recognize her right to occupy
any post at all—administrative, executive—any at all. That
is what they profess, but their attitude toward her remains
the same. She is a means of enjoyment. Her body is a
means of giving pleasure. And she is aware of this. It is a
form of slavery.

"Slavery is nothing but a state in which some people
reap the benefit of the forced labor of others. Slavery can
be abolished only when people no longer wish to reap the
benefit of the forced labor of others because they consider it sinful or shameful. But what they actually do is to
change the outer forms of slavery by forbidding the sale of
slaves, and then they fancy (and convince themselves) that
slavery has been abolished, not seeing and not wishing to
see that slavery continues to exist because people go on
wanting to reap the benefit of other people's labor and
consider it right and just to do so. So long as this is considered right, there will be found people who, being stronger and more cunning than others, will bring about slavery.

"So it is with the emancipation of woman. The slavery of
woman consists in having man consider it right and desirable to use her for his pleasure. And then they set about
emancipating her—they give her the same rights as man,
but continue to regard her as a means of enjoyment, train-
ing her to this in childhood and teaching it by means of
public opinion. And she continues to be the same debased,
profligate slave, and men continue to be the same profligate slaveholders.

"They emancipate woman in colleges and courts, but go
on regarding her as a means of enjoyment. As long as she
is taught (as we teach her) to look upon herself in this way,

she will continue to be a creature of a lower order. Either, with the aid of the dastardly doctors, she will prevent herself from conceiving, which means she will become a prostitute, one who has descended to the level not of beasts, but of things; or else she will be what she really is in most cases—miserable, hysterical, mentally unbalanced, incapable of spiritual development.

"Schools and colleges can do nothing about this. The only thing that can change it is a change in man's attitude toward woman, and of woman's attitude toward herself. It will only be changed when women come to consider a state of virginity the highest state and not the shame and disgrace it is now considered. Until such a time, the aspiration of every girl, no matter what her education, will be to attract as many men as she can so that she will have a chance to choose from among them.

"The fact that she knows mathematics or can perform on the harp will not change matters in the least. A woman is happy and has achieved her highest aim when she has captivated a man. And so her principal aim in life is to be able to captivate men. It has been so in the past, it will be so in the future. It applies to unmarried girls as well as to married women. Unmarried girls must be able to do this to insure themselves a choice; married women must do it to exert power over their husbands.

"The one thing that stops her efforts in this direction, or rather suspends them temporarily, is childbirth, and then only when she is not a monster, that is to say when she nurses her babies herself. But again the doctors step in.

"My wife, who wanted to nurse her children and did nurse five of them, was not well after the birth of her first child. The doctors, who shamefully stripped her and felt her all over (for which I was expected to thank them and pay them a fee)—these honorable doctors found that she ought not to nurse her first child, and so she was deprived of the only means of getting rid of her coquetry. A wet nurse was found for the child, which meant that we took advantage of a strange woman's poverty and ignorance to lure her away from her own baby and give her to ours, for which we dressed her in a starched cap with braid on it. But that is aside from the point. The point is that when my wife's confinement was over and she was released from nursing her child, the coquetry that had been lying dormant in her broke out with exceptional force. And in direct proportion to her coquetry I was tortured by a jealousy that had not given me a moment's peace since the first day of my married life, a jealousy that must inevitably torture all husbands who live with their wives as I lived with mine, which is to say—immorally."

XV

"Not for a minute during the whole of my married life was I free of the pangs of jealousy. But there were periods when my sufferings became more acute. One of these periods was after the birth of our first child, when the doctors forbade my wife to nurse it. I was particularly jealous at this time, first of all, because my wife experienced the anxiety which any mother would feel on having the natural course of things interrupted without any good cause; and secondly because, on seeing the ease with which she shook off the moral obligations of a mother, I justly (if unconsciously) concluded that she might just as easily shake off her conjugal obligations, especially since she was perfectly well and, despite the prohibition of the honorable doctors, nursed her other children herself without any ill effects."

"You waste no love on the doctors," observed I, having noticed a particularly spiteful glint in his eyes every time he mentioned them.

"It is not a question of loving them or not loving them. They ruined my life just as they ruin the lives of hundreds of thousands of others, and I cannot detach cause from effect. I can understand that they, like lawyers, are anxious to squeeze money out of their patients and I would gladly have given them half of my income (as would anyone else who understood the true state of affairs) if by doing so I could have kept them from having anything to do with my family life. I have not gathered statistics, but I know of dozens of instances (there are innumerable ones) when doctors killed either the baby in the womb, declaring that the mother was unable to bear children (although later she bore them very successfully), or the mother herself by subjecting her to some sort of operation. Nobody calls such deaths murder, just as in the Middle Ages the killings of the Inquisition were not called murder, because they were said to be done for the human welfare. The crimes doctors commit are countless. But all these crimes are as nothing compared with the moral corruption of the materialism they bring into the world, especially through the medium of women. Moreover, if we were to follow their advice we would seek to achieve a state of isolation one from another due to the infection to be found everywhere and in everything, instead of striving toward the unity of the human race; according to their teachings each of us should sit alone with a solution of carbolic acid in his mouth (although this, by the way, has recently been discovered to be ineffective). But that, too, is nothing. The main thing is that they corrupt people, especially women.

"Nowadays one cannot say, 'Your ways are bad, you must change them.' One cannot say this to oneself or to anyone else. If your ways are bad the cause lies in a disturbance of the nervous system or something of the sort, and you must go to the doctors and they will prescribe thirty-five kopeks' worth of medicine which you must take. You become worse, you go to more doctors and take more medicine. A splendid practice!

"But that is not the point. I only wanted to say that she successfully nursed her other children and that her pregnancies and periods of nursing were the only things that saved me from the sufferings of jealousy. If it had not been for them, what happened eventually would have happened much sooner. The children saved her and me. In eight years she had five children. And she nursed all five of them herself."

"And where are they now, your children?" I asked.

"My children?" he repeated with a frightened look.

"Forgive me; perhaps it is painful to be reminded of them?"

"No, it is nothing. My children were taken by my wife's brother and his wife. They would not let me keep them. I gave them all of my property, but they would not let me keep the children. I'm considered insane. I have just been to see them. I spoke to them, but they will not give the children to me. You see I would bring them up to be different from their parents, and they must not be different. Ah, well, what is to be done? Naturally they will not give them to me and will not trust me. And I am not sure I would have the strength to bring them up. I am afraid I would not. I am a ruin, a wreck. But there is one thing I have. Knowledge. Yes, I know things that it will take others a long time to learn.

"My children are alive and growing up to be barbarians, like everyone else. I saw them—three times. There is nothing I can do for them. Nothing. I am on my way to the south. I have a little house and a garden there.

"Yes, it will take others a long time to find out what I know. It will not take us long to find out how much iron and other metals are contained in the sun and the stars, but to find out things exposing our own bestiality—that is hard, very hard. . . .

"You, at least, listen to what I have to say. For that I am grateful."

XVI

"You mentioned my children. Again, what a false attitude is taken toward children! Children are a joy! Children are God's blessing! A lie. They may have been once, but they are not now. Children are a torment, and nothing else. Most mothers are fully aware of this and even say as much if they are caught off their guard. Ask any mother of the privileged classes and she will tell you that she does not want to have children for fear of their falling ill and dying, and if she happens to give birth to a child she does not want to nurse it for fear of becoming too attached to it and having to suffer. The delight taken in a child's loveliness—in its little hands and feet and body—all the delight a child affords is less than the suffering caused not only by its falling ill or dying, but by the very fear of its falling ill or dying. In weighing the advantages and disadvantages of having children, the disadvantages always outweigh the advantages, and that is why it is better not to have children. Women say this plainly, boldly, fancying that their feelings spring from a love of children—a good, commendable feeling, one of which they are proud. They fail to realize that this way of thinking is a denial of love and an assertion of selfishness. The joy they take in a child is less than the suffering it causes them, and therefore they do not want to have a child. It is not themselves they sacrifice for the sake of the loved one, but what might be a loved one for the sake of themselves.

"Clearly this is not love but selfishness. But it is hard to blame rich mothers for this selfishness—one cannot utter a word of protest if one recalls what the health of their children costs women (again thanks to the doctors) in aristocratic society. Even today a shudder passes over me every time I remember the life and the mental state of my wife in those early days when there were three or four children who took up every minute of her time and every ounce of her energy. She had no time for me at all. We lived under a constant threat of danger, of being rescued from this danger, of having it return, of making desperate efforts to ward it off, of being rescued again—as if we were on a sinking ship. Sometimes it occurred to me that this atmosphere was created on purpose, that my wife feigned anxiety for the children's welfare so as to insure her triumph over me; it was a very simple, tempting means of having all questions solved to her advantage. Sometimes I fancied that all she did and said was done and said hypocritically. But I was wrong. She was really dreadfully harassed, she was in a constant state of anxiety about the children, their health, their ailments. It was torture for her as well as for me. And she could not help being tortured. Concern for her children, the animal concern to see that they were fed, comforted, defended, was as strong in her as it is in most women, but she had something else that animals are free of—reason and imagination. A hen does not worry about what may happen to her chick, she does not know of all the many diseases that it may fall prey to, nor does she know of all the remedies that people fancy can prevent illness and death. And so for the hen offspring are not a torment. She does for them what she must do, and does it joyfully; for her, offspring are a joy. If her chick falls ill she knows exactly what to do: she feeds it and keeps it warm. And in doing this she knows she is doing all that is necessary. If the chick dies she does not ask herself why it died and where it has gone; she clucks a bit, gets over it, and goes on living as before. But this is not enough for our unfortunate women, my wife in particular. She heard and read a countless number of the most varied and variable rules on the education and upbringing of children, to say nothing of children's diseases and their cure. They must be fed this and that; no, not this and that, but that and this. Every week we, especially my wife, found out something new about how they should be fed, clothed, bathed, put to bed, taken for walks, given the air. As if children had begun to be born only yesterday. If one of the children fell ill it was because it had not been fed right, or bathed right, or at the proper time; in a word, my wife was to blame for the illness because she had not done what she ought to have.

"It was bad enough when the children were well, but if they fell ill, life became hell. It is assumed that diseases can be cured, that there is a certain branch of science dealing with this and there are certain people—doctors—who know how to effect these cures. Not all of them know how, but the best of them do. And so here we have a sick child, and we must find that very best of doctors, the one who knows how, and then the child will be saved; but if we do not find that particular doctor, or if we do not happen to live where he lives, the child is doomed. My wife was not the only one who believed this: all the women of our set did, and on every hand she heard nothing else 'Yekaterina

Semyonovna lost two children because she did not call in Ivan Zakharich soon enough.' 'Ivan Zakharich saved Maria Ivanovna's elder girl.' 'On the doctor's advice the Petrovs went to live in different hotels and the children were saved; if they hadn't the children would have died.' 'So-and-so's child was very frail; on the doctor's advice they moved to the south and the child was saved.' How could she help being perpetually worried and harassed when the life of her children, for whose welfare she was as concerned as any animal is, depended on finding out what Ivan Zakharich would say on a certain matter before it was too late? But nobody knew what Ivan Zakharich would say, he least of all, for he knew only too well that he knew nothing and could do nothing; he could only exert some chance influence to keep people from losing faith in him as a doctor who knew how. If she had been wholly an animal she would not have suffered these tortures; if she had been wholly a human being she would have believed in God and would have said and thought, as believers say and think: 'God giveth, God taketh away; nothing is done but by the will of God.' She would have thought that the life and death of all people, including her own children, was within the power of God and not of man, and then she would not have been tortured by the thought that she was able to prevent the illness and death of her children and would not have attempted to. But this was how she looked at it: she was entrusted with the weakest and most delicate of creatures, creatures who might fall prey to a countless number of ills; she felt a passionate, animal love for these creatures, she was responsible for them, and yet the means of preserving them was hidden from all but a few pundits whose advice and services could be obtained only for a large sum of money, and not always at that.

"My wife's life with her children, and consequently mine as well, was a torture rather than a joy. How could it be otherwise? She was in constant anguish. Sometimes in the calm following a jealous scene or an ordinary quarrel, I would hope to relax, I would long to read, to think, but no sooner would I set my mind on something than news would come that Vasya had vomited, or there were blood streaks in Masha's stool, or Andrei had broken out in a rash, and there I was—all my hopes dashed to the ground. Where must I go? What doctor must I get? How were we to isolate the child? And then—medicine, thermometers, enemas, doctors. . . . Scarcely was this siege over when another began. There was no such thing as a normal, well-regulated family life. In its stead there was, as I have said, a ceaseless rescuing of ourselves from real and imaginary dangers. That is how it is in most families. It was particularly true of my family, for my wife was extremely credulous and very fond of children.

"And so the coming of children poisoned our life instead of improving it. Furthermore, the children were a new cause of dissension. This became evident as soon as they appeared, and the older they grew, the oftener they were a means and an object of dissension. They were not only an object of dissension, they were a weapon of struggle as well. We fought each other with our children. Each of us had his favorite child and used it as his weapon. My thrusts were usually directed against our eldest boy, Vasya; hers, against Liza. As the children grew up and their characters developed they became prospective allies, whom each of us tried to win over to his side. They, poor things, suffered dreadfully from this, but we were too much engrossed in our constant state of war to think of them. Our daughter was on my side, our eldest boy (he resembled my wife and was her favorite) was on hers, and I often found him hateful."

XVII

"And so we lived from day to day. Our relations became more and more antagonistic. In the end it was not disagreements that gave rise to antagonism, but antagonism that gave rise to disagreements. I disagreed with anything she had to say before she said it, and she did the same.

"In the fourth year both parties concluded independently that we could neither understand each other nor be in accord. We no longer tried to come to an understanding. In the most simple matters, especially if they concerned the children, each of us kept to his own unwavering opinion. As I recall it now, the opinions I defended were not so dear to me but that I could have relinquished them; but her opinions were different, and so to have given in would have meant giving in to her. This I could not do. Nor could she. Probably she considered herself to be in the right; I was certain that I was. When we were alone together we were doomed to silence or to carrying on conversations that were practically on an animal level: 'What time is it?' 'Time to go to bed.' 'What are we having for dinner today?' 'Where shall we go?' 'What news in the papers?' 'We must send for the doctor; Masha has a sore throat.' If we diverged from these impossibly narrow subjects of conversation by a hair's breadth, we were sure to become exasperated. We flared up, vituperations were called forth by the coffee, the tablecloth, the carriage, a move in a card game—things that could not possibly have held the slightest importance either for her or for me. For myself I may say that at times my hatred of her reached a fantastic pitch. Sometimes as I watched her pouring our tea, swinging her foot, lifting a spoon to her mouth, or sipping tea, I hated her for the way she did it as much as if it were the most heinous of crimes. At that time I failed to notice that my periods of hate regularly and inevitably followed the periods of what is called love. A period of love, a period of hate; a weak period of love, a brief period of hate; an intense period of love, a prolonged period of hate. We did not then realize that this love and hate were different aspects of one and the same animal feeling.

"Life would have been a nightmare if we had understood the true state of affairs, but we did not understand, we did not see things as they really were. In that lies a person's salvation as well as his punishment: however wrong a person's way of life is, he is able to hide it from himself, to disguise the tragedy of his situation. That is what we did. She found distraction in strained, flustered household activities, arranging the rooms, dressing herself and the children, studying, looking after the children's health. I had my own means of intoxication—the intoxication of work, hunting, and cards. Both of us kept busy all of the time. Both of us felt that the busier we were, the nastier we had a right to be to each other 'It's all very well for you to make those faces,' I said to her mentally, 'you kept me awake all night with that row of yours, and now I have to attend a conference.' 'It's all very well for you,' she said not only mentally but aloud, 'but I was kept awake all night by the baby.'

"And that is how we went on living, in a sort of fog that kept us from seeing things as they really were. And if what happened later had never happened, I might have lived to a ripe old age, thinking to the day of my death that I had lived a good life—not particularly good, but good enough—the sort everybody lives; I would never have realized in what an abyss of misery and falsehood I was floundering.

"We were like two mortal enemies put together in the stocks, bound by a single chain, poisoning each other's lives and refusing to admit it. I was not yet aware that ninety-nine percent of all husbands and wives live in the same way, and that this is inevitable. At that time I did not know this about myself or about others.

"What strange coincidences occur in life, whether one is living the right or the wrong way! When parents reach a point at which life is quite unbearable, it becomes necessary to move into town for the sake of the children's education. We, too, were confronted by this necessity."

He grew silent and twice made the sound that was like a suppressed sob. We were approaching a station.

"What time is it?" he asked.

I looked. It was two o'clock.

"Aren't you tired?" he asked.

"No, but you must be."

"I feel suffocated. I shall take a walk and have a drink of water."

And, swaying on his feet, he walked off down the corridor. I sat there alone, going over in my mind all he had

said, and so lost in thought was I that I did not notice him
come back through the door at the other end.

XVIII

"I cannot speak calmly," he began. "I have spent much
time pondering over these things, I have come to look upon
many things differently, and I want to impart my view to
others.

"Well, we began to live in town. It is easier for unhappy
people to live in town. In town a person can live a hundred
years without realizing he has died and gone to dust long
ago. There is no time to 'know thyself.' Everyone is too busy.
Business affairs, social demands, health, art, the health of
one's children, the education of one's children. Today you
must entertain so-and-so; tomorrow you must call on so-
and-so. You must see this and hear that. In town there is
always one, or perhaps two, or even three celebrities who
are not to be ignored. This one, that one, or the other one
has to take treatments; there is the teacher, the tutor, the
governess; and on the whole, life is as empty as a barrel.

"That is how we lived, and the pain of our living together
was assuaged. During the first months we were occupied
with the fascinating task of settling ourselves in the new
flat, in the new town, and making trips from town to country and from country to town.

"One winter went by, and during the next there occurred
what seemed to be a trifling, insignificant circumstance, but
one that was directly responsible for what happened
eventually. She was not well, and those rascals declared
she must not have any more children and taught her how
to avoid having them. I found this repulsive. I did everything I could to prevent it, but she insisted on it with frivolous obstinacy, and I gave in. The last excuse for our bestiality—children—was now removed, and life became more
disgusting than ever.

"Peasants and workingmen have need of children; however hard it is to feed them, they have need of them, and

so their conjugal life is justified. But we of the upper classes
have children without any need of them, they are only an
extra care and expense, they are unwanted claimants to
the legacy, they are a burden. And so we are left without
any justification whatever for our bestiality. Either we use
artificial means of ridding ourselves of children, or we look
upon them as a misfortune, a mistake resulting from lack of
caution, which is the most disgusting of all. There is no justification. But we have fallen so low that we do not even see
any need of justification. The vast majority of educated
people today give themselves up to profligacy without any
pangs of conscience.

"And how could we suffer pangs of conscience when
there is no longer any conscience, unless we can call public opinion or the Criminal Code a sort of conscience? But
in this case neither the one nor the other is outraged: public
opinion cannot object because *everybody* does it, even Maria Pavlovna and Ivan Zakharich. (What? Would you have
us breed a lot of beggars or deprive ourselves of the opportunity of moving in society?) As for the Criminal Code—
there is nothing to fear here. It is only low women and
soldiers' sweethearts who throw their babies into pools and
wells; they, of course, must be put in prison, but *we* do everything in good time and antiseptically.

"For two more years we lived in this way. The rascals'
methods were effective: she blossomed forth, grew stronger
and more beautiful, like a flower in late summer. Aware of
this, she began to pay more attention to herself. There was
something challenging, something disturbing about her
beauty. She was a full-blown, thirty-year-old, non-child-
bearing, well-fed, spirited young woman. The sight of her
caused a fluttering of the heart. When she moved among
men she attracted their gaze. She was like a well-fed un-
exercised horse in full trappings that is suddenly given the
rein. There was no rein on her at all, as there is no rein on
ninety-nine percent of our women. I realized this and was
afraid."

XIX

He got up impulsively and took a seat at the window.

"I beg your pardon," he said, turning away. There he sat gazing out of the window for some three minutes. Then he gave a sigh and came back to sit beside me. His face was quite different, there was a pathetic look in his eyes and his lips were puckered into something like a smile.

"I am a bit tired, but I will go on. There is still a lot of time left—it is not yet growing light. Ye-es," he began, lighting a cigarette, "she grew fair and buxom when she ceased bearing children, and her illness—that incessant suffering because of the children—got better. Not that it disappeared entirely, but she was like one emerging from a drunken torpor, who suddenly sees the world about her with all its joys, a world she had forgotten about, that she had been unable to appreciate, that she had not understood, 'I must not let it slip by! Time is passing, it will never return!' That, it seems to me, is what she thought, or rather, what she felt, and she could not have thought and felt otherwise: she had been brought up to believe that there is only one thing worth living for—love. She had got married, and although she had received something from that love, it was far from being what she had expected, what she had been promised; on the contrary, it had brought her much disappointment and suffering, in addition to a quite unexpected form of torment—children. This torment had worn her out. And now, thanks to the solicitous doctors, she had discovered that one can avoid having children. She rejoiced, she enjoyed the new sensation, she was rejuvenated for the one purpose she knew in life—love. But not love with a sullied, jealous, spiteful husband. She began to dream of a different sort of love, something new and pure. At least so I fancied. And she began to look about her, as if awaiting someone. I saw this and became alarmed. Over and over again, when, as was her custom, she spoke to me through the medium of others—that is, when she spoke to others but addressed her words to me

—she said boldly and with a half playful air (seeming to forget that she had expressed the opposite view an hour before) that a mother's devotion to her children was a deception, that it was not worth sacrificing one's life for one's children when one was still young and could enjoy life. So she gave her children less attention, and what she gave lacked the old desperate intensity, and she spent more and more time on herself and her appearance, although she screened the fact by indulging in pleasure, and even in self-improvement. Once more she took up the piano, which she had quite abandoned. And that is how everything began."

His tired eyes wandered to the window again, but he instantly drew them back and seemed to be forcing himself to go on.

"And then came that man."

He paused and made his strange sound two or three times. I could see that it was painful for him to name the man, to recall him, to speak of him. But he forced himself to, and his voice was full of determination, as if he were tearing down barriers.

"He was a vile creature, I thought. And not because of the role he played in my life, but because he really was vile. His being vile, by the way, is proof of how irresponsible she was. If it had not been he, it would have been someone else—it was bound to happen!" Again he paused. "He was a musician, a violinist; not a professional violinist —half musician, half society man. His father was a landowner, my own father's neighbor. His father lost all his money and the children—there were three boys—went to work, all but the youngest, who was sent to his godmother in Paris. There he was enrolled in the conservatoire because he had a talent for music, and he finished as a violinist and played at concerts. As a man he was—" Evidently he had intended to say something beastly about him, but he restrained himself and went on quickly, "I can't say what sort of life he led there: I only know that that year he appeared in Russia and came to my house.

"Moist, almond-shaped eyes, smiling red lips, a waxed mustache, the latest style of hairdress, vulgarly good-looking, what the women call 'not bad,' a weak but not ugly physique with a well-developed backside such as women have, or Hottentots, so they say. Hottentots, too, are musical, I have heard. He became familiar if given the opportunity, but, being sensitive, recoiled at the slightest rebuff. He held himself with dignity, wore buttoned boots of a peculiar Parisian shade, bright neckties, and other things which foreigners pick up in Paris and which always impress the women because of their novelty and originality. He always assumed an affected, superficial gaiety, and had a manner of speaking in hints and snatches, as if everyone knew what he wanted to say and could finish it for himself.

"He and his music were the cause of everything. At the trial it was made to appear that everything happened because of jealousy. Nothing of the sort—that is, not nothing of the sort, but still—not that. At the trial it was decided that I was a wronged husband who had killed my wife in defense of my honor (that is the name they gave to it). And so I was acquitted. At the trial I attempted to show things in their true light, but they thought I was just trying to preserve my wife's fair name.

"Whatever her relations were with that musician, they meant nothing to me, or to her either. The only thing that meant anything was what I have already told you—my bestiality. Everything happened because there was that dreadful gulf between us; so great was the strain of our mutual hatred that the slightest provocation was enough to bring things to a head. Our quarrels had become terrible, and they were the more terrible in that they alternated with periods of intense animal passion.

"If that man had not put in an appearance, another would. If the motivating force had not been jealousy, it would have been something else. I contend that all men who live as I did must either become completely corrupt, or leave their wives, or kill themselves or their wives, as I did. Anyone who escapes is a rare exception. Before I ended things in the way I did, I had been many times on the verge of suicide, and she, too, had attempted to poison herself."

XX

"Yes, that is how things were not long before the end. We were living under a sort of armistice that we ought to have preserved. But then one day I remarked that a certain dog had won a medal at a show.

" 'Not a medal but a recommendation,' she said.

"We began to argue. We jumped from one subject to another. There were reproaches:

" 'Oh, everybody knows that; it's always like that. You said . . .'

" 'I said nothing of the kind.'

" 'In other words I'm a liar?!'

"I felt that we were on the verge of one of those terrible quarrels that made me want to kill her or myself. I was sure we were on the verge of it, I dreaded it like fire, I wanted to restrain myself, but my whole being was consumed by fury. She was in the same or even worse state; she intentionally distorted what I said, gave my words the wrong meaning. Every word she spoke was saturated with poison; she sought out my most vulnerable spots and was sure to make her thrusts there. On and on. I shouted, 'Hold your tongue!' or something of the sort. She jumped up and rushed into the nursery. I tried to stop her so that I could finish what I had to say. I seized her arm. She pretended to be hurt and cried out, 'Children! Your father is hurting me!'

" 'Don't lie!' I shouted.

" 'It isn't the first time!' she shouted back.

"The children rushed to her side. She tried to calm them.

" 'Don't pretend,' I said.

" 'For you everything is pretense; you could kill a person and then accuse him of pretending. Now I understand everything—that's just what you want!'

" 'I'll see you dead!' I shrieked.

"Even now I can remember how horrified I was by my own words. I had not supposed myself capable of saying such harsh, dreadful words, and I could not believe they had come out of my mouth. After shrieking them I ran into my study, sat down, and began to smoke. I heard her go into the hall and put on her things. I asked her where she was going. She did not answer. 'The devil with her,' I said to myself; and returned to my study, where I lay down and began to smoke again.

"Through my head passed a thousand plans for taking revenge on her, for getting rid of her, for patching things up and going on as if nothing had happened. There I lay thinking and smoking, smoking, smoking. I thought of running away from her, going in hiding, leaving for America. I reached the point of imagining life without her, how marvelous it would be, how I would join my life with that of another, a wonderful woman, utterly different. I would get rid of her by having her die, or by divorcing her, and I began to scheme how to accomplish this. I realized I was thinking things I ought not to think, and I smoked to keep myself from facing this realization.

"Life in the house ran its usual course. The governess came in and asked where the mistress was and when she would be back. The footman came in and asked if he should serve tea. I went into the dining room. The children, especially Liza, who was old enough to understand, cast looks of cold inquiry at me. We had our tea in silence. She did not come back. The evening passed and still she did not come back. Two feelings warred within me: anger with her for torturing me and the children by staying away when she knew she would only come back again, and fear that she would not come back but would lay hands on herself. I would have gone in search of her, but where was I to go? To her sister's? I would look foolish if I went and asked for her, and that was just what she wanted. The deuce with her! If she was so bent on torturing somebody, let it be herself. Otherwise the next quarrel would only be worse. But what if she were not at her sister's and intended laying hands on herself, or had already done so?

"Eleven o'clock, twelve . . . I did not go up to the bedroom—silly to just lie there alone and wait. I could not lie down in my study, either. I wanted to busy myself with something, to write letters, or to read, but I could do nothing. I sat alone in my study—angry, tortured by my thoughts, listening for the least sound.

"Three o'clock, four—still she did not come. Toward morning I fell asleep. I woke up. She had not come.

"Life at home went on, but everyone was perplexed and kept looking at me inquiringly and reproachfully, assuming that it was all my fault. And within me the same struggle was going on—anger with her for torturing me and anxiety about her.

"At about eleven o'clock her sister came as an emissary from her. She began in the usual way: 'She is in a dreadful state. What could have happened?'

" 'Why, nothing happened,' and I added that she had an impossible character and that I had done nothing at all.

" 'But things cannot remain as they are,' said her sister.

" 'That is up to her, not me,' said I. 'I refuse to take the first step. If we are to separate, we must separate.'

"My sister-in-law went away without any satisfaction. I had boldly declared that I would not take the first step, but when she was gone and I came out and saw the children looking so frightened and pathetic, I was quite ready to reconsider this. I would have been only too glad to take the first step, but I did not know how. Again I paced the floor and smoked. I drank vodka and wine for breakfast and gradually achieved what I had unconsciously been longing for: I lost sight of the baseness and stupidity of the stand I had taken.

"At about three o'clock she came home. She said nothing on seeing me. Supposing that she had repented, I began to explain that my words had been evoked by her reproaches. With the same stern and haggard face she said she had not come for explanations but to take the children, that we could not go on living together. I tried to say it was not my fault, that she had driven me to desparation. For a moment she stared at me harshly, gloatingly, then she said:

" 'Say nothing more; you'll only regret it.'

"I said I could not abide comedy. At this she shouted something unintelligible and rushed to her room. I heard the key turn in the door—she had locked herself in. I knocked, there was no answer, and I stamped wrathfully away. Half an hour later Liza came running to me in tears.

" 'What is it? Has something happened?'

" 'There's not a sound coming from Mama's room.'

"We went to the room. I pulled on the door with all my might. The lock did not hold and both halves of the door opened. I went over to the bed. She was lying unconscious, in an awkward position, in her skirts and boots. On the bed table lay an empty bottle of opium. We brought her to. Again tears, and at last a reconciliation. But not a real reconciliation; the old animosity remained in the heart of each of us, and to it was added the resentment for the suffering this quarrel had caused us and for which each blamed the other. But we could not go on nursing our resentment forever, and so life resumed its old course. Quarrels like this and even worse took place all the time—once a month, once a week, once a day. The same thing over and over. Once I applied for a passport to go abroad (our quarrel had lasted two days), but then there was a half explanation, a half reconciliation, and I did not go."

XXI

"This was the situation when that man put in an appearance. As soon as he arrived in Moscow (his name was Trukhachevsky) he came to see me. It was a morning visit. I received him. At one time he and I had been on intimate terms, and during our talk he felt his way, trying to restore our terms of intimacy, but I made it clear from the very beginning that I did not want to, and he adapted himself to my tone. I disliked him the moment I set eyes on him. But oddly enough, some strange, fatal force prevented me from repulsing him, from sending him away, and made me, on the contrary, encourage him. How easy it would have been for me to have received him coolly and sent him away without introducing him to my wife! But no, I had to talk about his playing, to say someone had told me he had dropped the violin. He denied it and said he was playing more than ever. He recalled that I had once played. I said I did not play any more but that my wife played very well.

"And an amazing thing: my relations with him from the very first day, from the very first hour, were such as they would have been had I foreseen the outcome of this visit. There was a certain tension between us; I noted every word, every expression either of us used, and attributed special significance to it.

"I introduced my wife to him. The talk immediately turned to music and he offered to come and play with her. My wife was handsomely and alluringly dressed (as she always was of late) and looked disturbingly beautiful. She seemed to like him from the first. She was also delighted with the prospect of playing piano and violin duets, for she especially enjoyed this and often hired a violinist from the theater to play with her. Her face expressed her joy. A glimpse of my face told her how I felt about it and she instantly changed her expression, and that game of mutual deception began. I smiled graciously, pretending to be pleased. He looked at my wife in the way all lechers look at women, but pretended to be interested only in what we were talking about, although he was not at all interested in it. She tried to appear indifferent, but she could not help being disturbed by the false smile of her jealous husband (a smile she knew only too well) and the lustful glances of our visitor. I noticed a special shine in her eye the first time she saw him, and probably it was my jealousy that caused an electric current to flow between them, making them duplicate each other's smiles, glances, and facial expressions. She blushed—he blushed; he smiled—she smiled. He got up to leave and stood there smiling, holding his hat against his quivering calf, glancing from her to me as if waiting to see what we would do. That moment is especially impressed on my memory because at that moment I could have refrained from inviting him back, and then nothing would have happened. But I looked at him, then at her, and said to her in my mind, 'Don't think I am jealous,' and to him, 'Don't think I am afraid,' and then I invited him to bring his violin some evening and play with my wife. She glanced at me in astonishment, blushed, and, as if afraid of something, protested that she played too poorly to accompany him. Her refusal to play only irritated me the more, and I insisted that he come. I remember the strange feeling with which I stared at the back of his head and noted a slitter of white neck that came and went under his black hair as he walked jerkily, with a birdlike hop, out of the room. I could not help confessing to myself that it was agony for me to be in his presence. 'It all depends on me,' I thought, 'whether I shall ever see him again or not.' But not to see him would mean that I was afraid of him. No, I was not afraid of him. That, I thought, would be too humiliating. And there in the hall, knowing that my wife could hear me, I insisted that he come with his violin that very evening. He promised, and went away.

"That evening he brought his violin and they played. But nothing much came of it: they did not have the right music (my wife could not play what they had without practicing). I was very fond of music and helped them to the best of my ability—set up a stand for him and turned the pages. They played a few things, some songs without words and a Mozart sonata. He played beautifully, drawing the most exquisite tone from his instrument. He also displayed a refinement of taste that was not at all in keeping with his character.

"Naturally his playing was much superior to my wife's, and he helped her, at the same time paying her respectful compliments. He behaved himself admirably. My wife appeared to be interested only in the music, and her manners were very simple and unaffected. I, too, pretended to be interested only in the music, but all evening I was tortured by jealousy.

"The minute their eyes met I saw that the animal crouching inside each of them, in defiance of all the rules of their social position, posed the question, 'May I?' and answered, 'Indeed you may.' I saw that he had not expected to find my wife, a Moscow woman, so charming, and was delighted with her. Not for a moment did he doubt that she would have him. The whole problem lay in getting round that insufferable husband. Had I myself been chaste I would not have understood this, but I myself, like most others, had taken the same view of women before my marriage, and so I could read his mind like a book. My tortures were increased by knowing beyond a shadow of a doubt that, outside of brief moments of sensuality, her only feeling for me was one of irritation, and that this man, because of his novelty and his elegant appearance, but especially because of his outstanding talent for music, because of the closeness arising from their playing together, and the influence wielded by music (especially violin music) over sensitive natures —that this man would not only make her like him, but that without a second's thought he would conquer her, dazzle her, wind her round his little finger, do anything he wanted with her. I could not help seeing this, and it caused me untold suffering. And in spite of this, or perhaps because of it, some force acting against my will made me treat him with particular consideration, made me even gentle with him. Whether I did it for my wife's sake, to show her that I was not afraid of him, or for my own sake, to deceive myself, I cannot say, but from the very first I found it impossible to be simple and direct with him. I countered the desire to kill him on the spot by being gentle with him. I treated him to expensive wines for supper, I went into raptures over his playing, I smiled graciously when speaking to him, and I invited him to dine with us on the following Sunday and play with my wife again. I said I would also invite some of our friends who were fond of music to hear him.

"On that the evening ended."

In a state of great agitation Pozdnyshev shifted his position and made his peculiar sound.

"Strange how that man affected me," he began again with an obvious effort to compose himself. "As I entered the hall on returning from an exhibition three or four days later my heart suddenly went heavy as a stone, and I could not tell why. It was because when passing through the vestibule I had seen something reminding me of him. It was only on entering my study that I became conscious of what it was, and went back to the vestibule to make sure. No, I

had not been mistaken: there hung his fashionable coat.
(Without realizing it, I took particular notice of everything
that was his.) I made inquiries. Yes, he was there. I went to
the reception room, not through the drawing room, but
through the children's classroom. My daughter Liza was
poring over her books and the nursemaid was sitting at the
table holding the little one and twirling a lid of some sort.
The door into the reception room was closed and I could
hear *arpeggios* and his voice and hers. I listened, but could
not make out anything. Evidently the piano was being
played with the intent of drowning out the sound of their
voices, perhaps of their kisses. Good God, what happened
to me then! The very thought of the beast that dwelt within
me at that moment sends shudders through me. My heart
contracted, stopped, and then pounded like a sledgeham-
mer. The dominant feeling was pity for myself (this is always true when a person is in a frenzy). 'In front of the
children! In front of the nurse!' I thought. I must have looked
terrible, judging by the odd way in which Liza looked at
me. 'What am I to do?' I asked myself. 'Go in? I dare not.
God only knows what I am capable of.' But I could not go
away either. The nurse was looking at me as if she understood my feelings. 'I must go in,' I said to myself, and I
swiftly opened the door. He was sitting at the grand piano
playing *arpeggios* with his white thumbs sticking up. She
was standing in the curve of the piano looking through
some notes. She was the first to see or hear me come in
and she looked up. Perhaps she was frightened, but she
pretended not to be, or perhaps she was not frightened at
all. At any rate, she did not start or stir; she only blushed,
and that not at once.

" 'How glad I am that you've come; we can't decide what
to play on Sunday,' she said in a tone she would never have
used with me if we had been alone. I resented her using
'we' in respect to herself and him. I greeted him without a
word. He shook my hand, and with a smile which appeared
to me sheer mockery, explained that he had brought music
for Sunday and that they could not come to an agreement
as to what to play—a difficult classical piece (Beethoven's

sonata for violin and piano) or some little pieces. He said it so simply and naturally that I could find nothing to take exception to, and yet I was certain that everything he said was false and they had come to a secret agreement to deceive me.

"A source of the greatest torture for those who are jealous (and in our form of society all are jealous) is the physical proximity of men and women sanctioned by our traditions. One would make of himself a laughingstock if he attempted to prevent physical proximity at balls, the physical proximity of doctors and their patients, the physical proximity of those studying art, painting, and especially music. Here are two people studying music, the most noble of the arts; their study requires physical proximity and there is nothing in the least reprehensible about this physical proximity; only the most foolish and jealous of husbands could find anything to object to. And yet everyone knows that it is precisely these studies, especially music, that give rise to adultery among people of our set.

"My own disconcertment seemed to be communicated to them; for some time I was unable to utter a word. I was like an upturned bottle out of which nothing can flow because it is too full. I wanted to upbraid him, to put him out of my house, but I realized I must be courteous. And I was. I pretended to approve of everything, and because of the contrariness that made me the more gracious the more painful I found his presence, I told him that I relied completely on his judgment and advised her to do the same. He lingered for just so long as was necessary to smooth over the unpleasant impression made by my startled entry and strained silence, and then he took his leave, pretending that at last they had decided what to play on the following day. I was certain that it made not the least difference to them what they played, so absorbed were they in something quite different.

"I was particularly attentive as I saw him out (how else is one to see out the man who has come to destroy the peace and happiness of one's home!). With particular warmth I pressed his soft white hand."

XXII

"I said not a word to her the rest of the day. I could not. Her presence roused such hatred within me that I feared the consequences. At dinner she asked me in the presence of the children when I intended leaving (I had to attend a regional convention the following week). I told her. She asked me if there was anything she could get ready for me. I made no answer. I sat at the table without speaking for a while, then, still without speaking, went into my study. Of late she had ceased coming to me in my study, especially at such an hour. I lay there nursing my anger. Suddenly I heard her step. Into my mind came the dreadful, the hideous thought that, like the wife of Uriah, she was coming to me at that unusual hour to conceal her sin. 'Can she really be coming to speak to me?' I thought as I listened to her steps approaching. 'If she is, then I am right.' An unspeakable hatred for her filled my heart. The steps came nearer, nearer. Surely they would pass by the door and go into the reception room? No, the door creaked and there she stood in the doorway—tall, beautiful, with a timid look of appeal in her eyes that she tried to hide, but which I detected and knew the meaning of. I held my breath for so long that I nearly choked. Still looking at her, I took out my cigarette case and lighted up.

" 'Is it nice to smoke when I have come to talk to you?' she said, sitting down close to me on the sofa and leaning toward me.

"I moved away so that she should not touch me.

" 'I see you are displeased that I am going to play on Sunday,' she said.

" 'Not in the least,' I said.

" 'As if I could not see it!'

" 'I'm very glad if you do. As for me, I see nothing but that you are behaving like a bitch. . . .'

" 'If you are going to swear like a cabby I shall go away.'

" 'Do. Only remember, if the honor of the family means

nothing to you, it means much to me—it's not you I care
about—you can go to the devil for all I care—it's the honor
of the family!'

" 'What? What are you saying!?'

" 'Go away! For God's sake go away!'

"Feigning not to understand (or perhaps she really did
not understand), she got up, hurt and angry. But instead of
going out, she stood still in the middle of the room.

" 'You really have become impossible,' she began. 'Not
even an angel could live with you.' Trying as usual to strike
my most vulnerable spot, she reminded me of the incident
with my sister (when in a fit of rage I had said all sorts of
coarse things to her; it was a very painful memory and she
knew it, and that was why she brought it up at this moment). 'After that, nothing you do can surprise me,' she
said.

" 'You would like to insult, humiliate, and disgrace me,
and then say I am to blame,' I said to myself. Suddenly I
was seized by hatred such as I had never felt before, and
for the first time I longed to give physical expression to my
hatred. I leaped up and made for her, but I remember that
just as I leaped up I became aware of what I was doing
and asked myself if it was right to give way to my feelings,
and answered that it was, because in that way I would
frighten her. And so instead of suppressing my hatred I
surrendered myself to it and rejoiced to feel it running riot
within me.

" 'Get out before I kill you!' I shouted, going over to her
and seizing her by the arm. I purposely stressed the tone of
hatred as I said it, and I must have looked terrible, for she
was so frightened she could not move.

" 'Vasya,' she said. 'What is the matter with you?'

" 'Get out!' I roared louder than ever. 'You drive me to
fury. I cannot answer for what I shall do.'

"Having succumbed to my fury, I exulted in it and wanted to do something extraordinary that would demonstrate
the extremity of my feelings. I wanted passionately to strike,
to kill her, but I knew I must not do this, and so, to give vent
to my passion, I snatched up the paperweight and hurled

it past her, shouting, 'Get out!' My aim was good and it went past without striking her. She went out, but halted in the doorway. And while she was still there and could see me (I did it with the express purpose of having her see me) I picked up the things on my writing desk, the candlesticks, the inkstand, and hurled them on the floor.

" 'Get out!' I shouted. 'Get out! I cannot answer for what I shall do!'

"She went away, and I instantly calmed down.

"An hour later the nursemaid came and told me my wife was in hysterics. I went to her. She was sobbing and laughing, could say nothing, and her body was twitching all over. She was not pretending, she was really ill.

"In the morning she was better and we enjoyed a reconciliation under the influence of the feeling called love. When, after our reconciliation, I confessed to being jealous of Trukhachevsky, she showed no embarrassment, she merely laughed the most natural laugh in the world and said it was ridiculous to suppose she would become infatuated with such a man.

" 'Could any decent woman feel anything for a man like that? Nothing but the pleasure that comes of the music. If you wish, I shall refuse to see him ever again, even Sunday, although the guests are invited. Write him a note that I am unwell and that will be the end of it. The only thing I regret is that anyone, especially he himself, should fancy he is dangerous. I am too proud to admit of such a thing.'

"She was not lying; she believed what she said. She hoped by these words to make herself despise him and to build up defenses against him, but she failed. Everything was against her, especially that accursed music. We said no more about it, and on Sunday our guests came and my wife and he played for them."

XXIII

"I think it is hardly necessary to say that I was a vain man; what is there to live for in our society if one is without vanity? And so I saw to it that the dinner and the evening of

music were arranged so as to do us credit. I myself bought
the food for dinner and invited the guests.

"At six o'clock they arrived, and he came too, in evening
dress, with diamond studs, showing his bad taste. He assumed a superior air and smiled condescendingly when
spoken to, as if everything one said and did was just what
he expected, don't you know. I took particular pleasure in
noting every mark of ill-breeding in him because it served
to soothe me and prove that, as she herself had said, he
was too far beneath her for her to stoop to an infatuation
with him. I no longer allowed myself to be jealous. In the
first place, I had already suffered so much from jealousy
that I was exhausted and needed a rest; in the second, I
wanted to believe my wife's asseverations, and so I did.
Despite the fact that I was not jealous, all during dinner
and the part of the evening preceding the music I could not
relax and be myself with either of them, but kept watching
the movements and glances.

"The dinner was like all dinners—stiff and boring. The
music began rather early. How every detail of that evening
is impressed on my mind! I remember his picking up his
violin, unlocking the case, removing the cover some woman
had embroidered for him, taking out the instrument, and
tuning up. I remember the air of indifference my wife assumed to hide her bashfulness (a bashfulness caused primarily by her playing) and her sitting down with this false
expression on her face. Then began the sounding of middle
C, the plucking of strings, the setting up of notes. I remember their exchanging looks, their glancing at the assembled
guests, their murmuring something to each other, then beginning. She played the first chord. I remember the grave,
strained, fine expression that came to his face, as, listening
for his tone, he pressed the strings with cautious fingers in
response to the piano. They had begun."

He stopped and made that strange sound several times
in succession. When he tried to speak again he could only
utter a choking sound, so he waited. Then:

"They played Beethoven's 'Kreutzer Sonata.' Do you
know that first *presto*? Do you?" he shouted. "Ugh! A

dreadful thing, that sonata. Especially that movement. And in general, music is a dreadful thing. What is it? I don't understand. Just what is music? What does it do to a person? And why does it do it? They say music has an elevating influence on the soul. Nonsense. A lie. It certainly does have an influence, and a terrible influence (I can only speak for myself), but it is not an influence that elevates the soul. It neither elevates nor abases; it merely excites. How shall I put it? Music causes me to forget myself and my true state; it transports me to another state that is not my own. Under the influence of music I fancy I feel things I really do not feel, understand things I do not understand, am capable of things I am incapable of. I explain it by the fact that music affects me like a yawn, or laughter: I am not sleepy, yet I yawn when I see another yawn; I find nothing to laugh at, yet I laugh on hearing another laugh.

"Music instantly throws me into the spiritual mood in which the composer found himself while writing it. My soul merges with his and I am taken with him from one mood to another, but why I should go through those moods I cannot say. The composer, on the other hand—let's say the composer of the 'Kreutzer Sonata,' Beethoven—knew why he was in that particular mood. The mood led him to the performing of definite acts, and so this mood had sense for him, but it has no sense for me. Music excites to no purpose. To be sure, if a military march is played, the soldiers march off and therefore the music achieves its end; if a dance is played, I dance, and again the music achieves its end. The same thing is true if a mass is played and I take the sacrament. In other cases it merely excites, without supplying an outlet for this excitement. That is why music wields so terrible, sometimes so frightful, an influence. In China music falls under the jurisdiction of the state. And so it should. Is it permissible that any chance person should hypnotize another (or even many others) and make him do whatever he likes? The worst of it is that often the hypnotist is a person of no moral principles.

"It is a dreadful weapon for chance individuals to wield. Take this 'Kreutzer Sonata'—the first movement. How dare

anyone play this *presto* in a drawing room where there are
women sitting about in *décolleté*—to play it, applaud it,
and then eat ices and exchange the latest gossip? Such
music must be played only in very definite and meaningful
circumstances, when very definite and meaningful under-
takings, corresponding to the music, are to be embarked
upon. Once it is played, the actions inspired by the mood
must be carried out. Otherwise the unspent feelings and en-
ergies, incompatible with the place and the time, are sure
to wreak havoc. On me, at least, this music had a devastat-
ing effect. It seemed to reveal to me entirely new feelings
and capabilities of which I had been utterly unaware. 'This
is how it is,' it seemed to say to me; 'not at all as you are
used to thinking and being, but like this.' Just what this
new way was I could not say, but the consciousness of the
new state brought me joy. I saw all the same people, including her and him, in an entirely new light.

"After the *presto* they played the delightful if common-
place *andante* with its vulgar variations and weak ending.
At the insistence of the guests they played a few other
pieces, an elegy by Ernst, it seems, and something else.
They were all very nice, but they did not make one-tenth
the impression on me that the first piece did. I heard them
against the background of the impression made upon me
by the first. I was gay and lighthearted for the rest of the
evening. Never before had I seen my wife as she was then.
The shine of her eyes, the graveness and significance of
her expression as she played, and her utter limpness and
her faint smile, blissful yet pathetic, when she finished. I
saw all that, but the only meaning I attached to it was that
she had had revealed to her, just as I had, new and un-
familiar emotions, evoked, as it were, from out the depths
of memory.

"The evening ended successfully and everybody went
home.

"Knowing that in two days' time I was leaving for the
convention, Trukhachevsky said on leaving that he hoped
the pleasure he had enjoyed that evening would be repeated the next time he came to our town. I took this to mean

that he considered it impossible to visit at my house while I
was away, and this pleased me. Since I would not return
from the convention before he had left town, I supposed I
would not see him again.

"For the first time I shook his hand with genuine pleasure
and thanked him for the pleasure. He took leave of my
wife, too, as if for a long time. It seemed to me there was
nothing in their manner but what was most natural and decorous. Everything was capital. My wife and I were both
highly pleased with the evening."

XXIV

"Two days later I left for the country, taking leave of my
wife with an easy heart and in the best of spirits.

"There are always no end of things to attend to in the
country; it is a world of its own, with its own peculiar way
of life. I attended the convention for ten hours at a stretch
on each of the first two days. On the following day they
brought me a letter from my wife. I read it immediately.
She wrote of the children, her uncle, the nursemaid, of
things she had bought, and then, in an offhand way, as if
speaking of the most ordinary thing, she mentioned that
Trukhachevsky had called to bring her some music he had
promised, and he had offered to play but she had refused.
I did not remember his having promised her any music; I
had been under the impression that he had taken final
leave of her, and therefore I was unpleasantly surprised.
But I was too busy to give the matter much thought until I
returned to my rooms in the evening and reread her letter.
It seemed to me then that, in addition to the unpleasant
news of Trukhachevsky's having called in my absence, the
whole tone of the letter was strained. The mad beast of
jealousy roared in its den and tried to rush out, but I forced
it back, so afraid was I of its brute force. 'What a low feeling jealousy is!' I said to myself. 'What could be more natural than the things she writes to me?'

"I went to bed and gave myself up to thoughts of the
next day's duties. Usually I have difficulty in falling asleep

in a strange bed, but that night I fell asleep very quickly. But, as sometimes happens, I woke up suddenly, as if roused by an electric shock. I woke up with thoughts of her in my mind, of my carnal love for her, and of Trukhachevsky, certain that he had had what he wanted of her. I was rigid with wrath and horror. But I began to reason with myself. 'It's all nonsense,' I told myself. 'No reason to feel this way; there is nothing and never has been anything between them. How can you lower her and yourself by supposing anything so dreadful? A sort of hired fiddler with a shady reputation, and a respectable woman, mother of a family, *your own wife*. What an incongruity!' This was one side of the argument, but the other was: 'How could there be anything but that? How could there be anything but that simple, ordinary thing, for the sake of which I married her, for the sake of which I live with her? The only thing I want of her, and the only thing that other men, including this musician, want of her. He is single and in good health (I recalled how he had ground up the gristle of a chop in his teeth, and how greedily he had sucked up a glass of wine with his red lips)—sleek, well-fed, a man who, far from being without principle, is guided by the sole principle that advantage should be taken of every opportunity that comes his way. And he and my wife are bound by bonds of music, than which there is no more refined means of exciting lust. What is there to restrain him? Nothing. On the contrary, there is everything to urge him on. She? Who is she? A mystery—the same mystery she has always been. I do not know her. I know only her animal nature. And an animal does not and ought not to know any restraint.'

"Only then did I recall the look on their faces that evening when, after the 'Kreutzer Sonata,' they played a passionate little piece—I've forgotten by whom—a sensual, voluptuous thing. 'How could I have gone away?' I asked myself on recalling that look. 'Is it not clear that everything took place between them that evening? Is it not clear that on that evening there were no longer any barriers separating them, and that both of them, especially she, felt ashamed of what had taken place between them?' I remembered the faint, pathetic, blissful smile she had given me, and the way she had wiped her flushed perspiring face as I came up to the piano. Even then they had avoided each other's eyes; it was not until supper, when he poured her out a glass of soda water, that they glanced at each other and smiled ever so slightly. I remembered with horror having caught that glance and that fleeting smile. 'All is over,' one voice told me, while another said something quite different. 'Something has come over you,' it said. 'You are brooding over what could not possibly be true.' I could not bear to go on lying there in the darkness. I struck a match. I felt afraid in that tiny room with its yellow wallpaper. I lighted a cigarette and smoked, as I always did when I found myself running in circles around some insoluble problem. I smoked and smoked—one cigarette after another—so as to blunt my senses to the insolubility of my problem.

"I slept no more that night. At five o'clock, resolving that I could bear the strain no longer and must leave for home immediately, I got up, woke the watchman who served me, and dispatched him for horses. I sent my colleagues a note saying I had been unexpectedly summoned to Moscow on urgent business and asking them to appoint someone else in my place.

"At eight o'clock I took my seat in a tarantass and rode off."

XXV

The conductor came in. Noticing that our candle had nearly burnt out, he extinguished it without putting in a new one. It was growing light outside. Pozdnyshev sighed deeply but said nothing so long as the conductor was in our carriage. He resumed his story only when he had gone out and nothing was to be heard in the shadowy compartment but the creaking of the windows of the rocking train and the snoring of the shop assistant. I could not see him at all in the faint light of dawn. I could only hear his voice, in which agitation and suffering became more and more pronounced.

"I had to travel thirty-five versts by horse and eight hours by railway. The ride in the tarantass was delightful. It was a frosty autumn morning with the sun shining brightly—you know the sort of morning, when the tires leave a sharp imprint on the moist road. The road is smooth, the light brilliant, the air invigorating. It was glorious, riding along. I felt better as soon as morning came and I was on my way. As I gazed at the horses, the fields, the people we passed, I forgot where I was going. At times I fancied I was simply out for a drive, and that the circumstances causing it were purely imaginary. I took particular joy in forgetting. Whenever I remembered where I was going I would say to myself, 'Don't think; everything will be clear in time.' In the middle of the journey something happened that delayed me and distracted my attention: the tarantass broke down and had to be repaired. This accident had enormous consequences; because of it I missed the express and had to take the post train, and so I arrived in Moscow not at five o'clock, as I had expected, but at twelve o'clock at night.

"A ride in a cart, repairs, the settling of accounts, lunch in a wayside inn, a talk I had with a yard porter—all of these things kept my mind occupied. By evening all was ready and I set out again, and it was even more pleasant riding in the dusk than in the daytime. There was a new moon, a slight frost, a splendid road, good horses, a jolly coachman, and I enjoyed myself to the full, hardly giving a thought to what was awaiting me; or perhaps I enjoyed myself to the full precisely because I knew what was awaiting me and therefore wished to have one last taste of the joys of life.

"But this state of composure, this ability to suppress my feelings, ended with the trip in the tarantass. The minute I entered the railway carriage I experienced something quite different. That eight-hour trip by railway was an agony I shall remember as long as I live. Perhaps it was because on entering the carriage I felt I was almost home, or because railway journeys always act on the nerves. Whatever the reason, from the moment I took my place in the carriage I was unable to control my imagination, which painted for me one picture after another to excite my jealousy, each new picture more obscene than the preceding, and all of them showing how she had been behaving in my absence, how she had been deceiving me. I was consumed by fury and indignation, and I almost exulted in the humiliation the contemplation of these pictures caused me. I could not dismiss them, could not tear my eyes from them, could not help conjuring them up. And the longer I contemplated these imaginary pictures, the more I believed in their reality. The clarity with which they presented themselves to my mind seemed proof that my fancies were reality. Against my will some demon was inventing and whispering in my ear the most dreadful suppositions. I remembered a talk I had had with Trukhachevsky's brother many years before, and with a sort of morbid ecstasy I lacerated my heart with recollections of this talk, applying it to the musician and my wife.

"It had taken place many years before, but I remembered it clearly. Trukhachevsky's brother, in reply to my question as to whether or not he frequented brothels, had said that no decent man would go to a place where he might catch an infection, and where in general it was sordid and filthy, when he could always find a respectable woman. And behold! his brother had found my wife. 'True, she is not as fresh as she might be, one tooth is missing on the left side, and she is a bit plump,' I reasoned for him, 'but it cannot be helped; one must take what is offered.' 'Yes, he is doing her a favor by making her his mistress,' I said to myself. 'But then, she presents no danger of infection.' 'But what are you saying? This is unthinkable!' I said to myself in horror. 'Nothing, nothing of the sort has happened. You have not the slightest grounds for supposing such a thing. Did she herself not tell you she found the very thought of being jealous of such a man beneath you? Yes, but she was lying, she was lying!' I shouted inwardly, and then it all began again. . . .

"There were only two other passengers in our carriage —an old woman and her husband, both of them very taciturn. At one of the stations they got out and I was left alone. I was like a caged animal: one minute I jumped up and went to the window, the next I staggered up and down, as if this could accelerate the speed of the train. But the train with its windows and benches went rocking along at its own speed, just as ours is doing now."

Pozdnyshev jumped up, took a turn or two, and sat down again.

"I am afraid, dreadfully afraid to ride in railway carriages; they always terrify me. Yes, terrify me," he went on. "I kept saying to myself, 'I must think of something else— for instance, of the inn where I had lunch.' And in my mind's eye I would see the bearded porter and his little grandson, a boy of the same age as my Vasya. 'My Vasya! One of these days he will come upon the musician kissing his mother. How the poor child will suffer! But that is nothing to her! She is in love! . . .' And again the same thing. 'No, no. I will think of our inspection of the local hospital. Of how that patient complained of the doctor yesterday. The doctor had a mustache like Trukhachevsky's. With what impudence he—and she too—deceived me by saying he was going away!' And again it began. Everything, every single thing I thought of, brought me back to him. I suffered horribly. I suffered mostly because of my ignorance, my doubts, my indecision, my not knowing whether I ought to love or hate her. So great was my anguish that I remember welcoming the thought that I ought to get out of the carriage, lie down on the rails, and end it all. Then, at least, I would no longer be tortured by doubt and uncertainty. The one thing that kept me from doing this was self-pity, followed invariably by a great hatred of her. My hatred of him was mixed with an awareness of my own humiliation and his triumph; for her I felt nothing but hatred, a terrible hatred. 'I must not commit suicide and let her go free; she, too, must be made to suffer: she must be made to understand what I have gone through,' I said to myself. At every station I got out of the train to distract my thoughts. In the restaurant at one of the stations I saw some men drinking, and I ordered some vodka myself. A Jew who was standing beside me also drank. He began talking to me, and to avoid being alone in my carriage I went with him into his dirty, smoky, third-class carriage, the floor of which was strewn with the shells of sunflower seeds. I sat down next to him and he chattered about a lot of things and told me many anecdotes. I listened but did not understand what he was saying because my mind was filled with my own thoughts. He noticed this and insisted that I be more attentive. I got up and went back to my own carriage. 'I must think it over,' I said to myself. 'I must know whether I am right in thinking what I do and whether there is any cause for me to suffer so.' I sat down to think things over calmly, but instead of thinking calmly, I began the same thing all over again. Instead of rational thoughts—pictures and fancies. 'How many times in the past have I been tortured like this!' I said to myself, recalling other fits of jealousy, 'and each time it turned out to be nothing. This time, too, I suppose—indeed, I am sure—I shall find her in bed sleeping peacefully; she will wake up and be glad to see me, and her words and looks will tell me that nothing has happened, that these are all wild fancies. Oh, how glorious it will be!' 'No; too often has it ended in that way. This time it will be different,' said the other voice, and again everything began. Yes, herein lay my punishment. Not to a hospital for syphilitics would I take young men to cure them of their lust; I would give them a glimpse into my soul, that they might see the demons rending it to pieces. The awful thing was that I claimed complete and unquestionable ownership of her body, as if it were my body, and at the same time I realized I was unable to own her body, that it was not mine, and that she could dispose of it as she wished, and she wished to dispose of it in a way I did not want her to. And there was nothing I could do either to him or to her. He, like Vanka-the-Warder in the song, would sing of her sweet kisses as he was led to the gallows. Even in death he would have the better of me. If she had not yet committed this crime, she wished to commit it, and I knew she wished to, and that made it even worse: it would be better if she had already committed it, and I knew it, and there was no longer any doubt. I could not have said what I wanted. I wanted her not to want what she could not help wanting. The whole thing was utter madness."

XXVI

"At the next to the last station, when the conductor came to take our tickets, I picked up my bag and went out on the carriage platform; the knowledge that I was almost there, that the dénouement was at hand, increased my excitement. I went cold and trembled so that my teeth chattered. Mechanically I followed the crowd out of the station, took an izvozchik, got in and rode off. As I rode I watched the few people in the streets, the yard porters, the shadows thrown by the street lamps, now in front of my cab, now behind it, without a thought in my head. When we had gone about half a verst I became conscious of the cold in my feet, and I remembered having taken off my woolen socks in the train and putting them in my valise. Where was my valise? Here? Here. And my basket? I had forgotten all about my luggage, but now that I remembered it and found my receipt for it, I decided it was not worth going back for and I continued on my way.

"Try as I may, I cannot remember the state I was in at that time. What did I think about? What did I want? I remember nothing except that I had a premonition of something terrible and of vast import that was about to take place. Whether this something of vast import took place because of my intentions, or because of my premonition, I do not know. Or perhaps my mind was a blank, and I just imagined afterwards that I had had such somber thoughts.

"I drove up to the entrance. It was nearly one o'clock in the morning. Several izvozchiks were standing in front of the house, whose lighted windows gave them promise of passengers (the lighted windows were in our flat—the windows of the drawing room and reception room). Without even wondering why there should be lights in our windows at such a late hour, I climbed the stairs and rang the bell, still with that premonition of something terrible about to happen. Our footman—kind, stupid, hard-working Yegor—opened the door. The first thing that met my eyes was *his* coat hanging in the vestibule among other wraps. I ought to have been astonished, but I was not; I seemed to have expected it. 'So I was right,' I said to myself. When I asked Yegor who was here he said Trukhachevsky. I asked if there was anyone else.

" 'No one, sir,' he replied.

"I remember the glad tone with which he said this, as if anxious to disperse my fears that there might be somebody else. 'No one. Ah!' was what I said to myself.

" 'And the children?'

" 'All well, praise the Lord. Asleep this long while.'

"I could scarcely breathe and could not control the trembling of my lips. "So this time it *is* different! Those other times I expected misfortune and did not find it; everything turned out to be all right. This time everything is not all right. It has come. Here it is. . . .'

"I almost broke down, but some demon whispered into my ear, 'What, will you weep and grow maudlin while they part with each other serenely, leaving no proof of their guilt? Do you wish to go on doubting and suffering torment forever?' And instantly my self-pity vanished and a new feeling took its place. You will scarcely believe it, but it was a feeling of joy that at last my sufferings were at an end, that now I could punish her, get rid of her, give vent to my fury. And I did give vent to my fury—I became a beast, a fierce and cunning beast.

" 'Wait,' I said to Yegor, who had turned to go into the drawing room. 'Here, take this receipt and go to the station for my luggage. There is an izvozchik waiting at the door.'

"He went down the hall for his coat. Fearing that he might frighten them, I accompanied him to his room and waited until he put on his coat. From the reception room that was beyond the drawing room came the murmur of voices, the clink of knives and plates. They were eating and had not heard the doorbell. 'If only they do not come out now,' I thought. Yegor got into his coat with the astrakhan collar and went out. I saw him to the door and locked it behind him. A feeling of awe came over me when I found myself alone and knew I had to act. How, I had not yet considered. I only knew that now everything was over, that there could no longer be any question of her innocence, and that the time had come for me to punish her and put an end to my relations with her.

"Formerly I had always wavered, had said to myself, 'Perhaps it is not true, perhaps I am mistaken.' Now I felt nothing of the kind. I was perfectly convinced. Alone with him at night, in my absence! That was throwing prudence to the winds. Or even worse: this boldness, this recklessness in committing a crime, might be a boldness assumed intentionally, as proof of innocence. Everything was clear. There could be no doubt. I feared only one thing: that they might yet escape, might think of some new stratagem to rob me of proof and the opportunity of punishing them. And so, to catch them the quicker, I tiptoed to the reception room where they were sitting, not through the drawing room, but through the hall and the nursery.

"The boys were sleeping in the nursery. The nursemaid stirred and almost woke up, and I imagined what she would think when everything was discovered, and such a wave of self-pity swept over me that I could not restrain my tears. For fear of waking up the children I rushed on tiptoe into the hall and into my study, where I collapsed on the sofa and gave vent to my feelings.

" 'I am an honest man, the son of my parents; all my life I have dreamt of having a happy family; I, her husband, have never been unfaithful to her, and yet here she is, with five children, making love to a musician because he has red lips! She is not a human being! She is a bitch, a loathsome bitch! With her children sleeping in the next room— her children, whom she has always pretended to love so dearly! And to have written what she did to me! And to fling herself upon him so brazenly! But what do I know? Perhaps she has always done that. Perhaps she has been having children of footmen and calling them mine. Tomorrow I would have come home and she would have met me with her charming coiffeur, her tantalizing waist, her graceful movements' (I saw every detail of her beautiful, hateful face), 'and the beast of jealousy would have been turned back and locked up in my heart, to gnaw it to pieces. What will the nursemaid think, and Yegor? And poor little Lizal She already has an inkling of how things are. The brazenness of it! The falseness! The animal lust that I know so well!'

"I wanted to get up but could not. My heart was pounding so hard I could not stand on my feet. I would have an apoplectic stroke. She would have killed me. That was precisely what she wanted. Should I kill her? Oh, no; that would be too easy. I had no intention of letting her get off so easily. But there I sat while they were eating and laughing, and— Yes, he had no compunctions about taking her, even if she was not as fresh as she might be: after all, she was attractive and, what was most important, did not endanger his precious health. 'Why did I not kill her then?' I asked myself, recalling a quarrel of the previous week during which I had driven her out of my study and thrown things about. I had a vivid remembrance of the state I had been in then; more than a remembrance—I now felt the same longing to break and destroy things. I remember what an urge to action I experienced; every thought but those essential to action was driven out of my mind. I was in the state of an animal or man whose senses are quickened by threat of danger, and who, in this state, acts precisely, unhurriedly, without losing a minute, subordinating everything to a single definite purpose."

XXVII

"The first thing I did was to take off my boots and go in my stocking feet to some weapons hanging on the wall over the sofa and take down a curved damask dagger that had never been used and was exceedingly sharp. I drew it out of its sheath. The sheath fell behind the sofa and I remember saying to myself, 'I must pick it up later or it will get lost.' Then I took off my coat, which I had kept on all this time, and went noiselessly out in my stocking feet.

"I crept up to the door and flung it open suddenly. I remember the expression of their faces. I remember the expression of their faces because it caused me a pang of joyful torment. It was an expression of horror. That was just what I wanted. To the end of my days I shall remember the expression of horror and despair that flashed across both their faces in that first second of beholding me. He, it seems, had been sitting at the table, but on catching sight or sound of me he leaped to his feet and stood with his back to the bookcase. The look on his face was indubitably one of horror. The look on hers was also of horror, but horror combined with something else. Had it been horror alone, perhaps what happened might not have happened. In her look there was also (or at least it seemed so to me that first moment) an expression of disappointment, of vexation that her lovemaking and her happiness had been interrupted. But the expression on both of their faces was fleeting. It was as if she wanted nothing but the happiness of the moment. His look of horror was instantly supplanted by one of inquiry: 'Is it possible to lie to him or not? If it is, then I must begin. If it is not, something is about to happen. But what?' He looked at her inquiringly. On catching his glance her look of disappointment and vexation changed, or so I thought, to one of anxiety for him.

"For a moment I paused in the doorway with the dagger behind my back. In that moment he smiled and said in a tone so casual as to be almost comic:

" 'We were just having a little music . . .'

" 'This is unexpected . . .' she said at the same time, copying his tone.

"But neither he nor she were given a chance to finish. I was possessed of the same fury I had known the preceding week. Again I felt the urge to smash, to destroy; I was in a mad frenzy, and I gave myself up to my frenzy.

"Neither of them had a chance to finish. That was happening which he feared would happen. that which instantly cut off what they were saying. I threw myself upon her, still concealing the dagger lest he prevent me from plunging it into her left side, just below the breast. I had chosen this spot from the very first. The moment I threw myself upon her he perceived my intent and seized me by the arm, a thing I had not expected him to do.

" 'Think what you're doing! Help!' he shouted.

"I snatched my arm away and hurled myself at him. His eyes met mine, he suddenly went white as a sheet to the very lips, a peculiar shine came to his eyes, and he ducked under the grand piano and made for the door, another thing I had not expected him to do. I would have pursued him, but some weight hung upon my left arm. It was she. I tried to free myself. She tightened her hold and would not let me go. This unexpected obstruction, her weight on my arm, the repulsiveness of her touch, incensed me the more. I felt completely mad, I knew I must look terrible and was glad of it. I wrenched my left arm away with all my force and in doing so struck her face with my elbow. She let out a cry and released her hold on my arm. I wanted to dash after him, but the absurdity of chasing my wife's lover in my stocking feet flashed across my mind; I did not want to be absurd, I wanted to be terrible. Despite the state of frenzy I was in, I was constantly aware of the impression I was making on them, and my actions were partly governed by this impression.

"I turned back to her. She had fallen upon the sofa and was staring at me, one hand over the eye I had injured. Her face expressed fear and hatred of me, her enemy. It was the expression of a rat when someone lifts up the trap in which it is caught. I, at least, could detect nothing in her face but fear and hatred. It was a fear and hatred for me that love for another was sure to inspire in her. But perhaps I would have restrained myself and not have done what I did do if she had kept silent. But suddenly she began to speak and to seize the hand that held the dagger.

" 'Think what you're doing! What is it? What has come over you? There is nothing between us, nothing, nothing, nothing! I swear to it!'

"I still might have hesitated, but those words, which

meant just the opposite to me, namely, that there *was* something between them, called forth a response corresponding to the state I had worked myself up into and which was developing in a crescendo and must go on developing until it reached its highest pitch. There are laws governing even frenzy.

"'Don't lie, you slut!' I shrieked, and caught her in my left hand, but she broke loose. Without dropping the dagger, I seized her by the throat with my left hand, threw her down on her back, and began choking her. How resistant her throat was! She seized my hand in an effort to tear it off her throat, and as if it was just this I had been waiting for, I plunged the dagger into her left side below the ribs with all my force.

"When people say they do not know what they are doing in a fit of frenzy, it is nonsense, it is untrue. I realized everything, and not for a moment did I stop realizing it. The more the steam that my fury generated, the brighter the glow of my reason, so that I could not possibly have failed to perceive everything I did. I knew what I was doing every second of the time. I cannot say I knew what I would do later, but at the moment I knew what I was doing, and I seemed even to know slightly ahead of time, for the purpose, perhaps, of being able to repent, to tell myself I might have stayed my hand. I knew I was striking her below the ribs and that the dagger would enter at that spot. I fully realized I was doing something dreadful, something the like of which I had never done before, something that would have terrible consequences. But the consciousness of this flashed through my mind like a streak of lightning, and the consciousness was instantly followed by the deed. The deed was perceived with striking clarity. I remember feeling the momentary resistance of her stays and something else, and then the passing of the blade into softness. She clutched at the dagger with her hands, cutting them, but not stopping the knife. Later when I was in jail, after the moral transformation I underwent, I brooded long over this moment, recalling it again and again and trying to plumb its meaning. I remember that for a second, a brief second before the deed, I was filled with the terrible realization that I was killing a woman, had already killed her, a defenseless woman, my wife. I remember the horror of this realization, I even remember vaguely that that was why, having plunged in the dagger, I instantly pulled it out, wishing to undo what I had done. For a second I stood motionless, waiting to see what would happen, wondering if what was done could not be undone. She leaped to her feet and shouted:

" 'Nurse! He has killed me!'

"The nurse, waked by the noise, was standing in the doorway. I went on standing there waiting and not believing. But from under her stays the blood came gushing forth. Only then did I realize that it could not be undone, and instantly decided that it ought not to be undone, that this was what I wanted and what ought to have happened. I waited until she fell and the nurse ran over to her crying, 'Dear God!' and only then did I throw down the dagger and make for the door.

" 'I mustn't get excited. I must calmly consider what I am doing,' I said to myself, refusing to look at her or the nurse. The nurse wailed and called for the maid. I went down the hall, sent the maid to her, and went into my own room. 'What must I do now?' I asked myself, and knew what I must do. Going into my study, I went straight to the wall, took down a revolver, examined it—it was loaded—and put it on the writing desk. Then I picked up the dagger sheath that had fallen behind the sofa and sat down on the sofa.

"I sat there for a long time. I thought of nothing, remembered nothing. I heard noises in the other rooms. I heard someone drive up and enter the house. Then someone else. I heard and saw Yegor bring my luggage into the room. As if I had any need of that now!

" 'Do you know what has happened?' I said. 'Tell the yard porter to notify the police.'

"He went out without a word. I got up, locked the door, took out a cigarette and some matches, and began to smoke. Before I had time to smoke a single cigarette I was overcome by sleep. I must have slept for two hours. I remember dreaming that she and I were on friendly terms; we had quarreled and made it up, there was a certain tension between us, but we were on friendly terms. I was waked up by a knock at the door. 'The police,' I thought on waking. 'I seem to have killed her. But perhaps it is she and nothing has happened.' There was another knock at the door. I did not answer, I was too busy trying to decide whether it had really happened or not. Yes, it had. I remembered the resistance of her stays and then the sinking in of the dagger, and little chills ran up and down my spine. 'Yes, it has. Now for myself,' I said. But even as I said it I knew I would not kill myself. Yet I got up and picked up the revolver. And a strange thing: I remembered how many times before I had contemplated suicide, as I had in the train on that very day; it had seemed an easy thing—easy because I knew what a punishment it would be to her. Now I could not so much as contemplate killing myself, let alone do it. 'Why should I?' I asked myself, and there was no answer. Once more came the knock at the door. 'First I must find out who is knocking. I can do it later.' I put down the revolver and covered it with a newspaper. I went to the door and pushed back the bolt. It was my wife's sister, a silly, kindhearted widow.

" 'Vasya! What has happened?' she said, and the tears that were always ready, overflowed.

" 'What do you want?' I asked her roughly. I saw that it was foolish and unnecessary to be rude, but I could not help it.

" 'Vasya, she is dying! Ivan Fyodorovich has said so,' Ivan Fyodorovich was the doctor, my wife's doctor, her adviser.

" 'So he is here?' I asked, and again I felt my anger rising. 'Well, what of it?'

" 'Vasya, go to her. Oh, how awful, how awful!' she moaned.

" 'Go to her?' I repeated to myself. And I answered myself that of course I must go to her, that it was the thing to do, that when a man kills his wife as I had done, the thing to do is to go to her. 'If that is the case, I must go,' I said to myself. 'If I must do the other, I shall have plenty of time,' I thought, having in mind my intention to shoot myself. 'There will be words, grimaces, but they will not touch me,' I said to myself.

" 'Wait,' I said to her sister. 'I will look foolish going in my stocking feet. At least let me put on some slippers.' "

XXVIII

"And strange as it may seem, again as I went out of the room and walked through the chambers I knew so well, there arose the hope that nothing had happened. But I was struck by the horrid smell of medicines—iodoform, carbolic acid. Yes, it had happened. As I went down the hall past the children's classroom I caught sight of Liza. She looked at me with frightened eyes. I even fancied that all five of the children were there and all were staring at me. I went to the door. The maidservant opened it to me and she herself went out. The first thing that caught my eye was my wife's pearl-gray dress flung on a chair, covered with blood. There she lay with her knees up, on our double bed, on my side of the bed, for hers was against the wall. She lay raised very high on a mound of pillows, and the jacket she had on was unfastened. Something had been placed over the wound. The air reeked of iodoform. I was struck most of all by the bruised swelling of her cheek, part of her nose, and one eye—the result of the blow of my elbow when she had tried to stop me. There was nothing beautiful about her whatsoever. I found her even repulsive. I stopped on the threshold.

" 'Go over, go over to her,' said the nurse.

" 'Perhaps she wishes to ask forgiveness,' I thought. 'Shall I forgive her? Yes, she is dying and so I can forgive her,' I thought, resolving to be generous. I went straight to her. With a great effort she raised her eyes, one of which was all swollen, and haltingly, with an effort, she said:

" 'So you got what you wanted . . . you killed me.' And through her physical suffering, through her consciousness of death, glimmered the old familiar expression of cold animal hatred: 'But I won't . . . give you . . . the children. . . . She' (her sister) 'shall have them.'

"She found what I considered the main thing—her guilt, her deception—not worth mentioning.

" 'I hope you enjoy the sight of what you have done,' she said, and, glancing toward the door, she gave a sob. There in the doorway stood her sister and the children. 'See what you have done.'

"I looked at the children, then back at her, at her bruised and swollen face, and for the first time I forgot myself, my rights, my pride; for the first time I saw her as a human being. And so insignificant seemed my jealousy and all that had injured my pride, and so significant seemed that which I had done, that I was ready to fall on my knees and press my face against her hand and say, 'Forgive me!' But I could not.

"She grew silent and closed her eyes, apparently lacking the strength to utter another word. Then her mutilated face quivered and contracted. Weakly she pushed me away.

" 'Why did you do it? Why?'

" 'Forgive me,' I said.

" 'Forgive you? Nonsense. If only I don't die!' she cried, raising herself and fixing feverish eyes on me. 'Yes, you got what you wanted! I hate you! Ah! Oh!' she cried, evidently frightened by something in her delirium. 'Kill me! Kill me! I'm not afraid! But everyone, everyone! Him, too! He's gone, he's gone!'

"She was delirious to the end. She did not recognize any of us. She died at noon of that same day. Long before that, at eight o'clock, they took me to police headquarters and then to jail. There, during the eleven months I awaited trial, I pondered over myself and my past and came to understand it. I began to understand on the third day. On the third day they took me back there. . . ."

He tried to go on, but, unable to suppress his sobs, he stopped. With a great effort he took himself in hand and resumed:

"I began to understand when I saw her in her coffin." He caught his breath and began to speak hurriedly. "Only when I saw her face in death did I realize what I had done. I realized that it was I, I who had killed her, that she had once been alive, warm, full of movement, and because of me she was now motionless, cold, waxen, and that this could never be undone—never, anywhere, by anyone. Only one who has lived through this can understand. Oh, oh, oh!" he cried several times, then was silent.

For a long time we sat without speaking, he whimpering and shaking with suppressed sobs.

"Forgive me. . . ."

He turned away and lay down, covering himself with a blanket. When, at eight o'clock in the morning, we reached the station at which I had to get off, I went over to him to say good-bye. I did not know whether he was asleep or only feigning, but he did not stir. I touched his hand. He threw back the blanket and I saw that he had not been asleep.

"Good-bye," I said, holding out my hand.

He gave me his with a faint smile that was so pathetic it moved me to tears.

"Forgive me," he said, repeating the words with which he had concluded his story.

1891

AFTER THE BALL

So you contend a man cannot judge independently of what is good and what is bad, that it is all a matter of environment—that man is a creature of environment. But I contend it is all a matter of chance. And here is what I can say about myself. . . ."

This is what our respected friend Ivan Vasilyevich said at the conclusion of a discussion we had been having about the necessity of changing the environment, the conditions in which men live, before there could be any talk about the improvement of the individual. As a matter of fact, no one had said it was impossible to judge independently of the good and the bad, but Ivan Vasilyevich had a habit of answering thoughts of his own stimulated by a discussion, and recounting experiences from his own life suggested by these thoughts. Often he became so absorbed in the story that he forgot his reason for telling it, especially since he always spoke with great fervor and sincerity. That is precisely what happened in the present case.

"At least I can make this claim with regard to myself. My own life has been molded in that way and no other—not by environment, but by something quite different."

"By what?" we asked.

"That is a long story. If you are to understand, I must tell it all to you."

"Then do."

Ivan Vasilyevich considered a moment and shook his head.

"Yes," he said, "my whole life was changed by a single night, or rather, a morning."

"Why? What happened?"

"It happened that I was deeply in love. I had often been in love before, but never so deeply. It took place a long time ago—her daughters are married women by this time. Her name was B., Varenka B. She was still strikingly beautiful at fifty, but in her youth, when she was eighteen, she was a dream: tall, slender, graceful, and majestic—yes, majestic. She always held herself as erect as if she were unable to bend, with her head tipped slightly backward; this, combined with her beauty and height, even though she was so thin as to be almost bony, gave her a queenly air that would have been intimidating if it had not been for her gay, winning smile, her mouth, her glorious shining eyes, and her whole captivating, youthful being."

"Ivan Vasilyevich certainly does lay it on thick!"

"However thick I were to lay it on, I could not make you understand what she was really like. But that is beside the point. The events I shall recount took place in the forties.

"I was then a student at a provincial university. I don't know whether it was a good or a bad thing, but in those days there were none of your study circles, none of your theorizing, at our university; we were just young and lived in the way of young folk—studying and having a good time. I was a very gay and energetic youth, and rich in the bargain. I owned a spirited carriage horse and used to take the girls out for drives (skating had not yet become the fad); I went on drinking parties with my fellow students (in those days we drank nothing but champagne; if we were out of money, we drank nothing, for we never drank vodka as they do now); but most of all I enjoyed parties and balls. I was a good dancer and not exactly ugly."

"Come, don't be modest," put in one of the listeners. "We've all seen your daguerreotype. You were a very handsome youth."

"Perhaps I was, but that isn't what I wanted to tell you. When my love was at its height I attended a ball given on the last day of Shrovetide by the Marshal of Nobility, a good-natured old man, wealthy, and fond of entertaining. His wife, as amiable as he was, stood beside him to receive us. She was wearing a velvet gown and a diamond tiara in her hair, and her aging neck and shoulders, plump and white, were exposed, as in the portraits of Empress Yelizaveta Petrovna. The ball was magnificent. The ballroom was charming, there were famous serf singers and musicians belonging to a certain landowner who was a lover of music, the food was abundant, the champagne flowed in rivers. Much as I loved champagne, I did not drink—I was drunk with love. But I danced till I dropped. I danced quadrilles, and waltzes, and polonaises, and it goes without saying that I danced as many of them as I could with Varenka. She was wearing a white dress with a pink sash, white kid gloves that did not quite reach her thin, pointed elbows, and white satin slippers. A wretched engineer named Anisimov cheated me out of a mazurka with her. I have never forgiven him for that. He invited her the moment she entered the ballroom, while I had been delayed by calling at the hairdresser's for my gloves. And so instead of dancing the mazurka with her, I danced it with a German girl I had once had a crush on. But I am afraid I was very neglectful of her that evening; I did not talk to her or look at her, for I had eyes for no one but a tall, slender girl in a white dress with a pink sash, with radiant, flushed, dimpled cheeks and soft, gentle eyes. I was not the only one; everyone looked at her and admired her, even the women, though she outshone them all. It was impossible not to admire her.

"Formally I was not her partner for the mazurka, but as a matter of fact I did dance it with her—at least most of it. Without the least embarrassment she danced straight to me down the length of the whole room, and when I leapt up to meet her without waiting for the invitation, she smiled to thank me for guessing what she wanted. When we had been led up to her and she had not guessed my nature, she had given a little shrug of her thin shoulders as she held out her hand to another, turning upon me a little smile of regret and consolation.

"When the figures of the mazurka changed into a waltz, I waltzed with her for a long time, and she smiled breathlessly and murmured 'encore.' And I waltzed on and on with her, quite unaware of my own body, as if it were made of air."

"Unaware of it? I'm sure you must have been very much aware of it as you put your arm about her waist—aware of not only *your* body, but of hers as well," said one of the guests.

Ivan Vasilyevich suddenly turned crimson and almost shouted:

"That may apply to you, modern youth—all you think of is the body. In our day things were different. The more deeply I loved a girl, the more incorporeal she seemed to me. Today you are aware of legs, ankles, and other things; you disrobe the ladies with whom you are in love, but for me, as Alphonse Karr has said—and a very good writer he was—the object of my love was always clad in bronze raiment. Far from exposing, we tried to hide nakedness, as did the good son of Noah. But you cannot understand this."

"Pay no attention to him. Go on with your story," said another of the listeners.

"Well, I danced mostly with her and did not notice the passage of time. The musicians were so exhausted—you know how it always is at the end of a ball—that they kept playing the mazurka; mamas and papas were rising from the card tables in the drawing room in anticipation of supper: footmen were rushing about. It was going on for three o'clock. We had to take advantage of the few minutes left us. I invited her once more, and for the hundredth time we passed down the length of the room.

" 'Will I be your partner for the quadrille after supper?' I asked her as I took her back to her place.

" 'Oh, yes, if they do not take me home,' she said with a smile.

" 'I won't let them,' I said.

" 'Give me my fan,' she said.

" 'I am sorry to give it back to you,' I said as I handed her her little white fan.

" 'Here, then, to keep you from being sorry,' she said, plucking a feather out of the fan and giving it to me.

"I took the feather, unable to express my rapture and gratitude except with a glance. I was not only gay and content—I was happy, I was blissful, I was benevolent, I was no longer myself, but some creature not of this earth, who knew no evil and could do nothing but good.

"I tucked the feather in my glove and stood riveted to the spot, unable to move away from her.

" 'Look, they are asking Papa to dance,' she said, indicating a tall, stately man who was her father, a colonel, in silver epaulettes, standing in the doorway with the hostess and some other women.

" 'Varenka, come here,' called the hostess in the diamond tiara.

"Varenka made for the door and I followed her.

" 'Do talk your father into dancing with you, *ma chère*. Please do, Pyotr Vladislavich,' said the hostess to the colonel.

"Varenka's father was a tall, handsome, stately, and well-preserved old man. He had a ruddy face with a white mustache curled *à la* Nicholas I, white side whiskers that met his mustache, hair combed forward over his temples, and the same smile as his daughter's lighting up his eyes and lips. He was very well built, with a broad chest swelling out in military style and with a modest display of decorations on it, with strong shoulders and long, fine legs. He was an officer of the old type with a military bearing of the Nicholas school.

"As we came up to the door the colonel was protesting that he had forgotten how to dance, but nevertheless he smiled, reached for his sword, drew it out of its scabbard, handed it to a young man eager to offer his services, and, drawing a suede glove on to his right hand ('Everything according to rule,' he said with a smile), he took his daughter's hand and struck a pose in a quarter turn, waiting for the proper measure to begin.

"As soon as the mazurka phrase was introduced he stamped one foot energetically and swung out with the other, and then his tall heavy figure sailed round the ballroom. He kept striking one foot against the other, now slowly and gracefully, now quickly and energetically. The willowy form of Varenka floated beside him. Imperceptibly and always just in time, she kept lengthening or shortening the step of the little white satin feet to fit his.

"All the guests stood watching the couple's every movement. The feeling I experienced was less admiration than a sort of deep ecstasy. I was especially touched by the sight of the colonel's boots. They were good calfskin boots, but they were heelless and had blunt toes instead of fashionable pointed ones. Obviously they had been made by the battalion cobbler. 'He wears ordinary boots instead of fashionable ones so that he can dress his beloved daughter and take her into society,' I thought to myself, and that is why I was particularly touched by his blunt-toed boots. Anyone could see he had once danced beautifully, but now he was heavy and his legs were not flexible enough to make all the quick and pretty turns he attempted. But he went twice round the room very well, and everybody applauded when he quickly spread out his feet, then snapped them together again and fell, albeit rather heavily, on one knee. And she smiled as she freed her caught skirt and floated gracefully round him. When he had struggled back to his feet, he touchingly put his hands over his daughter's ears and kissed her on the forehead, then led her over to me, who he thought had been her dancing partner. I told him I was not.

" 'It doesn't matter; you dance with her,' he said, smiling warmly as he slipped his sword back into the scabbard.

"Just as the first drop poured out of a bottle brings a whole stream in its wake, so my love for Varenka released all the love in my soul. I embraced the whole world with love. I loved the hostess with her diamond tiara, and her husband, and her guests, and her footmen, and even the wretched Anisimov, who was clearly angry with me. As for her father with his blunt-toed boots and a smile so much like hers—I felt a rapturous affection for him.

"The mazurka came to an end and our hosts invited us to the supper table. But Colonel B. declined, saying that he must be up early in the morning. I was afraid he would take Varenka with him, but she remained behind with her mother.

"After supper I danced the promised quadrille with her. And while it had seemed that my happiness could not be greater, it went on growing and growing. We said nothing of love; I did not ask her, nor even myself, whether she loved me. It was sufficient that I loved her. The only thing I feared was that something might spoil my happiness.

"When I got home, undressed myself and thought of going to bed, I realized that sleep was out of the question. I held in my hand the feather from her fan and one of her gloves, which she had given to me when I put her and her mother into their carriage. As I gazed at these keepsakes I saw her again at the moment when, choosing one of two partners, she had guessed my nature and said in a sweet voice, 'Too proud? Is that it?' then joyfully held out her hand to me; or when, sipping champagne at the supper table, she had gazed at me over her glass with loving eyes. But I saw her best as she danced with her father, floating gracefully beside him, looking at all the admiring spectators with joy and pride for his sake as well as her own. And involuntarily the two of them became merged in my mind and enveloped in one deep and tender feeling.

"At that time my late brother and I lived alone. My brother had no use for society and never went to balls. He was getting ready to take his examinations for a master's degree and was leading the most exemplary of lives. He was asleep. I felt sorry for him as I looked at his head buried in the pillow, half covered by the blanket—sorry because he did not know and did not share the happiness which was mine. Petrusha, our serf valet, met me with a candle and would have helped me undress, but I dismissed him. I was touched by the sight of the man's sleepy face and disheveled hair. Trying to make no noise, I tiptoed to my own room and sat down on the bed. I was too happy, I could not sleep. I found it hot in the room, and so without taking off my uniform I went quietly out into the hall, put on my greatcoat, opened the entrance door, and went out.

"It had been almost five o'clock when I left the ball;

about two hours had passed since, so that it was already light when I went out. It was typical Shrovetide weather—misty, with wet snow melting on the roads and water dripping from all the roofs. At that time the B.'s lived on the outskirts of town, at the edge of an open field with a girls' school at one end and a space used for promenading at the other. I went down our quiet little bystreet and came out upon the main street, where I met passersby and carters with timber loaded on sledges whose runners cut through the snow to the very pavement. And everything—the horses bobbing their heads rhythmically under their lacquered yokes, and the carters with bast matting on their shoulders plodding in their enormous boots through the slush beside their sledges, and the houses on either side of the street standing tall in the mist—everything seemed particularly dear and significant.

"When I reached the field where their house stood I saw something big and black at the promenade end of it, and I heard the sounds of a fife and drum. My heart had been singing all this time, and occasionally the strains of the mazurka had come to my mind. But this was different music, harsh and sinister.

" 'What could it be?' I wondered, and made my way in the direction of the sounds, down the slippery wagon road that cut across the field. When I had gone about a hundred paces I began to distinguish in the mist a crowd of people. They were evidently soldiers. 'Drilling,' I thought, and continued on my way in the company of a blacksmith in an oil-stained apron and jacket who was carrying a large bundle. A double row of soldiers in black coats were standing facing each other motionless, their guns at their sides. Behind them stood a fifer and a drummerboy who kept playing that shrill tune over and over.

" 'What are they doing?' I asked the blacksmith who was standing next to me.

" 'Driving a Tatar down the line for having tried to run away,' replied the blacksmith brusquely, glaring at the far end of the double row.

"I looked in the same direction and saw something horrible coming toward me between the rows. It was a man bare to the waist and tied to a horizontal gun held at either end by a soldier. Beside him walked a tall officer in a greatcoat and forage cap whose figure seemed familiar to me. The prisoner, his whole body twitching, his feet squashing through the melting snow, advanced through the blows raining down on him from either side, now cringing back, at which the soldiers holding the gun would pull him forward, now lunging forward, at which the soldiers would jerk him back to keep him from falling. And next to him, walking firmly, never lagging behind, came the tall officer. It was her father, with his ruddy face and white mustache and side whiskers.

"At every blow the prisoner turned his pain-distorted face to the side from which the blow had come, as if in surprise, and kept repeating something over and over through bared white teeth. I could not make out the words until he came closer to me. He was sobbing rather than speaking them. 'Have mercy, brothers; have mercy, brothers.' But the brothers had no mercy, and when the procession was directly opposite me I saw one of the soldiers step resolutely forward and bring his lash down so hard on the Tatar's back that it whistled through the air. The Tatar fell forward, but the soldiers jerked him up, and then another blow fell from the opposite side, and again from this, and again from that. . . . The colonel marched beside him, now glancing down at his feet, now up at the prisoner, drawing in deep breaths of air, blowing out his cheeks, slowly letting the air out between pursed lips. When the procession passed the spot where I was standing I got a glimpse of the prisoner's back through the row of soldiers. It was something indescribable: striped, wet, crimson, outlandish. I could not believe it was part of a human body.

"'God in heaven!' murmured the blacksmith standing next to me.

"The procession moved on. The blows kept falling from both sides on the cringing, floundering creature, the drum kept beating, the fife shrilling, and the tall, stately colonel walking firmly beside the prisoner. Suddenly the colonel stopped and went quickly over to one of the soldiers.

" 'Missed? I'll show you!' I heard him say in a wrathful voice. 'Here, take this! And this!' And I saw his strong hand in its suede glove strike the small weak soldier in the face because the man's lash had not come down hard enough on the crimson back of the Tatar.

" 'Bring fresh whips!' shouted the colonel. As he spoke he turned round and caught sight of me. Pretending not to recognize me, he gave a vicious, threatening scowl and turned quickly away. I felt so ashamed that I did not know where to turn my eyes, as if I had been caught doing something disgraceful. With hanging head I hurried home. All the way I kept hearing the rolling of the drum, the shrilling of the fife, the words, 'Have mercy, brothers,' and the wrathful, self-confident voice of the colonel shouting, 'Here, take this! And this!' And the aching of my heart was so intense as to be almost physical, making me feel nauseated, so that I had to stop several times. I felt I must throw up all the horror that this sight had filled me with. I do not remember how I reached home and got into bed, but the moment I began to doze off I saw and heard everything all over again. I jumped up.

" 'There must be something he knows that I do not know,' I said to myself, thinking of the colonel. 'If I knew what he knows, I would understand, and what I saw would not cause me such anguish.' But rack my brains as I might, I could not understand what it was the colonel knew, and I could not fall asleep until evening, and then only after having gone to see a friend and drinking myself into forgetfulness.

"Do you suppose I concluded that what I had seen was bad? Nothing of the sort. 'If what I saw was done with such assurance and was accepted by everyone as being necessary, it means they know something I do not know,' was the conclusion I came to, and I tried to find out what it was. But I never did. And not having found out, I could not enter military service, as it had been my intention to do, and not only military service, but any service at all, and so I turned out to be the good-for-nothing, that you see."

"We know very well what a 'good-for-nothing' you

turned out to be," said one of the guests. "It would be more
to the point to say how many people would have turned out
to be good-for-nothing had it not been for you."

"Now that's a foolish thing to say," said Ivan Vasilyevich
with real vexation.

"Well, and what about your love?" we asked.

"My love? From that day on my love languished. Whenever we went out walking and she smiled that pensive smile
of hers, I could not help recalling the colonel out in the
field, and this made me feel uncomfortable and unhappy,
and I gradually stopped going to see her. My love petered
out.

"So that is what sometimes happens, and it is incidents
like this that change and give direction to a man's whole
life. And you talk about environment," he said.

1911

NOTES

TWO HUSSARS:
Written in 1856. First published in the same year.

A HAPPY MARRIED LIFE:
Work on this story was begun in 1858. It was first published in 1859.

YARDOTION:
The story was conceived in 1856, but written only in 1863. After writing it, Tolstoy laid it aside until 1885, when he introduced changes into the text. It was first published in 1886.

THE DEATH OF IVAN ILYICH:
Written from 1884 to 1886. First published in 1886.

THE KREUTZER SONATA:
Written from 1887 to 1889. The censor prevented its publication until 1891.

AFTER THE BALL:
The first sketch was written in 1903. It appeared posthumously in 1911.

The modern abridgment of the
greatest novel ever written!

WAR AND PEACE

BY LEO TOLSTOY

Abridged by Edmund Fuller

For those who have never read WAR AND PEACE, the DELL version will be the best possible introduction to that giant among the world's masterpieces.

For those who have read the original, the Dell abridgment will be a revelation of the firm and unadorned foundation on which Tolstoy constructed his towering and complex literary edifice.

A LAUREL EDITION   **ONLY 75¢**

THE LAUREL SERIES OF GREAT SHORT STORIES

If you cannot obtain copies of these titles from your local bookseller, just send the price (plus 10c per copy for handling and postage) to Dell Books, Post Office Box 1000, Pinebrook, N. J. 07058. No postage or handling charge is required on any order of five or more books.

FOUR GREAT RUSSIAN SHORT NOVELS

A rich sampling of the short novel at its best, in the hands of four immortal Russian writers

TURGENEV: First Love

DOSTOYEVSKY: The Gambler

TOLSTOY: Master and Man

CHEKHOV: The Duel

A Laurel Edition   *50c*